TRULY MADLY DEADLY

A DCI ROBERT KETT NOVEL

ALEX SMITH

RELENTLESS
MEDIA

TRULY MADLY DEADLY
Published Worldwide by Relentless Media.
This edition published in 2024.

Edited by Hanna Elizabeth

15.2.0

www.alexsmithbooks.com
relentless.media

ALSO BY ALEX SMITH

The DCI Robert Kett Thrillers

Paper Girls

Bad Dog

Three Little Pigs

Whip Crack

Run Rabbit Run

Stone Cold Dead

Every Mother's Son

Sweet Briar Rose

Jaw Breaker

Knock Knock

King Rat

Knuckle Bones

Lucky Number Seven

Unholy Saints

Truly Madly Deadly

Cry Baby: A Novella

Other Books

Six Days, Six Hours, Six Minutes

The Harder They Fall

For Hanna

PROLOGUE

Sunday

Karen Dankworth had expected love to be many things. Exciting? Sure. Scary? Of course. Confusing? Well, that went without saying. She'd expected it to leave her breathless, or heartbroken. She'd expected adventures and horror stories. Love, she'd thought, would bring her the full gamut of emotions, because love was everything.

What she hadn't expected, though, in all her forty-three years of life, was for love to leave her feeling lonely.

She sat forward in the leather easy chair her husband usually occupied and checked her watch, realising that it was too dark to see the time. Night had crept in while she'd been sitting here, uninvited and unwelcome. It had filled the house like dirty water, its touch cold on her face, on her arms.

Shivering violently, Karen stood up and navigated her way across the living room. She'd had her leg tucked beneath her for what felt like hours and the pins and needles filled her foot instantly, making her limp.

"Ow," she said as she slid her hand over the cold wall. "Ow, ow, ow."

She found the switch and flicked it, banishing the dark like it was a flock of startled birds. The living room glowed, but the rest of the house remained unlit and quiet, and she felt it again, that feeling of being utterly, inescapably alone. It was the worst feeling in the world. Worse than grief, worse than anger, worse than betrayal or jealousy or bitterness. It made her feel like every single piece of who she was had been cut out of her, leaving an empty shell.

She was almost glad of the pins and needles, because at least she could feel *something*.

She clamped her jaw shut and took a breath, flexing her toes. Her watch told her it was a minute or so after six, and that wave of desolation almost hit her again until she started moving, making her way out of the living room and across the dark hall, switching on the kitchen lights. Her phone was on the counter, buried in breadcrumbs from the toast she'd made herself for dinner. She brushed them from the screen, along with a dollop of Lurpak.

Not that there was any need, of course, because there was clearly no message there from her husband.

"Wanker," she said, enjoying the shape of the word in her mouth. She said it again, louder. "Wanker. Wanker. Wanker."

She and Grant had been married for seven years, and together for two more before that. And on the days when she couldn't believe it was real, she only had to come here and see it for herself—over a decade of love radiating from the photographs along the kitchen wall.

There was the first picture ever taken of them both,

outside the pub on New Year's Eve with a group of friends, all of them looking like children. There was their wedding day, just a registry office, of course, not because they didn't have much money, although that had certainly been a factor, but because Grant hadn't wanted to make a fuss. But still better than she could have imagined, better than all the stories she'd told herself when she was a kid.

Their glorious trip to the Alps, then the disastrous holiday in Spain when they'd arrived to find the villa they'd booked hadn't even been built. Then three old houses, all rented, before they'd worked up the deposit and the courage to buy this place. There were the dogs, too, her Maisie and Grant's Spiff, who'd enjoyed four good years as step-siblings before cancer and old age had taken them.

No kids, of course. Grant had been so against the idea he'd had the snip when he was twenty-three. He'd finally got around to telling her that, a year after she'd met him at the end of the aisle.

She flicked open her phone and checked her messages anyway, just to be sure that she hadn't missed one. But there was only Grant's last text, from just after three.

It'll be fun, I promise.

'*It*' had been his idea of a night out together after she'd confronted him about the fact that tomorrow was Valentine's Day. He'd forgotten, of course, even though he'd fired up his charm in order to gaslight her. She'd never been able to see the bullshit in the early days because Grant was handsome, and he knew how to wrap her around his little finger. But after a decade or so it was hard to miss.

"Of course I haven't forgotten," he'd said, circling the island in order to rest his hand on her cheek. "But I can't do it tomorrow, I've got to work late. You know Mondays are bad for me. Which is why I arranged something for next weekend."

"What's wrong with tonight?"

She'd seen the flicker of annoyance, the glance at his watch, the weary sigh.

"I'll see what I can do."

And he'd walked out of the front door. That was their love, right there in a nutshell. Her watching him leave, day after day after day.

The loneliness was so bad it was actually painful. Karen put a hand to her heart, wondering for the millionth time whether she should just leave him. She could hit the road tonight and just keep driving. She could go anywhere. There had to be better places out there than this, better suburbs than Taverham, better cities than Norwich. Better weather, better schools, better jobs, better people.

Better husbands.

She wouldn't do it, though. Never had, never would.

She just wasn't the sort of person who could give up on love.

"Right," she said. "More toast."

There wasn't much that toast and marmalade didn't fix, along with a cup of tea, of course. She opened the fridge, the rattle of jars and bottles so loud that she thought she'd just imagined the knock on the front door. She hesitated, waiting for it to come again, cold air wafting over her arms, the smell of something on the turn in there making her nose wrinkle.

Nothing.

She closed the fridge anyway and walked into the hall, staring at the rectangle of patterned glass in the door.

The security light had been triggered.

She grabbed her fleece-lined jacket from the row of pegs and slipped it on, opening the door. She was braced for the cold, but the air outside seemed warmer than it did in the house, undisturbed by wind. There was nobody out there, which she was equal parts relieved and disappointed about. Past their small front garden was the street and its line of parked cars, the lights blazing in the houses opposite. The only sound was the hum of traffic from the main road and the rumble of somebody putting their bin out.

No Grant, of course.

Karen was pushing the door shut when something scuttled through her peripheral vision. Her body tensed like a trap, but when she looked at the stone slab of the doorstep it wasn't a mouse she saw there.

It was a box.

"What on earth?" she asked beneath her breath.

The box was small, just big enough to contain a single chocolate, perhaps. Or maybe even a ring box. It was immaculately wrapped in purple paper and tied with a pink ribbon. She couldn't work out why it had startled her so much, and now that the shock had passed, she felt some of that misery of abandonment leak out of her.

It was Grant. She'd asked for his love and here it was, topped with a bow. It wasn't the present itself that brought a smile to her face, it was the fact that he'd listened to her. He'd *heard* her. And didn't that mean that he cared, that he could change?

She crouched down and reached for the present, but it danced out of her reach—jerking back a couple of feet and rolling onto its side.

Karen stood bolt upright, not sure whether the pressure in her throat was a giggle or a scream. She scanned the street again, no sign of anyone in the dark spaces between the cars. The box sat there, waiting for her.

"Grant?" she said. "What are you doing?"

A car drove past, the driver oblivious to the fact she was standing in the open door. When it had gone, the quiet seemed unbearable.

"It's too cold for this," she called out. "Can you come in?"

She hated herself a little for the whine in her voice. She could imagine Grant's eyes rolling from wherever he was hiding. How many times had he said it to her?

You always claim you want fun, but the trouble is you're *no fun, Karen. You're no fun at all.*

"I am fun," she whispered to herself.

She stepped out of the house in her bare feet and lunged for the box. It retreated again, the paper catching the streetlights in a flash of purple. She hissed a laugh through her nose, the euphoria taking her by surprise as she ran down the path.

"Stop it!" she said. "I haven't got my shoes on!"

She kept chasing it anyway, all the way to their gate. Here, the box stopped moving, caught on the wooden struts. She snatched it before it could start again, holding it to her chest as she stared down the street.

"Grant?"

He didn't want to reveal himself, so she turned her attention to the box instead. It was so light it felt empty—no ring, then—the paper so thin it was in danger of crumpling in her grip. There was fishing wire taped to the bottom, invisible in the dark. It was impossible to see where it led.

Her feet were aching from the cold, so she scuttled back to the house and pushed the door to behind her—not closed, though, in case Grant made an appearance. Elbowing on the hallway light, she studied the box more closely.

The only markings were two letters drawn in black on the top, JV, inside a crudely shaped heart. It was so flimsy that the whole thing buckled as she tried to take the ribbon off, the paper tearing as she picked apart the tape. She unfolded the box to reveal nothing inside at all. On the reverse side of the paper, though, was some writing. She turned it around so that she could read it.

NR9 5NN. Meet me there. Come now.

I love you.

She felt it for a moment, a sudden glow that reminded her of the early days, the breathless excitement of something new. Grant had never been a man to say "I love you," only "I love you *too*," in response to the dozens of times a day she would say it. But here it was in black and white. He'd even taken time with his handwriting, the shapely letters far neater than his usual scrawl.

I love you.

She looked through the still-open door at the cold, quiet evening. Getting into her car and slogging through the dark to a random address wasn't exactly her idea of fun, but maybe Grant was right, maybe she needed to make a little more effort. After all, *he* was.

Besides, there wasn't a hope in hell of her staying here, was there?

Fun or not, she just wasn't the sort of person who could give up on love.

Karen slipped on her shoes, grabbed her keys, and bolted through the door.

AS FAR AS romantic locations went, this one sucked.

Karen followed the satnav on her phone north out of Taverham, her hopes of food and cocktails in the city dashed as the roads got narrower and darker. Other than the light from the

MG's headlights, the world had been erased, the night-drenched fields on either side of the road so immense that she felt like she was driving along a bridge over the abyss—one slip of the wheel threatening to send her spinning into oblivion. She hadn't even known there was so much countryside out here, as if Norfolk's towns and villages had burrowed themselves beneath the dirt to hibernate, leaving nothing but stubble and muck.

"What are you planning, Grant?" she asked, and she was answered by her phone, which lay on the passenger seat.

"Your destination is ahead."

"The fuck it is," she muttered, craning over the steering wheel.

The road angled slightly to the right, edged on both sides by tall hedges, and as she rounded the bend she spotted—*thank God*—a sign of civilisation: a tangle of fairy lights hanging from a tree. There was a break in the hedge here, barely big enough for her to steer the car into. Branches scraped the doors and windows like nails on a blackboard as she bumped the MG through the gap.

Ahead was a track, more fairy lights marking it out like the lights on a runway. They led towards the glow of a car's taillights maybe fifty yards ahead. There was nothing else here. No little boutique hotel where they might be staying the night, no spa retreat, no fancy restaurant, no camp site. Not even a toilet, which was worrying because every pothole made her feel like she was going to wet herself.

No, there was only a whole lot of dark mud beneath her tyres and a darker sky overhead, just those little lights to ward away the night.

It wasn't a car up ahead, she realised as she drew close to the other vehicle. It was a lorry, the kind you hired to move house. It sat with its back to her, an enormous heart drawn in red paint on the shuttered rear door, the letters JV crudely splashed in the middle.

The taillights seemed brighter than ever, turning the world a shade of crimson that might have been romantic anywhere else. More strands of fairy lights had been laid around the wheels of the lorry, and some on the lowered tailgate.

There was another car on the far side of the vehicle, but she could only see the front bumper. It looked like Grant's BMW.

Karen switched off the engine and opened the door, easing herself into the night. It was colder here than it had been back home, although the air was perfectly still.

Something caught in the back of her throat when she breathed in, sour and chemical. There wasn't a single sound other than the thump of her heart and, when she felt brave enough, the warble of her voice.

"Grant?"

Something moved inside the lorry, a dull clank. Karen hovered by the car.

"Grant, is that you?"

The reply was muffled by the walls of the truck, just a grunt that tripped an alarm bell in her stomach.

"Grant?" she tried for a third time. "Are you okay?"

"Yeah," came a shout. "I'm fine. I'm here."

She exhaled slowly, crossing the open space between the MG and the lorry like she was in no-man's-land, her arms folded tightly over her chest.

"Where are you?"

"In the back," said Grant. "You have to lift the door."

"What is this?" she said. "What's going on?"

I'm having fun, she almost added, before he could start complaining.

She climbed awkwardly onto the lowered tailgate, grabbing the handle of the shuttered door and wiggling it upwards. It was stubborn, but after a couple of attempts that left her arms burning she managed to open it far enough to see inside.

Not that there was anything to see. It was pitch black in there.

"Grant?"

"Hurry up, Karen," he said, and his voice had an edge she'd not heard before, something she couldn't identify. "Please."

"Okay," she said. "Hang on."

She hefted herself through the door, which was so low that she had to stay on her hands and knees as she crawled through. It was impossible to see anything, but the floor of the lorry must have been filthy because she could feel the dirt between her fingers, gathering under her nails.

"Jesus Christ, Grant," she said. "What is this?"

She cleared the door and stood up, her knees cracking. In the aching dark, vertigo almost took her, and she staggered sideways until her fingers found the metal wall. In spite of the cold and the dark, something still glowed inside her, the warmth of anticipation. Any second now, the lights would come on and she'd see... what? A meal for two? A makeshift spa? A *bed*?

"Please, Grant," she said. "Tell me what's happening."

Grant sniffed.

"I can't," he said. "I'm sorry."

She heard a clatter from behind her, then somebody yanked the shuttered door down so hard that the lorry trembled. The dark was thick enough to drown in and the scream left her mouth before she could stop it, an ugly sound that she'd never made before in her life.

"I did it!" Grant yelled. "I got her here. Let me go!"

His words plunged her into a terror she'd never known before. She opened her mouth, but before she could utter her husband's name a light blinked on overhead, so bright that she had to screw her eyes shut. She put her dirty hands to her face, squinting through her fingers, trying to find meaning in the glare.

"Let me go!" Grant called again.

Her husband was sitting on the far side of the lorry's enormous cargo hold, dressed in the blue jeans and maroon jumper he'd left the house in earlier. His dark skin was streaked with sweat and there was a stain in his hair that might have been blood. His eyes were so wide he didn't look like her husband. He looked like some awful waxwork dummy. When he squinted up at her, all she could think to do was laugh, because he wasn't real. None of this could be real.

"Karen," he said, quieter now, more urgently. "Karen, hurry up."

She didn't understand what he meant until he jiggled on his chair and she realised he'd been tied there.

"What?" she said, a stupid question if there ever was one.

"Now!"

She ran to him, the lorry rocking on its suspension with her movement. No longer night-blind, she realised there was a table behind her husband, an old wooden one littered with tools.

"What's going on?" she said as she dropped onto her knees beside him. The stench coming off him—sweat, maybe worse—was enough to make her recoil.

"I don't fucking know. I got a call to come out here, saying it was a work thing. Gave me an address, but when I got here they lamped me. Woke up in this chair."

It *was* blood in his hair, she saw. It had left a stain down the back of his ear, down the side of his neck, invisible in the maroon collar of his jumper.

He tugged at his ropes again and the cords of his neck jutted out like steel wire. The chair didn't so much as wobble, and she realised it had been bolted to the floor. Karen found the knot and began to work at it with her fingers, the impossible job made even harder by his movements.

"Hold still," she said. "I can't—"

Something hit the side of the lorry like a cannon shot, the echo rumbling back and forth like thunder.

Then, a shout from outside the back door.

"Grant and Karen Dankworth," it said. It was a man, that was all she could be sure of.

"Keep going," hissed Grant, and Karen obeyed, her fingertips aching from the effort, her hand muscles close to cramping.

Another thump on the metallic body of the lorry.

"I bring you here tonight in the name of love," the voice went on. It had moved, as if the speaker was walking down the side of the vehicle. He struck it again, like he was hammering a gong. "In the name of everything that love stands for."

"Fuck's he playing at?" said Grant, fighting the ropes, making her job infinitely more difficult.

Karen found the weak spot, picking at it.

"Hurry up, for fuck's sake," he said.

"What would you do for love, Karen?" the man outside continued.

The loop came undone and Grant ripped his hands free, pushing himself out of the chair. He ran to the shuttered door and tried to lift it, the lorry wobbling.

"Fucker's locked it," he growled, turning back to Karen like this was her fault. "What do we do?"

She thought of her phone in the car, hated herself for leaving it there. All she could give Grant was an expression of utter helplessness, and he, in turn, threw her a look of disgust. He turned back to the door and gave it a solid kick.

"Let me out!"

"What would you do for love, Grant?" answered the voice from close to the front of the lorry.

Grant kicked the door again, but it was made of sterner stuff than him. Karen turned her attention to the table, to the tools that had been left there: a sledgehammer, an axe with a rusted blade, a crowbar, and a collection of knives of all shapes and sizes. The knot in her stomach was tighter than the knot that had bound her husband, making every movement difficult.

"You claim to love one another," said the voice. "But that is a lie."

Grant lumbered past, nearly knocking her over as he approached the table. He picked up the sledgehammer, then dropped it to the floor and chose the crowbar instead. He lurched back to the door, so unsteady on his feet that he looked drunk.

"Grant, you are guilty of the betrayal of love," the man shouted.

Grant jammed the crowbar into the bottom of the door, the sound of it deafening in the enclosed space.

"Come on, you piece of shit."

Karen wasn't listening to him. She was trying to make sense of what she'd just heard from outside.

"How many times, Grant?" the man yelled. "How many women?"

"What?" said Karen.

Her husband stamped on the crowbar, trying to bust the latch, but the door wasn't giving in. He shot a look back at her.

"Do something!"

She was paralysed by fear, her thoughts scattering.

Grant picked up the sledgehammer, swinging it at the door, the sound of it driving Karen to her knees. She clamped her hands to her ears, her head full of broken glass. The pressure in her bladder had eased, but she couldn't bear to think about it.

"Love means nothing to either of you," came the voice. "It is a lie."

"You're fucking demented," Grant yelled, hitting the door again, the force of the impact making him stagger back. "You're dead, you hear me?"

An unpleasant tang caught the back of Karen's nose, instantly recognisable.

Smoke.

"And I, Jack Valentine, declare that this is your punishment," said the voice. "If love means nothing to you, then you are not worthy of it. Kill it dead."

Grant hit the door again, out of breath. He dropped the hammer and put his hands on his knees, panting. The smell was stronger now, and past the ringing echo of the sledgehammer, Karen could hear the crackle of fire.

"No," she said, as if that word had ever made a scrap of difference in her life.

It was getting hotter, which was no surprise, given that the metal shell of the lorry was basically an oven.

"Kill it dead," the voice said again. "Prove that your love does not exist."

"What are you talking about?" said Grant, the sweat rolling off him.

"One of you dies, one of you *leaves*," said the voice. "Or you both burn in hell."

"What?" said Grant. "You want us to kill each other?"

"You have, I'd say, three minutes before the fire kills you both," said the voice.

Karen watched her husband think about it for all of five seconds. He looked at her the way a butcher would look at a joint of meat, nothing in his expression but cold calculation.

Then he reached down and picked up the sledgehammer.

"Wait," said Karen, toppling from her knees onto her backside. "Grant, wait, it's not real."

Grant gripped the weapon in both hands. His entire body, the body she'd held night after night for nearly ten years, which had brought her so much pleasure, which had granted her protection from all the things that might harm her, was rigid with intention. And his face, that beautiful, dark-eyed face she'd fallen in love with almost at first sight, was now nothing more than an executioner's mask.

The fire outside was roaring now, the air shimmering. Smoke was pouring through the cracks in the shuttered door, through the vent that led into the cab.

This *was* real. She knew it, and so did Grant.

Karen scrambled back, her shoes scuffing the floor.

"Grant, just stop."

She coughed hard, the smoke reaching for her lungs.

"I'm sorry," he said, lifting the sledgehammer. "I really am. I'm sorry for everything."

Everything.

She retreated, the leg of the table jutting into her back. Grant was struggling to hold the heavy hammer, coughing hard enough to bring up a lung.

She took her chance, turning clumsily, grabbing the top of the table and hauling herself up.

It couldn't take her weight, teetering onto two legs then crashing down on top of her. Tools and weapons rained onto her face, something slicing open the flesh of her cheek, almost taking out her eye. She screamed, the table crushing her chest, pinning her tight.

Then Grant was there, standing over her, just a blur in the smoke. She was almost glad she couldn't make out his face.

"I'm sorry," he said again.

Karen swept her hands from side to side, searching, grasping, *finding*.

She didn't know what it was, but she gripped it tight and thrust it up with everything she had left.

A second of resistance, then the pop of a blade entering flesh.

Grant grunted, looked like he might topple.

Then he recovered.

"Forgive me," he said, just a whisper against the inferno. "I love you."

She'd lost the weapon, her hands slick with blood. But it didn't matter. The heat was too much, the fire closing in. And those were fine words to send you on your way.

She just wasn't the sort of person who could give up on love, after all.

"I lo—" she started.

Then the blunt head of the sledgehammer dropped.

CHAPTER ONE

Monday

DCI Robert Kett woke to the smell of the house burning down.

He lay still and sniffed a couple of times, the aroma of smoke scratching the back of his throat. The room was dark, but beads of light rested like birds along the top of the curtain pole. He sat up and checked his phone, seeing that it was just before seven. He noticed, too, that it was February 14th.

Billie was breathing gently beside him, and he rested his hand on her arm.

"Billie," he said.

He sniffed again, catching the faintest whiff of something burning. There were voices, too, coming from downstairs—hushed whispers.

It was this that kicked the last few dregs of sleep from his head, an unwelcome shot of adrenaline. In moments like this, halfway between dreams and reality, his thoughts always went to the same place, snapping like magnets.

There's somebody in the house. Bad men. They've come for you.

And in this case, they'd brought petrol and lighters.

But he forced the thoughts away before they could take root, closing his eyes, focussing on what he was smelling, on what he was hearing, seeing the truth of it.

Not whispers, but giggles.

Not men, but his daughters.

He breathed out slowly, inhaled, the smell of smoke stronger.

"Shit," he said. Because Hollenbeck were dead and gone. The idea of them destroying his house was now impossible.

The girls, on the other hand...

"Billie," he said again, giving her arm a squeeze.

"Billie's not here," she grumbled. "Please leave a message and she'll get back to you in an hour or three."

"The message is that it's nearly seven, and the girls are downstairs by themselves, and I think something's on fire."

She opened her eyes and sat bolt upright.

"Shit," she said.

They clambered out of bed together, Kett throwing Billie her dressing gown from the back of the door before grabbing his own. He shivered as he put it on, the house ridiculously cold, the floorboards like ice beneath his bare feet as he made for the stairs. They creaked out a warning and the whispers from downstairs turned into shouts and squeals of alarm.

"They're coming!"

"Alice?" said Kett. "What's going on?"

He crossed the hallway and entered the kitchen,

wafting a definite haze of smoke out of his face. All three of his girls stood in their pyjamas between the island and the sink, frozen in various poses like they were playing musical statues. Alice was holding the kettle, steam rising from the spout. Evie had a spoon in each hand, her arms stretched to the sides like the Angel of the North, her eyes wide above a huge grin. Moira was facing the other way and bent double, staring at him between her legs. She was chuckling uncontrollably.

It looked like every natural disaster known to man had taken place right here in the kitchen. A bottle of milk had been upended on the counter, its contents forming a puddle on the floor. All of the cereal had been taken out of the cupboard, stacked like Stone Henge. Rice Krispies crunched underfoot as he took a couple of steps forward.

He still couldn't see the source of the smoke, and he wasn't sure if that made him feel more or less worried.

"Uh..." said Kett. "What's going on?"

"What's burning?" added Billie from his side.

"Nothing!" said Alice, dumping the kettle onto the counter. "Go away!"

"You're not supposed to see," added Evie, turning her spoons to them like they were weapons.

"Why are you upside down?" added Moira, still peering at them through her legs.

"Just go back to bed," said Alice. "We'll bring it to you."

"Bring what?" said Kett.

"Breakfast!" squeaked Moira. She stood straight and spun around, swaying a little. "Dizzy."

"Don't tell them!" said Alice, glaring at her. "You'll ruin it."

"Ruin *what*?" said Kett.

"Breakfast," said Alice, turning her glare on him like all

of this was somehow his fault. "It was supposed to be a secret. For Valentine's Day."

"Oh," said Kett, smiling. "Well, that's... That's actually very sweet, girls."

"It is," said Billie, sliding her arm through his. "Very thoughtful. But what's burning?"

Alice shrugged.

"Cereal."

"You burned cereal?" said Billie.

Another shrug, like it was a ridiculous question.

"Right," said Kett. "I guess we'll go back to bed then."

"Just please be careful with that hot water, Alice," said Billie. "And try not to burn any more... cereal."

Kett hesitated for a moment before turning around, Billie taking his other arm and escorting him from the kitchen.

"You think it's okay to leave them?" he asked as they crossed the hall. "What if they try and microwave a saucepan or something?"

"Or blow up the fridge," added Billie.

"Or worse," said Kett. "Put peanut butter on my toast."

"The horror," said Billie with a laugh.

They were halfway up the stairs when somebody knocked on the door. Kett's arm was still locked in Billie's grip and he felt her body contract with shock. They both looked down to the door to see a silhouette in it.

"Who on Earth is that?" said Kett. "I'll get it."

"No, I will," said Billie, relaxing. "It'll be Albert from up the road."

"Again?"

Albert Smith was a neighbour who was well into his nineties, and who was sadly in the grip of dementia. For the last couple of weeks he'd taken to knocking on their door at all hours of the day and night, wanting to speak with his wife. It was a tough ask, because Morag Smith had passed away almost a decade ago.

"Go back to bed," said Billie as she made her way down. "I'll sort it."

Kett waited for her to open the door, just to be sure it really was Albert. The old man stood in his tartan dressing gown, a flat clap clenched in his hands, his worried face unknotting itself into a smile when he saw Billie.

"Come on, Bert," she said, slipping on her shoes and taking his arm. "Let's get you home, pop the kettle on."

Kett headed for the bedroom, burrowing himself into the warmth of the duvet. He closed his eyes, listening to the laughter of the girls downstairs, almost slipping back into sleep before the slamming front door brought him back. Billie charged up the stairs and into the room like a rhino, diving under the covers. Her hands were so cold he actually screamed.

"Bloody Nora," he said, wrapping her in a hug, rubbing her arms to warm her up. He kissed her forehead. "Valentine's Day, then?"

"It is. Although, when was the last time we bothered celebrating?"

"Years," said Kett. "You always told me it had more to do with greeting card company profits than true love."

"And I stand by that. Although..." She raised an eyebrow. "A card might have been nice."

"It's in the post," Kett told her. "Probably *lost* in the post. Sorry. I'll put in a complaint with Royal Mail."

"Good man."

"And *my* card?" he said.

"They didn't have any," said Billie.

"Who didn't?"

"The shops. All of the shops. No cards anywhere. Crazy."

She kissed him. Then they both turned to the door as the sound of laughter rose up the stairs. It was followed moments later by a parade through the bedroom door: Evie first, still clutching her spoons, then Moira, holding what looked like a homemade card, then Alice, who was doing her best to carry their largest tray. She had to turn sideways in order to enter the room, and in doing so managed to knock over one of the cups on the tray. A rain of tea pattered onto the carpet.

"Whoops," she said.

Evie and Moira hurled themselves onto the bed, Moira thrusting the card into her mum's face.

"I made it," she said.

"No, you didn't," Evie told her. "I made it. You just added the glitter."

"*So* much glitter," said Billie, a waterfall of purple sparkles pouring onto the bed as Moira opened the card. "And hundreds of those little sharp stars that the hoover won't pick up and that will remain in our sheets for the next year or so."

"Yay!" said Kett.

He had to admit, the card was sweet. Evie had drawn him and Billie on the front. At least, he *thought* it was him and Billie.

"Why do I have a beard?" he said.

Evie shrugged.

"And why is my tummy so big?"

"You're pregnant," she said.

"But I'm a man."

"Because it's a baby *boy*, obviously."

"Right..."

"It's beautiful," said Billie, turning the card over. "Did you write this too?"

"Dear Mummy and Daddy," Evie read aloud, beaming. "Happy Valentine's Day love from Evie, Evie and Evie."

"Hey!" said Moria. "You said you wrote my name!"

Evie rolled onto her back and burst out laughing, earning a thump on the arm from her five-year-old sister. Before Kett could tell either of them off, Alice had dumped the tray on the bed, more tea sloshing onto the duvet.

"Oh, hang on," said Kett, turning the cup upright. "It's soaking wet."

"Because it's tea," said Alice matter-of-factly. "You'll have to share."

"We made it," said Moira. "Eat it."

"Uh..." said Kett.

On the tray in front of him, swimming in tea, were two bowls. Both contained a smorgasbord of assorted cereals, *sans* milk, some slices of white bread, unbuttered, and what Kett hoped were raisins. There was more glitter in the bowls than there was in the card. A single cup of tea, the colour of parchment, stared sadly up at him.

"Wow," he said. "This looks... delicious."

"Such a good job, girls," said Billie. "And very kind of you."

All three of them beamed with pride.

"So much glitter," Billie said again.

"We'll be pooping purple for a week," said Kett, and Evie howled with laughter.

"Are you going to eat it?" said Moira.

Evie handed them each a spoon, and Kett dutifully scooped out a couple of Cheerios. The glitter crunched between his teeth like sand.

"It's the perfect breakfast, thank you," he said. "Now,

why don't you go and watch TV until it's time to get ready for school?"

They didn't need any more encouragement, especially considering the TV was usually banned on school days. Evie and Moira bounded off the bed, knocking over the second cup of tea as they went, and the three of them charged down the stairs like a herd of water buffalo.

Kett righted the cup, moving the tray to the bedside table in order to minimise the amount of tea that was dripping onto the already saturated duvet. He looked at Billie, shaking his head.

"Their hearts are in the right place," he said.

"Shame their heads aren't screwed on," she replied, looking sadly at the tray. "I could have done with a tea."

"Not that tea," he replied. "Looked like Porter made it."

He groaned out of bed, stretching his arms until he felt his spine crack. Pain needled through him, the collection of old wounds and injuries combining with what he was fairly certain was arthritis. He doubled up as he felt a cramp building in his lower back.

"Ouch," he said.

"You are a fine specimen of a man, Robert Kett," said Billie, and he wasn't sure if she was being sarcastic or not. "I love you."

"Love you too," he said, making for the door. "Happy Valentine's Day."

CHAPTER TWO

Two hours and four cups of tea later, Kett could still taste glitter.

He sat at his desk in the open-plan offices of Norfolk Constabulary's Major Investigations Team, running his tongue around his teeth and working out flecks of purple grit.

Most of the other desks were occupied as officers quietly worked their cases, the soft clack of keys strangely comforting. DC Kate Savage sat at the next station over, wearing her knitted red beanie—the one her boyfriend, PC Aaron Duke, had crocheted for her—even though the heating was on. She was studying a stack of paperwork with a serious expression.

Next to her, Porter had rocked his chair back on two legs as he stared at his phone. Every now and again, the big DI would splutter out a long sigh.

Kett plucked another piece of glitter from his tongue, flicking it away. His Valentine's breakfast wasn't doing much to help the sickness he still felt, even six weeks after their last case. It turned out that being force-fed pig shit wasn't very good for you, and he'd had to endure a hefty dose of antibiotics before he felt anywhere near back to normal. The bruises and cuts had taken longer, as they always did, adding a few more scars to the tapestry of his broken body.

But the physical injuries weren't the worst thing that had come from that case.

He turned his attention back to the screen on his desk, and to the woman who stared at him from a photograph.

Vicky Ledger.

He was still certain that Vicky had been responsible for the death of the two men they'd found inside the chimney of the cabin last Christmas: Craig Heilig and Magnus Metcalfe. She hadn't physically killed them, but she'd coerced others to do it for her; she'd all but confessed it to Kett when they'd caught her. But Vicky was a master manipulator. Not only had she convinced Saint Nicholas to kill, she'd also made him confess. Nick's trial had been a short one because he'd pleaded guilty to everything they'd thrown at him, and even though sentencing hadn't happened yet, he was looking at life behind bars.

Vicky, on the other hand, was free and clear. Kett had kept tabs on her, as much to make a point as to catch her doing anything illegal. She'd stayed in hospital for a few days to make sure her unborn baby was okay, and was now back at Nick's retreat. As far as Kett could tell, she'd kicked out everyone but the staff and some close friends and was living like a princess.

He'd had to stop prying when she'd filed a complaint against him, accusing him of harassment. But it didn't mean he was going to leave her alone. She deserved to be behind bars.

Not that he had any way of making that happen.

He heard Porter sigh again, the DI's lips flapping.

"You alright, Pete?" he called across.

Porter dropped his chair back onto four legs, still staring at his phone.

"Yes, sir," he said. "Sorry, can't get my head around it."

"What case are you working?"

"Case?" asked Porter with a frown.

"Yes, *case*," said Kett. "As in, your job."

"He's doing crosswords, sir," said Savage without looking up. Porter gave her a disapproving look.

"It's a workout, sir," he said. "A mental one. Helps me stay sharp. I'm usually alright with the Times one, but this clue's a bastard."

"What is it?" asked Kett.

"A crossword," Porter said.

"No, the *clue*."

"Oh, right," said Porter. "'*Pagans, strangely, hate barnyard birds*.' Eight letters."

He glanced hopefully at Kett.

"Uh..." said Kett, wracking his brain and finding absolutely nothing there at all. "Owls?"

"How can you spell owls with eight letters, sir?"

"Five o's?" suggested Savage.

Porter actually considered it for a moment before shaking his head.

"No," he said. "Not it."

"I don't know where you even start with crosswords, sir," Savage said, finally glancing up from her paperwork.

"Usually start with number one," Porter replied, deadly serious.

"Hang on," said Kett. "I think I've got the answer."

He paused for dramatic effect.

"Get back to work," he said. "That's the answer. Back to

work before the boss realises he's paying you to mess around."

As if he'd been waiting for a cue, the door to Superintendent Clare's office thumped open. Everyone swung their head towards it, the hum of chatter quietening as Clare stomped into the bullpen. He wiped his eyes with both knuckled fists like an exhausted toddler, snorting loudly. His obnoxiously brown suit jacket was unbuttoned, his shirt untucked. After a moment, he lowered his hands and blinked at the room like he was surprised to see anyone there.

"Everything okay, sir?" Kett asked him. "You look like you've just woken up from a nap."

"I never sleep, Detective," Clare shot back, his red-flecked eyes bulging. "What time is it?"

Kett checked his watch.

"Nearly ten," he said.

"In the morning?"

"Uh... yes, sir."

Clare advanced a few more steps, wiping white flecks from his thin lips. His mouth opened like he was going to yell at them, and then *kept* opening, as if he'd decided he was going to swallow them all whole. He groaned his way through a monstrous yawn, one that gave the entire Extreme Crime Task Force a good ten seconds to study his dangling uvula.

"Are you sure you're okay, sir?" Kett asked when the Super's jaw had snapped shut.

"I'm fine," Clare said, walking a little further into the room. "Although, if you must know, my wife's still on her celibacy kick. She's convinced it's made her look ten years younger. She's added another month to it. So now I'm doing it too, to give her a taste of her own medicine."

"You're going celibate, sir?" asked Kett, his nose wrinkling.

"I am. I'm holding back the goods, see how she likes it."

"I bet she's utterly devastated," Savage said quietly, the sarcasm audible even in her whisper.

"What?" barked Clare.

"Nothing, sir," she said. "Good for you."

Clare eyeballed her for a second before letting it go.

"What are you lot up to anyway? Hanging out here like a bunch of eunuchs' scrotums. I've been thinking about nicknames for you all, you know. Do you want to hear what I came up with?"

"Not really," Kett muttered.

Clare pointed a long-nailed finger at Porter.

"You're now called KitKat, do you know why?"

"Because I'm delicious, sir?" asked Porter.

"Because you're always taking a break. You." He pointed at PC Felicity Niven, who was close to cowering under her desk. "I'm going to call you Seaweed. Because you float around all day getting tangled around my feet."

He swung his arm around the room, addressing each copper in turn.

"You're Motion Sensor, because you only work when somebody walks past. You're now called Deck Chair, because you always fold under pressure. Butter Knife, because you're not the sharpest tool in the box."

The bullpen door opened and PC Duke sauntered in, whistling. He took one look at Clare and tried to wheel around and escape.

"And here comes Hodenkobold," said Clare.

Duke turned back.

"What, sir?" he said.

"Hodenkobold?" said Kett.

"Look it up, Detective," Clare replied. "You'll see how apt it is. Get over here, Hodenkobold."

Duke slouched to his desk. Porter was studying his phone, and he barked out a laugh.

"Hodenkobold," he said. "It means somebody extremely annoying."

"Bit harsh, sir," said Duke with a pout.

"Wait for it," grinned Clare.

Porter carried on reading, chuckling.

"The literal translation is testicle goblin! Sir, you've absolutely captured the essence of Duke."

"Why would you call me that?" said Duke.

"Face like a hairy bollock," Clare told him. "Now who's next, ah yes."

The Super turned his attention to Kett.

"You're new name is Zipper."

"Zipper, sir?"

"Because having you in my employment is more painful than getting Little Colin caught in the fly of my trousers."

Everyone grimaced.

"Little Colin?" mouthed Kett.

"Could be worse," said Porter, still grinning. "You could be bollock gremlin."

"Testicle goblin," Clare corrected.

"What about me, sir?" asked Savage.

"I'm just going to keep calling you Kate," said Clare with what almost passed as a smile. "Because I actually like you, and unlike the rest of these moist goat vaginas, you do your job."

"I'm literally doing my job right now," grumbled Kett beneath his breath.

"Have you got a nickname, sir?" asked Duke.

"Yes," said Clare with a twisted smile. "God."

Nobody was brave enough to contradict him. He gave them all another disgusted look, then turned back to Kett.

"You're needed, *Zipper*," he said. "In reception."

"Why, sir?" Kett asked.

"Because apparently some tosser has just come in claiming he's murdered his wife."

CHAPTER THREE

By the time Kett had made his way to the lobby, Savage along for the ride, it was mobbed. Close to a dozen uniformed officers occupied the space, two by each set of doors and the rest crowding one of the rows of chairs that were usually occupied by impatient civilians waiting for appointments. It looked like everyone had been evacuated, including the desk staff. Kett could see them all peering through the main doors from the car park, as wide-eyed as goldfish.

Only one man remained, perched on the very edge of a chair. His hands had been cuffed in front of him and his head rested between his knees. His back was arched so tightly that Kett could have counted the ridges of his vertebrae through the thin fabric of his black shirt. He was well-groomed and smartly dressed, although it looked like he'd run through hell and back. His shoes were caked in mud, and Kett could see streaks of crimson in his black hair, and on the dark skin of his neck. His hands were the worst, so much dried blood between his fingers that it looked like paint.

"What the hell?" Kett asked quietly, letting the reception door close behind him.

He walked over to the front desk, nodding to the sergeant who stood there.

"Tomlinson," he said. "What's going on?"

The sergeant looked at the man on the chair, his forehead creasing.

"Walked in ten minutes ago," he said in a smoker's whisper. "He's got a bad limp. Waited in the queue, if you can believe it. When he spoke to Shell he told her he'd killed his wife. Wanted to speak to whoever was in charge."

"He give you a name?"

"Grant Dankworth," said Tomlinson. "Said his wife's name is Karen. That's all he told us. Shell got an officer in, we cuffed him, and he's been sitting here ever since. No weapons on him, no phone, no wallet. Just keys. Hasn't said another word."

"Thanks," said Kett.

He walked through the throng of constables, collecting a chair as he went and positioning it in front of the seated man, sitting close enough to speak quietly, but far enough that he had some space to retreat if the man decided he wasn't done killing. Savage stood by his side, her body tense.

"Grant," said Kett. "That your name?"

This close, the smell of the man was overpowering—the tang of sweat and smoke. There was more blood on his trousers, and Kett saw a tear in the fabric and the hint of a serious wound in the skin beneath. He showed no sign of responding, the gentle rise and fall of his back the only clue that he was still alive.

"Grant," Kett said again. "My name's Robert, I'm a police officer here. First things first, I need to make sure you're okay. You're hurt, aren't you?"

The man's reply was too faint for Kett to make out, spoken to the floor in a voice that seemed drained of all strength.

"Can you lift your head for me, Grant?" Kett persisted. "Just so I can hear you better."

It was a struggle, that much was clear. Dankworth's body trembled like a clockwork toy as he ratcheted himself up, his feet scuffing the floor, his cuffed hands braced on his good leg. When it appeared, his face was so contorted with pain and exhaustion and grief that he could have been wearing a mask. His eyes were wild enough to cause the uniformed coppers in the room to shuffle to attention, a collective reaching for batons and tasers.

Grant caught Kett's eye for a fraction of a second before looking away, licking teeth that were stained red with blood. He was drenched in sweat, more bloodstains splashed on his throat, soaking the collar of his shirt.

"Thank you," said Kett, moving back in his chair before he even realised he was doing it. "Can you tell me what happened? Your wife is hurt?"

Dankworth licked his chapped and bleeding lips again, his eyes crawling in their sockets, seeing everything and nothing. Kett gave him all the time he needed, and after a minute or so he seemed to find what he was looking for.

"Karen's dead. I killed her."

Kett glanced at Savage, whose face was drawn.

"You killed her?" he repeated when he'd turned back to Dankworth. "By accident, Grant? Or did you mean to do it?"

He'd met a number of people who'd taken the life of somebody they loved by mistake. Far too many of them. The ones who'd been texting while driving their kids to school and who'd run their car off the road, the ones who'd drunkenly set fire to their house after falling asleep with a cigarette between their lips, the ones who'd punched a friend or a sibling a little too hard during an argument. Dankworth carried the same expression of horror and disbelief, the same awful remorse. Which was why it was such a surprise when he nodded.

"I meant to do it," he said, tears rolling down his cheeks, turning crimson by the time they dropped from his chin. "I meant to do it. I killed her."

"She's definitely dead?" said Kett. "Because often people can look—"

"She's fucking dead," the man spat. "I crushed... I crushed her..."

He lifted his cuffed hands like he was trying to imitate something, bringing them down onto his lap with some force. When he spoke again, his voice had gone up an octave, almost a scream.

"I crushed her *fucking head.*"

He dropped back between his legs as if he could disappear, shouting those same words three more times before quietening.

"Where is she now?" asked Kett.

"I... I don't know," Dankworth replied, his voice muffled. "I can't remember."

"Not at home? At work?"

"I don't remember," he said, and there was a touch of anger there now, a promise of violence.

Kett stood up, nodding to the sergeant.

"Don't like where this is heading," he said. "Can you take him down to an interview room? Get him secure, and get somebody to take a look at his leg."

"Yes, sir," said Tomlinson.

"How did he get here?"

Tomlinson held up a set of keys, giving them a rattle. "By car, I'm guessing."

"Kate, with me," said Kett.

He took another look at Grant Dankworth before he left, but there was no sense to be found in his hunched form, in his soft whimpers.

Kett pushed through the main doors into the chill of the morning, ignoring the puzzled stares from the crowd. Shelley, the receptionist, was doing her best to corral them into some kind of order, and he gave her a thankful nod as he strolled past.

"What's the model?" asked Savage as they entered the first row of cars.

"BMW," said Kett.

There were at least six in the lot, and Kett held the fob up high and pressed the button until he heard one of them chirp. It was a 3 Series with a 65 plate, its white body encrusted with mud. It had been reverse-parked almost perfectly two rows from the building.

Kett cupped his hand to the driver's window and checked the interior, but there was nobody else inside. He opened the door, leaning in. It was no surprise to find bloodstains on the black leather, the wheel and the gear stick smudged with crimson. There were red streaks on the windscreen as well.

"Where he's wiped it," said Savage, seeing the same thing. "Must have used his hand to clear the condensation."

"Anything in the glove box?" he said.

Savage opened it, releasing an avalanche of paperwork.

"Yep," she said. She selected a sheet of paper and scanned through it. "Service receipt. Grant Dankworth, lives in Taverham. Laburnum Avenue."

Kett inserted the key, made sure the car was in neutral,

then started the engine. He didn't want to sit on the seat because of the blood, so he craned over and used his knuckle to activate the satnav. This, at least, was clean. The last entry on the list of previous destinations was in Norfolk, a place in the middle of nowhere. It had been keyed in last night.

"Swannington," he said, seeing the name of the nearest village. "You know it?"

"Yes, sir," said Savage, still leafing through papers. "Tiny place, out by the Dinosaur Park."

"Anything there?"

Savage peered over the car's logbook at the screen.

"Grant Dankworth's wife?" she suggested.

Kett killed the engine and struggled out, his back aching as he straightened up. He closed the door and walked to the boot, popping the latch. The pneumatics must have gone because it didn't open, and he had to heft it up himself, wedging his shoulder under it to prop it up.

If he'd had any doubts at all about the man's innocence, they ended here.

A sledgehammer lay across the boot, its wooden shaft streaked with bloody fingerprints and its dull metal head caked in meat. There was hair on the hammer as well, clumps of dirty blonde matted with gore.

"Shit," he said, putting his hand to his mouth.

That used to be somebody's head, he thought, and he had to look away, had to sip cold air from over his shoulder. Savage appeared next to him, a low groan escaping her.

"I'll get Hay out here," she said. "But you should see something."

He made sure Savage was clear, then he dropped the lid of the boot. It closed like a bear trap.

Savage led him to the passenger door. She'd laid the

papers out on the seat, and on the top was what looked like a printed invitation. In the middle of it was a photograph of two people, a man and a woman, standing in what looked like a pub. Underneath that, in enormous pink letters, were a handful of words.

Join Grant and Karen for their anniversary drinks!

The Cock Inn (oo-er!), Sunday at 7.

No Gifts Required!

The paper was creased with age, and when Kett picked it up it almost disintegrated. He reached for his glasses before remembering he'd left them on his desk, holding the document at arm's length and doing his best to squint it into focus.

The man in the photograph was the same man he'd just met in the lobby, although he looked remarkably different here. He was younger, his eyes bright, his smile genuine. He had one arm over the shoulders of the woman next to him, pulling her close. Everything about their body language suggested nothing but love.

With more than a little reluctance, Kett turned his attention to the woman in the photograph. She was recently in her forties, he guessed. Her hair was a darker blonde and tied back to reveal a round face. The photographer had caught her mid-laugh, her mouth open at a slightly odd angle but her eyes bursting with joy. She was clutching the hand that Grant had looped over her shoulder, pulling it to her chest. She wore a loose green dress, which bore a design Kett couldn't see without his glasses.

They were a beautiful couple, there was no doubt about it.

Or they had been, once. Now one of them was being led to an interview room.

And the other was, more than likely, dead.

"Karen Anne Dankworth," said Savage. "Born in 1979. She's named on his insurance."

"Forty-three," said Kett. "How old's he?"

"Same age. They've almost got the same birthday, too. He's March, she's April."

"What happened between then and now?" Kett asked, looking at the photograph for a moment more before folding it up and sliding it into his pocket.

Savage didn't answer, reaching for her phone. Kett shuffled through the papers while she spoke to Hay, finding bank statements, insurance renewal forms, travel documents, a couple of parking tickets, but nothing much else. Everything here corroborated what the photograph had told him, that this was a relationship with very little in the way of problems.

Everything except the sledgehammer, that was.

He stepped back and shut the door, turning to Savage when he heard her hang up.

"Hay's on her way, sir," she said. "She'll be a minute or two."

"Thanks," he said.

"You want me to go to their house?"

Kett hesitated for a moment, then shook his head.

"Grant said he couldn't remember where he'd killed her. I don't think she's at home. I'll send a uniform to check, but I think our best bet is the satnav. Take Duke and try to find out what Grant was doing in Swannington last night."

"Will do, sir," said Savage. "Where are you going?"

Kett looked over the roof of the BMW, trying to blow HQ away with a sigh.

"I'm going to try to work out what the hell is going on."

CHAPTER FOUR

When he returned to the reception, it was like nothing out of the ordinary had happened. Shelley was back behind her desk, arguing with the first in a long line of people who were waiting to be seen. A few of the seats had filled up, but there was a noticeable gap where Grant Dankworth had been sitting. Kett guessed the chair had been taken away to be cleaned.

He walked the short way to the MIT office in silence, pushing through the door to see Superintendent Clare in the middle of the bullpen. Porter and Duke sat at their desks scribbling notes while DS Alison Spalding read from a sheet of paper she was holding. She glanced at Kett without missing a beat.

"Dankworth's a sales guy, works for an internet company in the city. Blast."

"What's the matter?" said Clare.

"No, Blast is the name of the company. He's their content director. According to their website, he's not local. Grew up in Croydon, moved here when he was twenty-four, after uni. His hobbies include MMA and jigsaws."

"Mixed Martial Arts and jigsaws?" said Duke. "You reckon he does them at the same time? Like Chess Boxing?"

"No, Hodenkobold," said Porter. "I don't reckon he does."

"He's never been in trouble, never been on our radar," Spalding continued. "But his house was broken into four years ago, couple of electronics stolen. Happened during the day. Nobody was home, nobody was ever arrested for it."

She flicked to the next sheet of paper.

"He married Karen Cubbage in 2015, up in the Castle. Registry office thing. She's the same age as him. She works for the city council, but when I called them, they told me she's been off for a few months with an illness. I'm guessing it's a mental health thing, by the way they were talking. Wouldn't tell me what. They said nobody's heard from her for a while. I called the house, no answer, there's a unit on its way there to check."

"Maybe she's not dead, then," said Clare. "Maybe she's just missing."

"There's a bloody sledgehammer in the back of Dankworth's BMW that says she's dead," said Kett.

Clare pulled a face.

"I hate you, Kett," he said.

"I didn't put it there, sir. Hay's on her way up. The last address in the satnav is from last night, somewhere near Swannington. I think that's our best shot."

He turned to Duke.

"Aaron, Kate's waiting for you outside. Check it out."

"Yes, sir," said Duke, offering a salute before jogging to the door.

"Dankworth's in an interview room, you want him?" said Clare.

"Not particularly," said Kett.

"Wrong answer, Zipper."

"Fine. Pete, you coming?"

"Yes?" said Porter, with enough reluctance that it sounded like a question.

The DI grumbled his way out of his chair and they left together. The drop in temperature as they walked deeper into the building was like stepping into a freezer, enough to punch the air from Kett's lungs.

"Christ," said Porter. "Have they not had the heating on back here?"

There were two constables standing outside the second interview room, both of them shivering.

"He's in this one, sir," said the first, hitching her thumb at the door. "Won't let anyone look at his leg, got pretty aggressive. He's secured."

"I hope so," said Kett.

He passed between the PCs and opened the door, shuddering his way into the frozen room. The cold wasn't necessarily a bad thing when it came to interrogations. People tended to cave in earlier when their teeth were chattering, especially when you promised them a nice, hot cup of tea when they'd finished.

Not that it mattered in this case, of course. Dankworth had already confessed.

The man sat behind the desk, his cuffs secured to the metal clip. The stench of him had filled the room, the bitter aroma of smoke the strongest of them all. The cold seemed to have perked him up a little because he sat upright, his eyes like a hawk's as Kett and then Porter entered. It was brighter in here than in reception, and every streak of blood on the man was illuminated in grotesque detail. The wound in his leg glistened like a mouth through the hole in his trousers.

"Grant," said Kett as he closed the door behind them. "How are you doing?"

"I need my solicitor," he said, his voice so much louder and clearer than it had been back in reception that he could have been a different man. "Now."

"We'll get right on that," said Kett, taking a seat on the other side of the table. Porter joined him, shoulder to shoulder, a welcome warmth in the frigid room. "But while we wait, do you mind if we ask you a few questions?"

"Look," he said, his cuffs rattling against the clip as he tried to lift his arms. He was still sweating profusely, his face grey. It was the wound in his leg, Kett thought. The pain must be excruciating. "I didn't know what to do, okay? I didn't know who to tell, because I didn't... I didn't *want* to do it."

Kett clicked the button on the digital recorder.

"Hang on," he said. "This is DCI Kett and DI Pete Porter interviewing Grant Dankworth."

He gave the time and the date, then motioned for the man to continue. Dankworth leaned over the table as best he could, fixing Kett with a stare that seemed to be getting stronger by the second.

"You're not allowed to talk to me without my representation," he said. "I want to talk to my solicitor."

"We didn't arrest you, Grant," said Kett. "You came to us. There must have been a reason for that. As soon as we straighten a few things out, we'll call your brief. Before we start, do you and your wife have kids we should know about?"

He shook his head.

"Okay. Where's Karen now?"

Dankworth recoiled when Kett spoke his wife's name, as if he'd been slapped. He gazed at the wall and Kett knew he was seeing her death. He would be seeing it for the rest of his life.

"She's... she's where I left her," he said, shaking his head.

"Middle of the countryside? Near a village called Swannington?"

Dankworth frowned.

"How do you know that?"

"Last entry in your car's satnav," Kett told him. "From yesterday. What happened?"

The man shook his head again, more in disbelief than in denial. He seemed utterly different to the person Kett had spoken to less than half an hour ago, and he wondered if the man was suffering from some kind of psychosis.

"We found the sledgehammer," he added as motivation.

Dankworth's newfound confidence was stripped away in an instant. He rested his head on the desk, his body rattling from the cold and from shock.

"Did you use the sledgehammer to kill Karen?" asked Kett, feeling the tremble of his own voice. The room seemed to be getting colder by the second.

After a few moments, Dankworth nodded—as best he could, anyway, given that his head still rested on the table.

"But you said you didn't want to do it. What happened?"

"You can't be arrested if somebody makes you do something, can you?" he said quietly. "That wouldn't be fair."

"Somebody made you kill her?" asked Kett.

Dankworth sat up, and for a second Kett thought he was going to topple off his chair. The frown still buckled his forehead, as if he couldn't remember. The smell of smoke grew stronger with every movement, and Kett used it to jog the man's memory.

"Where was the fire, Grant?"

"It was everywhere," he said.

And he petered out again, as if the words had simply drained out of him.

"Okay, start from the beginning," said Kett. "Tell us why you drove to the countryside."

Dankworth settled himself with a breath. He seemed to have forgotten all about the solicitor. He studied the walls as he spoke, as if reading an invisible script.

"We had drinks after work. Me and a couple of the lads. I was just leaving when I got a text. It told me to drive out to an address, so I did."

"Did it say why?" asked Porter before Kett had the chance.

Dankworth shook his head.

"Did you know the sender?"

"No."

"Are you in the habit of following anonymous texts to the middle of nowhere?" said Kett. "Because if that had been me, I'd have ignored it."

Dankworth sucked in a breath, then spat it out.

"I thought it was a Tinder thing," he said quietly. "A hook-up."

"That happen a lot, then?" asked Porter, making a point of staring at Dankworth's wedding ring.

"No," he said, an obvious lie. "Just a bit of fun. You know how it is."

"No," said Kett, his voice as cold as the room. "We don't. What happened next?"

"I don't remember." He lifted his hands as if to touch his head, but the cuffs stopped him. "I got there, and I saw this van. Or a *lorry*. Big one. I just figured it was, you know... Like, some people prefer it in vans and cars and stuff. So I walked over to it, then somebody must have... I don't remember what happened. I just woke up inside the lorry, tied to a chair. He'd lamped me, got this bloody great lump on my head."

He turned his head so they could see. He wasn't lying, it was like somebody had stitched an egg beneath his scalp.

"You were tied to a chair inside the lorry?" asked Kett.

"Yeah, I was," Dankworth said, as if he sensed nobody believed him.

"You didn't see who attacked you?"

"No, but I heard him. He was outside. I think his voice woke me up."

"What was he saying?" asked Kett, adjusting his position in the uncomfortable chair.

"Uh... I don't remember. My head hurt too much. But he was talking about Karen; he knew her name. He was talking about me and her, asking how much we loved each other. He..."

Dankworth closed his eyes, groaning.

"I feel like I'm having a stroke or something," he said. "My head."

"We'll get you something for it," said Kett. "Carry on."

"He said Karen was going to join me, then we were going to have to do something. I can't remember what he said, the pain was too much. Then she came."

"Karen drove out to meet you?"

"I heard a car, and I heard her voice and I told her to..."

"To what?" asked Kett. "To run? To get help?"

"The man said he'd kill me if I gave her any warning, or if she left. I had to get her inside the lorry. So I told her to come in and she did. She got me out of the chair and..."

His face crumpled, an outpouring of pure grief.

"She helped me, and I... I..."

Nobody spoke, waiting for him to find his way.

"The man shut the door when Karen climbed inside, he locked us in. Then he set fire to it."

"To what?" asked Kett. "The lorry?"

Dankworth nodded furiously.

"He set the whole thing on fire and told me that... that only one of us was allowed to leave. There were weapons in the van. Knives, stuff like that. A... a..."

"A sledgehammer," said Kett when he couldn't finish.

Dankworth nodded again.

"I didn't have a choice," he said. "The van was burning, I could see the flames. The heat, it was..."

Kett knew what it was like, he'd been there more than once. Even here, in the fridge of the interview room, he could feel the choking, blistering horror of a fire.

"I wasn't going to do anything, I swear," he said. "But Karen had a knife, she stabbed me with it."

He looked down at his leg, his face morphing once again as if it was the first time he'd seen the wound.

"She fucking stabbed me, so I... I hit her. I hit her. I hit her until she... I killed her, but I didn't want to. *He* made me do it. I didn't want to."

Kett shared a look with Porter, the DI pale.

"Then what happened?" asked Kett. "The man let you out?"

"The door opened," Dankworth said, nodding. "Just a crack, but I managed to get my hands under it, lift it. I got out. The lorry was a fucking bonfire. Whole thing was up in flames. I just ran."

"You ran," said Kett. "To your car?"

"Yeah."

"You didn't see the man?"

"I didn't stop to look. I didn't care about anything, I just wanted to get the fuck out of there."

"You cared about one thing," said Kett. "You cared enough about the sledgehammer to bring it with you."

"No, I..." he said, shaking his head. "Wait, I mean, I guess I *did*, but only..."

He struggled, his mouth opening and closing.

"He might still have been out there," he said eventually. "That's right, I wanted to bring it in case he attacked me."

"So you went to your car, opened the boot—which is no small feat, given your pneumatics are gone—dropped the hammer in there, then walked back to the driver's seat and got in?"

"Yeah," said Dankworth.

"Seems remarkably composed for somebody who's just murdered their wife."

"I didn't murder her," Dankworth said, leaning over the table. "I just told you. Somebody made me do it."

He glanced at the tape recorder, his tongue darting across his lips.

"Wait, I told you I wanted to speak with my solicitor," he said. "You shouldn't be doing this."

"We're just having a chat," said Kett. "And we're almost done. What time did you get to the lorry, Grant?"

The man didn't look like he was going to answer, but after a minute or so of silence, he shrugged.

"Five?"

"And what time did Karen get there?"

"I don't know. They took my phone, and my watch. I don't know how long I was out for."

"That's what I find strange," said Kett. "This all happened yesterday evening, didn't it? Or last night. But you only got to us at," he checked his watch, "just after ten? Where have you been since Karen died?"

Dankworth opened his mouth and let it hang there, as if every word in the English language had abandoned him. Kett filled the silence with the inevitable.

"Grant Dankworth, you are under arrest for the murder of Karen Dankworth. You do not have to say anything, but it may harm your defence if you do not mention when questioned something you later rely on in court. Anything you do say may be given in evidence."

"I told you," he shot back. "I didn't kill her. Somebody made me do it."

Kett stood up and made his way to the door, opening it while Dankworth continued to plead his case.

"Just go out there, you'll see," he said. "The real killer might still be there."

Then his voice was trapped behind the closing door.

Kett pulled out his phone as they walked back to the bullpen.

"What now, sir?" asked Porter.

"I need to call Savage," he said. "And warn her that they might not be on their own out there."

CHAPTER FIVE

It didn't take as long to drive out of the city as Savage had feared, although the journey seemed far longer than it really was thanks to Duke's incessant humming. Over the last few weeks, she had tried every technique in her armoury to try to get him to stop—from giving him a punch on the arm every time he put his lips together, to flat-out threatening to break up with him if he ever so much as *hmmmm'd* the first line of *We Will Rock You* again.

Nothing had worked.

She'd come to the understanding that it was simply a glitch in Duke's programming. The second he got in a car, he started to hum. He'd told her he'd done it since he was a travel-sick kid, which made it a minor miracle that he was still on speaking terms with his mum. It was a good thing he had a few redeeming qualities, Savage thought as she followed the satnav's instructions.

He turned one of those qualities to her now, beaming a giant smile.

"What?" she said, feeling the heat in her cheeks.

"Have you forgotten?"

"No," she said. "Forgotten what?"

"That it's Valentine's Day!" he said with the squeak of a little boy.

"Oh, right."

"Come on," said Duke. "It's the most romantic day of the year."

"It's really not," said Savage. "It's like the *least* romantic day of the year. Nothing but corporate pressure to buy your other half a dozen red roses that will be dead in a week. The whole thing was cooked up by shops and restaurants to bring in a bit of extra cash in the quiet weeks after Christmas, you must know that."

"But it's *Valentine's*," he said. "The god of love and all that."

Savage took her eyes off the road for a moment to see if he was being serious, but his face was made of stone.

"The god of love?"

"Yeah, you know," Duke waved his arms in a way that made it clear he did *not* know. "Valentine's."

"He wasn't a god, he was a saint," said Savage. "As in Saint Valentine. You know he was arrested and dragged before the prefect of Rome, then condemned to death. He was beaten with clubs and then he had his head cut off."

"Ew," said Duke, horrified. "That's not very romantic. What did he do to deserve that?"

"He wouldn't stop humming in his girlfriend's chariot," said Savage.

She stopped at a junction, then turned left.

"I think he got in trouble for marrying young couples," she said. "Which meant the men couldn't go off to fight for their country. The emperor didn't approve."

"So they chopped his head off?"

"Violent times," she said, squinting into the brutal winter sky.

"Well, I booked us a table at the Mexican place you like," he said, some of the enthusiasm gone from his voice. "The one with the hats."

She reached over and rested her hand on his for a second.

"That's sweet of you, Aaron, thank you."

"You're wel—"

"But it will be absolutely mobbed. Let's stay in, eat Ben and Jerry's in front of the telly."

"We can't," he said.

"Why?"

"Because there's something I need to do, Kate. Something important."

She gave him a suspicious side-eye.

"I can't say anything," he said. "It will ruin the surprise."

She had so many more questions, but they were probably best left unasked. Fortunately, they were approaching their destination. Savage followed the road around, trying to make sense of the field that was hidden on the other side of a scraggly hedge. She caught a flash of white up ahead, slowing down.

"There," said Duke, pointing to a break in the hedge.

Savage slowed the car to a halt next to the gap, cutting the engine and putting her hazards on. There wasn't much room to get by here, but they hadn't seen another car in the last five minutes and she didn't want to risk disturbing any tracks in the mud. She got out, halfway around the car before she heard her phone ring. It was Kett.

"Sir," she said. "I think we've found it."

"That's why I'm calling," came his reply, muted by static. "Grant Dankworth told us he was forced to kill his wife, that somebody locked them in the van and set fire to it, would only let them out if one of them killed the other."

"Seriously, sir?" she said, watching Duke get out of the car and stretch his arms over his head. "That sounds a little... far-fetched. You think he was telling the truth?"

"Kate?" said Kett. "I'm losing you. Just be careful, if it looks like somebody else is there, back off and call for reinforcements."

"Will do, sir," she said.

"Kate?"

She hung up and fired a text back: *I'll be careful. No sign of anyone else here.*

It wasn't a lie. She trudged carefully through the mud, avoiding the lines of tyre tracks and holding onto the prickly branches of the hedge to stop herself from falling.

Duke wasn't so lucky, making it three steps into the quagmire before his heavy feet slid out from under him. He did the splits in slow motion before his legs buckled, depositing him on his backside.

"Shit a brick!" he cried out.

Savage wanted to offer words of encouragement, but as soon as she opened her mouth, her body saw it as permission to laugh. She slapped her hand to her mouth to stop it, wincing at the look Duke threw her way.

"I'm so sorry," she said when the giggles had passed. "That was not very kind of me."

"Too bloody right," Duke moaned, doing his best to stand up without having to plant his hands in the mud. It was a losing battle, and after a few minutes of what looked like inept breakdancing, he crawled to the side of the muddy path, using the hedge to pick himself up. "Fucking fuck," he muttered, brushing his hands together. "Serves me right, I guess."

"Why?" asked Savage as she hopped off the track onto the relative safety of the grass.

"For having such an impressive top half," he said, giving her a little flex through his uniform. "My centre of gravity is off."

"Is that the problem, is it?" she said with a smile.

She ignored his reply, squinting against the February sun to see a narrow field fringed by woodland. The gnarled trees had gathered like an army, reaching for her with bare-boned fingers. The only sign of life was the throbbing purr of pigeons and the distant rumble of farm equipment. But it wasn't peaceful. There was something about the uneven ground, about the ugly trees, about the cruel winter light and the stench of rotting vegetation, that made her feel a deep sense of unease.

It really is bleak out here, she thought. *It really is a horrible place to die.*

The lorry sat in the middle of the field, burned to its shell. It was a big one, rigid rather than articulated, easily twelve metres long and four in height. All four tyres had blown out, the walls of the cargo hold almost completely black—just a fringe of white near the roof, like the icing on a cake. The shuttered rear door was slightly open, the faintest outline of a heart visible in the soot. There might have been letters there too, an L, perhaps, or a J? She couldn't be sure.

Only the lorry's cab remained relatively intact, she saw as she circled it. The glass in the doors and windscreen had shattered, but it had retained its colour.

Smoke still rose from the wreck, but it was just the ghost of the fire. The burning had stopped a long time ago.

"Arson," said Duke. He was pointing a muddy finger to the space beneath the lorry and she saw a little collection of melted petrol canisters there. Ducking down, she counted five of them.

"Jesus," she said, standing. "If they were all full, this thing would have gone up in seconds. I'm amazed it didn't explode."

She approached the back of the truck, coughing the haze of smoke from her lungs. Up close, she saw that the first letter inside the heart was definitely a J, but she couldn't make out the other. The shuttered door was only open a couple of feet, a slit of absolute darkness.

"Careful," said Duke from behind her.

"Well, you can always go first, Aaron."

"I was going to," he said. "I just can't move very fast or I'll bugger over again."

She stood back to let him pass, and he pulled out his torch as he approached the back of the lorry. The tailgate was down, thankfully, and he leaned on it in order to shine the light through the gap. She caught sight of the mud on his trousers, but the lorry had removed any further urge to laugh.

"Stinks," he said. "Can't see anything at all."

He laid the torch on the tailgate, then clambered up, staying on his belly as he shuffled through the gap. There was a moment, when he pushed his head into that lightless slit, that she almost screamed for him not to. She imagined it slamming down like a guillotine, beheading him like Saint Valentine.

"What a mess," he said, his voice echoing inside. "Loads of shit in here, but I can't see a body."

Savage hopped onto the tailgate and crouched down next to him.

"Careful, it's hot," he said.

It was warm, if anything, but it was remarkable the lorry

was still radiating any heat at all after the cold night. There was a fine layer of ash on the tailgate, greasy to the touch, but she ignored it, worming her way through the gap. The smell was unbearable, the caustic stench of burnt plastic and metal. She stood on the other side of the door and clicked on her torch, her watering eyes making it impossible to see anything until she'd blinked the tears away.

If this was Karen Dankworth's tomb, it was a tragic one. The lorry would have become an oven within minutes, but with any luck, Karen hadn't burned alive. Judging by the sledgehammer they'd found, she'd been dead by the time the flames had spread.

If that was the case, though, then where was the body?

Savage didn't want to step too far into the lorry in case she contaminated the evidence. She methodically swept her torch from left to right, pausing at lumps of darkness that might have been knives or tools. But there was nothing here big enough to have been a person.

Had the heat been enough to *cremate* her?

She shuddered, shooing Duke out of the way just as he'd clambered through the door. She escaped back into the day, rolling off the tailgate and doing her best to brush the soot and the ash—*the remains of Karen Dankworth*, she tried not to think—from her suit.

Sucking in the cold, damp air, she walked to the lorry's cab. The plastic handles had been melted, drooping like candle wax, so she grabbed the lip of the broken passenger window and hoisted herself up. The cab was remarkably unscathed given the damage to the rest of the lorry, the leather seats blistered but still intact. The air freshener hung from the mirror, fluttering wildly in the breeze as if determined to extinguish the smell of the fire.

Savage tugged on the glove box, but it was melted shut.

"Anything?" asked Duke behind her.

"Nothing," she said. "Can you take a look around the field, see if they left anything else?"

She heard him trudging off, and leaned further through the window in order to investigate the tray between the front seats. This, too, was empty.

She dropped back to the ground and walked along the front of the lorry. It was a DAF, the registration from 2013. She made a note of it before hopping up the other side and craning through the driver's window. The van had been emptied, the wide dash clear and nothing on the floor.

The only thing that still remained was the key.

Savage yanked a glove from her pocket, using her elbow to cling to the door while she wrestled it on. She suspected the key was melted into the ignition, but when she gave the leather fob a gentle tug, it slid free. She hopped to the ground and laid it in her palm. The key was a standard one, nothing special about it at all.

The fob, though, was the shape of a heart. And on it were two letters, etched messily into the leather.

JV.

"Can't see anything else," yelled Duke from the other side of the narrow field. "Plenty of tracks, though. Car ones, not people. You found much?"

"Not sure," she called back. "Do the letters JV mean anything to you?"

"JVC?" he replied. "They make lorries. Diggers and stuff."

"No C, just a J and a V. I think they're written on the back of the truck as well, in paint, on the door."

She made her way back around to see, holding the key fob up to compare. It was impossible not to see it now, the loop of the J and the sharp point of the V a deeper shade of black against the charred metal door.

"JV," she said to herself, trying to figure it out and coming up blank.

"Julie's Van?" asked Duke as he traipsed around the lorry. Incredibly, he'd managed to get himself even muddier, his boots caked and his trousers brown up to his shins.

"What on earth have you been doing, Aaron?" she asked.

"Puddle," he said.

"Julie's what?"

"Julie's Van. JV. Just throwing things out there. Joe's Van. Justin's Van. Jamie's Van. Uh..."

He stared at the sky for a moment.

"Jumpy Vampires. Jello Vegetables. Juicy Vagina."

"Aaron!" said Savage.

He held up his hands in apology.

"Sorry, it was out before I could stop it."

He leaned in, staring at the key fob in her hand.

"Could be anything," he said. "You think it means something?"

She studied the heart on the key fob a moment longer, then turned her attention back to the lorry.

JV.

"I'm hoping it means *everything*," she said.

CHAPTER SIX

"What are you thinking, Pete?" asked Kett as Porter led the way back into the bullpen.

There was a buzz in the room that hadn't been there this morning, a palpable excitement. It wasn't every day that somebody turned up at the station claiming to have staved in his wife's head with a sledgehammer. There was no sign of the Superintendent, so Kett made his way through the door and down the corridor, heading for the Incident Room.

"I don't know," said Porter after he'd had a chance to think. "His story's wild. It feels too insane to be a lie, you know?"

"That's what I was thinking," said Kett. "If you kill your wife, you don't concoct a tall tale about somebody locking you in a van and making you fight to the death. You do it discretely, you hide the body, you claim innocence."

"And then we catch you anyway," said Porter. "Because it always happens sooner or later. At some point, you'll slip. So maybe he thought, 'Fuck it, I'll come up with a story so nuts that everybody will assume it's the truth.'"

"He'll still get done for it, though," said Kett as he opened the Incident Room door. "So what's the point?"

DS Spalding was in the room, pinning a couple of photographs to the wall. She must have caught the end of their conversation because she called out to them.

"Because he'll get a manslaughter charge, most likely," she said. "Not murder. Ten years instead of twenty."

"Still, that's a lot of time behind bars, especially when he could have asked her for a divorce," said Kett.

"Some men think murder is easier," Spalding said. "And cheaper. If you can get away with it. I was watching the interview; he seems like the kind of man who'd put a sledgehammer through his wife's face if it made his life more convenient."

Kett puffed out a sigh, walking over to look at the photographs. Grant was there, and Karen too, their close-ups taken from the invitation that they'd found in the BMW and blown up to life-size.

"They look so happy," he said. "Let's just say, for a moment, that he was telling the truth. Somebody targets them, lures them to a lorry in the middle of nowhere, sets fire to it, then asks them to fight each other to the death."

Spalding lifted an eyebrow.

"My cat could come up with a better story than that," she said.

"Yeah," agreed Kett. "But let's argue for a moment that this is what happened. It still feels off."

"How?" asked Spalding.

"Because... I mean, Pete, if this was you, if you and Allie were in this situation, the van is burning, you've been asked to kill each other. You know it's real, there's no doubt in your mind. There's a sledgehammer right there. What do you do?"

"Knock the bloody door down," he said. "It's a sledgehammer."

"Let's say you tried that," Kett went on. "There's no way out, you're literally cooking in there, Allie's about to die the most horrific death imaginable. You have maybe a minute to do something or you're both finished. What do you do?"

Kett knew what he was going to say, he just needed him to say it.

"I smack myself in the head with the hammer," Porter said. "Or cut my throat with a knife. If it's me or Allie, then it's her. She's the one getting out of there."

Kett nodded.

"Me too," he said, trying not to imagine the horror of it. "I die, Billie lives. It goes without saying, doesn't it? She's the kids' mum, they need her."

"That's pretty decent of you both, sirs," said Spalding, and for once she didn't sound like she was being sarcastic. "I mean, I'm not married, but if I was, I'm pretty sure I'd make the same decision as you."

She pondered it for a moment.

"Although it depends how annoying my imaginary other half is, I guess. She might be awful."

"And even if I did decide I wanted to kill her so that I could get away," said Kett, "I'm not sure I could do it. Even in the heat of the moment, so to speak, I don't think I could physically bring myself to crush Billie's head with..."

Even the thought of it turned his stomach.

"Nope, I couldn't. There's no way."

"I'm guessing Grant Dankworth didn't have the same feelings of love and respect for his wife that you both have for yours, sir," said Spalding. "I did a little digging and his name came up on a couple of dating sites."

"How did you find that?" asked Porter. "Aren't they confidential?"

"They are, but these sites are targeted by hackers all the time. Email addresses get released, names are exposed. Remember Ashley Maddison?"

"The website where married folk went to hook up with other people?" asked Porter, followed immediately by a shake of his head. "I mean, no, never heard of it."

Kett raised his eyebrow.

"I joined before I was married," Porter protested. "When I was single. I didn't know it was for affairs. I thought it was just to meet people. I was going through a dry spell. I only met one woman on there and she was about thirty years older than her photograph and she tried to get me drunk on sherry and I never saw her again."

Kett and Spalding stared at him.

"Okay, I saw her once more, but only because she was nice, and she wasn't married either, she was widowed, and she seemed lonely and—"

"Pete," said Kett, lifting a hand. "We believe you."

Porter flapped his hands to cool down his crimson cheeks.

"Her name was Doris," he said quietly.

"Christ, Pete, how old was she?"

"As I was saying," Spalding continued, sparing Porter the misery of having to answer. "Leaks from sites like these happen all the time. I found Grant's email from his work and typed it in on the off chance, based on what he confessed about Tinder. It pinged up again on three other leaks, from three sites. All are illicit dating services for married people."

"What a prick," said Porter.

"Indeed, sir," said Spalding. "But that seems like a

motive to me. You're bored of your wife, you're stepping out, you meet somebody else and you start to yearn for freedom. Happens all the time."

"Except most people don't execute their spouse," said Kett. "But this is good. It shows there was a rift between them, that he's a risk-taker."

"And that he's good at lying," said Spalding.

Kett nodded, pulling his phone from his pocket when he felt it buzz. It was Savage, and he put it on speaker.

"Hello, sir," she said, and her voice was about two octaves deeper than usual.

"Yikes," said Porter. "What happened to you?"

"It's Duke, sir," came the reply. "I'm on Kate's phone. She's driving."

"You find much out there?"

"We found the lorry, sir. It's been burned out, no sign of a body."

"Were there bones? Anything like that?"

"No, sir. No other cars, although lots of tracks. Maybe three vehicles in total. Lorry still had its plates. You got a pen?"

Kett didn't, but Spalding did. She scribbled the registration number down when Duke read it out, then walked out of the room.

"There was something else, sir," said Duke. "The key fob was a heart, and it had the letters JV in it. The same letters had been painted onto the back of the van, inside a heart."

"JV?" asked Kett.

"Yes, sir. We're heading back, unless there's anywhere else you need us to go."

"There is," said Kett. "Can you head over to Taverham and have a proper look at the Dankworth place?"

"Sure, sir," said Duke.

"I'll text you the address."

Kett hung up, placing his phone on the nearest desk.

"No body," he said, drumming his fingers on the tabletop.

"Could have been cremated," said Porter with a shrug. "Metal lorry, big fire."

"But there would have been bones," said Kett. "Cremation ovens just turn the fleshy bits to ash. They grind the bones afterwards."

"They what?" said Porter.

"They grind them, when they come out of the oven," said Kett. "You must have known that."

Porter shook his head.

"I just thought the whole thing went..." He *whoofed* his arms into the air. "You know."

Spalding walked back into the room, holding a sheet of paper.

"Plate came back registered to a William Briggs, but it's for a Volkswagen Beetle, not a lorry. An older model, 1981. Red."

"They switched the plates?" asked Kett.

"Looks like it, sir," said Spalding. "Briggs lives in Yarmouth. Want me to check out his place?"

"I'll go," said Kett. "Can you text Kate the Dankworth address?"

"Sure. By the way, Clare's calling for you both."

Sure enough, Kett could hear the Super's voice hollering from the bullpen like a rutting moose.

"He could come to me for a change," he muttered as he picked up his phone and left the room. Porter trotted along beside him, and by the time they'd walked through the door, Clare's words were crystal clear.

"Zipper! KitKat! Jesus Tossing Christ!"

Clare was standing in the middle of the room, his face flushed and his fists clenched. Everyone was doing their best to ignore him, but it couldn't have been easy. As soon as Kett and Porter entered the room, the Super angled his body around to face them, looking like a mantis about to behead its prey.

"Where the bloody hell have you been hiding? I've been shouting for hours."

"In the Incident Room, sir," said Kett. "Studying the *incident*. You could have called."

"Like I've got time for that, you steaming bellend," said Clare. "Hay's outside, she wants you."

"*She* could have called," muttered Kett.

Outside, the day was brighter than ever, although the cold still meant business. The vehicles around Dankworth's BMW had been moved, allowing all four doors to be opened. Three forensic technicians in white overalls and face masks busied themselves around the car, cataloguing the contents and dusting for prints.

Two constables held the boot open for Hay, who offered a wave when she saw Kett and Porter approaching. When Kett rounded the car he was surprised to see Emily Franklin there as well, the young pathologist bent double as she studied the sledgehammer.

"Morning," yawned Kett as they squeezed past the PCs.

"And what a morning," Hay replied in her distinctive Trinidadian accent. "Hello, Pete."

"Hey, Hay," Porter said. "Hey, Emily. Happy Valentine's Day."

Franklin looked up, one eyebrow cocked. Her dungarees were covered in little embroidered hearts of all shapes and colours, her jacket puffy enough that it could double as a Zorb ball if she was to ever roll down a hill.

"Why are you wishing me a Happy Valentine's Day, Pete?" she asked.

"Because it's what you're supposed to do," he replied. "It's like Christmas, or Easter, or Halloween."

"No it isn't," said Franklin. "Pretty sure you only say it to your Valentine crush."

"What?" blurted Porter. "That's not true."

Franklin grinned mischievously.

"Am I your crush, Pete?"

"No!" he protested.

"Leave him alone, Emily," said Kett. "He's taken."

Porter nodded, and Kett couldn't help himself.

"Doris would be devastated if she knew he had another love."

He did his best to stop the laugh from exploding out of his nose, but it was a battle he couldn't win.

Porter had daggers coming out of his eyes.

"Sorry, Pete," Kett offered. "Where are we at with this thing?"

The sledgehammer lay where Kett had last seen it, a collection of forensic bags and bottles laid around it. If anything, it looked even worse than it had before.

"This is a murder weapon, for sure," said Hay, using her shoulder to wipe away a bead of sweat that had rolled down the smooth dome of her shaven head. "Or at least it was used to destroy a human body very soon after death."

"Real blood, then?" asked Kett.

"Well, it isn't ketchup," Franklin replied. "Very real, but it's not the blood that worries me."

She pointed a gloved finger at the heavy metal head of the weapon.

"Skin," she said. "And hair. You see?"

Kett nodded. Porter emitted a quiet heave, stepping back.

"Grim," croaked the DI.

"I've collected some of it," Franklin went on, "but judging by the sheer volume of material that has accumulated here, we can assume it was used several times."

"You mean the attacker struck more than once?" asked Kett.

"Oh, yes," said Franklin. "Generally speaking, a single strike from a weapon of this weight will do significant damage. Easily enough to kill, if it hits with enough velocity and at the right angle—and in the right place, of course. But it wouldn't collect this many souvenirs."

"Souvenirs?" said Porter, gulping air.

"There would be blood, maybe a couple of hairs if the strike was to the head, but the speed of the strike and the force of the impact, not to mention the relative density of a human head, would leave the weapon fairly clean. A second strike, however, would hit a significantly weakened target—and we know it was the head, because of the hair. The sledgehammer would meet with less resistance, sinking further into the broken bowl of the skull."

"Nope," muttered Porter.

"It would collect some matter on the second strike, especially if it became wedged in the bone. But to look this messy, I'd say your attacker struck five or six times. There's some brain here, you see? And I found a tooth on the underside."

"Christ," said Kett. "You're sure?"

"I'm sure it was more than once," said Franklin. "Unless your attacker has superhuman strength, or unless he added the little bits of skin and hair afterwards, like some kind of craft project. Blood makes for a great glue. Did he seem like that sort of person?"

"Uh, no," said Kett, his skin crawling.

"Then the simplest solution wins again," said Franklin. "He struck her several times with the sledgehammer, in the face or the side of the head."

"She'd have been dead after the first one, right?" Kett asked.

Franklin shrugged.

"Not my place to say. I'll know for sure when I have a look at the body."

"Body's gone AWOL," said Kett. "Can you tell me anything else?"

"There are prints," said Hay, gesturing to the wooden shaft of the sledgehammer. "Dozens, all marked in blood. You have the suspect, don't you?"

"We do," said Kett. "He's already confessed, but these won't hurt. I'll get you his prints as soon as we have them."

"I can send some of this off for DNA testing too, if it helps?" said Hay. "But it won't come back for a while."

"I don't think the suspect or the victim were in our system," said Kett. "But the suspect claims he wasn't alone, says he was made to do this by somebody else, so it wouldn't hurt to find a third set of DNA."

He breathed out slowly.

"What a mess."

"He told you he was forced to kill his victim?" asked Franklin, frowning. "Who was it?"

"His wife," said Kett. "Why?"

"He must have really hated her," she said, staring into the boot of the BMW. "This isn't just murder, it's... It's *eradication.* He wanted to obliterate every last trace of her. You don't use a weapon like this, in this way, for anything else."

"Good point," said Kett. "Cara, we found the van where we think the killing took place. It's been burned out, no body, but there has to be something there. Can you take a look?"

"My pleasure," said Hay. "I'm done here anyway."

Kett nodded his thanks, walking past the PCs—who both looked like they were starting to struggle with the weight of the broken boot door—and heading back across the car park.

"I'm going to see if I can find this William Briggs guy, find out why the plates from his VW were on our lorry," he said. "You coming, Pete?"

"Not like I've got anything else to do, sir," said Porter.

"Great job," he said, throwing him the keys. "You can drive."

CHAPTER SEVEN

Taverham felt like the closest thing to an American suburb that Norwich had, the large houses set far apart, the gardens wide and well-tended. Kids too young for school braved the February chill, riding scooters and trikes up and down the quiet pavements while their parents chatted on the corners. People were making the most of the break in the rain they'd had for the last few days, the crisp blue sky promising a much-needed dose of vitamin D after the bleak winter.

Savage steered the Audi through the maze of the town until they reached Laburnum Avenue. A police IRV sat halfway down, its lights off, and she parked the Audi in front of it. The properties here were almost exclusively bungalows, most of them chalets that seemed a little quaint for a married couple who weren't yet fifty.

She got out and slammed the door, the echo of it bouncing back and forth along the quiet street. People were watching from pretty much every window she could see, although most of them were ogling Duke as he made giant strides down the pavement in his mud-caked uniform. He opened the gate of the Dankworth's chalet and approached the door, Savage right behind him.

"Should I knock?" Duke asked.

"I think our guys are in there," she replied, glancing at the empty IRV. "But sure, go ahead."

Duke lifted a fist and brought it down on the door.

Once.

He stood back, then noticed that Savage was staring at him.

"What?" he asked.

"Have you never knocked on a door before, Aaron?"

"Of course," he said. "I just did."

"Nobody knocks *once*, that's just weird. You have to knock two times, or three."

"But once is fine," he said as the sound of footsteps came closer. "See."

The door opened to reveal a uniformed copper.

"Did you knock?" he asked.

"Yes," said Duke. "I did."

"Just, I only heard one," the man said. "Wasn't sure if somebody had knocked or if a pigeon had hit the window."

"One is enough," protested Duke, following the PC inside.

"Unbelievable," said Savage as she stepped into the cramped front hall.

"There's no body here," said the PC. "I mean *nobody*, but also no dead wife. Searched the entire house and the garden, it's clean as a whistle."

"How'd you get in?"

"Back door was unlocked," he said. "Hopped the fence."

He stepped into the kitchen and Duke followed, but Savage remained in the hallway. There was a small sideboard next to the front door, a brightly-coloured bowl on top. It was full of loose change and a couple of keys. One had a fob, but it was a plastic one bearing the Blast logo, for Grant Dankworth's work, presumably. There were no car keys. Carefully framed photographs decorated the hallway, Grant and Karen beaming from every single one of them. Two looked like they were from the young couple's wedding, and the happiness seemed to shine out of it, warming the cold house.

Savage rifled through a stack of paperwork, finding nothing but bills, then made her way into the kitchen. It wasn't huge, a dining table squeezed into the gap between the enormous breakfast bar and the French doors at the back. There were more photographs on every wall, each one hand-selected, it seemed, to present the relationship in the best light possible.

The joy didn't seem to be a lie, Savage thought. She'd rarely seen a love that looked more genuine.

"You find any dogs?" she asked, seeing two of them in the gallery of pictures.

"No," said the PC. "No bowls or cages or anything either. Doesn't smell like a dog lives here."

"Can smell something, though," said Duke, his nose wrinkling.

Savage opened the fridge and caught it too, something off. She closed it again, a little harder than she needed to, causing a cascade of empty carrier bags from the top. The counter was messy, she noticed, covered in crumbs. A half-eaten piece of toast sat on a plate next to a tub of Lurpak, the lid half-off.

"Looks like they left in a hurry," she said. "Especially if the back door was unlocked."

She made her way out of the kitchen, checking a small living room before heading upstairs. There were only two bedrooms in the chalet, one a master and the other a small office. There was a laptop on the desk by the window, but when she opened it she saw that it needed a password. There was no indication that the Dankworths had children.

The bathroom had been tiled in the most obnoxious shade of pink imaginable. At least half a dozen air fresheners were positioned on the windowsill, the reek of them enough to make Savage's temples throb. The toilet had a fuzzy pink cover, something that should have been outlawed years ago.

She made her way back downstairs, peeking through the French doors for long enough to see a small garden, not even a shed out there. With no garage, and nothing else to explore, she escaped through the front door. The doorbell was an old one, no camera, so she walked back to the street and searched the front of the neighbours' houses.

"Come on," she said. "Come on..."

There, on the opposite side of the street—not a doorbell camera, but a Tesla Model S. She crossed the road, squeezing past the car on the narrow drive and knocking on the door. She was answered by barks, a microscopic furry shape appearing at the bottom of the frosted glass pane, bouncing off the walls.

"No cold callers," came a voice. "Or the dog will get you."

"I'm not a cold caller," Savage called out. "Although I am cold. It's the police. Can you open the door?"

A larger shape filled the glass, bent down to scoop up the dog, then straightened again. The door swung inwards to reveal two creatures that, were it not for the difference in size, could have been related. The dog was a little black Pomeranian and looked like a toupee. If it hadn't been for the beady eyes and the fact that its little pink tongue was poking from its mouth in a desperate attempt to lick her from three feet away, she would have assumed it belonged on the head of the man who held it.

He, too, was remarkably fluffy. His hair, the same colour as the dog's, stuck up at such extreme angles she thought he must have recently electrocuted himself. His beard was equally disordered, extending upwards almost to the bottom of his eyes and right down to his neckline. His eyes were as small as the dog's, and as he studied Savage his own tongue jutted out, running along his lips.

She couldn't work out if they were both growling, or if it was just the dog.

"Hi," she said, holding up her warrant card. The man studied it, the dog tried to eat it. "My name's DC Kate Savage. I'm with the Norfolk Constabulary."

"So it says," the man replied. "I'm Trevor. To what do you owe my pleasure?"

It was difficult to gauge the man's age. Somewhere in his forties, Savage thought, but the black turtleneck jumper he wore, which had been tucked into black corduroys that had been pulled up past his waist, made him seem so much older.

"I'm here because of a disturbance across the road," she said, throwing a thumb over her shoulder. "The Dankworths. Do you know them?"

"Yes," he said. "Are they okay?"

"We're not sure," said Savage. "Do you remember if you saw them yesterday?"

"I saw Grant in the morning," Trevor said. "Just to wave to. He leaves early."

"You didn't see him again? Or Karen?"

"My office is in the garden," he said. "I don't really see anyone once I've locked myself in there for the day.

You're lucky you caught me during a digestive biscuit break."

He licked his lips, and the dog yapped loud enough to make Savage's ears ring.

"Trevor loves a digestive," he said.

"Trevor?" asked Savage, wondering if he was talking about himself in the third person. "You mean *you*?"

"No, the dog," he said.

"Wait, I thought your name was Trevor."

"It is."

"You're *both* called Trevor?"

"It's a good name," he said. "Shame to waste it."

"Right," said Savage. "Look, I'm trying to work out what happened to Karen last night. It would really help us if we had an idea of when she left the house."

"She's missing?" asked Trevor—the *man*—with a frown.

"I can't see any cameras on the street," Savage said, ignoring his question. "But I notice you've got a Tesla."

"Oh, yes, I do!" the man said, his voice brightening. "Trevor."

"Trevor... the Tesla?"

He nodded.

"It's a good name," she said. "You don't happen to have Sentry Mode switched on, do you?"

"Always," he told her. "People say it drains the battery, but I say who cares. You can never be too careful. Caught a man peeing up it once in a car park in Swansea. Got the whole thing on camera. Reported it to the police, not that they did anything."

He gave her a disapproving look, as if she was responsible for this disappointment.

"I'm sorry to hear that," she said. "That's Wales for you. We'd have caught him if it had happened here."

This seemed to mollify him. He pushed his feet into a pair of fluffy grey slippers by the door, and Savage stepped out of the way as he carried the dog to the car.

"Trevor will have to join us," he said. "He doesn't like being left alone."

He opened the back door and lowered the dog onto the seat. Then he opened the passenger door for Savage.

"All on the phone, you know," he said as she lowered herself onto the seat. "I can control the whole car from my pocket. Very clever. But the screen in here is bigger. Can you close the door, in case Trevor tries to make a run for it?"

She did as she was asked. The dog was going ballistic in the back seat, running back and forth and making a noise like a hot water bottle in a blender. After a few seconds of this, it planted its front feet on the central console and eyeballed her like a tiny, angry pirate.

Trevor opened the driver's door and clambered in, giving the dog a pat that almost cost him his fingers.

"Little blighter," he said. "Doesn't like women much."

Savage guessed it was because Trevor didn't have many female visitors.

He tapped a few options on the large screen, navigating to the Tesla's security settings.

"Here we go. Last night, you say?"

"Yes," said Savage. "I don't know what time."

"If something happened, Trevor will have caught it," said Trevor, and Trevor the dog barked in agreement.

There was a list of incidents on the screen, and the man diligently cycled through them all. Most were simply cars on the street, or pedestrians passing in front of the house. Savage could see the Dankworth's chalet in surprising detail through the car's rear camera, and in one clip she caught sight of a woman standing in the front window.

"Hang on," she said before Trevor could cycle forward. "That's Karen?"

"Yes," he said, leaning in. "Spends a lot of time staring out the window, poor lass. I think she's lonely."

There was something ghost-like in the way Karen stood there, staring at the street. She hadn't moved by the time the clip ended.

"Grant is always at work," said Trevor. "I'm usually watching the TV when he comes home. Eight, sometimes nine o'clock."

The time stamp on the clip was 4:38 pm, and they worked their way through a few more, day slowly turning to night. It was just after six by the time Savage spotted somebody else at the house, a figure that walked down the dark path.

"There," she said, jabbing the screen and earning a stern *tut* from Trevor. He used his sleeve to wipe away the smear of her fingerprint, accidentally jogging the clip back to the beginning.

Savage resisted the urge to slap his hand away, watching the replay of the figure. It was hard to tell if it was a man or a woman because their head and body were concealed by a hooded raincoat that stretched almost to their knees. The figure walked slowly, their shoulders hunched low. They looked left and right, as if to check that the coast was clear, and crouched down by the Dankworth's front door.

"Is that Grant?" Savage asked.

"I don't think so. Maybe. I've never seen him do anything like this before."

Trevor leaned forward, crowding the screen.

"Back up a bit," she told him.

It looked like the visitor was placing something by the door, something delicate. The quality of the feed wasn't good enough to be sure. They seemed to give it a little pat, as if it was a living thing, then they stood up and knocked—loud enough for the car to pick up the sound.

After that, the person moved fast, retreating up the path and onto the pavement. They were doing something weird with their hands, Savage saw, as if they were feeding something out. They darted to the left, disappearing out of the scope of the camera.

A handful of seconds later, the front door of the house opened and Karen Dankworth appeared, just a silhouette against the hallway light. She craned out into the night before retreating, and she'd almost closed the door again before she caught sight of whatever had been left on the front step. She bent down to pick it up, and Savage almost yelped as the object danced out of her reach.

"What just happened?" Trevor asked, leaning in again.

This time Savage grabbed his arm and hoiked him back, an act which seemed to outrage the man and the dog in equal measures. She ignored their complaints, watching the screen as Karen dived for the object again. It scuttled back down the path like a mouse, and she gave chase, finally claiming it.

No matter how close Savage got to the screen, it was impossible to see what the woman was holding. She couldn't gauge her reaction, either, the resolution simply wasn't good enough.

After a few seconds, Karen turned and walked back into the house. Only for a minute or so, though, before she appeared again, slamming the door shut and running for the street, putting her coat on as she went. She was out of sight in seconds, but past the growl of Trevor's dog, Savage heard the sound of a car starting. It must have gone in the other direction, because it didn't pass the Tesla's camera.

"How strange," said Trevor. "What on earth was that thing? It *moved.*"

Savage didn't have an answer for him. He reached for the screen but she blocked him with her hand.

"Hang on, it's not finished."

He tutted at her again, fuming in his seat. The clip scrolled on, nothing but the empty street until, just as the dog was reaching an apoplexy of distress in the Tesla's back seat, a car drove past.

Savage paused it before it could leave the shot. It was instantly recognisable as a Volkswagen Beetle, an old one. And it was bright red.

"Love Bug," said Trevor.

"What?"

"That's what we used to call those cars when I was a kid. Love Bugs. After the Herbie films."

Savage took a photograph of it, making a note of the time: 6:07pm. She pressed play, counting down the seconds until the clip ended. The next saved file was nearly forty minutes later, and when she pressed it she saw Trevor the man shuffling past onscreen, Trevor the dog straining on the end of a lead.

"The camera really does add twenty pounds, doesn't it?" Trevor said, frowning at his backside on the screen.

"Thank you," Savage told him. "Can you export the file for me? I'll send somebody over to collect it."

He nodded, although he didn't look too happy about the request. Savage opened the door and escaped. Trevor the man squeaked, making a grab for Trevor the dog as it tried to vault the seats. She slammed it shut before it could escape.

"Sorry!"

She walked back across the street, calling Kett as she went.

"Kate," he said when he answered, the sound of an engine drowning out his voice. "How's it going?"

"Got lucky with a camera on the street," she said. "Somebody knocked on Karen's door a few minutes after six. Couldn't see who, but they left her a gift. Something small. It... it moved when she tried to pick it up."

Saying it aloud triggered something in Savage's head, something she couldn't quite wrap her thoughts around.

"It moved? Like it was alive?"

"No, sir, like it was..."

She saw the visitor feeding something out through their fingers as they retreated from the house. She saw the way the parcel jerked, as if it was being tugged by an invisible force.

"Like it was on a *string*," she said. "Like somebody was pulling it out of her reach."

And there it was again, something right on the edge of her mind.

"Karen left almost immediately after the parcel had been delivered, sir," she went on. "6:06. Sounded like she got in her car and drove."

"That must have been how they got Karen to the lorry," said Kett. "A note, maybe."

"About a minute after Karen left, another car drove by the house," Savage said. "A red Beetle."

"Shit," said Kett. "Like the one Briggs owns? The one whose plates were swapped with the lorry?"

"Can't be certain, sir, but how often do you see a red Bug in the city?"

"Literally never seen one," he replied. "We're almost in Yarmouth. I'll let you know if we get a lead."

A lead.

"Kate?"

"A lead," said Savage, thinking of Trevor tugging his dog on a lead, thinking of the parcel being dragged along the path. A thought materialised, as bright as the winter sun overhead. "Sir, I think I know what JV is."

"Yeah?" said Kett, his voice fizzing with static.

"Yes, sir. I think it's Jack Valentine."

CHAPTER EIGHT

"Head into the town, Pete," said Kett, the phone hot against his ear. "Hang on, Kate, I'm going to put you on speaker."

Porter drove the Volvo along the main road into Great Yarmouth, the sun blasting through the windscreen and giving Kett an instant headache. He used his free hand to pull the visor down, switching the call to hands-free and holding the phone up so that Porter could listen in.

"Okay, Kate, tell us what you know."

"I don't *know* anything, sir," she replied, her voice breaking up as Porter drove them over the bridge. "But it all suddenly made sense when I saw the package that was delivered to Karen's house, the way it danced out of her reach. It's a local tradition. Jack Valentine. You must have heard of it?"

"Assume we haven't," said Kett, although it did sound familiar.

"It's been going on since Victorian times, sir," Savage explained. "The legend says that Jack Valentine walks the streets on the night before Valentine's Day, leaving gifts for children. And for couples in love, I think. I can't remember."

"Okay," said Kett.

"His whole thing is that you never see him," Savage went on. "Like Santa, or the Tooth Fairy. He leaves a gift and disappears. But he's a trickster too. That's what made me remember. He's supposed to tie a string to the gift he leaves outside your door, then when you try to pick it up he pulls it out of your reach."

"Sounds like an arsehole," said Porter. He honked the Volvo's horn at the truck in front of them, which hadn't noticed the lights changing.

"He always lets you have the gift eventually," Savage said. "But it fits, right, sir? JV. Jack Valentine. The hearts we found on the lorry and the key fob, the gift outside the Dankworth house, the date, somebody must be using the legend, sir."

"Maybe," said Kett. "Although I don't get why somebody would imitate a local weirdo in order to lure a victim out of their house."

"Could have been Grant," said Porter. "A way of trying to throw us off his scent."

Kett nodded, seeing the thin, grey line of the sea appear ahead. He studied the houses that lined the street approaching the promenade. They were all enormous, built when Great Yarmouth was a thriving port.

Not the dump it was today.

"It's that one, Pete," he said, pointing his free hand at a stately Victorian mansion on the left. "Kate, can you go back to HQ and fill the Super in on what you've just told me? Try and get a profile down for somebody who would want to imitate Jack Valentine."

"Yes, sir," she said.

Kett hung up. There was nowhere to park on the busy road, and the house's enormous driveway was sealed by a formidable metal gate, so Porter bumped the Volvo onto the pavement and switched off the engine. Kett waited for a bus to drive past before climbing out, almost losing his elbow to a Deliveroo driver who tore past on his bike, screeching obscenities.

"This definitely the right address?" asked Porter.

"Yeah," said Kett.

"It's a bloody palace."

The house really was huge, a four-storey brick mansion with a tower making up the left-hand wall. Ornate woodwork and beautiful wrought iron details on the balconies made it look like the building was boasting, but it was a hard sell.

The closer Kett looked, the more he saw the façade was a lie. There was an enormous crack in the brickwork to the right of the tower, and several of the windows on the top floor had been broken. Through the bars of the gate, he saw that there was no front garden to speak of; it had been dug up and replaced with a featureless concrete slab littered with wheelie bins and three impressive sports cars, one of which was bright green.

Porter whistled as he took in the vehicles.

"Two R8s and a Porsche," he said. "Somebody's doing okay."

"No sign of a red Beetle, though," added Kett.

"These houses would have been amazing back in the day," said Porter. "Bet there's twelve bedrooms in there, at least. They're all HMOs now, packed full of immigrants, students and druggies, all paying two hundred quid a month for a damp room and a shared toilet. It's criminal."

"Criminal is why we're here," said Kett. "Although I'm

guessing for reasons other than a shoddy landlord. Any reason a House of Multiple Occupancy would need a gate like this?"

It was sleek and black and electric, probably the most expensive thing on the street other than the cars. The control panel had been fixed into the six-foot brick wall and Kett pressed the button. There was a buzz, but nobody answered. He pulled out his warrant card and held it up to the camera in case anyone was watching.

"Police," he said. "Open up."

The camera stared at him, and the speaker remained quiet. Kett pressed the buzzer again and stared through the bars of the gate, trying to see anything through the dark windows of the house.

"Boiler's on," said Porter, pointing to the steam billowing from the exhaust pipe on the first floor. "Somebody's home."

There was an alleyway down the side of the house, shaded by trees, and Kett walked into it, dodging a minefield of dog shit all the way to a sturdy metal side gate that was taller than he was. He gave it a shake, but it was locked. The wall next to it, though, couldn't have been more than five feet tall.

"Never ceases to amaze me," said Porter, bracing his hands on the top of the wall and hoisting himself up. "You pay a thousand quid for a gate, but literally anyone could get over this."

He looked at Kett for permission, and he nodded.

"Here we go," said Porter, getting his leg over the wall and dropping down the other side.

Kett planted his hands on the cold brick, pushed his boot against the wall, and jumped. He managed to get his chest over the top before gravity pulled him back down. He tried again, his boots scuffing the wall, his chest aching as it rubbed against the rough masonry.

"I say it again, sir," said Porter, who was watching with some amusement, "literally anyone could get over this."

Kett dropped to the ground again, cursing beneath his breath. He glanced at the windows along the rear of the house, his cheeks burning as he imagined somebody watching him.

"My mother could get over this, sir," said Porter. "And she's been in a wheelchair for six months."

"I'm bloody doing it," said Kett.

He backed away a few paces, took a run-up, and launched himself at the wall. This time he managed to get his arms over the top, and thanks to sheer perseverance, he kicked his way upwards. Porter grabbed his elbows, giving him a gentle tug.

"I don't need your help, Pete," Kett panted, although when he swung his legs over the top of the wall and felt himself slipping down the other side, he was grateful the DI was there. Porter caught him, holding onto him for a second or two before letting go.

"Got there in the end, sir," he said, brushing brick dust from Kett's shirt.

Kett slapped his hand away, giving him a glare before turning to the back of the house. A lot less time and effort had been spent on this side of the building. There was a sprawling web of cracks that looked ready to bring the house to its knees, plus a cage of dense ivy, minus its leaves. All of the ground-floor windows were boarded up, and the back door was sealed with another barred gate. The garden was a dump, literally. Half a dozen mattresses sat in a teetering stack, surrounded by dozens of black bin bags and assorted broken furniture. Judging by the pit of ash that sat nearby, somebody had been trying to burn it.

"I'm guessing drugs," said Kett, as they stepped carefully through the mess. "All these gates, boarded windows, too many cars. Doesn't feel like an HMO."

"Agreed," said Porter. "You smell that?"

Kett sniffed the air, inhaling the welcome scent of cigarette smoke. He nodded, reaching the back gate to see that it was open a crack. The smell was stronger here, and he could hear a voice, a woman talking quickly and quietly in a language that wasn't English.

He glanced at Porter to make sure he was ready, then he took hold of the heavy gate and pried it open. Beyond that was an old wooden door, and this too was ajar. He pushed it with his fingertips, wincing as the hinges squealed in alarm. Ahead was a dark, cold corridor, the walls black with mould and the wooden boards splintered like teeth. The woman carried on chattering from somewhere inside.

"Not sure I like this, sir," said Porter. "Shouldn't we knock?"

"We did," said Kett. "At the front gate. They chose not to answer."

He switched on his phone's torch and walked down the corridor, the boards like an out-of-tune piano beneath his feet. He stopped at the first door on the right, finding an empty kitchen that looked like a hurricane had passed through, the cupboards doorless and the floor covered with broken crockery. Past that, on the left, was a staircase that doubled back towards the rear of the house.

Kett glanced up at it as they passed, seeing a young woman sitting on the top step, speaking into her phone. She was dressed in a pink satin négligée that didn't leave much to the imagination, her bare feet scuffing the worn carpet of the stairs.

She flinched when she saw Kett and Porter, curling her legs up beneath her, shrinking into herself. But she carried on with her fast-paced conversation as if they weren't there. Her accent was Eastern European, Kett thought.

"Hey," he said, offering a wave. Porter had moved further down the corridor, towards the front of the house.

The woman didn't respond, angling her body into the wall as if she hoped she might turn invisible. Kett eased himself onto the first step, his arms up so as not to frighten her. He left his warrant card in his pocket for now, because he was fairly sure she'd bolt if she saw it.

"Hello," he said again. "Can I have a quick word with you?"

No reply, just that incessant chatting. Kett looked back to see Porter returning.

"Empty," he said. "Front door's barricaded, proper prison shit."

Kett nodded, then turned back to the stairs to see that the woman had gone. He heard footsteps overhead as she bolted, the chatter of her voice fading. Dust rained from the ceiling, landing in his hair, gritty between his teeth.

He grabbed the rickety bannister and lurched up the stairs, reaching a landing that was much brighter and more welcoming than the ground floor. There were six rooms up here, every door closed. Another set of stairs led up.

Somebody on the floor above was moaning seductively.

"What on earth is this place?" asked Kett, switching off his torch and sliding his phone into his pocket.

"Brothel," said Porter. "Has to be, right?"

The DI pushed open the closed door, revealing a large bedroom that was dominated by a king-size, four-poster bed.

Pink net curtains diffused the sunlight, the dust dancing in delicate swirls. A strong scent of incense caught at the back of Kett's throat, enough to make his eyes water.

"Yep, brothel," he said.

A tripod stood at the foot of the bed, although there was no camera.

"Do me a favour and call out some local units, will you?" said Kett.

Porter nodded, retrieving his phone. Kett tried the next door to reveal another room, smaller but no less sumptuous. There was a tripod here as well, and this one had a mobile phone attached to it. He could hear the same woman talking in the room across the hall, but her door had been closed.

He started up the next flight of steps, the operatic moans growing louder as he breached the mansion's second floor. It was even brighter up here, and warmer too. Three doors led off this landing, the sounds emanating through the closed door of the front room. The boards under him squeaked so violently as he walked that he was amazed nobody had come out to investigate—although whoever was making the noises did a good job of drowning out every other sound.

Kett checked to make sure Porter was behind him, then he rapped his knuckles on the door. Almost instantly, the noises stopped, followed by a furious whispering.

"Police," Kett shouted. "I'm going to give you ten seconds to get decent, then I'm coming in."

"What the actual fuck?" came a man's voice from inside the room. Kett heard the heavy thump of footsteps, more whispering. "No fucking way."

"*Nyet,*" said a woman.

"Move," came the reply, and a second later the door was ripped open with such urgency it almost came off its hinges.

A man stood there dressed in nothing but pale denim jeans, his muscular body covered in a sheen of sweat and a tapestry of tattoos. He was young, in his late twenties, thirty at the oldest, his hair black with bleached tips, his cheekbones like scalpels beneath the tight skin of his face. He wore a large diamond stud in each ear, and another flashed in his tongue. The look he gave Kett had some anger in it, for sure, but there was something else there too, an amused curiosity.

"Who the fuck are you?" the man asked, just the faintest trace of an accent in his voice—possibly Irish.

"Police," Kett said again, holding up his warrant card. "DCI Robert Kett, and this is DI Peter Porter."

"Peter Porter," the man said in his singsong accent, his smile growing. "Peter Porter picked a peck of pickled pepper, no?"

"Close," said Kett.

He glanced past the man to see another enormous bedroom. Lying on the bed was a young woman, the covers pulled up to her chin, her eyes full of fear. Past her, sitting on an easy chair by the window, manspreading so much that it looked like he was trying to do the splits, was another guy. He was older, his buzzcut more grey than brown and his beard whiter still. He wore camouflage trousers, army boots and a black T-shirt. He stared at Kett with undisguised contempt, a phone gripped in one hand.

"Is one of you William Briggs?" Kett asked.

"You want Willy?" said the man at the door, grunting a laugh. His accent was definitely Irish, although it had faded. "Can't help you there, pal, sorry."

"You want to tell me your name?"

"Not really," said the young man. "Not even sure why you're in here, if I'm honest. You're one of Dawson's?"

"Dawson?" asked Kett.

"Shut up," growled the man at the back of the room. At first Kett thought he was speaking to him, but the way the guy at the door fell silent made it clear he was the target.

"Who are you, then?" Kett asked the second guy.

"None of your fucking business," he growled back, his accent local. He leaned forward in the chair, clasping his hands in front of him. There was some serious muscle on him, and his forearms, which peeked out from the rolled-up sleeves of his shirt, bore what looked like military tattoos.

"You're probably right," Kett said, feeling the first rev of adrenaline. "But since you're being such an arsehole about it, I'm going to make it my business."

The man stood up, and the guy at the door lifted his hands.

"No need for this to escalate," he said, an edge of panic there. "Nothing illegal going on here, apart from maybe you lot wandering in without a warrant."

"The door was open," said Kett.

"Because we're all law-abiding folk. This is all legit, isn't it, sweetheart?"

He was looking at the woman in the bed, and after a second or two she nodded.

"What's your name?" Kett asked her.

She looked at the older man for permission—or possibly for an interpretation—and when he didn't react she turned back, saying nothing. She looked afraid, but Kett wasn't sure who she was afraid of—the men, or the police.

"Put some clothes on," he said to her. "My colleague is going to have a word with you out here."

"No need for that," said the first guy, laughing nervously. "You're here because you want to be, Stella, tell him."

"I am here because I want to be," she said in a heavy accent that had to be Russian, or maybe Balkan.

"All the same, he still wants a word," said Kett. "It will only take a second."

"Look," said the first guy, one hand on the door like he was ready to slam it into Kett's face. "Whatever you want, you're going to have to talk to Dawson, so—"

"Go," said the older man, gesturing to the woman. "Speak with them. Then they can fuck off."

Kett turned away as the woman climbed out of bed. A handful of seconds later she pushed past, wearing nothing but a dressing gown. Kett met Porter's eye for a moment and the DI nodded, leading her gently towards the stairs. She kept glancing back at the man in the door, her eyes wide and bright.

"You've got nothing to worry about, pal," the guy said, although he sounded more than a little worried. He called out a little louder. "She wants to be here, and she'd better remember that."

"Hey," said Kett. "That's enough. What's your name?"

He, too, had to look back at the other man for permission. This time, the older guy nodded.

"Luke," he said.

"Luke what?"

"Briggs," he said.

"You're William's brother?"

Luke nodded.

"And you?" Kett asked the other man.

"People call me the Archduke," he said.

"I don't want to know what your *Dungeons and Dragons* friends call you," he said. "I want to know your name."

The man smiled, but it was like cut glass. He stared at

Kett like he wanted nothing more than to grind his face beneath his heel, and judging by the way he flexed his hands into fists, he was seriously considering it.

Kett tuned into the outside world, hoping he'd hear sirens. But the only clue that anything beyond this house still existed was the relentless shriek of the seagulls.

The man in the chair still showed no sign of offering up his identity, so Kett turned back to Luke.

"You have any idea where your brother is?"

"He's his own fella," he replied with a shrug. "Could be anywhere."

"When was the last time you saw him?"

"Well now," said Luke, making a big show of thinking about it. "Maybe yesterday, maybe the day before. Time's a slippery bugger. Any reason you're chasing him?"

"We found the plates for his car on a lorry where a woman was murdered," Kett said.

Luke whistled.

"You're gonna have to say that again, Officer. Few too many words there for me."

"Your brother drives a Volkswagen Beetle? A red one?"

"Aye, and it's a piece of shit."

"The plates for that car were fixed onto a lorry. Last night, a woman was murdered in that lorry. She had her head caved in with a sledgehammer."

"Nice," said Luke, with no hint of sarcasm.

"Your brother's car was also seen at the same woman's house, a little while before she was murdered."

"Fascinating," said Luke.

"So what I want to know," said Kett, "is who was driving that car yesterday, and who would have switched the plates."

"Wasn't Willy. He loves that car."

"You've got a number for him?" asked Kett.

"No," came the answer, but it was from the older man. He was making his way across the room, taking slow, deliberate steps. He was taller than Kett by a few inches, and everything about him seemed designed to be intimidating. "We don't know shit about him, or about any lorry, or any woman. And I'm getting a little tired of your bullshit. You can tell Dawson if he sends any more of you pricks here, then he's going to wind up in a cement casket at the bottom of the Scroby Sands. Understood?"

"Why does everyone keep mentioning this guy called Dawson?" said Kett.

It looked like the Archduke was about to answer, but he was cut off by a shout from the bottom of the stairs. It could have been Porter, Kett thought, but the scream that followed certainly wasn't. It tore through the old house, echoing from the walls, a cry of pure terror.

"What the—" said Kett.

He turned to the stairs behind him, and by the time he heard the thunder of feet from the bedroom he realised he'd made a mistake.

Strong hands grabbed his arms, pushed hard, and before he even knew what was happening, he was over the bannister and falling fast.

CHAPTER NINE

There was no time to cry out, no time to do anything.

Kett landed hard at the bottom of the stairs, every molecule of oxygen ejected from his lungs. For a blissful moment he couldn't feel a thing, then his body realised what had happened to it and a fire broke out in his neck, blazing down his back and into his arms.

Fuck, he tried to say, but there wasn't enough air for him to get the word out. He was lying on his back, his feet pointing up the stairs, and when he tried to move, the agony stopped him as effectively as a straitjacket.

Footsteps thundered along the landing, raining dust. Kett glanced up to see Luke Briggs and the man who called himself the Archduke at the top of the stairs. They clattered down them so fast the whole house seemed to shake.

Fuck!

He kicked backwards, sliding down the last few steps and managing to roll away just as the men reached him. Somebody's bare foot crunched into the side of his head, no real force behind it. There was a hand in his hair, hoisting him up, doing its best to scalp him.

"Oi!" came a bellow from nearby.

Kett's ears were roaring too loud for him to know who was speaking. There was a thump and the fist in his hair vanished, dropping him to the floor. He rolled onto his back, pushing himself away from the shapes that wrestled above him. Porter was there, grappling with the older guy while Luke Briggs geared up for a punch.

"Pete," croaked Kett. "Watch out!"

Porter saw the punch coming, twisting out of the way, his fists by his ears like a boxer in the ring. The Archduke threw an uppercut that glanced off the DI's ribs. Then Luke tried again, catching Porter in the cheek with the sound of a baseball bat hitting a joint of meat.

"Enough!" Kett said, still just a whisper.

He grabbed the bannister and dragged himself up, his spine wrapped in barbed wire, his arms numb as he lumbered into the fray. The two men were focused on Porter, drumming punches into his sides.

The Archduke took a step back, bouncing on his heels, adjusting his body like he was about to launch a kick. Kett tackled him before he had the chance, driving his body towards the second set of stairs. The older guy threw his head back, trying to crunch it into Kett's nose with relentless force.

He had to let go of him, and the Archduke spun around, throwing a mean right hook. Kett ducked under it—more by chance than by skill—and threw himself at the man again. They hit the bannister together, splitting it in two before tumbling through the gap.

And for the second time in as many minutes, Kett was falling.

This time he had a softer landing, the Archduke grunting as he hit the stairs first, gargling with agony as Kett's knees dropped into his stomach. Kett tried to stay on top, but the angle was too steep and he tumbled away, hitting the ground floor corridor. Above him came a chorus of screams and shouts and he forced himself to his feet again, the whole house seeming to sway as he limped back up the stairs.

"Don't fucking move," he told the older guy, stepping over him. It was an unnecessary command because the Archduke was still lying on his back, his hands to his gut and blood running from a wound over his ear.

Kett reached the top of the stairs to see three women standing in the doorway of one of the bedrooms, all watching with horror as Porter and Luke Briggs grappled on the floor of the narrow landing. None of them were screaming, though, and when the noise came again, Kett realised it was Porter who was making the sound.

"Pete!" he yelled, trying to see between the flailing limbs, wondering if Briggs had a knife. He couldn't think of another reason the big DI would be making such an awful sound.

Then he got a little closer and realised Luke's head was planted firmly in Porter's crotch, his teeth clamped tight.

"Christ," said Kett.

"Get him off me!" wailed the DI, his eyes almost exploding from his head.

Kett stepped over Porter's squealing form and grabbed Luke under his bare armpits. When he tried to heft him backwards, though, the volume of Porter's cries grew to ear-shattering levels.

"Don't pull him!" he shrieked. "He's biting it!"

Luke was growling like a dog, his arms wrapped tight around Porter's arse and locking him in place.

"Get him off!" the DI screamed, thumping his fist into Luke's head.

"I don't know what you want me to do," Kett replied, panicking.

He pulled his phone from his pocket and crouched next to Luke, jamming it between the man's teeth. He worked it up and down, trying to loosen his jaw. Finally, Luke pushed himself away, wiping his mouth with the back of his hand. Incredibly, he was laughing.

Porter curled up, his hands over his crotch. Kett glared at Luke.

"You move," he said breathlessly as he struggled to his feet, "and you're going out that fucking window. Pete, you okay?"

Porter was frantically undoing his belt. He unbuttoned his trousers, took a wild-eyed look into his pants, then dropped his head to the carpet and breathed a sigh of relief.

"Fucker," he said. "Just give me a minute, sir."

Kett wasn't sure they had a minute. Luke was ready to bounce back onto his feet, and when Kett looked over the bannister he saw the Archduke on his way up, his face a mask of blood.

"This is going to end badly for both of you," said Kett.

"You reckon?" said the Archduke. "Because you're in *my* house."

"Pete, get up," said Kett.

He offered Porter a hand, helping him to his feet. The women watched from the safety of the doorway. Their expressions were unreadable, but one thing was clear enough: violence was nothing new to them.

It was nothing new to Kett, either, but he was flagging

fast. He put one arm against the wall, not enough air in here to fill his aching lungs.

The older guy had reached the top of the stairs, blocking their way out. Luke was back on his feet too, licking his lips.

"Last chance," Kett told them.

"Fair enough," said the older guy. "Your lucky day, anyway."

Kett wasn't sure what he was talking about until he heard the wail of a siren past the hammer blows of his pulse. The flood of relief that spilled through him was like stepping into a warm bath on a cold day and he pushed himself away from the wall. Porter pulled a set of cuffs from his pocket, offering them up.

"Who wants them?" he asked.

"Him," said Kett, nodding to the Archduke.

"Should snap them on your cock, you prick," Porter told Luke. "See how you like it."

"I'm game if you are," he said with a grin.

The siren grew louder, followed shortly by the sound of slamming doors from outside. There was a window at the end of the hall and Kett walked to it, bypassing Luke on the way. Through the dirty glass, he spotted an IRV on the kerb in front of his Volvo. Two men were getting out, one in uniform, one in a suit.

"It's Dawson," said Luke from right behind him. Kett spun around, but the young man held up his hands in surrender.

"We were just having a bit of fun, pal," he said. "Nothing wrong with a bit of rough and tumble."

"You bit me in the dick," said Porter.

"You're a big lad," Luke said, laughing. "How else am I gonna get you to submit?"

"Enough," said Kett. "Porter, cuff that twat. And you." He pointed a finger at Luke. "Go open the door."

Luke made his way past the Archduke, trotting down the stairs like he didn't have a care in the world. Kett waited for a moment in case the older man resisted, but he was smiling too, his teeth crimson.

"I have no idea what you're laughing about," said Kett. "Won't be so funny when you're behind bars."

"Good luck with that," said the man.

Porter snapped the cuffs on his wrist, then bent his arms behind his back to finish the job. Kett made his way gingerly down the stairs, both arms full of pins and needles and his back on fire. Luke was unlocking a monstrous metal bar from the front door, hurling it to the ground with a bell-like clang. He twisted four Yales onto the snib, then tugged the stubborn door open.

The two coppers were already on the doorstep. Kett wondered whether they'd scaled the wall, but when he glanced past them, he saw that they'd managed to get the front gate open.

Or somebody had opened it for them.

The first man was a young PC, his expression wary as he studied Kett. Standing next to him was a man in his late fifties with lanky grey hair surrounding a puckered bald spot, a pair of lopsided, tape-mended glasses perched on the end of his long nose and what looked like a week's worth of ketchup stains in the stubble around his mouth. He sniffed as he looked Kett up and down, his mouth a straight line but the slightest hint of annoyance in his sharp eyes.

"What in the name of Zeus' beard is going on here then?" he said in a pronounced Cockney accent, his arms out by his sides as he looked around. He was wearing a dark grey suit, but there was more ketchup on his shirt than there was on his face, mustard too, by the look of it. He looked like he hadn't changed his clothes for days, and the smell coming off him was pure, undiluted fish and chip shop. He squinted at Kett through his filthy glasses. "You lost, Robert?"

The way he addressed him made Kett feel like they'd met before, but he was pretty sure he would have remembered him.

"Dawson?" he asked.

"Well, well, well," Dawson said, his smile revealing small, white teeth. "It's like visiting the palace and the Queen knowing your name. Except this isn't your palace, is it? To what do we owe the pleasure?"

"You're police?" asked Kett, and Dawson pouted.

"Come on, man," he said. "Look at me. You think any other profession would reduce a person to a state like this? Piss and ketchup, that's me all over. Or should I say, all over me?"

He saw that Kett wasn't impressed and pulled a warrant card from his pocket. There was no ketchup on this, only a faint crust of what might have been egg yolk.

"You know how to dent a man's ego, Kett, I'll give you that."

"DI Charles Dawson," Kett said, reading the card.

"Chuckles," said Dawson.

"Huh?"

"My friends call me Chuckles. I still haven't figured out why."

He chuckled. Kett didn't.

"You're based out here?"

"For my sins," Dawson said, trying several times to return the wallet before it finally slid into place. He seemed a little drunk, Kett thought, but that surely couldn't be the case. "Literally. Got bumped from the Met to Norwich fifteen years ago, then from there to here, all because of some innocent mistakes that may or may not have cost the Force a lot of money and a couple of lives."

He smiled, but there was nothing pleasant in his eyes.

"I'm joking. Probably. But it still leaves me wondering what on Earth is going on here, and how you two city slickers blundered into it."

Kett glanced inside to see Porter at the bottom of the stairs, one hand on the Archduke's shoulder. Luke Briggs leaned against the wall, his arms folded over his chest. Neither of the men seemed bothered by the fact they were about to get arrested. Several of the young women had clustered around the broken bannister, all in lingerie or dressing gowns as they watched the events unfold.

"We're investigating a murder," said Kett. "A woman called Karen Dankworth was killed last night, just outside a village called Swannington."

"Swannington?" said Dawson. "Christ, might as well be the other side of the world, man."

"We found her in a lorry," Kett told him. "The lorry's plates had been switched. They belong to a car owned by William Briggs. A red VW Beetle that was seen at the victim's house before she was killed."

"I know it well," said Dawson. "Looks like a haemorrhoid on wheels."

He looked over his shoulder at the car park.

"Not here though, is it?" he said.

"This is the listed address for Briggs," said Kett, growing tired of the man's insolence. "We arrived, the back door was open, we made entry. Then Tweedle-Dee and Tweedle-Dum here attacked us."

"That right?" said Dawson. "These two wallies got the

better of the mighty Robert Kett and that bollocking big barn door down there? A little embarrassing, that, isn't it?"

"This twat bit me in the dick," Porter yelled from inside.

"Better hope he's got some mouthwash then," said Dawson, pulling a face. He peered into the dark hallway. "That what happened?"

"Gate was shut," said the Archduke. "They climbed the wall."

"Doesn't sound particularly kosher to me," said Dawson, tutting. "So how about we say it was open? That works better for everyone, I think."

"Fine," said the Archduke. "It was open."

"You walked in, they thought you were burglars, a scuffle ensued, your colleague almost lost his todger to Mrs John Wayne Bobbett there, but all's well that ends well."

Kett actually laughed. He stepped out of the front door so that he was almost chest-to-chest with the DI. He had the advantage of a good four inches, making Dawson crane his neck back. The guy had so much dandruff that it sparkled on his suit like glitter.

"I don't know who you are, Dawson," he said quietly. "But I know your name came up long before you arrived. They were expecting you. But what's weirder is that we put in a call for backup, and you arrive within minutes. *You*, a detective."

Dawson's smile started to slip, and he licked his dry lips.

"This place doesn't concern you, Kett," he said. "You—"

"That's *sir*, Dawson," said Kett. "In case you've been out here too long to remember how to address a senior officer."

"Put it away, *sir*," said Dawson, scratching his scalp. "Before Gnasher takes a nibble. I'm a lowly provincial plod who just wants to retire. You're Kett the Almighty, front-page stuff. I'm not interested in becoming another of your statistics. I couldn't give a rat's bollock if you arrest these rat's bollocks. You'll be saving me a pile of paperwork. But I've been working this job long enough to know that in a courtroom, no jury is going to look favourably on two rogue cops breaking and entering a property and picking a fight with the residents and their girlfriends. I can tell you exactly what they'll think. So let me do you a favour. Bugger off, leave these suppurating anal glands with me, and I'll get you whatever information you need."

Dawson took a few steps back, rubbing the back of his head.

"Giving me neck ache, sir. Old bones."

Kett took a deep breath of stagnant sea air, holding it in his lungs. Dawson was right, of course, they'd had no reason to enter the house, even considering the crime they were investigating. The right solicitor could throw the case out in a heartbeat, and the two men would be back home, free and clear.

But so much about this place felt wrong.

"You're telling me these women are in a relationship with these men?" he asked.

"Love is a strange beast," said Dawson. He pulled a packet of cigarettes from his pocket, Marlborough Reds, and took one out with his teeth. He used a match to light it, sucking in a lungful before breathing it over his head. "Who are we to say what love is, and what it isn't? Ask them, any of them."

Kett turned to Porter.

"What did she say, the woman you spoke to?"

"Said exactly that," Porter replied. "She's with Luke, she's happy, she's safe, and she's in love."

"See," said Dawson. "What a beautiful thing this is, and here we are, a couple of unromantic turds planted on the rose petal bed of their happiness, doing everything we can to ruin their day. What do you say we step away and leave them to it?"

He took another long drag, and this time he blew it into Kett's face.

"Sir."

Kett breathed in through his nose, savouring the nicotine hit, eyeballing Dawson until the other man looked away.

"On two conditions," said Kett. He pointed back at the Archduke. "His name."

"That crusty old fart stain is called Perry Paul," said Dawson. He took another hit on the cigarette before hacking up yellow phlegm, spitting it onto the driveway. "A ridiculous name if there ever was one. It's no wonder he doesn't want people to know it. He calls himself the Archduke, although if he's the son of the Emperor of Austria, then I'm the Pope's favourite dildo. What's the other condition?"

"Tell me where we can find William."

"Can any of you badger fingering vagina spatulas answer that?" asked Dawson, looking past Kett.

"Last I heard, he was down the pub," said the Archduke. "Spack saw him there last night."

"The Bull?" said Dawson, and the man nodded.

"There you go," he said. "The Iron Bull, it's on the south side of town. But be careful if you leave your car there, you'll lose your wheels. Maybe your shoes, too."

"I'll be back," said Kett, leaning in so that only Dawson could hear him. "You know I will. You don't think I know a bent copper when I see one?"

"Bring flowers next time, man," said Dawson, and he

actually had the temerity to give Kett a gentle double-slap on his arm. "Some chocolates, maybe."

Kett shouldered past him, heading for the open gate, Dawson's final words chasing him all the way to the street.

"And don't forget the lube!"

CHAPTER TEN

The pain followed Kett all the way to the car, a long groan escaping him as he dropped into his seat. Porter climbed behind the wheel, checking his face in the rear-view mirror before turning to Kett.

"You okay, sir?"

"No," said Kett. "But I don't want *them* to know that."

He glanced through the window to where Dawson and the PC were still watching from the driveway of the house. Dawson gave a condescending little wave and Kett had to resist the urge to reply with his middle finger.

"Drive, Pete," he said.

Porter did as he was told, waiting for a break in traffic before pulling the Volvo off the kerb and heading towards the beach.

"Who the fuck was that, then?" he asked.

"Charles Dawson," said Kett. "Hang on."

He pulled out his phone and called Clare, putting it on speaker.

"How's your... you know?" he asked Porter as it rang.

The DI gave himself a delicate squeeze.

"Still attached, sir," he said. "But who *does* that? Who bites another man in the winkie?"

"Briggs was right about one thing," said Kett. "Biting you in the dick was the only way he was going to get you on the floor."

"Jesus Christ, Kett," said Clare, who had answered the phone midway through the sentence. "Here I am about to spoon a mound of honey-flavoured Greek yoghurt into my mouth and suddenly you're in my earhole talking about men biting each other in their bellends. You really know how to fuck up a man's lunch."

"Sorry, sir," said Kett.

"Who bit who in the what, then?"

"We followed the lorry's plates to a house in Yarmouth, sir," Kett said, starting from the beginning. They'd reached the promenade, the sea a giant slab of slate-coloured water broken only by the enormous wind turbines of Scroby Sands. Kett pointed to the right and Porter steered them around a mini roundabout. "William Briggs' place. It's not a normal house, that much is obvious. The rooms are full of women with very little clothing on."

"Brothel?" barked Clare.

"I think so," said Kett. "Although I didn't see any guys there other than William's brother, Luke, and another man called Perry Paul. They both seemed to be running the place. I think it's a webcam house, or whatever you call them. The girls record themselves, stream it on adult websites, probably pay most of their earnings to the men. They all sounded like they came from Eastern Europe, maybe Russia."

"So you went to the house, you knocked, they let you in?" said Clare. His tone of voice didn't seem particularly optimistic.

"Yes, sir," said Kett. "I mean, kind of. The door was open. Paul and Briggs didn't take kindly to us being there, it got physical."

"It got *physical*, did it?" said Clare, and Kett was glad he was twenty miles away. "Got *physical*? Is that what we're calling it these days?"

"Sorry, sir," said Kett. "It wasn't that bad."

"I got bit on the dick," said Porter in protest.

"Yeah, Briggs bit Porter on the dick."

"Can you stop putting that bloody image in my head, Kett!" growled Clare.

"And you got pushed down the stairs, sir," said Porter. "Twice."

"Like I said, not that bad," Kett insisted, switching the phone to his other hand to relieve the ache in his shoulder. "But it got weird, sir. We called for backup and a detective rolled up. DI Charles Dawson. You know him?"

"Know the name," said Clare. "Can't picture the face."

"Hard to see his face, he's got so much ketchup on it. He says his friends call him Chuckles."

"Jesus Christ," said Clare. "I know exactly who you mean. Looks like somebody pulled him out of a skip?"

"That's the one. He showed up with a constable, and it's pretty obvious he knew Paul and Briggs. They mentioned him to us before he even got there, asked us if we were one of *his*."

"He's dirty," said Clare.

"In every sense of the word, sir," said Kett. "He made it clear that we'd breached the house illegally, asked us to leave. He was acting more like Perry Paul's lawyer than a copper."

"Except he was right," grumbled Clare. "You did breach the house illegally."

"I mean... kind of," said Kett. "Probable cause."

"I'd need to talk to some colleagues of mine, but there have been rumours about Dawson for years. He got kicked out of the Met, although it was all hush-hush. He was here, too, but not under me. He worked for that other lawless prick you took down."

"Holy shit, Wallace Marshall?"

They'd met retired Superintendent Wallace Marshall on the Jaw Breaker case two years ago. He'd been bent, sure, but for different reasons—a murderous vigilante who was currently serving twenty-three years in Belmarsh for his crimes.

"Yeah. It's how Dawson ended up in Yarmouth. He's not been accused of anything, as far as I know, and part of that is he's actually a pretty decent detective. Closes a lot of cases."

"He doesn't look like he could close a suitcase," said Kett. "My gut's telling me he's in on it with the men in the house, probably offering them protection in return for a backhander."

"In return for some kind of 'hander,' sure," said Clare, and Kett grimaced. "What is it with Great bloody Yarmouth and bent coppers? As if Marshall wasn't bad enough."

"Dawson's no Marshall, sir, but he's worth us keeping an eye on, and probably worth us bringing in."

"Hold fire on that," said Clare. "I'll ask around. Dawson won't be the only one. The corruption runs right up the food chain. There's a lot of temptation out there. Too much money flowing through those docks. It's the Wild West."

"Wild East, sir," said Porter.

"Shut up, Pete," said Clare. "Forget about Dawson for now. Any leads on the Dankworth murder?"

"According to Paul, William Briggs was drinking in a

pub called the Iron Bull last night. We're on our way there now."

"Watch your pockets," said Clare. "That place is wretched."

"Yes, sir."

"And don't Kett anything else up, you twat."

Clare ended the call and Kett rested his phone on his thigh, watching Yarmouth roll by through the window. The town was busy for February, although most of the people walking the wide promenade were couples, all wrapped up in winter gear and each other's arms.

"You doing much for Valentine's, Pete?" asked Kett.

"Flowers," Porter replied. "And nappies."

"Nappies?"

"For Bobby, not for Allie, sir. Hard to be romantic with a soon-to-be one-year-old."

"You'll get the romance back," said Kett. "In another seventeen years or so."

Porter laughed, turning off the main road into the warren of streets that hid past the seafront.

"Take it your Valentine's morning wasn't particularly romantic then, sir," he said.

"There was plenty of glitter, put it that way," Kett replied. "I think it's right down there."

Porter followed Kett's finger, squeezing the Volvo past lines of parked cars until the narrow road opened out. Directly across from the junction was a pub that looked as tired and beaten up as Kett felt. The ugly brick building sat back from the tightly packed houses, squatting on the edge of a small car park. A raggedy Union Jack flag hung from a white pole over the door. Several of the rusted letters on the wall were missing, the rest spelling TH RON BU L.

"Looks nice," said Porter. There were only two other

cars in its car park, and one of them didn't have any wheels—the chassis mounted on bricks, all of its windows broken. "Thought they were just joking about losing our tyres."

He pulled up in front of the door and cut the engine. Kett prepared himself for the pain, gritting his teeth as he got out. The cold wind numbed his face but brought every other ache into sharp relief.

"You know, when I took on the job of DCI, I thought I was going to be behind a desk all day," he said. "Not quite sure what happened there."

"You'd probably just end up getting into a fight with the desk, sir," Porter said. "We'd walk into the bullpen to see you strangling a stapler. Or wrestling your chair. You'd be slamming your own head in the fridge door."

"Little harsh," grumbled Kett.

Porter nodded to the other side of the street.

"Got company."

Three teenage boys had gathered outside one of the houses, their skinny wrists and ankles poking out of track-suits that looked far too small for them. They were all watching Kett and Porter intently.

"We're police," Kett yelled across the road. "If any of you so much as come near this car, then I'm going to be using *you* as tyres. Understood?"

None of the lads replied.

"That's a really vague threat, sir," said Porter. "How would that even work?"

"Stay with the car, Pete," Kett told him.

"Yes, sir."

Kett pushed his way through the pub's front door, assaulted by the smell of stale beer and piss. The interior of the Iron Bull was every bit as awful as the outside, the walls plastered with British flags and portraits of sour-faced politicians: Maggie Thatcher, Winston Churchill and Boris Johnson chief amongst them. Above the wide walnut bar was a mural of four Spitfires, and in between them a handwritten message: *We won two world wars, if you don't like Britain... piss off!*

"Yikes," said Kett as he approached the bar. There was nobody in sight anywhere, and the place was deathly quiet. He cleared his throat. "Hello?"

He was answered by the sharp crack of breaking glass from the open door behind the bar.

"Hello?" he said again.

"Fuck," came a woman's voice.

Kett stepped past the bar, approaching the door. Above it was a photograph of two people who both looked like they'd been carved from a slab of gammon. The man on the left was completely bald, his fat cheeks red, his small eyes glaring and his teeth bared in what might have been a smile. The woman next to him could have been the same person, just in a dirty blonde wig. Both were wearing Union Jack jumpers.

Something else smashed, followed by a run of muttered swear words.

"I'm police," Kett said.

"Hang on."

Kett poked his head around the door, finding himself in a small kitchen lined with shelves. A hatch in the floor was open, leading into darkness. In the centre of the room, kneeling on the floor with her back to Kett, was a woman. She was dressed in black dungarees and a pink T-shirt, her arms almost completely covered in bright tattoos. In her hands was a dustpan and brush, and she was doing her best to sweep up shards of broken glass. Enormous curls of sandy hair cascaded down her back, and when she glanced over her shoulder, it fell across her face, blinding her.

"Hang on," she said. "Sorry, sorry."

"It's fine," said Kett. "Take your time. You want some help?"

"I can manage," she said, trying to blow the hair out of her face. "Just give me a sec."

Kett did as she asked, returning to the bar. He pulled out a stool in order to sit down, then changed his mind when his fingers stuck to the wood. He scrubbed them down his trousers instead, realising for the first time since he'd left the Briggs house that he was absolutely filthy.

There was a clatter of broken glass, then the young woman appeared. Her cheeks were red and sweaty, but she managed a nervous smile.

"Sorry," she said again. "Honestly, I'm such a butterfingers. I'm amazed we've got any glasses left."

"It's no bother," said Kett, holding up his warrant card. "My name's DCI Robert Kett. Do you mind if I ask you some questions?"

"Not at all," she said. "Can I get you a drink?"

"Some water would be great, thank you."

The woman grabbed two glasses from over the bar, almost dropping one, and filled them from the dispenser. She passed one to Kett, and he drank the whole thing in one go.

"You needed that," she said, putting her own glass down after the smallest of sips. "You okay? You look like one of the punters in this place after fight night."

"I'm okay," said Kett. "Fight night?"

The woman laughed.

"That's every night," she said. "I'm Sophie Welch."

She extended her hand and Kett took it, surprised at the strength of her grip.

"No wonder you've broken so many glasses," he said. "This can't be your place, Sophie."

"The pub?" she asked, looking around. Her tattoos were like a comic strip, random images running down both arms and crossing her collarbone. Kett spotted more than one rainbow, as well as two female signs interlinked with each other. She caught him looking and laughed again. "Oh, the pub," she said. "Yeah, if you look past all the ink, I'm a foaming-at-the-mouth nationalist."

This time it was Kett's turn to laugh.

"It's my parents' place," she said, nodding to the photo over the door. "Or it was, anyway. Mum passed a few years back, Dad last Autumn."

"I'm sorry to hear that," Kett said.

"They weren't as bad as they look," she said. "They had a lot of love, they just didn't know how to spread it very wide. And they raised me, so they can't have been all that bad."

She did a little twirl behind the bar, her clouds of hair fanning outwards.

"I got Dad to agree to a gay night, if you can believe it," she said. "Every Thursday for the last two years. Folk love it, they think the whole Tory, Brexit, BoJo-loving thing is ironic."

"The locals don't object?" asked Kett.

"You kidding? It's half-price drinks all night, and the music's better than the rest of the week. Half the punters in here turn up in their fanciest pink shirts. They're like Mum and Dad, you'd think they goosestep their way to the pub, but they're just people. They just want to be part of something. They just want to be happy."

"That's very wise," Kett told her. "I like it."

"But you're not in a pink shirt," she said. "And it's not Thursday. So I'm guessing you're not here for bottomless margaritas."

"Sadly not," he told her. He pulled out his phone and found the photo he wanted, sliding it across the bar. "This is William Briggs. Do you know him?"

She barely glanced at it before nodding.

"Willy," she said. "He okay?"

"As far as I know. We're looking for him in connection to an incident that happened last night. When was the last time you saw him?"

"Last night," she said. "He was here until closing time, just after eleven. He's usually one of the last to leave, and it's usually at the end of a solid kick. Nice enough guy, but he can really put it away."

"Was he here alone?"

"Last night he was, yeah. Usually he's with his girlfriend, Darcey. He comes in alone when they've fallen out. Didn't say much about it."

"Darcey..." Kett prompted, and Sophie shrugged.

"All I know is she's local. In Yarmouth."

"Did he say where he was going last night?"

"No, but he got a lift home," she said. "Saw somebody driving him out of the car park in his fancy Beetle thing."

"You know who was driving?"

"No, but he quite often gets picked up. Darcey doesn't drive. I mean, she can, but she doesn't have a car. It's mostly his brother, who is *not* a nice enough guy, for the record. Luke doesn't drink. Sometimes it's somebody else, older guy, real prick. I won't let Willy drive himself, although God knows he tries sometimes."

"Luke didn't pick him up last night," said Kett. "I've

already spoken to him. I don't suppose you've got CCTV here?"

"Used to have a great camera out the front," she said. "But the kids kept throwing stones at it before they knocked off the cars, so Dad took it down. There's one down the side, though. Stops the punters pissing up the walls."

"You mind if I have a look?"

"It's all on my phone," she said, retrieving it from the front pocket of her dungarees. "You want last night?"

Kett nodded, and she poked the screen a couple of times before passing it over.

"Motion controlled," she said. "I never look at it, sorry. Some things should never be seen."

Kett slipped on his glasses and scanned through the list of clips. Most, it seemed, had been triggered by some kind of horrific, bug-eyed monster that was lurking down the side of the pub.

"What is *that*?" he asked, and Sophie craned over the bar to take a look.

Kett pressed play, realising that the monster was actually a spider making its web in front of the camera.

"Terrifying," said Sophie.

Kett exited the clip and scrolled backwards through the night until he saw the time stamp for yesterday evening. He clicked the entry for 11:13, watching five men stroll into sight and walk down the side of the pub. All of them stood in a line, pulled their trousers and pants down to their ankles, and began to piss up the side of the wall.

"Those absolute bastards," said Sophie, as the men all looked at the camera and started jeering.

Kett didn't wait for the mass urination to finish. He moved to the next clip, which showed a couple more punters walking across the car park and onto the street. As he was manoeuvring to the next one, a text pinged onto the screen. He'd read it before he could stop himself.

But I'm doing it for you. I love you.

Sophie deftly flicked the text away with her finger.

"Sorry," she said. "Ignore that."

Kett picked the next clip, watching a man teeter into sight. He was walking like a true drunk, two steps forward then three back, his arms wheeling.

"That's Willy," said Sophie. "Took him ten minutes to get from the front door to the edge of the car park."

"You were watching him?"

"No," she said, a little defensively. "I mean, not like *that*. A couple of times he's snuck back in while I'm cleaning the bar. I got him out and locked the door. Checked the car park a couple of minutes later to make sure he was gone and saw him being driven off. Watch, you'll probably be able to see it."

William staggered across the car park, hanging onto the fence like the ground had given way beneath his feet. He was shouting something, but even when Sophie turned the volume all the way up, Kett couldn't make out what he was saying.

As he waltzed towards the street, another text pinged onto the screen.

You don't love me back?

This time, Kett saw the name of the sender.

Jax.

Sophie dismissed the text, her cheeks blazing.

"Everything okay?" Kett asked.

"God, Sorry," she said. "You've caught me in the middle of an argument. A quiet one. Wouldn't be Valentine's Day without one, would it?"

Kett didn't answer, because on-screen Briggs had

reached the street. He was waving at somebody, and a second or two later, a car crept into the shot. The night vision turned it grey, but the shape of it was instantly recognisable. The VW Beetle slowed down, the bonnet disappearing behind the wall of the pub.

"That's his car," said Sophie. "I asked to buy it off him once, because you can't get hold of them these days. Good ones. But he loves that thing more than anything, except maybe Darcey."

It was too dark to identify the driver as they leaned over and opened the passenger door. Briggs lurched towards it, sidestepping out of sight for a good four seconds before reappearing. He reached for the car and missed, reversing almost halfway across the car park and, by some miracle, managing not to fall on his arse. As he tried again, the door of the Beetle opened and the driver stepped out.

Kett paused it, using his thumb and forefinger to increase the size of the shot. It was too blurry to see much, but he was pretty sure the driver was wearing a raincoat, the hood pulled up.

"Wasn't raining last night, was it?" said Kett.

"No, but it was chuffing cold," Sophie replied.

Kett zoomed out and pressed play. The driver walked around the front of the car, which meant Kett couldn't see them past the pub wall. They entered the shot again a few seconds later, just as Briggs had reached the car for a second time. The drunk man started to retreat again, although this time it seemed like a conscious decision—as if he was trying to turn around. Then the driver grabbed hold of his arms, pushing him into the car.

"You recognise that person?" asked Kett.

"No, sorry," said Sophie.

Whoever it was, it looked like they were using some

force to keep Briggs inside the car. They threw what might have been a punch, then they slammed the door shut and ran around the front of the vehicle again. Here, they stopped for a moment, looking up at the pub, but their face was a circle of shadow inside the hood, as if they didn't have a head at all.

They dropped into the car and drove off before the door had even closed, out of sight in less than a second.

"Shit," said Sophie. "That's about when I looked out the window. I didn't see any of that other stuff. I just saw him being driven away. Honest."

Her cheeks were still red, and the look she threw Kett seemed something more than just apologetic.

"Honest," she said again. "You think he's okay?"

"No," said Kett. "I don't. Don't suppose there's any chance I can keep this?"

"The phone?" She shook her head. "No, I've got my life on there, can't function without it. I can try to email it?"

Kett nodded, pushing himself away from the bar and fishing a card from his wallet.

"I might need to speak with you again," he said, laying it on the bar. "Thank you for your help."

"Any time, Detective," she said.

He walked away, hearing the ping of another text behind him. He glanced back when he reached the door to see the young woman looking at her phone.

Even in the shadows of the bar, he couldn't miss the smile on her face.

CHAPTER ELEVEN

WHEN KETT STEPPED OUT OF THE PUB INTO THE brilliant sunshine, he was surprised to see Porter standing by the Volvo, surrounded by the three teenage boys that had been across the street. They were all facing away from the pub and laughing at something on Porter's phone—loud enough that nobody heard Kett crunching his way over the car park.

"That was a bastard," said Porter. "I couldn't get the wires out and the fella who owned it was coming out the front door with a kitchen knife. The only reason I got away was because I was at the top of a hill, just put it in neutral and rode it all the way down while the guy ran after me in his pants. Hopped out at the bottom and scarpered."

"Scarpered?" asked one of the boys. He was about fifteen, a slug of fair hair perched on his top lip. He spoke with an accent.

"You know, I legged it," said Porter. "Bolted. Scrammed. Ran away."

The lads laughed again.

"But what I was saying," the DI went on, "is that I

turned it all around after that. Gave me such a shock that I stopped twocking cars, went straight. If I hadn't done all that, I probably never would have become a copper."

"Done all what?" Kett asked.

Porter flinched, almost dropping his phone. He spun around, a guilty look on his face.

"Was just telling these lads that I used to be like them, sir," he said. "And that it's not too late to change." He looked back at them. "You lot ever thought about joining the police?"

They laughed like he'd told the funniest joke they'd ever heard. Then they bolted, tearing up the street and shouting to each other in a language that Kett didn't recognise.

"You really got through to them, mate," said Kett. "And probably not a great idea to advertise the fact you used to be a car thief."

"I was their age," Porter said. "Wasn't easy growing up in the East End. And this lot have it a million times harder. They've been dragged away from their own country, they're not at school, too young to find work. The whole world's fucked them over, and then we blame them when the uniforms pick them up for dealing or B&E. They're good kids in a bad place."

Kett nodded.

"I know. But we can't save them all."

"We can try," said Porter.

Kett dropped into the passenger seat and Porter climbed behind the wheel. He patted his pockets, turning pale.

"What?" asked Kett.

"The little shits stole my keys."

"Your keys?" said Kett. "Those are *my* keys."

Porter attempted an apologetic smile.

"Sorry, sir."

"For fuck's sake," said Kett. "Bloody go and get them back."

The boys had vanished, spiriting themselves into the alleyways between the run-down houses. Porter stared forlornly out of the windscreen, both hands gripping the wheel like he could will the engine to start by using the sheer power of his mind.

"I could always hot-wire, it, sir," he said after a moment.

"Christ," said Kett, fetching his phone. "I'll call Savage and tell her to swing by the house, get the spares. And I'm going to stay right here so that when they come back to boost the car, I can yell at them."

"What about me, sir?" asked Porter.

"You are going to go out there and find an address for William Briggs' girlfriend. She's called Darcey something. She's local."

"Will do," he said. "Sorry, sir."

Kett waved him out of the car. Porter slammed the door behind him, slouching down the street. Kett called Savage.

"Sir," she said when she'd answered. "How's Great Yarmouth?"

"Anything but great," he said. "I've lost my keys. Any chance you could pick up the spares from the house and meet us out here?"

"I could, sir," she said. "But I was about to head out with Hay. She's on her way to the lorry and I was going to go with. It's not easy to find."

"Send Duke, then," said Kett. "You're better off at the crime scene. You found anything else?"

"Nothing worth reporting, sir," she said. "You?"

"Too much to fit into this conversation," said Kett. "But there's video footage of William Briggs being forced into his car last night. At least, that's what it looked like. Outside the Iron Bull pub in the town, just after eleven."

Kett hesitated, wondering if he'd seen it right.

"He was drunk. Maybe whoever picked him up was just annoyed with him. I don't know. Couldn't see the driver's face because of a hood."

"A hood, sir?" asked Savage. "The person who dropped off the gift at Karen Dankworth's house was wearing a hood. A raincoat."

"That can't be a coincidence," said Kett. "Before you head out, can you see if you can find the Beetle on the system? Speed cameras, ANPCs, anything like that. They might have left a trail."

"Yes, sir," she said. "Did it still have its plates when you saw it?"

"I don't know, I couldn't see. Why?"

"Because from what Grant Dankworth was saying, he murdered Karen before Briggs was picked up. The plates from the Beetle were on the lorry when it burned."

"Good point, Kate," said Kett. "The killer must have taken it earlier in the day, because he was inside it when he was at the Dankworth place. Check the system, see what you can find."

"Anything else, sir?"

Kett looked through the windscreen to see that Porter had stopped walking, his shoulders slumped as he looked back over his shoulder. He resembled a dog that had been driven to the middle of the woods and then abandoned.

"Yeah, can you see if there are any women called Darcey associated with William Briggs, local to Yarmouth?"

"Darcey as a first name, sir?"

"Yeah, I think so. Call Porter if you find anything."

"Will do, sir. Duke shouldn't be long."

"I hope not," Kett said after he'd hung up. He pulled the collar of his coat around his neck, shivering in the fridge of his Volvo. "I'm freezing."

YOU'RE A BLOODY FOOL, *Pete.*

Porter traipsed down the street, mentally kicking himself for being such an idiot. Twenty years on the job and he'd still fallen for the oldest trick in the book. The three boys had looked so cold on the other side of the street, so *lost*, that he'd felt sorry for them. He'd called them over for a chat because he'd honestly believed he could get through to them. After all, it hadn't been *that* long ago he'd been in the same boat—or car, if you were going to be pedantic. He'd been fifteen when he'd boosted his first set of wheels, a 1983 BMW 5 Series that had been so knackered the exhaust had fallen off after two miles. The Audi he'd wheeled downhill three years and about two dozen cars later had been the last of them. Somehow, he'd never been caught, because a TWOC record would have scuppered his career before it had even started.

But what he'd said to Kett hadn't been a lie. If he hadn't spent so long breaking the law, it never would have entered his head that he had the power to mend it.

Still, he should have known better than to let three kids crowd around him. He was lucky they'd only taken his keys and not his wallet and his phone and his trousers too.

He realised he'd stopped walking, and when he looked back, he saw Kett fuming at him through the Volvo's window. He gave the DCI a nervous wave before scuttling around the corner.

You're a bloody fool, he told himself again, patting his pockets in case the keys had magically reappeared.

They hadn't, of course.

He pulled off a glove with his teeth and then opened Google on his phone, typing 'William Briggs, Darcey, Yarmouth' into the search bar. The first thing to come up was Briggs' Facebook page, which showed nothing except the logo for Gorleston Football Club.

His privacy settings stopped Porter from going any further, so he navigated back to the search page and started scrolling. He was surprised to see a LinkedIn page a few entries down, and he clicked on it. There was still no photo, but several jobs had been listed, two in Dublin and the rest in London. They were all programming gigs. His location was listed as Great Yarmouth.

He was clicking on the entry for his latest workplace when his phone began to ring. It was Savage.

"Hi, Kate," he said. "You okay?"

"Yes, sir. Kett just asked me to look into something for you. You're looking for a woman called Darcey?"

"Yeah," he said. "But I'm on it, don't worry."

"You've found her?"

"I mean, I'm getting there," he said.

"Darcey DeCarlo?"

"DeCarlo," Porter echoed. "Yeah, that's her."

"Darcey with an E."

"Dearcy, yeah."

"No, an E after the C, sir. You saw the Companies House listing?"

"I... did," he lied.

"Briggs and DeCarlo are co-directors of a defunct company, streaming services. It's registered to the same Yarmouth address as the car."

"Yes, I definitely think I saw that," Porter said.

"But her address is on there too, down in Gorle—"

"Gorleston," Porter guessed. "That's what I was thinking."

"Stanton—"

"Stanton Street," he said.

"Aven—"

"I meant Avenue. Stanton Avenue."

"Number..."

Porter waited.

"Number twenty..." Savage teased.

"Two," he said. "Three. Four. Five."

"Twenty-five," Savage confirmed. "Great work, sir."

"Too bloody right it's great work," he said. "Thanks, Kate."

He heard her laughing as she hung up.

"Darcey DeCarlo," he said to himself before he could forget. "Stanton Avenue."

He Googled the street to see that it was twenty minutes away on foot, then hunkered down and set off into the wind. It was tough going, the cold leeching through his overcoat and his suit, creeping down his collar and up his trouser leg where it at least helped with the pain in his crotch. He upped his pace to get his heart going, the warmth bleeding back in after a few minutes.

Around him, Great Yarmouth continued its gradual descent into dystopia. Half the shops he passed were closed, most boarded up and daubed with graffiti. Gangs of youths crowded the doorways, eyeballing him as he passed, and cars revved their engines aggressively at the traffic lights. But the sun was doing its job well, brightening the streets, bringing a smile to the faces of the families he passed.

He texted Allie as he walked.

Hope you and Bobby are having a better Valentine's Day than I am.

Then he took a selfie of himself in front of a chip shop and sent that too, so busy looking at his phone that he almost collided with a lamppost.

"Bloody thing," he muttered, glaring at it.

He'd walked a few more paces before the smell of the shop caught up to him. The temptation was too great to resist, especially as he hadn't had lunch yet, and five minutes later he strolled out of the shop with a tray of chips almost drowning in ketchup. He didn't trust himself not to drop them if he ate on the go, so he perched on the edge of the little wooden bench outside the window, savouring them.

When he'd dumped the rubbish in the bin, he pulled the collar of his overcoat up against the cold and walked as fast as he could without giving himself a stitch, following the directions through a tangle of narrow streets south. It took a lot longer to reach Stanton Avenue than Google had promised him, and when he rounded the corner, he was surprised to see a police car parked on the side of the road. The door opened as he approached it, and Duke got out, stretching like an enormous cat.

"You have got to be kidding me," Porter said, wiping his leaking nose. "How the hell did you get out here so fast?"

Duke checked his watch.

"It's been forty minutes, sir?" he said. "Stopped at Kett's house, drove out, handed them over. Kate gave me the address."

Porter checked his own watch.

"You could have let me know you were on your way, you could have picked me up."

"Sorry, sir," said Duke. "But then you wouldn't have had a chance to eat your chips."

"Huh?" said Porter.

Duke extended a finger.

"You've got ketchup on your shirt, sir."

Porter glanced down to see that Duke was right. There was a red stain the size and shape of a kidney, lurking beneath the knot of his tie.

"That's not ketchup, Constable," he said. "It's... blood."

"Blood, sir?"

"From the fight. I'm sure Kett filled you in."

"Right," said Duke nodding. "Lot of blood, sir. You sure you don't need to go to the hospital?"

"I'm fine," Porter said. "Takes more than a little blood to stop Peter Porter."

He turned away from Duke's knowing smile to look at the properties along the side of the road. They were all bungalows, identical to every other bungalow he'd ever seen on the job. Sometimes it seemed like all there was in the world was bungalows.

"That's it," he said, nodding to the one with a rusting 25 on the gate. It was a little neater than the others, but not by much. In the middle of the overgrown front garden was a fake wishing well, a plastic cat curled up where the bucket should be. The curtains in both front windows were drawn.

"Bit weird for the middle of the day, sir," said Duke, noticing the same thing.

The gate was low enough for Porter to step over, and he made his way up the short path to the front door. As he was passing the well, the cat leaped upwards with a gargled howl of panic. The noise Porter made wasn't far off, and he clutched a hand to his heart in order to stop it from exploding through the ketchup stain on his shirt.

"Jesus fucking bastard Christ," he said as the cat disappeared into the bushes that separated this house from the next. "I thought it was an ornament."

"You want me to knock, sir?" asked Duke as he overtook him.

Porter nodded. Duke lifted his fist and cracked it into the wooden door—just once—before standing back.

"What was that?" Porter asked.

"A knock, sir," Duke replied.

Porter shook his head in disbelief.

"Have you never—" he started, then a shape appeared in the frosted glass, followed by the sound of a key turning.

"See," said Duke. "Once is enough."

The door swung open to reveal a woman in her thirties wearing pink pyjamas covered in little hearts. She was in the process of doing up her hair, a clip pinched between her lips. She glanced at Porter, then spent a little longer looking Duke up and down before muttering something that nobody could understand.

"Hi," said Porter, shouldering Duke out of the way. He held up his warrant card. "DI Peter Porter, Norfolk Police. We're looking for Darcey DeCarlo."

The woman took the clip from her mouth and slid it into her hair, although not well enough to stop a lock from falling in front of her face. She blew it away.

"Darcey?" she said. "She okay?"

"She's not here then?"

"No," said the woman, leaning against the door to keep it open. "Haven't seen her today."

"She lives here, though? Miss..."

"Tabitha," she said. "Do you need my surname?"

"Tabitha is fine," said Porter. "Darcey lives here?"

"Yeah, we rent it together," said Tabitha. "Well, *I* rent it, she gives me money whenever she hasn't handed it all to her boyfriend to spunk on the dogs."

"He does *what* on the dogs?" asked Duke.

"Spunks on them," she said. "Spaffs it all away. You know, gambling."

"Oh," said Duke, evidently relieved.

"The boyfriend is William Briggs?" asked Porter.

"Willy, yeah. He's a bit of a waste of space, although you must know that already or you wouldn't be here. I've been telling her to get rid of him all the time I've known her. He in trouble?"

"I'm not sure," said Porter. "Can you tell me when you last saw Darcey?"

"Yesterday," she said, shivering in the cold. "We sometimes have Sunday lunch together if we're not working. We take turns. I did it yesterday, although it weren't much. All frozen."

"What time was that?"

She shuddered again, wrapping her arms around her chest.

"We can go inside, if you like?" Porter told her.

She took a lingering look at Duke again, seemed to think about it, then shook her head.

"Better not," she said, although she didn't explain why. "We ate probably around four? I was working after, left the house about six."

"Working where?"

"Up the club," she said. "Mercy. Got home after three, no idea if she was here or not."

She frowned.

"Her door was open, though. I remember that. So she must have gone out. She always shuts her door when she's in bed."

"Do you have any idea where she might have gone?"

"Probably out with old Scrote-Faced McGee."

"William?"

"That's the one, yeah. If she's not here, she's usually with him. He's got this house over by the seafront, massive place. But it's not really a house, it's..."

She clamped her lips together, unwilling to say any more.

"We know what it is," said Porter. "I don't think she was with William last night. He was in the pub by himself until after eleven."

Unless it was Darcey who picked him up, he thought.

"How tall is Darcey?" he asked. "Does she have a raincoat?"

"Those are some random questions," Tabitha said, one eyebrow arched. "She's five-three and her waist is the same size as my forearm, although a little bigger the last couple of weeks. I don't know where she was, sorry. But she doesn't have a lot of friends in town, and she doesn't go out much except with William, or if she's at church, so unless she's got some kind of secret life thing going on..."

She shrugged.

"Highly doubt it, though, she's a real church mouse. No tats, won't even get her ears pierced. As delicate as they come, which makes it all the weirder that she picked *him.*"

Porter pulled a business card from his wallet and handed it over. She took it, and smiled up at Duke.

"Have you got one too?" she asked him. "My Tinder Valentine's just stood me up."

"He's got a girlfriend," said Porter.

Tabitha pouted.

"And I'm married," Porter added, showing her his ring.

She grimaced.

"Thanks for your time," he muttered.

He made his way back up the path, Duke clomping along behind him. They both stepped over the gate onto the pavement. The cat was there, licking its paw and watching Porter like it was planning on giving him another heart attack. He hissed quietly at it.

"Where now, sir?" asked Duke.

He didn't have time to answer before he heard the sound of a door opening again. Tabitha jogged up the path in her bare feet, using one hand to scoop the hair out of her face.

In her other hand, she held something small and colourful.

"I almost forgot, I found this," she said. "Last night, when I came home. It was in the bin. Maybe it's important."

She held it out, and Porter took it in his gloved hand.

It was a paper box that had been unfolded into a crude cross, three of the edges torn. On the plain side, somebody had written six words in spidery black pen:

Midnight. Come dance with me, baby.

They'd added a postcode beneath it.

Porter carefully turned the paper over in his palm. The reverse side was purple and plain, except for a large heart drawn in black pen. Inside the heart were two letters.

JV.

"Shit," he said. "Is that William's handwriting?"

Tabitha shrugged.

"What is it?" she asked. "Is it bad?"

"Thank you," Porter told her. "We'll be in touch."

But the answer to her question buzzed inside his head like a wasp.

Yeah. This is really bad.

CHAPTER TWELVE

Savage perched on the bonnet of the IRV, rubbing her arms through her coat to try to get some feeling back into them. The sky was a perfect shade of winter blue, the sun so bright it had given her a headache. But it was a lie, because the temperature had dropped to somewhere near freezing, the air deadly.

She could have been sitting in the car with the heating on, of course. If Porter or Kett or even Duke were here, that's what they'd be doing. But it felt too rude when the forensic team was ferreting around the shell of the burned-out lorry, clouds of breath billowing from their facemasks, their chattering teeth audible every time they got too close. In their white suits, they looked like an army of confused snowmen shambling over the frozen field.

This thought, at least, made her laugh.

"If you've found something funny here, please share it."

The voice was Hay's, and it was coming from the back of the truck fifteen yards away. The shuttered door was open, but only by a couple of feet, and Hay's face peeked out of the gap. Savage pushed herself off the bonnet of the car and walked over, trying not to trip on the hard, uneven ground.

"Sorry, Cara," she said. "Was in a world of my own. How's it going?"

"It's very odd," Hay replied. "You coming in?"

"Do I have to?"

"No."

Hay crawled out through the gap, her overalls absolutely caked in soot. Savage offered a hand and Hay took it as she dropped to the ground. She pulled off her facemask, her skin slick with sweat.

"I hate fire," she said, spitting into the dirt. "You can never get rid of the smell, or the taste."

"Or the dirt," said Savage, trying to scrub the soot from her hand.

They both turned to the open lorry, and Savage took a moment to study the shapes that had been crudely painted on the shuttered door in what she hoped was red paint: the *J* and the *V* inside a heart.

"Odd?" she said after a moment. Hay seemed to stir from a daydream.

"Yes. Odd. The husband said he killed Karen inside the lorry?"

"He did, but there's no body, is there?" said Savage. "Unless it burned up?"

Hay chewed on something for a moment, frowning.

"There's blood. A lot of blood. It's hard to see because of the soot, because it forms a barrier that prevents chemical enhancement. But some gentle cleaning and liberal doses of luminol revealed a significant blood pattern on the floor towards the back of the lorry. I have scraped and swabbed and we should be able to get DNA, unless the fire exceeded eight hundred degrees. It will be close."

"Is the blood on the floor?" asked Savage. "Grant Dankworth claimed he crushed his wife's head with a sledgehammer while she was sitting or lying down."

"It is, mostly," said Hay. "There's a large puddle with a four-foot streak, which does seem to corroborate a powerful blow to the head. I haven't cleaned the walls yet, so I may change my mind, but yes, this could well be a strike from a heavy hammer."

Savage closed her eyes for a moment, trying to think about anything other than what had happened here. It took her a few attempts to open them because of the cold. Hay was staring into the back of the lorry, shivering.

"I found handprints in the blood," she said. "I have counted seven so far, but there may be more."

"Handprints?" said Savage. "You think they're Grant's?"

Hay shook her head, sighing out a cloud of breath that was so thick it could have been cigarette smoke.

"I think they're the victim's, Kate. The pattern suggests that the attack didn't kill her. The prints lead towards the door, but do not quite make it. She may have been struck again here, and a third time, but there are still handprints. She really did not want to die."

"God," said Savage, putting her hand to her mouth. "She bled out?"

"There isn't enough blood," said Hay. "I think the fire took her."

Again, Savage tried not to imagine it, and again it was all she could think about. The sledgehammer had struck Karen in the head three times, but it hadn't been hard enough. She'd crawled through the burning truck until she couldn't go any further.

And then she'd burned to death.

"The lorry was definitely on fire when Karen and Grant were fighting?" Savage asked. "That's what he claims."

"We'll know more when we've finished our tests," said Hay. "But it seems that way. There are several layers of fire damage and blood, from what I can see. The blood is on the burnt metal of the floor, and there is another layer of soot on top. This suggests that the fire was burning whilst the attack was taking place. Either that, or the lorry had been burned before."

Savage nodded, watching a technician pick something from the frozen mud and put it into an evidence bag.

"What happened to the body?" she asked.

"That is the million-dollar question," Hay replied. "I think it was removed. There are traces of burnt flesh on the ground, like food inside an oven. There are also marks where the soot has been scuffed. It's easier if I show you."

Savage looked at the open back door of the lorry.

"It's fine," she said. "You can just tell me."

Hay held her hands a foot or so apart.

"The marks are this wide, and there are five of them. I can't be sure, but the first thing I thought of was a spade."

"A spade?"

"They were using it to scrape the body off the floor," said Hay, and Savage felt her stomach roll over. "The lorry has a metal bed, and the fire was directly underneath it. It would have been hotter than a grill. Retrieval would have been impossible while the lorry was burning, and by the time it had finished, the body would have been fused in place. It would have taken some effort to remove it."

"So why bother?" asked Savage. "Why go to all that

effort and risk being caught? Anyone could have seen the flames and called for a fire engine. It must have been burning for ages."

"I don't think it was," said Hay, pointing to the upper half of the lorry, which was relatively unscathed. "I think it was extinguished fairly promptly."

"You'd need some hefty gear to put that out," said Savage.

"I don't know for sure," said Hay. "But I will keep searching for answers. The fire was started with gasoline cans, did you see?"

Savage squatted to get a look beneath the truck, seeing the warped plastic.

"Was the lorry's tank full?" she asked, and a ghost of a smile appeared on Hay's face.

"This is why I like you, Kate," she said. "No, the tank was empty."

"Empty?"

"Not just low, but drained," said Hay. "There's no sign of fire damage inside the tank."

"So the blaze wasn't intended to kill," Savage said. "The truck wasn't meant to explode. The fire was supposed to scare them."

"That's what I think too," said Hay.

"It set a timer," said Savage. "Dankworth claimed the man who imprisoned them in the lorry told them he'd only let them out when one of them was dead. The fire was a motivator, but he didn't want them to burn up before they had a chance to go at each other."

Hay remained silent, listening intently.

"Which seems to support Dankworth's theory," Savage went on. "Unless he set the fire himself, of course. But that's a bit of a risk."

"So is killing your wife," said Hay. "For some people, the risk is what makes it attractive."

"True," said Savage. "Thanks, Cara."

Hay nodded, walking to the tailgate and pointing at the painted heart.

"By the way, your heart up there, it's blood. The letters too."

"Really?" said Savage.

"Really. But it will take me a few days to work out if it's the same as our victim's."

"Or our killer's," said Savage.

She watched Hay clamber back into the lorry, then walked back to the car. The pain of the cold finally trumped her politeness, and she got in, switching on the engine so that the heat would start working. The vents were blowing so hard that she almost didn't hear her phone, and by the time her numb fingers had worked it out of her pocket, the call had ended.

It was Kett, and she rang him back.

"Kate," he said, accompanied by the roar of an engine and the wail of a siren. "You in Swannington?"

"Yes, sir," she said.

"We've found a paper box with the letters JV inside a heart," said Kett. "Somebody wrote a message inside it and gave an address. It was at Darcey DeCarlo's house, and nobody has seen her since last night."

"Shit," said Savage. "What's the address?"

"It's about five miles away from the lorry where Karen was killed," said Kett. "We're on the way from Yarmouth now, but it will take us a while. Can you go look?"

"Yes, sir," said Savage.

"Just a look, though, Kate. We don't know what we're going to find there. Or *who*."

"I'll be careful, sir," she said. "What's the address?"

"It's a postcode. Hang on."

He read it out, and she typed it into the IRV's satnav.

"Aylsham Road, it's up near Skeyton," she said. "Five minutes. I'll call you when I get there."

"Just a look," said Kett, and she hung up, putting the IRV in gear and bumping it in a wide semi-circle over the field. She flicked on the lights and the siren as she reached the road, pulling out slowly before flooring it.

The barren countryside opened up around her, the frosted fields resembling foam-flecked waves, the bare trees like shipwrecks reaching for the sky. She turned south-west first, flipping the visor down against the glaring sun, then the road took her around in a circle until she was travelling east, past remote houses and quiet farms, past the occasional car and a solitary rider on a black horse. The road she arrived at could have been the same one she'd left seven minutes ago, nothing on either side but fields, the entire scene enclosed by dark woodland.

Only one thing stood out, a dark monolith that she caught sight of as she passed a break in the hedge, so black that it looked as if somebody had taken a knife to the day and cut the shape right out of it.

The verges were too high to mount, so she left the IRV in the middle of the road and exited into the cold. She could smell the fire from all the way back here, the chemical reek of petrol and soot catching in the back of her throat. She wondered if she'd brought it with her.

Cutting through the hedge she saw there was no track here, just a swathe of mud that had frozen solid, preserving the tyre tracks that crisscrossed through it.

The black shape she'd seen from the road sat fifty yards away. It was another lorry, its back facing her. Unlike the first one, this had been burned to its shell, the vehicle completely ravaged. The grass around it had been burned away, an almost perfect circle.

Savage scanned the field, no sign of anyone or any other cars. She pulled out her phone as she approached the lorry, calling Kett.

"Kate," he said. "You're there?"

"I am, sir. It's another lorry, in the middle of a field. Just like the last one. It's been almost completely destroyed by fire."

Kett swore.

"I'm putting you on speaker," he said. "It's safe?"

"It's safe, I think," she said. "There's nobody else around."

The field seemed to get bigger as she walked, the truck moving further away—the illusion made worse by the fact the blinding sun sat right over the black ridge of its roof. Savage cupped her free hand to her forehead until she walked into the lorry's shadow.

Unlike the shuttered rear of the other lorry, this one had two hinged doors. They were closed, although the one on the right hung precariously at an angle. If there had been a heart drawn on the back of this one, the fire had erased it.

"The damage is a lot worse here, sir," she said, walking around the lorry. The cab had contracted in the heat like a fist, the interior an unrecognisable sculpture of metal and plastic. "The whole thing's melted. Hang on."

The lorry's registration plate had fallen off and lay upside down half a dozen feet from the wreck. Savage bent down beside it and used her knuckle to flip it over.

"Got a plate, sir," she said, reading out the details.

"I'll check it," Kett said.

Savage made her way down the other flank of the lorry, returning to the rear doors.

"I think I can get it open, sir," she said.

"Be careful," Kett replied. "Could still be hot in there."

It wasn't. The cold had sapped every last bit of warmth from the fire.

The heat wasn't what worried her, though.

"Hello," she shouted, her voice bouncing back from the lorry before being swallowed whole by the field. "Police. If there's anyone in there, make yourself known."

Inside the truck, something shifted, and Savage only just managed to lock her throat around a scream. She took a couple of steps backwards.

"What is it?" said Kett.

The noise came again, a patter like falling rain.

Or like fingers desperately scratching.

Savage pictured Karen Dankworth, her head staved in, the fire crawling over her, burning her skin, igniting her hair.

Still alive.

She slipped the phone into her pocket and ran to the lorry. The right-hand door hung off its hinges, and when she pulled it, it split from the frame and crashed to the ground like a ringing bell—as if it wanted her to see what lay inside.

Savage could hear Kett calling her name from inside her pocket, but she ignored him. She stepped up to the lorry and peered inside.

The body that sat in the middle of the cargo bay was definitely not still alive. It was hard to tell that it had ever been human. The sculpture of flesh sat cross-legged, mummified in char. Its head was bowed, its hands in its lap, as serene as a Buddhist statue. Soot rained down from the roof of the lorry, drumming the floor.

Savage pulled out her phone.

"Kate?" said Kett, desperate now.

"I'm okay, sir," she said, hoping he wouldn't hear the lie. "But there's bad news."

She took a breath, wondering if the whole world now reeked of smoke.

"We've got a body."

CHAPTER THIRTEEN

By the time they'd followed the satnav to the postcode that had been written on Darcey DeCarlo's box, the country road was completely mobbed with police cars. Porter pulled the Volvo up behind the last of them and switched off the engine. The heat plummeted almost immediately.

"Do we have to get out, sir?" he said, nodding through the side window. "I can kind of see it from here."

Kett squinted through the straggly hedge, making out a black smudge in the middle of the field.

"Come on, Pete," he said, clambering out. The cold air wrapped him up in a brutal hug. "It's bloody awful."

Duke pulled up behind them in his IRV, the bumper almost kissing the back of the Volvo. Kett waited for him to get out before leading the way down the narrow road, squeezing past three IRVs and a familiar Mercedes.

Even if he hadn't seen Superintendent Clare's car, there was no denying he was here. His brash voice carried over the hedge, about three decibels short of a squeal.

"Great," muttered Kett.

A constable stood by a break in the hedge and Kett nodded to her as they passed. Clare paraded in the middle of the field, his gangly arms waving, his long legs doing their best to keep him upright on the slippery ground. He was wearing his Big Tossing Jacket, which resembled the carcass of a dead camel more and more every time Kett saw it, and a black hat that was pulled so far down his forehead that it hid his eyes.

All in all, he looked like he had escaped from some kind of facility.

He must have heard them coming, because he turned to face them, craning his head back to enable him to peek under the brim of his hat.

"Well, if it isn't Zipper, Kit-Kat and Hodenkobold," he said. "Back from your holidays, are you? Flight got delayed, did it?"

"Hodenkobold, sir?" said Duke.

"Yes, Constable," said Clare, his beady eyes black beneath his hat. "Your new nickname, as I pointed out this morning."

"When?" asked Duke, confused.

"That's it, I'm changing your name to Sieve," said the Superintendent. "Because anything that goes in slips right out again."

"Technically, sir," said Duke, "only water comes out. Sieves collect all the juicy bits."

"I'm about to collect *your* juicy bits, Constable," said Clare, on the verge of apoplexy. "And put them in a tossing *jar*. Shut up and get over here."

They scuttled the last few yards. Kett took in the lorry as he walked. Even though it was completely black, he could see that it wasn't identical to the last one. It was a little smaller, for one, and the back doors opened outwards rather than rolling up. One of the doors lay on the ground.

This lorry held a body. It had been turned to charcoal, the rough shape of the person it had once been almost perfectly preserved. All of the finer details, though, had been burned away. The face was a mask, the eyes and mouth nothing but scratches scattered between the nubbins of its nose and ears. There was no hair, no clothes, just ravaged flesh.

"Shit," said Kett, putting the back of his hand to his mouth.

"Yes, Detective," said Clare. "Shit is exactly what this is. Unbearable shit, hurled onto my plate by you horrible, thoughtless bastards."

"Again, sir," said Kett, "*we* didn't do it."

"So hurry up and tell me who did," said Clare. "Two lorries, both burned out, presumably last night. We have one man telling us he was forced to murder his wife in the first one, although there's no body to confirm his story. And this lorry has a body, but we don't know who it is."

"I think we have an idea who it is," said Kett. "Pete."

"It's not Pete, you twat," said Clare. "He's standing right behind you."

"No, I mean... Pete, show him what you found."

Porter approached the Super with caution, holding out an evidence bag containing the unravelled paper box. Clare pushed his hat back from his eyes and leaned in.

"This was at Darcey DeCarlo's house, sir," Porter said.

"Who?"

"She's in a relationship with William Briggs. We found his plates on the other lorry. We've just visited Darcey's house and her housemate told us she found this in the bin this morning. She doesn't know where it came from. JV, just like on the first lorry."

He turned the bag over to reveal the handwritten note on the other side.

"The postcode leads here."

"Nobody has seen Darcey since yesterday," said Kett. "We found footage from a pub in Yarmouth showing William getting picked up just after eleven, in his own car. He was off his face, could barely walk. We couldn't make out the identity of the driver, but they were wearing a hooded raincoat, just like the footage Savage found of the person who dropped off the gift at Karen Dankworth's house. I'm thinking that Karen got a box just like this one, telling her where to go. She thought she was meeting Grant, and maybe Darcey thought she was meeting William."

"There's a mark on it, sir," said Porter, turning it back over. "There. Looks like somebody could have peeled some tape off it. Maybe there was string."

"Because the killer likes to play games," said Clare.

"Like Jack Valentine," said Savage as she walked out from behind the lorry, her phone to her ear. Her face was gaunt, although Kett wasn't sure if it was because of the cold, or the horror of what she'd found here. She nodded to Kett as she walked over, then studied the box in Porter's hand. "JV. Again."

"Whoever is doing this, he likes to mark his territory," said Kett. "We know any more about this Jack Valentine character?"

"Not much, sir," said Savage. "But I might have an idea about that. Hang on... Hi."

She turned away, speaking into the phone.

"Any leads on the lorries?" asked Clare.

"I gave the plate number to Spalding, sir," said Kett. "She's running it."

As if on cue, his phone rang. Clare lifted an eyebrow as the *Mexican Hat Dance* pealed out over the field.

"Sorry," Kett grumbled, answering the call. "Alison, any luck?"

"Your plates don't belong to a lorry, sir," said Spalding. "They belong to a 2013 model Renault Vivaro campervan that's been listed as SORN for four years. Last recorded owner was a woman called Anna Greer, forty-four. She lives in Aylsham."

"Thanks, Alison," said Kett.

"You're welcome, sir," she said. "Least I can do, considering you're out there in the cold and I'm sitting by the radiator with a cup of tea in my hand."

"Wait, my desk is the one by the radiator," said Kett, but Spalding had hung up.

"What did she say?" asked Clare, ogling.

Kett's phone dinged, a text from Spalding listing Greer's address.

"The killer switched the plates again," said Kett. "Spalding's found the owner. She's local."

He turned to Duke.

"Can you go grab her, Aaron?" he asked. "I don't know what she's got to do with this, but she's safer with us."

"Yes, sir," said Duke, turning around and lumbering off.

"Aaron," Kett called after him. "You need her name. And her address."

"That I do," Duke replied, spinning back.

Kett handed the PC his phone, seeing that Savage was off hers.

"William Briggs and Darcey DeCarlo weren't boyfriend and girlfriend," she said. "They were husband and wife."

"What?" said Kett. "How did we not know this?"

"They got married last week," Savage said. "Wednesday. Records haven't been updated yet."

"Nobody knew," said Kett. "Nobody at the Briggs house mentioned it."

"Neither did Darcey's housemate," said Porter.

"They were keeping it a secret," said Savage. "But why?"

Nobody could answer her.

"Where was the ceremony?" asked Kett.

"Yarmouth," she said. "St Margaret's. It's a Catholic church."

"The housemate said she spent time in church," said Porter.

"Okay," said Clare. "This is good. Kett, find out what you can from St Margaret's. Savage, keep working this place until Hay gets here. She done at the first murder scene yet?"

"Not quite, sir," said Savage. "But somebody definitely died inside the lorry. The sledgehammer did the damage, but it was the fire that killed her."

"Fuck," said Porter.

"Also, the truck's petrol tank had been emptied. Completely. There was enough fuel beneath the vehicle to start a fire, but there was no danger of it exploding."

"The killer wanted a slow burn," said Kett.

"That's what I think, sir," said Savage. "He wanted to scare them enough that they'd turn on each other, but he needed to give them time to do it."

"Or somebody wanted to feed us enough bullshit to make his murder believable," said Clare. "This could still be Dankworth, going out of his way to present himself as a victim, not a killer."

"Maybe, sir," said Savage. "But we'd need to find a link between him and William Briggs and Darcey DeCarlo."

"So go and bloody do it then," said Clare, pulling his hat down so low that his eyes were almost covered again. "I'm going back to HQ until you bag of bollocks can sort yourselves out."

He stormed off, almost going arse over tit on the icy mud. Kett could hear him yelling obscenities at the ground all the way to the hedge.

"Celibacy does not suit that man," he said.

"Does it suit anyone, sir?" asked Porter.

Kett reached for his phone before remembering he'd given it to Duke.

"Has Aaron gone?" he asked, not seeing the PC anywhere. Savage nodded. "He's taken my bloody phone. He was supposed to copy the address and give it back, the giant prat."

He breathed a cloud of frustration into the air.

"Jesus Christ."

"Want mine, sir?" asked Porter.

"No," he said. "You can come with me. Let's go talk to the priest."

CHAPTER FOURTEEN

The Catholic Church of St Margaret was one of the few remaining glimpses of the town that Yarmouth had once been. It stood tall on the pedestrianised main street just a stone's throw from the beach, as if holding its nose up at the run-down greasy spoons and sweet shops and tourist attractions that surrounded it. By the time Porter parked the Volvo outside, the evening was drawing in. The dark slid off the sea, pooling in the corners, gathering like an invading army.

"After you, sir," Porter said, switching off the engine. "Age before beauty and all that."

Kett was too cold to argue, hauling himself out of the car. He made his way through the open gate and opened one side of the ornate oak doors. Past the cold porch was a grand space that—as he'd always found was the case with churches—seemed far too big for the outside walls to contain. Rows of wooden pews filled the nave like ribs, dozens of sculptures the colour of bone watching with blind eyes. Even the stained-glass windows struggled to hold their colour. The temperature inside was only slightly warmer than outside, but at least when Porter closed the door, the wind couldn't follow them in.

There wasn't a soul in sight.

Kett glanced at Porter to see him making the sign of the cross over his chest, kissing his fingers when he'd finished.

"Didn't think you were religious, Pete," he said, his voice echoing back and forth between the stone walls.

"Force of habit," he said. "From being a kid. These days I just need to ward off the vampires."

Kett breathed out a laugh.

"Speaking of which..." said Porter.

A woman emerged from a door at the far end of the church. She was very tall and very thin, and she walked with a stoop as if she was carrying a wooden cross on her back. Her hair was scraped back so tightly that her face had been pulled out of shape, her eyes held open as if they were on hooks. In the light of the church, her pale face looked almost green.

"I heard the door," she called out to them, her quiet voice filling the church with ease. "Came to make sure you're not planning on stealing the candlesticks. Or the lead from the roof. Or whatever else you can get your grubby mitts on."

"Our hands are clean," said Kett, pulling out his warrant card. "DCI Robert Kett, Norfolk Police."

"So you *are* here about the roof?" said the woman, crossing the transept but stopping next to the first line of pews. She seemed to expect Kett and Porter to come to her, and Kett obliged.

"I'm afraid not," he said when he'd reached her. The echo of his footsteps seemed to take too long to fade. "This is about something else."

"Shame," said the woman, fixing him with a stare of

some intensity. "Because at some point they'll take so much that the roof will simply collapse, and the church will be lost. Think of the cost of that, Detective, will you? Next time you're putting your resources into removing a handful of petty criminals from the streets."

She turned her gaze to Porter.

"Can you imagine it? A world without buildings like this? We're losing them, one by one. And we're losing everything they stand for."

"You work here?" Kett asked, and she tutted.

"I do."

"Can I ask your name?"

"You can," she said, a small, triumphant smile letting him know she was well aware of how annoying she was being. Kett didn't give in to her, holding her eye until she tutted again. "Valerie."

"I need to ask you about a woman who attends your church, Valerie," said Kett. "Darcey DeCarlo. Do you know her?"

The answer was clear in the way the woman grew tense, her back straightening. She really was tall, Kett saw. Taller than him, for sure, and maybe even Porter's height. She was broad, too, and Kett wondered if she'd taught herself to walk with her back bent in order to hide her height, the way so many tall kids did.

"No," said Valerie, her answer surprising Kett.

"You're sure?" he said.

"The church has a large congregation. Am I expected to know every single one of them?"

"No," said Kett. "But I assumed you'd remember somebody who got married here last week."

Two spots of colour grew in Valerie's cheeks, almost

perfect circles. But the hardness didn't leave her face. It seemed to take an age for her to speak.

"It does not surprise me one jot that a man such as yourself sees no sanctity in the power of marriage."

Kett lifted his left hand, flashing his ring—which, he noticed, was well in need of a polish.

"I beg to differ," he said, and the woman laughed in his face.

"You wouldn't know love if it danced on your grave," she said quietly.

"Hello?" came a voice from the back of the church. "Valerie?"

The woman flinched as a man emerged from the same door that she had. He was older than her by a good decade, somewhere in his late fifties, and his black robes—which he was frantically doing up as he trotted towards them—made it very clear he was a priest.

"Sorry," he called. "Sorry, sorry, sorry."

Kett wasn't sure who he was apologising to until he reached them. He shot Valerie a wary look, then did his best to smile at Kett.

"You are welcome," he said. "More than welcome, whatever else has been said."

He glared at Valerie a second time, although she didn't notice. Her attention was still squarely on Kett.

"My name is Father Jack Odling," he said, clearing his throat. He smelled strongly of cigarette smoke, and there might have been alcohol there as well. He seemed to read Kett's mind, pulling a packet of Polos from his pocket and tipping two into his mouth. He offered them to Kett, who shook his head, then to Porter, who took one.

"Thanks," said the DI. "Haven't had a Polo since I was a kid."

"One of my many vices, I'm afraid," said Odling. "You're police?"

"Is it that obvious?" asked Kett, holding up a warrant card that the priest barely glanced at.

"Sadly, yes," Odling said. "You see more than your fair share of trouble when you're in the calling."

He caught the way Porter was staring at him and quickly shook his head.

"Not *that* sort of trouble, young man," he said. "We're not all tarnished with the same brush."

"They were asking about a member of the congregation, Father," said Valerie. She stood a good few inches over the man and he seemed to know it, shrinking away from her. "A name I did not recognise."

"Darcey DeCarlo," said Kett. "I'm afraid I don't have a photograph. She's twenty-three, and she lives just up the road."

"Darcey," said the priest, and Valerie cleared her throat aggressively. He avoided meeting her eye, shrinking away even further. "I know Darcey, yes."

Valerie made a noise of outrage, then she sat down in the pew hard enough to shunt it backwards.

"We can't lie to them, Val," said Odling. "Not *here*."

He looked up at Kett the way a schoolboy would look at a headmaster, his hands clasped together in front of his chest.

"Darcey was married here a few days ago," he said. "To her boyfriend, William."

"William Briggs?" asked Kett, and the priest nodded. "Why is it such a secret? People get married every day."

"It's not a secret," said Father Odling. "Not from you, anyway. From her parents."

Something clattered deep inside the church, from the

door the priest and the woman had walked through. Odling flinched, but he didn't turn to look.

"Darcey and William have been together for as long as I have known them," the priest said, clutching compulsively at his robes. "They came through those doors together two years ago and have been part of our community ever since. William is... He's an interesting young man, but he has his troubles. He and his brother live in the town too, in a house of..."

"Ill repute," offered Valerie.

"We know," said Kett.

"But Miss DeCarlo is from different stock altogether. She hails from the Lakes, and her family are devout Catholics. I think they always planned to get married eventually, but fate forced their hand."

"Fate?" asked Kett, hazarding a guess. "She was pregnant?"

Valerie tutted again and Father Odling rolled his eyes at her.

"It happens, Val, as well you know."

"It *shouldn't* happen," she shot back. "As well *you* know."

Kett thought of the lorry they'd found, the charred figure in the back.

Please don't let it be her.

"They came to me a week last Sunday and presented their news. Poor Darcey was distraught; she thought it was the end of the world. If her father found out that she'd borne a child out of wedlock then she would have been ostracised from the family. William asked if I could marry them immediately."

He sighed.

"And me being a fool for love, agreed."

"They were married on Wednesday?" Kett asked.

"In the evening," said Father Odling. "We had another service in the day, that was the only slot open. There were no attendees, just Darcey, William, myself and Valerie, who reluctantly served as a witness."

"Who was the other witness?" asked Kett. "I'm pretty sure you need two."

"You do," said Father Odling, a note of disapproval in his voice. "It was William's brother, Luke."

"He didn't mention it when I spoke to him this morning," said Kett.

"I'm not surprised. I don't think he knew what was going on. He was as high as a kite for the entire service. But I made the decision to ignore it. He was sober enough to sign the papers, and I had no doubt that William and Darcey were doing the right thing. It's rare to see a love as committed as theirs in this day and age. It's comforting to know that it still exists."

Valerie made a noise like there was a chicken bone caught in her throat.

"It was a perfunctory service," Odling went on. "Limited readings, and very short intercessions. No mass, of course. But the gospel reached fruition, their marriage was sanctioned."

The clattering noise from the other end of the church came again, and this time the man looked back. Judging by the expression on his face he seemed to expect to see the Devil himself stride out of the door.

"Everything okay?" asked Kett.

"I was about to ask you the same thing," he replied, turning back. "Is Darcey alright? Why are you asking about her?"

"That was the last time you saw her? The wedding?"

"I saw her the following day," he said. "They both came around with a bottle, to say thank you. That was around dinnertime, five maybe. She was like a different person, Detective. She was glowing. After that, I didn't see them again."

Valerie was studying the priest like a hawk, her head subtly shaking from side to side.

"And you?" Kett asked her. "When was the last time you saw them?"

"At the wedding," she said, making a point of locking eyes with him.

"Is she okay?" Odling asked again.

"We don't know," said Kett. "We're trying to find Darcey and William. We've got footage of William being picked up outside the Iron Bull last night after eleven, by somebody driving his Beetle. The driver was tall, and they were wearing a raincoat."

The priest cleared his throat, casting his gaze towards Valerie again.

"I never once saw Darcey in a raincoat," he said. "And she isn't a tall girl. She didn't drive, either, as far as I know."

"Can you think of anything else?" asked Kett. "Anyone who fits that description? Anything that might help us find her?"

"You'd be best looking at *his* place," said Father Odling with a sneer. "William wasn't an unpleasant man, but he came from a rotten house filled with rotten people. I don't think anybody there wanted him to be happy, not even his brother. William and Darcey often spoke about moving away, about starting fresh somewhere, and I don't think his brother wanted him to go. But there's another man who calls the shots. I get the feeling he would be capable of anything if it helps him get what he wants."

"Perry Paul, calls himself the Archduke?" asked Kett, and the priest nodded.

"A vile man, and even he isn't the worst."

"Don't," said Valerie. She'd meant it as a whisper, but the church betrayed her, broadcasting it from wall to wall. "That's enough."

Kett waited for the priest to continue, but he just glanced at Valerie again, his expression unreadable.

"I think that is enough, for now," Father Odling said. "I will ask around and see if anyone has seen Darcey or William. Despite what appearances may suggest, this is a close-knit town, people here care for one another."

"Thank you," said Kett, passing the man a business card. "Anything else, call me. Either of you."

Valerie made a point of turning away from him on the pew.

Kett nodded to the priest before heading for the door. He heard the same noise as he went, an echoing crunch from deep inside the building. This time he stopped, staring at the door that lay on the other side of the transept.

"What is it, sir?" Porter asked quietly.

Kett waited a moment more, then shook his head.

"Nothing," he said, making his way towards the door again. "Just on edge."

He stepped outside, surprised at how dark it had grown in the ten minutes or so they'd been in the church. The lights on the pedestrianised street had come on, the shops glowing. Porter closed the door behind him.

"Now I remember why I stopped going to church," he said, pulling the collar of his overcoat tight against his neck. "Creepy."

"Yeah," said Kett. "They were definitely hiding something, right?"

Porter nodded, leading the way back towards the Volvo.

"Did you notice anything else, sir?" he asked.

Kett got into the passenger seat and Porter climbed behind the wheel, both of them slamming their doors.

"Notice what?" Kett asked.

"Their names, sir," Porter told him as he started the engine. "Jack and Val."

"Shit," said Kett. "You're right. That's some coincidence."

"Or not," said Porter as he put the car in gear and drove off.

CHAPTER FIFTEEN

SAVAGE HEARD THE THROB OF EMILY FRANKLIN'S TVR long before she saw it, the powerful engine cutting through the respectful peace of the crime scene. Hay's forensic team hadn't arrived yet, but a troupe of miserable constables searched the circumference of the field, looking like crows in their black uniforms. Night had fallen, a rig of halogen lights doing its best to extend the day.

The lorry sat with its rear doors open, the burned body still sitting perfectly upright inside, swathed in shadow. From where Savage was standing, two dozen yards away, the corpse could have still been alive. She kept expecting it to simply stand up and walk away, and the thought of it made her want to scream.

The TVR rattled into silence and Savage heard a car door slam. A few seconds later, a round silhouette that could only be Franklin in her puffer jacket walked through the gap in the hedge. A stray branch caught in her hair and she wriggled herself free, hefting her bag over the muddy field. She offered a smile to Savage and then an even bigger one to the lorry.

"Never rains, but it pours," she said when she was in earshot. "What's the equivalent? Never smokes, but it burns? No, doesn't work. Never burns, when it..."

"Blazes?" offered Savage.

"Better than anything I could come up with," she said, dropping her bag at Savage's feet and catching her breath. "How are you? You look... awful."

"Thanks," said Savage.

"I mean, your awful is still most people's gorgeous," Franklin went on, turning to the lorry. "That the body?"

"Yeah," said Savage. "Hay's not here yet, nobody's been in."

"I think Cara and I are interchangeable at this point," she said. "Sometimes I wake up and I think I'm her. Might even shave my head one of these days."

Franklin collected her bag, and they walked over together, the lights casting their long shadows across the stubbled field.

"Any sign of the first body yet?" asked Franklin.

"Not yet," said Savage. "Although it isn't impossible that this is her."

It seemed unlikely that anyone would scrape the charred corpse of a woman from one lorry and place it into a second burned vehicle—and it would surely be impossible to bend a fire-damaged body into this position—but then everything about this case seemed unlikely and impossible.

Franklin dumped her bag beside the open back door, ducking down to unzip it. She handed Savage a torch that was almost as thick as her forearm. Then she pulled out an equally impressive lantern and set it on the lip of the truck's cargo hold. When she switched it on, Savage had to throw a hand over her face.

"That's like looking at the sun, Emily," she said.

"It's a bit of a beast," Franklin replied.

Savage blinked the light from her eyes, watching Franklin pull on a pair of latex gloves.

"Little help?" she said, and Savage laced her fingers together, allowing Franklin to step into them. The pathologist grabbed the handle on the side of the remaining door and hauled herself inside. She offered a hand, but Savage shook her head, using the lorry's rear grill as a ladder.

Illuminated by the harsh glow of the lantern, the interior of the lorry was every bit as awful as Savage had expected it to be. The floor and walls had been charred black, the smell of burning plastic hanging in the air like poison. The roof had survived the blaze, but only just, the canvas filthy with smoke and soot.

The body sat cross-legged by the door, its head bowed, its hands resting on its lap.

"This is very unusual," said Franklin, kneeling beside the corpse. "You hardly ever see bodies in this position. It's almost like it's been posed."

"They wouldn't have died like this in the fire, would they?" said Savage. "They must have already been dead, surely."

"Possibly," said Franklin. "Have you ever seen the photos of the monks who set themselves on fire in protest? They sit like this, and their bodies are perfectly preserved."

"It's horrific," said Savage.

"Indeed, it is."

Franklin pulled a digital camera from her bag and began taking photos. The corpse had no clothes left to speak of, its body too warped by the flames to make out any distinguishing features.

"Adult, for sure," said Franklin. "No way of telling how old without a look at the teeth."

"Male or female?" asked Savage.

"Can't be sure," she said. "I'll probably need to get it onto my table. There are studs in both ears, which makes me think it might be a woman. But that's probably awfully sexist of me."

Savage leaned in as close as she dared, seeing the lumps in each withered earlobe—a spark of gold from the one on the right as Franklin's flash went off again. The stench of burnt flesh entered her nose, and she belched acid, turning away with a hand to her mouth.

"Horrible," she said, studying the rest of the lorry through watering eyes.

The cargo area was smaller than the last one, and it looked like it had been set up the same way. Towards the back was a charred slab of tabletop, the legs completely burned away. The metal frame of a chair sat close by, bolts where it had been secured to the floor, the plastic seat melted away. In between were several blackened lumps. Savage switched on the torch Franklin had given her, seeing the vague shape of a hammer, and the longer shaft of what could only be an axe.

"It's exactly the same as the first lorry," she said, coughing the smell from her lungs. "If Dankworth's story is to be believed, he and his wife were both locked inside the lorry and made to fight. The killer would only release the survivor. Looks like it happened that way again."

"You know the names of these guys?" asked Franklin, still snapping away.

"We think it was William Briggs and Darcey DeCarlo inside the lorry," she replied, turning back. "We just need to work out which one of them that is."

Franklin put her camera away, moving in front of the

corpse. The sound of Savage's phone bursting to life made both of them jump.

"Sorry," she said, seeing Porter's name on the screen. "Sir?"

"This just got a little more complicated," said a voice, not Porter but Kett. "You were right about William and Darcey being married. They got hitched under the radar because she was pregnant."

Savage felt the blood drain from her head, the vertigo like the lorry was moving again. She stepped carefully to the wall and put a hand to it so that she wouldn't tumble into the corpse.

"Pregnant, sir?"

Franklin looked up, her face serious.

"About six weeks, I think. Probably not enough to show, although she was slim. Franklin there yet?"

"Yes, sir. She's looking at the body now."

"Can you let me know if she finds anything?"

"Will do, sir," said Savage. "But it looks like whoever was inside the lorry was made to fight. There are weapons here, just like the last one."

"Keep me posted," said Kett, and he hung up.

"Come and look at this," said Franklin.

The corpse was so close to the back doors that there was no room for Savage to kneel next to Franklin. She jumped back down to the ground instead, more than a little grateful to be back in the fresh air. Franklin had a scalpel in her hand, and she was using it to peel back the burnt skin of the corpse's chest.

"See this nubbin?" she said. "Definitely not organic."

Savage glanced at the body, but only for a second.

"Can I take your word for it, Emily?"

"It's metal," she said, her gloved fingers exploring.

"Right here, looks like it's slipped between the ribs and the xiphoid process."

"A knife?" asked Savage.

"That would be my guess. There's a metal prong here that would have sat inside the wooden handle. The rest of it must have burned away. Looking at the angle, I'd say it was an upward thrust into the lungs, possibly the heart. I can't say how long the blade is, but if it was more than three inches then at least death would have been quick."

She sighed.

"Excruciatingly painful, but quick."

"You still can't tell if this was a man or a woman?" asked Savage. "Because Kett just told me that the woman we think was trapped in here might have been pregnant."

"I heard," said Franklin. "There's no underwire here from a bra. Do you know if she was buxom?"

"Skinny, I think," said Savage.

"I won't know until I can get inside. There may be enough left downstairs to figure it out. If not, it's relatively easy to determine with a full autopsy. But looking at the body..."

She hopped down next to Savage and did exactly that.

"I don't know. Shoulders are wider than I'd expect to see on a woman, the lumbar curve is a little shallower. Maybe I was wrong. Some guys wear studs."

"Thanks, Emily," she said. "Let me know if you find anything else."

"You'll be the first person I call," she said. "Aaron taking you anywhere nice for Valentine's tonight?"

"This is the only date I'm getting," Savage said. "Story of my life."

"Preach, sister," said Franklin, returning to her work.

Savage took a moment, sighing deeply as she studied the

corpse, as she thought about the person it had once been. She felt bad for hoping that the body had once belonged to a man called William Briggs, and not a woman called Darcey DeCarlo. Murder was murder. It shouldn't have mattered.

But it did, of course.

She walked back to the road, calling Porter as she went. It was Kett who answered.

"Franklin can't be sure if the body's male or female," she said. "It's got a stud in both ears, though. You know if Darcey or William wore earrings?"

"No," said Kett.

"Wait," came Porter's voice. "Earrings?"

"Yeah."

"I'm almost positive Darcey's housemate said she didn't have any piercings. She called her a church mouse."

"You're sure?" asked Kett.

"Pretty sure, sir. No tattoos, no piercings."

"Luke had his ears pierced, though," said Kett. "William's brother. Both of them, and his tongue."

"Let's hope it runs in the family, then," said Savage. "Emily found what she thinks is a knife in the victim's heart. Must have been driven in with some force, all the way up to the hilt."

"Shit," said Kett. "You heard from Duke?"

"Not yet, sir," she said. "Want me to call him?"

"Please," said Kett. "And tell him to bring my bloody phone back."

He hung up before she could answer, and she found Duke's name on her phone. It had almost rung off before he answered. He sounded out of breath.

"Hey, sorry."

"You okay?" she asked.

"Yeah, just running back to the car. There was a hill. I

went to Alison Greer's house and spoke to her. She lives with her mum. They confirmed the campervan was Alison's, but she doesn't drive it anymore. Her ex-girlfriend does. Apparently, she stole it and won't give it back."

"You get a name for the girlfriend?"

"Got more than a name," he said. "Got her address too. It was just down the road. That's where I'm running back from now."

"Why are you running, though?" asked Savage.

"Because it's cold. Anyway, the woman's name is Jaye Moore, and she wasn't in."

"You knocked?"

"Of course I knocked."

"I mean, you knocked more than once?" Savage said. "Because otherwise, people don't know it's a knock."

"Once is fine," said Duke. "But she wasn't there. I had a good look around, nobody home, and no car."

"That isn't good," said Savage. "Can you call Kett and tell him what you just told me?"

"Will do," he said.

"But call Porter."

"Why?"

"Because you've got Kett's phone."

"Oh, yeah," he said. He blew out a sigh. "And I'm still hoping we get a moment at some point today. I really need to talk to you about something. Something important."

"Sure, Aaron," she said. "We'll probably get to go home at some point."

She blew him a kiss and hung up, turning to the lorry. Franklin was back inside, kneeling next to the statue-like corpse as if she was praying to it.

What she'd said to Duke was a lie, she knew.

They wouldn't be going home anytime soon.

CHAPTER SIXTEEN

By the time they'd made it back to HQ it was after six, and the darkness was absolute. Porter reversed the Volvo into a space and cut the engine, rubbing his tired face with both hands.

"Come on, Pete," said Kett, forcing himself to get out of the car. "We can do it."

He walked between the parked cars, heading for the lights of the main building. He was only halfway there when he heard the slam of a door behind him, followed by a high-pitched voice calling his name.

"Robbie!"

Kett glanced over his shoulder to see a familiar face wobbling down the road towards him. It was Norman Balls, one hand holding his glasses to his nose as he jogged, the other gripping his belt to stop his trousers from descending.

"Shit," said Kett, turning back. "Keep walking. Pretend we haven't seen him."

"Robbie!" yelled Balls, the patter of his feet growing faster. "Robbie! Robbie!"

"I think he wants to talk to you, sir," said Porter.

"Robbie! Robbie!"

Kett upped his pace, almost running.

"Robbie! It's me, Norman! Robbie! Robbie!"

Kett reached the door and almost ripped it off its hinges in his desperation to get inside. Porter ran in after him, and to Kett's horror he held the door open for Balls—beaming a smile at Kett as he did so.

"You bloody bast—" Kett started, then Balls burst into the lobby, panting furiously.

The strange little conspiracy theorist planted his hands on his knees and sucked in a breath. His shirt was untucked, a sheen of sweat on his balding head. He looked like he'd just run a marathon, not a thirty-yard dash.

"It's me," he said. "Norman. Your best friend."

"Not my best friend, Norman," said Kett, glaring at Porter.

"Didn't you hear me? I was calling your name."

"Sorry, mate," said Kett, jamming a finger in his ear. "Losing my hearing in my old age. What are you doing here?"

Norman stood upright, looking left and right, then leaning in and speaking quietly.

"I heard about the murders," he said. "The body in the lorry. Hey, that rhymes."

"Not really," said Kett. "How on earth did you find out?"

Balls tapped his nose and winked.

"Your police scanner," said Kett. "I keep meaning to talk to you about that, Norman. It's illegal to have one. And police radio is encrypted. How can you even listen to it?"

"Because I'm Norman Balls. And Balls knows it alls."

Kett sighed, pinching the bridge of his nose where a headache was brewing.

"Sure. But it doesn't explain what you're doing *here*."

"Aren't friends allowed to drop in on each other from time to time?" said Balls.

"We're not—"

"But the real reason I'm here," Balls interrupted, "is because I have some information you might need."

Kett sighed again, louder this time.

"Norman, if this is about your stepdad again, I really can't help you. Your mother is entitled to date whoever she likes."

"It's not about Ron," said Balls. "Although I've got some stories about that man, I can tell you."

"Please don't."

"Maybe later, then," said Balls. "No, it's about who's committing these murders. JV. I know what that stands for."

Kett waited for a couple of uniformed constables to pass by, heading into the cold, before replying.

"Jack Valentine, we know."

Balls' face dropped.

"How?" he asked.

"Because we're police," he said. "It's what we do. We know things."

"Ah, but I bet you don't know what Jack Valentine has to do with missing people," said Balls. "Or why he's doing what he's doing."

Kett sighed a third time, so dramatically that half the heads in reception turned to look at him.

"Fine," he said. "Give it your best shot."

Balls looked shiftily behind him.

"Not here," he said. "You never know who's listening."

"Norman, nobody is listening to you," said Kett. "Nobody *wants* to listen to you, especially me."

"Follow me," said Balls.

He shouldered the door a few times before remembering to pull, then he beetled into the night.

"Why the hell did you let him in?" Kett asked Porter, who was still grinning.

"Look at him, sir," the DI said, nodding through the glass to where Balls was practically vibrating with excitement as he retreated into the car park. "He just loves you so much. Who am I to get in the way of a man and his best friend?"

"He's not my bloody best friend," Kett hissed. "For fuck's sake, I'll go speak with him. Can you get everything up on the board?"

"Will do, sir," said Porter. "Have fun."

Kett yanked the door open and chased after Balls. By the time he'd caught up with him, he was sitting inside his enormous Rover with the engine running. He motioned for Kett to get into the passenger seat. After breathing another enormous sigh of frustration, he gave in. There was a bunch of white flowers on the back seat, he noticed, as well as a box of chocolates and a bottle of champagne.

"Please tell me this isn't a date, Norman," he said.

He closed the door to keep in the heat, then immediately regretted it when the aroma of the car clawed into his sinuses. It was unlike anything he'd ever smelled before, a mix of BO, Pepperoni, Deep Heat and Lynx. He put a hand to his mouth.

"Christ, Norman, what *is* that?"

"That is the smell of a man in love, Robbie," said Norman, sniffing his own armpit. "*Eau d'Balls*. If I bottled it, I could make a fortune."

"If you bottled it, they'd arrest you on terrorism charges," said Kett. He went to open his door again, but to his horror Balls put the car in gear and started reversing out of the space. "Wait, what are you doing?"

"I need your help," Balls said, engaging the central locking with his elbow. He drove towards the exit, using his hand to smear the fog from the windscreen. "We can talk on the way."

"This is technically kidnapping," said Kett. "If you don't tell me where we're going, I'm going to arrest you."

"You can't," said Balls, the Rover accelerating over the roundabout and heading for the dual carriageway. "Best friends don't arrest each other."

Kett groaned, buckling his seatbelt and resigning himself to the trip.

"So talk," he said. "Jack Valentine. What do you know?"

"Not much," said Balls.

"*What?*"

"I mean I know the basics, but folklore isn't really my field. I'm conspiracies and urban legends, the interesting stuff. Luckily for you, I know the foremost expert on local folklore, and I'm taking you to her now."

"Your mum?" asked Kett.

"No, of course not."

"I didn't think you knew any other women."

"I know plenty of women," said Balls. "Three of them, in fact."

"Including your mum?"

He didn't answer. The Rover roared its way towards the city, Balls craning over the wheel in order to see where he was going. He had to keep pushing his glasses up his nose, and every time he did so, the car wobbled alarmingly. Even though they were barely doing fifty miles per hour in the slow lane, Kett gripped the strap above the door. He didn't let go even when Balls steered them off the A11 ten minutes later, heading up the slope into the suburb of Cringleford.

"You're not going to tell me where we're going?" Kett asked.

"To see a lady," said Balls. "A lady I have a very intimate connection to."

"That isn't an image I want in my head," muttered Kett.

"Not like that, you philistine. She's an intellectual, like me. No need for base desires. We have a relationship with one another, and I'd like to move it to the next level."

"And I fit into this how?"

"You're giving me an excuse to see her," said Balls. "You get info, I get the love of my life."

"And she gets to be sick in her mouth," Kett said quietly.

"What?"

"Nothing, Norman. Is it much longer?"

It wasn't. After navigating the streets for a while, Balls pulled the Rover up in front of an attractive semi-detached house with a large front garden and an ancient Citroen 2CV in the driveway. The downstairs curtains were open, the lights on, and through the window Kett saw a woman sitting on the sofa staring intently at a laptop. She was in her early thirties, dressed in pyjamas, her enormous head of curly hair such a bright shade of ginger that it shone like copper wire.

"Give me a second," said Balls, folding down the sun visor and studying himself in the mirror. He licked the palm of his hand and ran it over what little hair he had left, giving himself a wink. "Come on. Can you bring the chocolates?"

He was out of the car before Kett could answer, retrieving the flowers and the champagne from the back seat and trotting to the front door. Short of stealing Balls' car and driving back to HQ, there wasn't much that Kett could do except grab the box of Dairy Milk and follow him. Balls must have rung the bell, because Kett saw the woman rise from the sofa and leave the room. He jogged up the driveway, reaching Balls just as the door opened.

"Oh God," she said when she saw who was standing there. She looked at Balls, aghast, then turned to Kett with even more horror.

"Madelaine," said Balls, bowing deeply before holding out the bunch of flowers. "First and foremost, these are for you. White lilies, of course, to symbolise the purity of my love."

"Norman," the woman started, but Balls wouldn't let her finish. He offered the bottle.

"And the finest nectar, of course."

Madelaine looked at Kett for a moment more, the confusion creasing her brow. Then she turned her attention to the flowers and the champagne.

"Tesco's Finest sparkling wine," she said, refusing to take either of the gifts. She looked back at Kett as if he was responsible for what was happening.

"Hi," said Kett. "Sorry."

"There are no apologies necessary here," claimed Balls, his hands dropping to his sides, white petals raining onto the path. "We are but three best friends congregating in the night."

"We're not best friends," said Kett and Madelaine together, a perfect coincidence which broke the tension a little. Balls didn't seem to notice.

"May we come in, dear? We have important matters to discuss."

Madelaine looked at Kett again, a hint of caution in her eyes.

"I'm police," he said, using his free hand to fish his

warrant card from his pocket. "DCI Robbie Kett. I'm sorry to drop in like this, I didn't have much choice."

"I brought him with me," said Balls. "He can be our chaperone, in case things get heated."

"Oh," said Madelaine, clearly horrified.

"And I thought you could help him with his case."

"I really am sorry," said Kett when Madelaine didn't reply. "I can come back another time. Or speak on the phone. This really isn't how I was planning to spend my evening."

He glared at the shiny bald spot on the back of Balls' head, hoping the man could hear the names he was silently calling him.

"It's fine," said Madelaine, finally standing back from the door. "I'm heading out in a bit, but I'm happy to talk."

"Heading out?" asked Balls, frozen to the doorstep. "Not on a date?"

"Not sure that's any of our business, mate," said Kett, pushing past him and entering the house. Balls flustered in behind him, and Madelaine closed the door. It was roasting in here, and Kett shrugged off his overcoat. The woman took it from him and hung it up on a jam-packed coat rack, nodding at his feet.

"Shoes, if you don't mind."

Kett groaned as he took off his boots, the ache in his spine worse than ever after a day in the cold. Balls did the same with his boat shoes, revealing one bright red sock with the *Star Trek* logo on it, and one bright green sock covered in cartoons of what looked like Oscar the Grouch from *Sesame Street*. Kett and Madelaine both looked at them, then at each other.

"I wasn't expecting to have to remove my footwear today," said Balls as an explanation.

"Norman, nobody cares about your socks," said Kett.

"Why are you here?" Madelaine asked, still cautious.

"Two reasons," said Balls, holding out his gifts again. "The first, because it's Valentine's Day."

"That's not a reason," said Madelaine.

Balls licked his lips, some of his confidence waning. He stared at the flowers and the bottle in his hands.

"Oh, for the love of..." Madelaine said.

She took them from him, marching into the living room. Kett followed, finding an equally ordered space with a TV in one corner and a record turntable in the other. There were bookcases everywhere, containing a mix of dusty tomes, vinyl records and boxed action figures. What little wall space remained held framed pictures, and when Kett took a closer look he saw that most were articles cut out from various newspapers and magazines. The name at the top of each one was the same.

"Madelaine Fielding," said Kett.

"The one and only," she replied, studying him with a nervous smile. "Am I in trouble?"

"I was about to ask you the same thing," said Kett. He looked at Balls as he made himself comfortable on the sofa, the little man oblivious as he fluffed up the cushions. "One word and I can take him away."

Madelaine laughed.

"He's harmless, I *think*."

"You two know each other?"

"Online," she said. "He has his website, *Balls Knows It Alls*. You've seen it?"

"Unfortunately, yes."

"I have one too, although unlike his, it's not mainly photos of my own face and made-up testimonials from the local newspaper." She smiled. "You know he claims he's an official police consultant?"

"Is that right?" said Kett.

"It's on his home page. He calls himself Deputy Balls."

"Because I am," said Balls, tuning in. "Isn't that right, Robbie?"

Kett was too tired to argue. He perched on the end of the sofa, while Madelaine hovered by the window. She seemed to remember the flowers and the wine, putting them down on the coffee table. Kett added the box of Milk Tray.

"Right," he said. "So, tell me why you brought me here, Norman."

"Because of the murders," Balls said.

Madelaine went white. Kett thought he could literally see the blood draining out of her face, revealing freckles as dark as pinpricks. She brushed a swathe of thick, red hair from her eyes.

"*Murders?*"

"Two dead," said Balls. "One body yet to be found, the other burned in the back of a lorry."

"Christ, Balls, hang on," said Kett. "None of this is public knowledge, Madelaine. But yes, there have been two murders. Both inside lorries abandoned in fields. The only other thing we have to link them are two letters left at the crime scenes. J and V."

"Jack Valentine," said Balls.

"We don't know that," said Kett, wishing he could eject Balls from the front door. Or the window. "We think two of the victims were lured to the scene by a gift of some kind, left outside their front door. A paper box, purple, with the letters J and V inside a heart. On the reverse side of the paper was a message and a postcode. We also found the same letters inside a heart painted on the back door of the first lorry, and again on the key fob. As Balls blurted out just now, we're working on the theory that JV stands for Jack Valentine."

"And as you are the leading authority on local folklore," said Balls, "I thought I would bring the police to you."

"Right," said Madelaine, looking back and forth between them like she was watching them play tennis. "I mean, I'm really *not* the leading authority. You'd be better off talking to somebody at the university."

"Balls," said Balls. "You wrote a book on him, didn't you?"

"No," said Madelaine. "I mean, I wrote a book, of sorts, for my PhD, years ago. There was a chapter on Jack Valentine, that's all."

"See!" said Balls, smugly. He leaned back on the sofa, crossing his arms over his chest.

Madelaine pulled a book from a shelf and handed it to Kett. It was a slim paperback with a cover that looked homemade—a crude, pixelated illustration of Black Shuck, the legendary wild dog of Norfolk.

"Could have done with you a few years ago," said Kett, thinking about the Bad Dog case. He read the title. "'*The Ghosts, Ghouls and Goblins of East Anglia*, by Madelaine Fielding.' Impressive."

Madelaine blushed, sitting on the corner of the coffee table.

"He's chapter four," she said, and Kett flicked through the pages, finding himself face to face with a creepy linocut image of a grinning man in a black hat. His too-long arms were stretched out to his sides, a wrapped present in one, the other reaching for the front door of a house. His eyes had been drawn with spirals, making him look wild, making him look insane.

"Yikes," said Kett. "That's Jack? Who is he?"

"Nobody knows where the legend started," said Madelaine. "But he's been going for nearly two hundred years."

"He's a romantic thing, then?" asked Kett. "Something about couples? Love? It has to be, right, because of his name?"

"Originally he was more like Santa," said Madelaine. "He brought presents for children, left them on the doorstep for them to find on Valentine's morning. It was the parents, of course. Couples got in on the act after a while. People would leave gifts for their loved ones in Jack's name. Neighbours and friends would do it too. It never really caught on outside Norfolk, but it's been going strong here since Victorian times."

"Okay," said Kett. "So if a killer is using the name Jack Valentine—and Madelaine, I must stress, this is all highly confidential at the moment—what are they trying to tell us?"

Madelaine's mouth opened, but nothing came out. After a few seconds, she shrugged.

"I have no idea, sorry. I can't think why anybody would do that. Jack's a nice person. It's generally a happy legend."

"He doesn't look particularly nice here," said Kett, looking at the illustration. "He looks like a monster. Like that man from *Chitty Chitty Bang Bang*. Remember him?"

"The Child Catcher," said Madelaine with a shudder. "Gave me nightmares for years when I was a kid. Yes, there is an element of that, especially with Jack's alter ego."

Balls was quietly unwrapping the chocolates, as if he hoped nobody would notice.

"Alter ego?" asked Kett.

"There was another version of Jack said to stalk the streets," Madelaine went on. "He was called Snatch Valentine, and in some versions of his tale he was a trickster."

"He'd tie string to his gifts and tug them away," said Kett, remembering what Savage had told him.

"Yes, or he'd wrap up an empty box, leaving only a letter inside, something cruel. He'd often do this to people who were unlucky in love, taunting them for being a failure."

"That's what happened to our victims," said Kett. "A note. The boxes had string on them too. Or fishing wire. The killer tugged them away as the victim reached for it. The notes had a message and a destination, a postcode."

"Jack would sometimes go even further," said Madelaine. "He'd leave a rotting fish inside the box, or worse."

"What's worse than a rotting fish?" asked Balls as he chewed on a toffee. There was a dribble of chocolate spittle on his chin and he wiped it away with the back of his hand, plucking another chocolate from the box.

"I thought those were for Madelaine?" asked Kett.

"It's a date," said Balls. "People share things on dates."

Madelaine still looked horrified at the idea, her body a tightly wound coil as if she was preparing to run away from Balls at a second's notice.

"Pretty sure it's not a date, mate," said Kett.

Balls swallowed noisily.

"It's a da—"

"Anyway," said Kett. "You were saying, Madelaine?"

The woman swept her hair out of her face again.

"I'm really not sure I'm being any help," she said. "Folklore and tradition are one thing, but I wouldn't know why somebody would take on the identity of such an obscure character. I've never done anything like this before; I've never even spoken to a policeman before. I just write articles for a local magazine, self-help columns and word searches and the occasional horoscope when Brian is ill. I'm not like those people on the telly who can give you a profile."

She lifted her hands apologetically.

"You're doing great," said Kett. "This is all really helpful. If you can think of anything else, though, now's the time to say it."

"Nothing that isn't in there," said Madelaine, nodding at the book. "Like I said, the character of Jack, or Snatch, got quite dark at times. If you turn the page, you'll see what I mean."

Kett did as he was asked, seeing another illustration. This one looked newer, more stylised, and it was even more sinister than the first. Jack was in the centre of the picture, dressed in the same stovepipe hat and long coat. His features were as crooked as a Punch doll's, his long nose and chin resembling a crescent moon, and his eyes still held that coil of insane glee.

Over his shoulder was a sack, and sticking out of it was a pair of woman's legs.

"Jesus," said Kett.

"This was Jack Valentine's worst prank," said Madelaine. "He'd knock on your door on Valentine's Eve, when you were waiting for a visit from your beloved. And when you answered, he'd snatch you up and take you away."

Despite the heat of the room, Kett felt a shiver run up his back, lifting the hairs on his neck.

"Why?" he asked.

Madelaine had gone paler still.

"I don't know," she said. "But it's nothing good, is it?"

"No," said Kett, gently closing the book. "It's not. You mind if I take this?"

"Of course not," she said, blushing a little harder. "It's

not very good, but it got me my doctorate, so I can't complain."

"If I have any questions, can I call you?" he asked.

Madelaine glanced at Balls, who was still gorging himself on Dairy Milk.

"He won't be there," he said quietly.

"I guess so, then," said Madelaine. "Shall I get you my number?"

Kett nodded.

"Thanks," he said, looking at Balls again. "I guess the only question I have left is, what do you want to do about him?"

CHAPTER SEVENTEEN

"But I brought you gifts!"

Kett stood outside Madelaine Fielding's front door, one arm around Norman Balls' substantial waist as he tried to pull him out of the house. The little man had his fingers wedged in the frame and was resisting with all his might. He was surprisingly strong.

"Gifts!" he wailed. "Like all good suitors should."

"Come on, mate," said Kett. "We really do need to go."

"The flowers!" Balls wailed.

"That's really sweet of you, Norman," said Madelaine from where she stood inside, both hands on the door as if she was tempted to slam it shut on Balls' fingers. "But who brings white lilies to a date? They're funeral flowers."

"They are not! And the chocolates, I brought you chocolates."

"You *ate* the chocolates," she said. "All of them."

"I left you the Orange Truffles," Balls protested.

"Nobody likes the Orange Truffles!"

Kett doubled his efforts, but Balls was hanging onto the door like an orangutan.

"Let go, Norman!"

"Can we just crack open the champagne?" Balls said. "We'll all feel better after a drink. And when I say all, I mean me and you. Robbie's got somewhere to be."

Madelaine winced.

"That's really sweet of you, Norman," she said. "But no. I'm already in a relationship. I'm supposed to be meeting him right now. In fact, I think he's here."

Kett followed the direction of her gaze to see a small van parked up the street. It was an old one, painted in various shades of pastel green and pink with the letters Happy Wheels stencilled on the side. A furry creature with big eyes and a wide smile peered over the top of the words. Kett couldn't work out what it was. He couldn't see the driver from here, but there was definitely somebody looking at him through the side mirror, their expression full of shock.

"What?" said Balls, looking back and relaxing his grip on the door.

Kett saw his chance. He yanked hard, like he was doing the Heimlich, and Balls popped free, both of them almost tumbling onto the path.

"Shut the bloody door!" Kett yelled.

Madelaine did exactly that, a guilty look on her face. It slammed so hard the letterbox rattled.

"Sorry, Norman," she yelled from inside.

"I saved you the Orange Truffles!" Balls wailed.

"Come on," said Kett, taking Balls' arm and leading him towards the road.

The little man started storming towards the van, and Kett heard the click of the locks snapping shut—the face in the mirror more worried than ever. Kett grabbed hold of his sleeve, wheeling him towards the Rover.

"First rule of anything, mate," he said. "No means no."

Balls looked like he was about to protest, and then the wind left his sails.

"But what if they all say no?" he asked, looking up with round, wet eyes.

Kett didn't have an answer. He slung his arm around the other man's sagging shoulders and steered him towards the car. Balls climbed behind the wheel.

"Thanks for being a friend, Robbie," he said as he started the engine. "I'm going home to drown my sorrows. I'm destined to be alone forever."

"No you're bloody not," said Kett, diving into the passenger seat before Balls could drive off. The little man looked at him with an expression of pure hope.

"You're coming with me?" he said. "Because we're friends?"

"No," said Kett. "I just need you to drive me back to the station."

THE OPEN-PLAN OFFICES of the Major Investigation Team were bustling with activity, but Kett couldn't see many members of the Extreme Crime Task Force amongst the sea of faces.

The Investigation Room, too, was empty when he poked his head around the door. There was an odd smell, an aroma of what might have been fish. Somebody had started to pin photographs from the case on the walls. Kett saw Karen and Grant Dankworth there, the picture from their anniversary party at the pub. He saw separate photos of William Briggs and Darcey DeCarlo, too, both professional headshots by the look of it.

The sight of them made him wonder how many dead the walls of this room had held over the years.

Too many to count.

Not too many to remember, though. The name and the face of each and every one was etched inside his head, a gallery of horror.

Cheery, he told himself.

He sniffed the room again, his nose wrinkling, then he made his way back to the bullpen.

"Anyone seen the boss?" he asked, and a PC nodded towards the far side of the room.

"They're all in the kitchen, sir," she said.

That could only mean one thing, and sure enough he heard the bubble of the kettle as he opened the door. Sitting at the small table in the middle of the room were Porter, Savage and the Superintendent. Duke was standing by the counter, drumming his fingers as he waited for the kettle to boil. They all turned to Kett.

"How's your Balls?" asked Porter.

"Don't ask," said Kett, taking a free seat and clicking his fingers at Duke. "Aaron, phone."

"Oh, yeah," said Duke, rummaging in his pocket before handing it over. Kett checked it for messages before looking up.

"What's going on in here?"

They all turned to Duke, who held up his hands in protest.

"It wasn't that bad!" said the PC.

"Lies," snapped Clare. "It smelled like an elephant's vagina."

"What?" said Kett.

"Aaron had a tuna sandwich for his dinner, sir," said Savage.

"If that was tuna, I'm a tossing ballerina," said Clare. "I've pulled corpses from the river that smelled better than that."

"It must have been bad," said Kett. "It still reeks in there."

"It was fine," grumbled Duke.

"He left it in his locker," said Savage, grimacing.

"It was fine," said Duke. "Everything's okay out of the fridge for a little while, isn't it?"

"Aaron, you've had that sandwich in your locker for *three days*," said Savage, who looked like she was considering a breakup.

"Which is roughly how long we're going to have to quarantine the Incident Room," said Clare. "Another cup, Testicle Gremlin. Zipper, anything useful?"

"I learned never to go on a date with Norman Balls, sir," said Kett, placing Madelaine's book on the table. "He took me to see a friend of his." He hesitated. "Friend's a little strong. Colleague, maybe. She's got some knowledge about the legend of Jack Valentine. In some versions of the story, he was supposed to kidnap women, carry them away in his bag. I read a little on the way over, mainly just to distract myself from Balls' sobbing. Jack Valentine actually had a pretty vindictive streak, mainly against people who he felt were unlucky in love, or who didn't deserve love."

"That kind of fits what we've seen on the case, sir," said Savage.

"How so?" said Clare, rocking his chair back on two legs.

"Grant and Karen Dankworth didn't seem like the most loving pair, sir," she said. "He certainly didn't have a lot of respect for her, and he was almost certainly sleeping around."

"What about Darcey and William, though?" said Kett. "Pregnant, newly married, they look every bit the young, devoted couple."

"Pregnant out of wedlock, sir," said Savage. "It's the kind of thing some people frown upon."

"Maybe a hundred years ago," said Porter.

"Jack's more than a hundred years old," said Kett. "He started back in Victorian times. Maybe our killer's a prude?"

"Bollocks," said Clare, and Kett had to admit it didn't seem massively convincing. "What else do we have?"

"I left Franklin at the second lorry, sir," said Savage. "She found what looks like a knife in the chest of our victim, but she wasn't able to tell whether it was a man or a woman. The damage from the fire was too bad."

"Still no word from William Briggs or Darcey DeCarlo?" asked Clare.

"Nobody's heard from them since last night, sir," said Porter. "But we found a box from JV at Darcey's house, looks the same as the gift that was left outside the Dankworth place. Security footage shows William being collected from the pub by what looks like the same man that was at the Dankworth house just hours earlier."

"It's a pattern," said Savage. "Right? The killer takes one person by force, like Grant and William. I mean, William wasn't attacked, but only because he was so drunk he got into the car. The other person in the relationship, the woman, is given a box with an address."

"Maybe William got into the car because he knew the driver," said Kett. "It could have been his brother, Luke, or that twat Perry Paul. Or Dawson."

"I asked around," said Clare. "Dawson's been festering in Yarmouth for years now. Nobody likes him, but he's never given off vibes of anything other than sheer incompetence. I didn't get the impression from anyone that he was seriously bent."

"He's so bent he was practically folded in half, sir," said Kett. "Whatever the Briggs brothers have got going on in that house, he's a part of it, even if he's just turning a blind eye."

"Maybe he's making a move on the Briggs brothers and masking it as some kind of serial killer thing," said Porter.

Kett shook his head.

"Doesn't feel like that," he said. "I don't think the Dankworths have any links to crime. But I don't know. It's worth keeping an eye on him."

"Light years ahead of you, Kett," said Clare, still rocking back on his chair. "I've got some good friends in the Yarmouth office. They're going to tail Dawson for the foreseeable, see what he's up to."

A waft of fragrant steam entered Kett's nose as Duke poured hot water into the cups.

"Anything new happened with Grant Dankworth, sir?" he asked, his mouth watering.

"He's still in holding," said Clare. "CPS wants to charge him, but they don't know what with. He's still protesting his innocence, but he isn't particularly convincing. It's very clear that he had nothing but resentment towards his wife. He's blaming her for the fact that this happened."

"Nice guy," said Savage.

"You get anywhere with the plates on the second lorry?" asked Kett.

Duke poured milk into the cups and ferried them to the table, sloshing tea everywhere.

"Christ, Duke, I want to drink it, not swim in it," said Clare.

"Sorry, sir," said the PC, using his sleeve to wipe up the

spill and earning a tut from Savage. “I went to Jaye Moore’s house and there was nobody there. I left cards with some of the neighbours and one of them called me back. Moore is out of the country. Canada. The camper has been off the road for weeks, in storage. They didn’t know where.”

“I’ve posted a unit on their street,” said Clare, “just in case JV shows up there. Although he’d have to be a brainless tossbag to give us a clue like that in advance. He must know we’re not stupid.”

Clare pushed his chair back onto two legs again, teetering there for a moment, his eyes bulging before he was able to land safely.

“Careful, sir,” said Kett. “My kids bugger over like that all the time. I’m constantly amazed none of them have cracked their head open on the floor.”

“Do I look like one of your kids, Kett?” growled Clare.

“No,” he said. “Thank God. Did Porter tell you about the church?”

“He did,” said Clare. “Jack and Val. Spalding did some background and there’s not a thing on either of them. Clean as a whistle.”

“Valerie seemed like she disapproved of the Briggs and DeCarlo wedding,” said Kett.

“She seemed like she disapproved of everything,” added Porter. “Miserable as sin.”

“She was tall, too,” said Kett. “Broad, like whoever was wearing the raincoat.”

Clare nodded, rocking back again.

“Maybe it’s worth having another talk with them,” he said. “But I can’t spare any more units to babysit.”

“I’ll go back tomorrow, sir,” said Kett. “Even if they don’t have anything to do with this, they know more than they’re letting on.”

"Just can't see an old priest and an old woman managing to get one up on four people," said Porter, shaking his head. "You could have blown them both over with a strong wind."

"Careful with the word old, Porter," said Clare. "That priest is the same age as me, and I'm about as strong as they—"

Clare rocked too far, toppling backwards. His eyes almost exploded from their sockets and his arms pinged out to his sides in the vain hope of finding something to grab onto. Fortunately, Duke was still standing by the counter, and the PC managed to catch him before he hit the floor.

"Jesus Fucking Bollocking Christ!" Clare screeched as Duke tilted him back onto four legs. Clare glared at him, one hand to his heart. "What did you do that for?"

"Do what, sir?" said Duke.

"Try to kill me, you great steaming pile of giraffe's tossings! You're bloody fired, you hear me?"

"He just saved your life, sir," said Kett. "You were about to go arse over tit."

"I was not!" said Clare, pushing himself to his feet and jabbing a finger at Kett. His face was redder than Kett had ever seen it. "I had it completely under control. You're fired too, you badger's bellend."

"Sir!" said Savage. "He caught—"

"You're all bloody fired!" Clare shouted.

He stormed out of the kitchen, slamming the door shut behind him, his muffled voice bellowed back.

"But not until you've solved this arsing case. So get back to work."

"Is there anything we can do to get his wife to end her celibacy streak?" asked Porter when they were sure the Super had gone.

"Not sure what's worse, sir," said Savage. "The image of

him screaming at us, or the image of Fiona's celibacy streak actually ending."

Everybody around the table shuddered.

"Bagsy his tea," said Kett, grabbing two mugs from the table. He took a sip from the first—too hot, but utterly welcome.

"What now, sir?" Porter asked him. "If the plates from the second lorry don't lead anywhere, we're kind of at a dead end."

"At least until Franklin and Hay find something useful," said Kett, knocking back more tea. He slammed a fist against his chest as it burned its way down, glancing at the clock. It was well after seven. "How about you guys get home, recharge for a bit. You must have Valentine's plans."

"Just nappies," said Porter, taking a sip of his own tea. "But it'll be nice to hang out with the wife. You sure?"

Kett nodded, turning to Savage and Duke.

"What about you two?"

"No plans, sir," said Savage, at the same time Duke said, "Something pretty romantic." They looked at each other, both laughing.

"Nothing romantic," Savage insisted. "Do you and Billie have plans?"

"Yeah," he said. "Probably involving burnt toast and plenty of glitter."

"Not sure I want to know," said Porter.

Kett laughed, polishing off both teas then standing up.

"Go on," he said. "Make the most of it. I get the feeling we're not going to get much time to relax."

CHAPTER EIGHTEEN

Kett walked through the front door of his house half an hour later, feeling like he'd left a fridge and entered a sauna. He hung his coat on the peg over the hall radiator, which felt hot enough to cook eggs on, and made his way into the kitchen.

Billie was loading the dishwasher, the clatter of crockery so loud that she didn't hear him until he was right behind her. She jerked up, losing her grip on a plate which, thankfully, landed on the cutlery basket and remained intact.

"Robbie!" she said, a hand to her heart. "Of all people, you should know not to sneak up on me like that."

"Sorry," he said, gathering her into a hug and planting a kiss on her forehead. "I thought you'd heard me."

"I was miles away," she said, leaning back and putting a hand to the bruise on his cheek where Luke Briggs had lamped him. "What did you walk into this time?"

"An arsehole," he said, resting his hand on top of hers. "But I'm fine. I left it all outside."

She nodded approvingly.

"I saved you some spaghetti bolognaise," she said, returning to the dishwasher.

"Oh, great," he said, taking off his jacket and throwing it over the back of a chair. "I'm starving."

"But me and the girls decided to give it to Albert," she added. "He popped round again, I packed it up for him to take home. I don't think he's eating right."

"You're sweet. Did you have something?"

"Yeah, sorry," she said. "I wasn't sure when you'd be back, and I figured you probably wouldn't fancy a Valentine's thing after what happened today."

"You saw?" he asked, opening the cupboard above the kettle and pulling out a packet of chocolate digestives.

"It was on the news tonight," she said. "They were warning people about gifts left on their doorsteps, to call the police if they find a little paper box. Jack Valentine, I don't even know what that is."

"It's—" he started, and Billie held up a hand.

"I don't want to know, either," she said. "As long as it's nothing to do with us."

"It isn't," said Kett. "Whoever this is, we're not on his radar."

She didn't look convinced.

"That's the trouble with being you, though, isn't it? Sooner or later, the job puts you on everyone's radar."

He didn't know what to say to her, so he made a show of looking for the kids instead.

"Quiet in here," he said.

"A little too quiet," she replied. "I thought they were in the living room."

Kett peeked around the living room door, but even though the TV was on, there was nobody there. He double-checked behind the chair to make sure they weren't hiding, then popped his head into the toilet under the stairs, and finally into the dining room.

"Girls?" he called out. "It's Daddy, I'm home."

Usually, that would have kickstarted a stampede, but the house remained deathly silent. Billie appeared in the kitchen door, drying her hands on a tea towel. She was smiling, but it didn't do much to chase the sudden chill from his bones. He'd come too close to losing them before.

"They're fine," said Billie, reading his mind the way she always could. "I think they wanted to plan a surprise for you. They'll be upstairs."

He grabbed the bannister and hauled himself up onto the landing, feeling a rush of pure relief when he heard a chorus of stifled giggles from the bedroom on the right, where Evie and Moira slept.

"Shush!" whispered Evie. "He'll hear you!"

"Girls?" he called out, playing along. "Where are you?"

He made his way to the master bedroom, stomping his feet like a giant.

"In Mummy and Daddy's room?"

More giggles, then Alice's voice called out.

"We're not playing hide and seek, Dad."

"Oh," he said, making his way back down the landing to Evie and Moira's room. Alice was sitting cross-legged on the floor, and Evie was bouncing on her sister's bed, grinning like a loon. There was no sign of the little one.

"You okay?" he asked. "Where's Moo-moo?"

Evie laughed, and Alice smiled.

"You have to find her," said Alice.

"I thought we weren't playing hide and seek?"

"We're not," said Evie, her face bright red from bouncing, and from the heat. "It's another game."

"Yeah," came Moira's voice, muffled by whatever she was hiding in.

"Shush!" demanded Evie.

"Right," said Kett, entering the room. "Where are you, Moo-moo? Under the bed?"

It took an extraordinary effort to get down onto his hands and knees, and it wasn't worth it because the only thing he found beneath the beds were old board games, crumpled underwear and a lot of dust. His attempts to get up were scuppered when Evie threw herself onto his back, grabbing the collar of his shirt in an attempt not to fall off. Pain lanced through his back.

"Urk," he said. "I'm not a horse."

"Yes, you are," she said. "Giddy up!"

"I want to ride the horse," said Moira.

"Shut up," Alice told her, a little meanly. "You're hiding."

Kett rose gently until gravity peeled Evie from his back. She plopped onto the bed.

"No fair, horsey," she said, pouting.

"Right," said Kett, loosening his tie. "Where else could she be?"

There were only two options left. The first was the cupboard, which was usually too full of toys and clothes to allow anyone access. The second was the chest at the foot of Evie's bed. He waited for a moment, hearing a clunk that definitely came from inside the chest.

"She must be in the cupboard," he said, crossing the room in three giant steps. He ripped the door open, unleashing a wave of teddy bears. "What? That's impossible! Where else could she be?"

Evie tumbled back onto the bed, laughing insanely. Alice rolled her eyes, more than aware of the fact that he already knew where his youngest daughter was. It was hard not to, because it sounded like Moira was doing somersaults inside the box. The lid was bumping up and down as she moved around, a thump as if she was kicking out. He wondered if she was stuck in there, if maybe she was running out of air.

The thought reminded him of something, and he couldn't put his finger on what.

It was nothing good, though.

"Ah-ha!" he said. "She must be in here!"

He lifted the lid of the chest and Moira sprang up like a sweaty-faced jack-in-the-box, her eyes so wide that she looked drunk.

"Hi," she said.

"No, you're supposed to do the thing!" said Alice.

Moira frowned at her big sister.

"The thing," echoed Evie. "With the glitter."

"Oh," said Moira. "I forgot."

"It's fine," said Kett. "We don't need any more—"

Moira threw both of her hands in the air and released two fistfuls of pink glitter right into his face. Kett screwed his eyes shut too late, feeling like he'd been pepper sprayed. He backed away, feeling it beneath his eyelids like glass, hearing it pop between his teeth.

"And the card!" yelled Alice.

"Oh yeah," said Moira. "Happy Valentine's!"

Kett squinted through watering eyes to see Moira still standing in the chest. She was holding a heart-shaped card proudly over her head, and Kett took it from her.

"We wanted to jump out of a giant cake like they do on TV," said Evie. "But we didn't have one."

"It's great," said Kett, sitting on the edge of the bed and furiously wiping his eyes. The card was homemade from a cereal box packet and covered in about an inch of red glitter. He read the message on the other side. "'Dear Daddy, thank you for being our Valentine. We love you, even though you are a farty butt cheese.'"

"I added the last bit," said Evie, cackling.

"It's beautiful, girls, thank you," he said. "Best Valentine's card I've ever had."

"Hey!" said Billie, who was leaning through the door.

"Apart from Mummy's," Kett added quickly. "Even though she didn't get me one this year."

"That makes two of us," said Billie.

"How come you made another one, girls?" he asked. "You gave me one this morning."

"We're writing cards at school," said Evie. "But not just Valentine's ones. We're using them to tell people how we feel."

"Cool," said Kett.

"I told Emily she's a meanie," Evie went on. "And that she smells like a toilet."

"I got a phone call about it," said Billie.

"That's not very nice, Evie," said Kett.

Evie shrugged.

"She's not very nice to me."

"Well, this card's lovely," he told her. "Thank you."

"Right," said Billie, "I said you could stay up to surprise Daddy, but it's bedtime. *Past* your bedtime. Teeth, now!"

The girls groaned, but one by one they filed past her onto the landing. Kett rubbed his face, feeling like he was being exfoliated.

"So much glitter," he said.

"*So much* glitter," she repeated.

"Can we please stop buying the stuff?"

"I don't buy it. Nobody buys glitter. It just *appears*."

Kett laughed. Billie walked over and offered him a hand, hefting him off the bed.

He helped Moira brush her teeth, then put the two little ones to bed, reading a chapter of Evie's book even though they were both far too tired to listen. He almost drifted off himself, his eyelids weighed down by glitter. He had to force himself to get up, walking to Alice's room and giving her a kiss on the head, which he didn't think she even noticed because she was so engrossed in her iPad.

"Night, lovely," he said.

Billie was waiting for him downstairs, two glasses of wine on the living room coffee table. The TV was on, but she had an open book in her hand. She rested it on her knee as he sat beside her.

"Nearly put myself to sleep with a bedtime story," he said, yawning.

"Easily done. Wasn't sure if you wanted some wine or not, but I poured you one."

"Thanks," he said.

He passed Billie her glass then took his own, leaning back into the sofa and cradling it against his chest. Something wasn't sitting right with him, the feeling he'd had when he'd heard Moira moving around inside the toy chest, the thump of her feet, the clatter of her fists.

The idea of her not being able to get out.

"You okay?" asked Billie, and he realised she was waiting for a toast.

"Huh? Sorry." He clinked his glass against hers. "I love you, Billie. Happy Valentine's."

She took a long sip of her wine, studying him.

"Where are you, Robbie?"

"I'm here," he said. "I'm right here."

"Except you're not," she said, but there was no ill will, only a touch of sadness and a whole lot of resignation.

Kett set the wine back on the table, resting his elbows on his knees. He thought about the thump of Moira inside the chest, understanding that it wasn't the first time he'd heard the noise that day.

"Where are you?" Billie asked again.

Inside a church, he thought, thinking of the way Father Odling and Valerie had looked at each other when they'd heard the noise that echoed through the door, thinking of the fear in their expressions.

He glanced at Billie, and she saw it in his face.

"It could save a life?" she asked.

"I'm not sure," he said. "Maybe."

"Then you don't need to ask my permission."

She put her cold hand to his cheek.

"I love you, Robbie," she said. "Go get them."

CHAPTER NINETEEN

"And voilà!"

Savage looked over her shoulder as Duke walked into the dining room of the house he shared with his mother, a little Victorian terrace to the north of the city. There was a large tray in his hands, and the smell of whatever sat on it had reached her already, something fatty and flavoursome that was making her mouth water. He set it down on the table hard enough to make the cutlery clatter, gravy spilling off both plates and pooling on the tray.

"Shit, sorry," he said, reaching out to grab a napkin and knocking Savage's wine glass over. Thankfully, it hadn't been filled yet. "Shit, sorry!"

"It's fine," said Savage, setting the glass upright. "It's all fine, Aaron. There's no need to panic. It looks amazing."

It really did. An enormous duck leg sitting in between sautéed potatoes and a selection of vegetables that looked too bright to be real. The whole thing was steeped in a rich gravy that contained a hint of sherry.

"Hopefully it's okay," Duke said, using one hand to pass a plate to her, his other arm behind his back like a waiter.

He would have dropped the whole thing on her lap if she hadn't grabbed it.

"Are you okay?" she asked him. Duke had been clumsy for as long as she'd known him, but he was setting new records tonight.

"Yeah," he said. "I'm good. I'm great. Sorry."

He took his own plate from the tray and sat opposite her. He'd only just managed to pull his seat in when he changed his mind and sat at the end of the table instead. Then, after a moment's thought, he moved back to where he'd started. His movements made the candles on the table wobble, the smoke bringing back the headache she'd had earlier. Savage raised an eyebrow as she watched him start to get up again.

"Sit down, Aaron," she said.

"Sure, yeah, I am."

He picked up his knife and fork.

"Uh, I'm happy to present my duck *à l'orange*. It's duck. With an orange sauce."

"Thanks for translating," said Savage. "I never would have guessed."

"I hope it's okay," said Duke.

He looked seriously worried. It was weird, because he'd cooked for her so many times she'd lost count, and he'd never been this nervous. He didn't *need* to be nervous, because he was really good at it. Part of that was because he still lived with his mum, and Delores Duke—who had the coolest name in the world, as far as Savage was concerned—would secretly help him out in the kitchen whenever Savage came over for dinner. Being secretive wasn't one of Delores' skills, because she was almost as tall as her son, and twice as loud, especially after a gin and tonic. But fortunately, cooking definitely *was* in her skill set. Savage didn't think there had been a time in her life when she'd eaten as well as she did here.

The other reason Duke didn't have to be nervous was because he obviously loved being in the kitchen. The same enormous hands that dropped plates and cups and pretty much everything else he tried to hold were somehow perfectly suited to small knives and kitchen implements, and he would lose himself in the art of whatever he was preparing. He cared about what he made, and he cared about who he served it to. It was lovely.

"Don't worry," she told him, jamming her fork into the leg of duck, and sawing at it with her knife. "I'm so hungry you could serve me a carrier bag and I'd still think it was delicious."

"Right," said Duke with a frown.

Savage put the duck into her mouth, and it practically melted on her tongue. She groaned.

"Oh my God, Aaron," she said before she'd even swallowed. "This is *amazing*."

"Better than a carrier bag, then?" he said.

She laughed, diving into the dish with far less care than he had taken to prepare it. She really was starving, though. She'd not had time to stop for lunch, running on the fumes from the bowl of porridge she'd had before her run thirteen hours ago.

She wolfed down the potatoes and the vegetables, using her knife and fork for as long as she could before picking the duck leg up in her fingers and nibbling off the last scraps of meat. She'd have eaten the bone too if she could.

It was less than five minutes after Duke had set the meal down that she cleared her plate, sitting back in her chair with a contented sigh.

"That really was incredible," she said, both hands on her belly. "Don't suppose there's any more?"

Duke shook his head.

"Sorry," he said. "Ducks only have two legs."

He was only halfway through his, showing none of the zest for his own cooking that he normally did. After another delicate bite, he set his cutlery down and pushed his plate away.

"You sure you're okay?" Savage asked him. "You're not coming down with something, are you? Spalding had that awful cold last week."

"I'm not coming down with anything," he said. "I mean, maybe I am, but it's not a cold."

"Flu?" asked Savage.

"No," said Duke, obviously flustered. "I mean, it's not an illness, I might be coming down with..."

He swallowed hard, his hand moving to the pocket of his jeans. He was wearing a black polo shirt which was struggling to contain his muscles, and he'd had his hair cut and his beard trimmed—something she hadn't noticed until right now. Looking at him still gave her the same tingle in her stomach that it always had. He left his pocket alone and stretched his hands over the table. She scrubbed the duck grease off her fingers before taking them.

"Look, Kate," he said, tripping over the words. "These last few months have been the happiest of my life. I never thought I could be this happy, this content. You make me the happiest man on the planet. When I'm with you, I feel so..."

"Happy?" she said when he struggled.

"Yeah," he said. "I love you so much, Kate. I love you so much I feel like I'm going to explode with it sometimes."

The heat was rising in Savage's cheeks, along with

another feeling, one she couldn't quite put her finger on. It felt a little like she was about to explode as well.

"You know I'm not very good with words," he went on, beads of sweat forming on his face. "But I've got four of them I've been wanting to ask for a long time."

"Oh," said Savage. "Aaron, I..."

Duke opened his mouth to continue, but before he could get anything else out, Savage's phone started to wail from her pocket. In the quiet dining room, it felt obscenely loud.

"I'm so sorry," she said.

She tried to pull her hands free from Duke's, but he held on tight. The phone continued its tantrum, oblivious.

"I should probably get that," Savage said.

"Can't it wait?" asked Duke.

The phone cut off, plunging the room into an awkward silence. Duke squeezed her hands, looking her in the eye.

"Like I said, there are four words I want to say to—"

Her phone started to ring again, shrieking like a banshee. Savage pulled hard, the duck grease allowing her hands to slide free. She found her phone and saw Kett's name on the screen.

"I'm really sorry," she said to Duke, who looked crestfallen. She answered it. "Sir?"

"You in the middle of anything, Kate?" asked Kett.

"Uh..." Duke had obviously heard, because he nodded furiously. "I mean, yeah, kind of, sir. Why?"

"Because I'm on my way to Yarmouth," Kett said. "And I could do with an extra pair of hands."

Duke slumped into his chair with a sigh. Savage gave him an apologetic smile.

"How about two pairs, sir?" she asked.

DUKE DROVE them in his mother's car, the little pink Fiat 500 almost taking off as it hit sixty on the Acle Strait. It was coming up for ten by the time they reached the town, barely any traffic on the roads and even fewer pedestrians braving the cold night.

Duke had barely spoken on the journey, and she was pretty sure his, "I'm fine, don't worry," weren't the four words he'd promised her over dinner.

He spun them around Yarmouth's one-way system a few times before they found their way to the right part of town, the tower of St Margaret's guiding them along the last few roads onto the pedestrianised shopping lane. Aside from the fairy lights that hung over the main doors, the church was a monolith of shadow against the darker sky, serious and unwelcoming.

Duke left the Fiat 500 right outside the gate, switching off the little engine. He angled his enormous body to face her as much as the steering wheel would let him, taking a deep breath. Savage listened to the soft lullaby of the sea and the song of a distant seagull for as long as it took him to speak.

"I really need to say this, Kate," he said. "It doesn't matter where, it just matters that you hear it. It's really important, because I love you and I don't want to wait anymore. I—"

Somebody rapped on Duke's window and he actually screamed. He spun in his seat to see Kett gurning in, the DCI's face yellow from the sulphuric streetlights, and strangely sparkly.

"Bloody hell," said Duke, his voice an octave higher than usual.

Kett knocked again, making the motion to wind the window down. Duke did as he was asked, the sour aroma of the street filling the car instantly.

"You almost gave me a heart attack, sir," said Duke.

"I'll try harder next time," Kett replied. He nodded to Savage, his face sparkling even more than before. "Thanks for coming. Both of you."

"No problem, sir," said Savage. "Is that glitter?"

Kett rubbed his cheeks furiously.

"I've washed my face about ten times," he said. "It won't come off."

"Why are we here, sir?" said Savage.

"Honestly, it might be nothing," Kett replied, which earned a quiet grumble of annoyance from Duke. "But my gut is telling me I missed something when I was here earlier. Something important."

He stood straight and Savage unbuckled her belt, getting out of the car.

"Porter not around, sir?" she asked as the cold took hold of her.

"Didn't want to bother him," said Kett. "With the baby and everything. You guys said you weren't up to much tonight."

"Yeah, nothing much at all," said Duke, slamming the door behind him. "Zero things."

"Great," said Kett, turning to the church. It was bigger than Savage had first thought, as if it had grown in the few minutes they'd been here, and with no lights on it looked more like the stone wall of a castle. "I spoke with the priest, Father Jack Odling, and a woman who works here, Valerie. They admitted to marrying Briggs and DeCarlo in a private ceremony, but they seemed very cagey about it. I could hear noises coming from deeper inside the church. Sounded like somebody banging."

"Gross," said Duke. "Why would anyone do that in a church?"

"Banging on a door, Duke," said Kett.

"Oh, right."

"Like I say, it might be nothing."

"Or it might be everything," said Savage. "Are you thinking it's one of our missing couple? William or Darcey? Whoever isn't in the lorry?"

"Yeah," said Kett. "Grant Dankworth told us he and Karen were kidnapped and forced to fight. Karen died, he escaped. If the same thing happened to Darcey and William, whoever survived the fight might not have been able to get away. They might still be with whoever took them."

"They might still be here," said Savage, nodding. "How do you want to do this? Tactical?"

"Not yet," said Kett. He glanced at her, and there was almost a smile on his face. "Just a—"

"Look?" she finished for him, shaking her head.

He laughed quietly, then opened the gate and walked into the churchyard. It was pitch black in here, and Savage pulled her slim torch out of her pocket, casting Kett's shadow onto the wall of the church. He left the path, walking away from the main doors towards the rear. Savage followed, one hand on the cold wall of the church so she wouldn't trip in the knotted grass.

"Round here," whispered Kett as he reached the end of the building.

Savaged followed him through a narrow gap between the stone wall and the overgrown hedge. Beyond was a microscopic courtyard hemmed in by outbuildings, the weeds growing through the flagstones almost knee-high. There was a much smaller porch here, the door rotting out of its frame. Kett gave the handle a rattle, but it didn't open. He looked back at Duke.

"Can you try this, mate?"

"Sure, sir," said Duke. "You want me to kick it down?"

"No, we're not allowed to do that. Just give it a wiggle. You're stronger than me."

Duke stepped up to the door and turned the handle.

"Little harder," said Kett.

Duke twisted the handle and gave the door a bump with his shoulder. The frame split with a sound like a pistol shot, Duke almost tumbling through.

"Easy, Aaron," said Kett. "I didn't mean break it open."

"Sorry," said Duke from inside the porch. "That was an accident. I can fix it."

Kett gave Savage a knowing smile that she met with a stern frown.

"What?" he said.

"Nothing, sir."

They filed into the porch, Kett opening the door on the far side. The church was an abyss, so dark that she couldn't see the far wall. It seemed to leech all of the cold from her bones, her skin crinkling into goosebumps, her scalp shrivelling. She couldn't remember a time in her life when she'd felt more like an intruder, and she had the notion that if she walked through that door into the belly of the church, it would never let her go.

"Bagsy not going first," whispered Duke.

"I'll go," said Kett. "Just keep an ear out."

"For ghosts?" asked Duke.

Kett fired up the torch on his phone and walked through the door, the church gathering him into its folds of shadow.

Savage went next, clutching her torch like it was a weapon. It felt ten degrees colder in here than it did outside, the air so frozen it felt more like water. She sucked in breath after breath as she walked into the middle of the enormous nave. The quiet was immense, as if the entire world beyond these ancient walls had been erased.

Kett pointed down the central aisle towards the end of the church and they moved together, the echo of their shuffling footsteps whispering off the walls. There were two doors here, a central one that had to lead up to the tower, and a smaller one on the left. Kett pointed his phone towards the second one.

"That's where the noises were coming from," he said quietly. "Both the priest and the woman came out of that door earlier."

"Maybe *they* were banging," said Duke.

Kett tried the handle of the door and it opened willingly, not the slightest squeak of hinges. Beyond it was a spiral staircase leading down into a darkness that was even deeper than the rest of the church.

"Nope," said Duke, craning over Savage's shoulder.

She would have said the same, except there was a noise drifting up the stairs, quiet but unmistakeable.

Somebody was crying.

Kett put a finger to his lips, nodding down the stairs. He took the lead, his body tense. Savage went to follow, but Duke put a hand on her shoulder before squeezing past her, his huge frame blocking the stairwell. She wasn't sure whether to be grateful or annoyed.

The sound of crying grew louder as they dropped down the stairs. They were sniffles, rather than sobs, but there was no missing the grief in them. The way they whispered from wall to wall made them sound almost ghostly, and Savage kept glancing back over her shoulder to make sure the door above them was still open.

After a few steps, though, she couldn't see anything behind her at all.

Kett reached the bottom of the stairs, Duke hugging his back. Both of them had to duck beneath the vaulted ceiling, the narrow corridor barely big enough to hold them.

There was no space down here, no air, black spots exploded in the corner of Savage's vision as she gasped for breath.

Kett edged forward impossibly slowly, approaching a door in the right-hand wall. It was open, and it seemed as if the crying was coming from in there. A second door capped the corridor up ahead, this one closed.

Careful, she wanted to say, but she couldn't get the word past the lump in her throat.

Kett glanced back, as if to make sure she and Duke were still there, then he poked his head around the open door. Savage heard him gasp, and a second later the cries became a deafening scream.

"Shit!" said Kett.

He ran into the room, and Duke was about to follow when the door at the end of the corridor opened and a shape threw itself onto him. Duke's scream was louder than whoever was inside the room. He tumbled backwards, crushing Savage into the wall.

"Aaron!" she grunted.

"Fuck!" somebody roared, followed by the thump of a fist on flesh.

Savage grabbed hold of Duke's arms, trying to pull him out of the way of whoever was attacking him. But he wasn't having any of it, jerking out of her grip.

"Police!" he bellowed, driving his attacker back through the second door into the darkness beyond.

Savage pushed herself off the wall, making it three steps down the corridor before somebody ran out of the door on the right. There was enough light to see that it was a young woman, and she was moving fast, thumping into Savage hard enough to knock her against the wall again. She reached out to grab her but missed, seeing the woman launch herself up the stairs.

"Police!" Savage grunted.

"Stop!" came a shout from the room the woman had just left. Savage peered around the door to see a small chamber, a bed in one corner. There was an older man lying on it in his pyjamas, his round, flushed face full of terror. He was trying to get up but Kett had one hand on his chest, pinning him to the bed. He turned and saw Savage.

"Go get her!"

She nodded, retreating. Duke was fighting somebody in the other room, she could hear the crash of crockery. But he could handle himself. She climbed the steep stairs as well as she could, on all fours as she reached the top. Footsteps reverberated off the stone like rolling thunder, she couldn't make out where they were coming from. It was too dark to see anything.

"Police!" she called again. "Stop running."

She aimed her torch past the rows of pews, sweeping it towards the back of the building, then along the far wall. It was only when she stumbled into the nave, shining the light at the wall behind her, that she saw the open door.

The one that led up towards the tower.

She ran through it, pulling out her phone as she went and calling 999. The tower was as dark as everything else in the building, the stairs leading up in a crooked spiral. She could hear somebody climbing them at speed, their desperate breaths echoing down.

"Police," Savage yelled, hearing the call connect. "Hey, this is DC Kate Savage, Norfolk Police. I'm in St Margaret's Church in Great Yarmouth, multiple attackers, we need backup immediately."

She waited long enough for the operator to repeat the information, then slipped her phone into her pocket and climbed the stairs. After a small eternity she reached an open door, the cold wind kicking through it letting her know it led outside. She passed through carefully, in case the woman was waiting for her there, but when she walked out she saw her on the far side of the open tower, facing away, both hands braced on the crenelated wall like she was planning to throw herself over.

"Hey!" Savage called, lifting her free hand as if she had any hope at all of reaching her. "Hey, stop, I just want to talk."

The woman didn't move, her soft sobs carried off by the wind. Yarmouth lay beneath them, a tapestry of streetlights on one side and the lightless gulf of the sea on the other.

"Darcey?" said Savage.

This time, the young woman looked back, her eyes as bright as the moon overhead. She was wearing a tracksuit that looked far too big for her, her feet bare. Her hair hung over her face in wild tangles and she still clung to the top of the wall like an Olympic vaulter. Her entire body was rigid, the wind up here surely strong enough to blow her to her death.

"Darcey," Savage said again. Every instinct was telling her to run to the woman before she could jump, but she forced herself to stay by the door. "That is your name, isn't it?"

It took an age for the woman to nod.

"I'm Kate, I'm police. You don't have to be afraid."

She seemed *more* afraid, if anything.

"We're here to save you," said Savage. "We can take you home."

Darcey shook her head.

"You and your baby, okay?" said Savage, a strong gust of wind taking her breath away. She clung to the stone frame of the door. "But we have to get you off the tower, it's dangerous."

The woman turned slowly, bracing her back against the low wall. She put both her hands to her stomach, shaking her head.

"You're safe," Savage said again. "They're not going to hurt you anymore."

She saw the confusion on Darcey's face.

"They did this to you, didn't they?" she asked. "The priest, Father Odling? You don't have to worry about him, he's under arrest. He can't hurt you again."

"No," said Darcey, still shaking her head. "No, it isn't like that."

"Just come with me, come down," said Savage. "We can talk in safety, I promise."

"I can't," said Darcey, doubling up. "I can't. I can't."

"They can't hurt you," said Savage. She forced herself to walk onto the tower, the wind making her feel like she was on a rocking boat. "I'm going to take you somewhere safe."

"There is nowhere safe," said Darcey. "Not for me, not anymore. I just want to... It's better if I..."

She put her hands on the wall behind her, mounting it.

"No!" Savage said, making it halfway across the roof of the tower before Darcey screamed for her to stop. The young woman teetered on the wall, her hands grasping at the stone, her face full of panic.

"Don't come any closer," she said. "I know you're lying, I know what you're going to do."

"I'm not lying," said Savage. She'd dropped the torch and she held both hands out. "Please, I'm not going to hurt you."

"Yes you are," said Darcey. "You're going to take me away, take me away from my baby. I'll never see her."

"Of course you..." Savage said, then she realised what the woman was scared of. "He's dead, isn't he? William?"

Darcey screwed her face up, looking again like she might tumble silently off the tower.

"You killed him?" said Savage.

The woman groaned, a noise of pure misery that was even louder than the wind.

"We know it wasn't your fault," she said, risking another step while Darcey's eyes were closed. "We know they made you do it. Odling, right? And Valerie?"

The woman opened her eyes, that same look of confusion.

"They didn't," she said. "They didn't make me do anything. They... How did you know about Willy?"

"We know it wasn't your fault," said Savage. "We know somebody made you kill him. They put you in a lorry, right? They started a fire. Either one of you died, or both of you burned."

Darcey studied her like she couldn't believe what she was hearing.

"You're not the only one," Savage said, taking another step. Maybe a dozen yards between them now, still too far if Darcey decided to lean back, or if the wind picked up. "It's happened before, to another couple. We know you didn't have a choice."

From the bottom of the steps, Savage heard somebody shout her name. Darcey flinched.

"You're not in any trouble, I promise you," she said. "We know this wasn't your fault. Come with me, please. Let's get you inside, you and the baby."

"I can't," said Darcey. "I didn't kill him. I didn't touch him. He did it himself, and..."

Her face warped again, drowning in emotion.

"He did it, he did it, and I just want to be with him again. I want us to be together again. I'm sorry."

She met her eyes, and Savage saw the moment she made her decision.

"No!"

Darcey rolled backwards like a diver on a boat, falling noiselessly over the edge of the roof. Savage ran, slipping on the smooth stone and almost tumbling after her. Her stomach lurched, the shot of adrenaline enough to tear her head off, the roar of blood in her ears loud enough to drown out the sound of screaming until she looked over the edge of the wall and saw Darcey there, the hood of her tracksuit caught on the spout of the tower's guttering. She thrashed beneath it like somebody on a noose, the tracksuit working its way off her torso.

"Shit," said Savage. "Shit, wait there."

She leaned over the crenulations, grabbing hold of the hood. Darcey's hands slapped at her, her nails gouging her skin as she tried to fight her off. The world below was steeped in shadow but Savage knew that fifty feet or so beneath them was the concrete path that surrounded the church.

A quick, inevitable death.

"Kate!"

Somebody grabbed her jacket, trying to haul her back onto the tower.

"No!" she said. "Help me!"

Kett appeared beside her.

"Jesus Christ," he said. "Duke! Get up here!"

Darcey was slipping out of her hoodie, her legs kicking at the air. Her hand gripped Savage's again and this time it held on, the weight nearly pulling her off the edge.

"Darcey, you need to stop moving," she said, the stone wall cutting into her stomach, her chest.

If the young woman heard, she made no sign of it, tugging on Savage's hand like she was deliberately trying to pull her over. With every second she slid further over the low wall.

"Hang on," said Kett, and she felt his hands around her waist. "Pull, Kate!"

She did, screaming into the wind as she tried to hoist Darcey up the wall. Kett helped, his arms hauling her backwards until she felt like she was going to be torn in two. Inch by inch, they dragged the woman higher, until suddenly Duke was there on Savage's other side. He reached with both hands and grabbed Darcey beneath the arms, flipping her over the wall.

Together, all four of them tumbled to the stone floor of the tower. Savage rolled onto her back, the agony pulsing through her with every frantic beat of her heart. She tried to sit up to make sure Darcey didn't jump again, but a cramp rolled through her abdomen. She arched her back, not enough air to scream with.

Darcey wasn't going anywhere, though. She had curled herself into a ball, her hands over her belly, her face hidden by her hair as she sobbed and sobbed and sobbed.

"You okay, Kate?" wheezed Kett as he struggled to his feet. She didn't have time to answer before Duke skidded down beside her, one hand under her head as he pulled her close.

"You okay?" he echoed.

She managed a nod instead, resting her hand on Duke's arm, giving him a squeeze. The cramp fluttered away, but it had left her speechless. She said the words inside her head as the wind snapped across the tower, chasing Darcey's cries into the night.

This fucking job.

CHAPTER TWENTY

IT WAS ALMOST MIDNIGHT, BUT THE PARADE OF POLICE cars and ambulances parked outside St Margaret's made the street glow like it was the middle of the day. Kett stood by the main doors, shivering hard—as much the adrenaline run-off as the cold. His eyes kept drifting up to the top of the immense stone tower, which looked twice as tall now as it had when he'd first arrived. He kept imagining a different ending to what had just happened, Darcey DeCarlo tumbling earthwards, impaled on the railings below.

Followed by Savage.

He didn't really understand what was going on. All he knew for sure was that he'd well and truly Ketted this one up.

Again.

He'd been right, though. He'd trusted his gut and it had led him here. What had happened less than an hour ago was already a blur of adrenaline, and he forced himself to remember it. He'd walked through the door in the cellar to find a small room, the priest lying in the only bed wearing his pyjamas, Darcey on her knees beside him. She'd thrown herself up in her panic, thrashing her way out of the room before he could stop her.

Then the priest had been on his feet, coming at Kett in a hail of blustering shouts. It had taken everything Kett had to throw the man back onto the bed, and he'd had to leave him there to help Duke—the PC was in the next room over, Valerie's arms locked around his neck, her knees driving into his stomach and his crotch. It had taken both of them to subdue her, and by that point they'd heard Savage's screams from the tower.

"You want them in a car, sir?" asked Duke as the big PC limped to the doors, one hand still massaging his groin. He was doing his best to appear calm, but he was rattled. He kept glancing at the ambulance where Savage was being treated, his body tense like he expected to have to run over and save her.

"The priest?" asked Kett.

Duke nodded.

"No, leave them in the church for now," he said. "Let them stew."

Kett walked onto the street, passing Savage's ambulance and nodding to her through the open back door. The paramedic had just finished wrapping her stomach in gauze where the wall of the tower had left a nasty graze. She tilted her head to him in reply, but her face was as cold and as stony as the church.

He walked past two IRVs to the first ambulance that had arrived. The back doors were closed, but Kett had watched them load Darcey into it a few minutes ago. Duke had carried her down the stairs from the tower like a baby, her face pressed into his neck, the sobs endless. He could still hear her crying now, he realised, and when he knocked on the door he did so quietly, so as not to startle her.

"Busy," came a voice from inside.

"It's the police," said Kett. "Any chance of a quick word?"

He heard soft voices inside, and a few seconds later the door opened.

"It'll have to be quick," the paramedic whispered. "I need to get her back."

The woman offered Kett a hand as he climbed into the ambulance, closing the door behind him. It was warm in here, but Darcey DeCarlo shivered beneath her blankets, just her eyes visible as she sobbed quietly. She watched Kett like he meant to drag her back up the stairs and hurl her to her death.

"Hey," he said. He stood to the side and bumped into a tray of equipment, knocking something to the floor. Darcey flinched, and so did he. "Sorry, bit cramped in here."

"Because it's not an interview room," said the paramedic, shooing him out of the way to collect whatever had fallen.

Kett walked to the edge of the stretcher, ducking his head beneath the low roof, feeling like a giant next to the woman who lay there.

"How are you, Darcey?" he asked.

She didn't answer, she just stared at him. He didn't think she'd blinked once since he'd walked in. She wasn't crying anymore. She looked too frightened to cry.

"My name's Robbie," said Kett. "I didn't get a chance to introduce myself in the church. I'm a policeman. My colleague, Kate, told me everything that you said up there."

Darcey flinched again.

"You're not in any trouble," he said. "We know what happened to you, we know about William. You haven't done anything wrong."

She didn't react, other than to swivel her eyes up to the ceiling—as if she could see through it to the tower where she had almost died.

"But I need to ask you some questions, Darcey," he said. "Is that okay? Because what happened to you and William also happened to somebody else. There was another death. And we don't know if this is the end of it."

He heard the paramedic tutting, saw her tapping her watch.

"I don't want this to happen to anybody else," said Kett. "I want to find who did this to you, and to William, and I want to stop them. So please, think hard. Can you tell me what happened?"

Darcey made a noise like she was swallowing a mouthful of nails. He saw her hands move beneath the blanket, cradling her belly. When she spoke, she did so in a whisper that Kett had to lean in to hear.

"He's dead, isn't he?"

Kett waited a moment, thinking of the charred corpse.

"We found a body in the back of a lorry," he said. "We don't know who it is yet."

"It's Willy," Darcey whispered. "He did it."

"He killed himself?"

"He didn't have a choice," she said, her words muffled by the blanket over her mouth. "Even though he was drunk, he knew he didn't have a choice. It was on fire, couldn't see anything for smoke. I thought somebody was playing a joke, but he knew. There were weapons in there, on a table. We were supposed to use them against each other. He..."

"Who told you that you had to use the weapons?" asked Kett when she tailed off.

"I don't know who it was. They were outside. Shouting. Said only one of us could leave, or neither of us. Then the fire started and Willy, he just knew. Told me to... told me to look away but I didn't. Couldn't. Tried to stop him but... He didn't even hesitate, did I say that? He did it for me, for..."

Her hands wound tighter around her stomach.

"This was yesterday?" he said, glancing at his watch. "The thirteenth, right?"

She nodded.

"How did you end up there, Darcey?"

"I was home," she said, sniffing. "In bed. Somebody came to the door, but they weren't there, there was just a box."

"What time was this?"

"Late," she said. "After eleven. It was the strangest thing, it moved when I tried to get it, chased it all the way to the street. I thought it was Willy, because he's always playing jokes."

She sniffed again, her teeth chattering.

"Couldn't see anyone, and there was nothing in the box, just a note."

"We saw it," said Kett. "A postcode."

She nodded.

"You went out there? How?"

"Ben," she said. "Guy from church, he lives on my street. He didn't want to take me, and didn't want to leave me there because it was the middle of nowhere, but I told him it was okay. He knows Willy, and we saw his car in the field so we knew it was... knew it was him."

"His car? The Beetle?"

"No, he's got another one, a Ford. He told me the Beetle had been nicked or borrowed or something."

"When?"

She shrugged.

"Can you tell me what happened next?" asked Kett.

Darcey's eyes roved in their sockets as she replayed it.

"I don't remember," she said. "It's all too... It was so dark, just these fairy lights. I thought he was doing something romantic. There was a lorry, the doors were open. So I got in, and..."

Kett gave her the time she needed.

"He was sitting there, in a chair. I thought he was joking, because he was... he was *drunk*. Then somebody shut the doors, and Willy was screaming. He was screaming, and he was tied to the chair, I had to..."

She made a sawing motion beneath the blanket, as if she'd forgotten the word.

"You got him out?" said Kett.

"Yeah, but then somebody was banging on the lorry, shouting at us. A man. He told us..."

The horror of it was too much for her. Kett thought, for a moment, that he could see the reflection of the flames in the pools of her eyes—the illusion gone in an instant.

"The lorry was burning," she said. "I didn't know what to do."

The paramedic bustled past, taking Darcey's temperature. She turned to say something to Kett, but he blurted out another question before she could tell him to leave.

"What happened to William?"

"I already told you," she said. "Willy was panicking. He tried the door, we both did, but it was too hot. I couldn't see. He just picked up a knife from this table, and he told me... He told me he loved me, and he..."

"He killed himself," said Kett when she couldn't finish.

"He did for me," she said, cradling her belly. "For us."

"What happened next?"

"He must have unlocked the door," she said. "The man. It was open. Didn't want to leave Willy but I couldn't move him and the fire... I got out, I just ran, because I didn't know if he was coming after me. Took Willy's car and... the keys were in it, I just drove till I got here."

"You didn't see the man who did this to you?"

No reply.

"It was definitely a man, though?"

Darcey nodded.

"Can you tell me anything about his voice?"

"Loud," she said. "Really loud. *Scary* loud."

"Did he have an accent? Did he use any words that sounded odd, or unfamiliar?"

Nothing.

"You came to the church after you got away? Why?"

"Didn't know where else to go," she said.

"You could have called us, Darcey. You could have called the police."

"You'd have thought I did it," she said, her eyes sliding back to him. "You wouldn't have believed me, and I couldn't go to prison, not with the baby. But I didn't kill him, he did it to himself, I swear."

"I believe you," said Kett. "Father Odling and Valerie were here when you arrived?"

Darcey didn't respond.

"It's important that we—"

Somebody hammered violently on the back of the ambulance, Kett's heart shattering like glass. The door was wrenched open before anyone could reply, and DI Charles Dawson hauled his raggedy frame up onto the step.

It was impossible to miss the sound that escaped Darcey's lips when she saw him, a soft cry. She had curled herself into a ball beneath her sheet, her eyes liquid with terror.

"Hey!" the paramedic yelled. "You can't be here."

"Forgive me," said Dawson, his hoarse breaths carrying more than a hint of rum. He patted his pockets then held up his empty hands. "I'm police. Looks like you beat me to it, sir."

"What are you doing here, Dawson?" said Kett, barricading the door as best he could in case Dawson tried to enter.

"Just heard about what happened," the DI said, swaying like the ambulance was moving. "Wanted to come along and see if I could help, this being my backyard and all."

"You both need to leave," said the paramedic, one hand on Kett's arm.

"She's not wrong," said Dawson, grinning at the woman in the bed. "Looks like you could do with a warm bath and a cuddle, love."

Darcey was paralysed with fear.

"Out, now!" the paramedic insisted.

"Alright, alright, don't rush an old man," said Dawson, stumbling down onto the street. He turned back, offering that same smile to Kett along with an extended hand. "Need some help there, sir?"

Kett tried to turn back to Darcey, but the paramedic gave him a shove that almost sent him flying. He landed hard on the street, taking a couple of steps to regain his balance. When he looked back, he saw Dawson closing the ambulance door, giving it another solid whack with the flat of his hand.

"What the fuck was that?" said Kett.

"What was what, sir?" said Dawson, licking his fingers before working them through his mop of greying hair. "I was just going to ask a couple of questions. Not my fault we got kicked out."

He frowned at Kett.

"Is that *glitter*?"

Kett rubbed his face with a growl.

"She say anything?" asked the DI, walking a little too close. "She talk? Because a woman like that, you can't really take her word as gospel, you know what I mean?"

"No, I don't know what you mean," said Kett, taking a couple of steps to get away from him. The man smelled like he'd downed a bottle of Bacardi before bathing in a bucket of fried chicken. "You're drunk."

"Off duty," said Dawson. "As are you, sir. Am I right? Off duty, and yet still working. No getting away from the job, is there? Eats you alive. One minute you're prying around looking for answers, the next you're pushing up daisies."

The smile was still on his face, but his eyes had narrowed.

"How about you leave the interrogations to me, sir?" said Dawson. "Everybody around here knows old Chuckles, they'll talk to me."

"Darcey seemed to know you," Kett said. "She was terrified."

"Of me? No. She's just been through a lot."

Kett turned away before the urge to throttle him became too strong to resist. He wove a path through a throng of Dawson's uniformed coppers back to the church.

"What's his problem?" said Duke, who was waiting by the door, still in civilian clothes.

"He's an arsehole," Kett replied. "Where's the priest?"

"Chancel."

"What's that again?"

"The chancel, sir?" said Duke. "The bit at the front."

"Stay here," Kett said as he walked past him. "Don't let that prick anywhere near the church."

"He outranks me, sir," said Duke. "But I'll do my best."

Kett made his way to the far end of the church. The lights were on, but they felt muted, as if the building was ashamed of what had happened here. Father Odling sat on one of the pews that filled the chancel, still dressed in his red velvet pyjamas. He was staring at the altar as if he might find answers there, but he looked up when he heard footsteps, his round face etched with fear. A bruise had formed on his left cheek, although Kett didn't know how it had got there.

There was no sign of Valerie.

"Now look," said the priest, starting to stand. Kett put a hand on his shoulder, returning him to his seat with enough force to let him know not to try again. He sat next to him, taking a breath of frigid air before speaking.

"Now *you* look, Jack," he said, his voice filling the whole church. "I'm going to give you one chance to tell me what happened here. One chance, okay? Because the way I see it, you were keeping a young, vulnerable woman in the cellar of your church after her boyfriend was viciously murdered. Not only that, but you seemed to be sharing a bed with her. Nothing about this story is going to make your trial an easy one."

The man's mouth opened so far it looked like a trapdoor, his tongue squirming as it tried to work its way around a word.

"I was... What are you saying?" he managed. "I wasn't sharing her bed!"

"It was her bed, and you were in it," said Kett.

"Not like *that*," said Odling, whose face had gone such a severe shade of crimson Kett worried he was having a heart attack. "I was talking her through her prayers."

"In your pyjamas?"

"It was late!" the man protested. "I..."

He scrubbed his eyes with his fists.

"Lord give me strength," he said. "What a night. What a night."

He dropped his hands, composing himself.

"I see how it looks, Detective. I really do. But please look beyond what you think you've found here. I told you before, I have known Darcey a long time. I have watched her grow, fall in love, get with child. I married her to her soulmate. I love her, as I would love any member of this congregation. I would never keep her against her will, or hurt her, or do... *that* to her."

He puffed out a sigh, looking at the altar once again.

"Darcey turned up here last night."

"The thirteenth?" asked Kett.

"Yes. Although it was long after midnight, so it would have been the fourteenth. Today, really. She was in hysterics, out of her mind with worry, with trauma. She was covered in blood, and at first we thought something had happened to her baby."

"We?" said Kett. "You're talking about Valerie?"

"Of course," said Odling. "She lives with me in the house. She opened the door to Darcey, let her in. It goes without saying that we both wanted to call the police, but Darcey was adamant that we didn't. She threatened violence against herself unless we agreed to keep her hidden."

"She told you what happened?"

"Eventually," said Odling. "Sometime later, after we had bathed her, and fed her, she calmed down enough to explain that William had died, that he had taken his own life. Her story seemed... it seemed a little far-fetched. I wondered if perhaps he had threatened her, and she had killed him in self-defence. Or if maybe one of William's accomplices had been involved, and she was trying to cover for him. I explained before that William has a chequered past."

"What did she say, exactly?" asked Kett.

"I don't remember *exactly*," Odling said. "Although Valerie would. She has a much better brain for words than I do."

Kett scanned the church for the woman, but he couldn't see her amongst the pockets of police.

"Where is she?"

"She went off with one of your lot," said Odling. "Perhaps to use the bathroom."

"Fair enough," he said. "Tell me how you fit into all this."

"I don't fit into it at all," he said. "We just helped Darcey, the same way we would help anyone."

"She showed up here in William's car? After midnight?"

The priest grasped the pew, his knuckles white.

"She did, yes. We hid it in the Marina car park. Darcey told us we had to keep her safe, and keep her hidden. You have to understand she wasn't thinking straight, she was beside herself. My first duty is to my parish. Always."

"Did she say anything about her attacker? Did she see him?"

"She did not," said the priest. "She didn't say anything..."

The words petered out as he looked past Kett towards the front of the church. Kett turned to see that Dawson had slithered his way inside. He was sitting on a pew, a lit cigarette between his lips as he watched them. Duke stood in the doorway behind, offering an apologetic shrug.

"Ignore him," ordered Kett. "Carry on."

"I've said enough," Odling said, watching Dawson with the same expression of fear that Darcey had worn. "I don't know anything else, I swear. But we weren't doing anything wrong, we were just looking after her. You can arrest me for that if you want."

"I'm planning to," said Kett, causing the other man to gasp in outrage. "You should have called us. Whoever is doing this isn't planning to stop anytime soon, I'm pretty sure about that. Your hesitation might cost somebody their life. But there's still time to talk. If you know anything else, tell me now."

The priest wouldn't take his eyes off Dawson. He shook his head, his lips clamped shut.

"Is he the reason you're not saying anything?" Kett asked. "Because I can get him out of here. He can't hurt you."

"I've said enough," muttered Odling. "Do with me what you must."

"Then you're under arrest for obstruction of justice," said Kett, and he rattled off the police caution.

Father Odling bowed his head between his knees as if in prayer, sighing deeply.

"Don't go anywhere," Kett told him, his back cracking as he stood up. He made his way down the church to where Dawson sat in a cloud of smoke. The DI was lifting the cigarette to his mouth for another drag and Kett snatched it from him, grinding it beneath his boot.

"Come on, man," said Dawson. "I don't have many pleasures left, at least let me have that one."

"What's going on here, Dawson?" said Kett. "What aren't you telling me?"

"You could write a book about everything you don't know, sir," the man replied. He smiled, and there was nothing friendly there. He patted the pockets of his filthy trench coat. "Out of fags now, it's a fucking tragedy."

Kett half thought about arresting Dawson too, but there was no charge for being a prick, and he'd have had a hard time justifying it to the Superintendent.

"Where's Valerie?" he asked.

"Who's Valerie, sir?" said Dawson with a shrug.

Kett walked to the exit, collecting Duke on his way.

"Sorry, sir," the PC said. "I tried to stop him coming in, but he just wouldn't listen. He's a..."

"Yeah, he is," said Kett before Duke could finish.

He pushed through the porch doors into the night, finding the street strangely deserted. It was only when he walked past the row of parked cars that he spotted a commotion further up the road—half a dozen uniformed coppers milling around, their shouts echoing off the shuttered shops.

"What now?" Kett said, forcing his aching body into a jog.

The PCs parted as he arrived, revealing a body in the middle of the road. It was a woman, and even though she was facing away from him, there was no mistaking who it was. Valerie's tall frame and long limbs were splayed in an almost perfect cross, but the angle of her head made it very clear she was dead.

"Fuck," said Kett, stepping around the body and kneeling beside her. The woman's face was utterly serene, her open eyes so full of peace that Kett put his fingers to her neck just to make sure.

"No pulse, sir," said one of the PCs.

"What the hell happened?" asked Kett.

"Found her like this. Looks like a hit-and-run."

They were at the junction with a bigger road, the crossing concealed by the corner of a building and everything soaked in darkness. If Valerie had been running, there was a good chance she could have stepped in front of a car.

"Who was watching her?" said Kett, looking up at the coppers to see that nobody was willing to take responsibility. "She was supposed to be under escort."

"Just found her like this, sir," said the same officer. "Sorry."

"What the fuck is going on?" said Kett, standing up and turning to the night for answers it wasn't willing to give.

CHAPTER TWENTY-ONE

Tuesday

It was after five in the morning by the time Kett managed to get away from St Margaret's, and his exhaustion made the world burn like a fever dream. Darcey DeCarlo was long gone, taken by ambulance back to the city. So was Savage, although she'd been given the all-clear to go home. Kett had let Duke go with her, mainly because the big PC had pulled such a convincing puppy dog face that he hadn't really had a choice.

Father Odling had left the scene in the back of a police car a few hours ago, a portrait of despair. Kett was pretty sure the priest didn't know anything about what had happened to Darcey, but the fact remained he should have called the police. Any chance they'd had of following the killer's trail from the second lorry was long gone, and Father Odling was one of two people who could be blamed for that.

The other was dead.

Valerie had taken her last ride in the second ambulance, and no matter how much Kett asked, nobody could tell him what had happened to her. There were no witnesses, no passersby, and none of the shops at this end of the street had cameras. Valerie had gone from being inside the church and safely under police custody to being dead on the street in less than ten minutes, and he couldn't figure out how it had happened.

Only DI Dawson seemed amused about the affair, but Chuckles—as he insisted everyone call him—had left to buy cigarettes just after one and hadn't come back. Kett would have summoned him, but his phone had died, and none of Dawson's constables seemed to know how to get hold of him.

All in all, it was a mess.

He drove home fast, because his eyes kept closing and he needed the adrenaline to stop him dozing off. The day was waking up by the time he arrived at his house, but it was still dark enough that he didn't see the car parked in his driveway until he almost drove into it.

"Nope," he said as he squeezed the Volvo in next to the ugly brown Mercedes. "Nope, nope, nope."

He got out, closing the door as quietly as he could so as not to wake the girls—although he could see that the front bedroom light was on, a warm glow seeping through the closed curtains. The birds were celebrating the morning like it was their first, but the sound of them only made Kett feel his exhaustion more. He yawned so hard he felt his jaw crack, hearing the sound of a car window rolling down.

"Quit your bloody yawning, Kett," said Clare from inside the Mercedes.

Kett snapped his mouth shut, walking to the Super's car.

"What are you doing here, sir?"

"Well since you couldn't be arsed to answer your phone, I thought I'd pay a house call. What the bloody hell is going on?"

"It's... complicated, sir," said Kett. "Let me freshen up and I'll come straight in. I just need a cup of tea and maybe a five-minute nap."

"And maybe a nappy change and a cuddle from mummy?" said Clare. His door squealed as he opened it, and the sound of it closing could have woken the whole street. "You're not a baby, get on with it."

"Oh, right," said Kett. "Well, Darcey DeCarlo is—"

He was interrupted by the front door opening. Billie stood there in her pyjamas, embraced by light, her smile the most welcome thing in the world. Kett felt a sudden urge to tell Clare to go stuff himself, run inside, and never leave the house again.

The job wouldn't let him, though.

"Hey," she said to Robbie.

"Hey."

"Hi, Colin. You want to come in?"

"No, he's fine," said Kett, although Clare was already halfway to the door. "For fuck's sake," he grumbled, following the Superintendent in.

Billie greeted Kett with a kiss as he took off his coat.

"You okay?" she asked, and he shook his head. She kissed him again. "Kettle's on."

"Girls awake?"

"Moira's on her iPad, Evie's asleep, and Alice's room is such a tip I'm not sure if she's in there or not."

Clare had already made his way into the kitchen. He pulled out a dining chair and dropped into it like a sack of potatoes. Everything about the man seemed potato-like, his skin the colour of mash, his face drooping. Kett chose the sofa instead.

"Well?" the Super demanded.

"Like I said, it's complicated," said Kett. The sofa had been a mistake. As soon as he'd sat on it, he'd felt sleep gather him up in a hug. He stifled another yawn with his hand, speaking through it.

"I can't understand a thing you're saying," said Clare.

"Sorry. Darcey DeCarlo was in the second lorry with William Briggs. Same scenario. The killer set fire to it and told them to fight to the death. Briggs chose to..."

He glanced at Billie, who had grown considerably paler. She flipped the switch of the kettle before it could fully boil.

"Look, sir, can we talk about this outside?" asked Kett. "It's—"

"It's okay," said Billie. "I'll check on the girls."

"Sorry, Billie," Clare told her as she left the room.

"Briggs killed himself rather than fight Darcey," said Kett when he'd heard her scale the stairs. "The killer let her go, and she drove to the church. It was where she felt safe. Father Odling and Valerie kept her hidden in the cellar for near enough twenty-four hours. God knows what they were planning to do with her in the long run."

"You've arrested them?"

"Odling, yes," said Kett. "Valerie's dead."

"What?"

"You didn't hear, sir?"

"I've only just woken up," said Clare. He had rocked the dining chair back on two legs and was in danger of tumbling right back through the bifold doors. Kett didn't have the courage to tell him off.

"Valerie was killed in a hit-and-run outside the church. Nobody saw it. She was supposed to be under police supervision. I'm still trying to work out what happened."

"*You* happened," muttered Clare.

"Little unfair, sir," said Kett. "We almost lost Darcey too. She tried to jump from the tower. Kate saved her."

"Unbelievable," said Clare. "Where does this leave us, then?"

"Uh..."

"I'll tell you where it leaves us, Kett. We've swum up a whale's tosshole and we don't have a paddle. We're way past the urethra, we're approaching this blubbery bastard's prostate and unless he decides he's going to flipper himself to an orgasm, we're stuck inside his enormous, flaming todger. Is that an accurate assessment of where we are?"

"God, *no*, sir," said Kett. "Not even close."

It looked like Clare was about to go on, but he was cut off by the thunder of feet on the stairs. Seconds later, Evie and Moira ran into the room, approaching the sofa with such enthusiasm that Kett almost screamed. They hurled themselves onto him, their bony knees everywhere as they planted kisses on his face.

"Where have you been?" yelled Evie. "Where did you *sleep*?"

"In a whale's todger," muttered Clare.

The girls were too excited to hear him. They were kissing Kett so furiously that he had to close his eyes.

"Easy," he said. "It's lovely to see you too."

He gently pushed them away, and found that no matter how hard he tried he couldn't open his eyes again. He leaned back into the sofa, aware that Clare was talking but too tired to pay him any attention.

"Wake up, Daddy, it's morning," said Moira.

"We should get some glitter," said Evie. "Glitter wakes

everyone up."

"No glitter," mumbled Kett.

The girls jumped off him and ran from the room.

"Agreed, Kett?" asked Clare.

"Sure, sir," he said, although he had no idea what the man had said.

"Good. Then get some rest."

Through the fog of sleep, Kett was almost grateful, until the Super finished.

"And I'll see you at the station in half an hour."

FOUR HOURS LATER, and somewhat sheepishly, Kett walked into the offices of the Major Investigation Team. He'd managed an hour's sleep on the sofa after the girls had gone to school, but it had left him feeling worse than he had before he'd sat down. He felt like a badly made toy as he crossed the bullpen, every joint loose and his head rattling on his shoulders.

Savage was sitting at her desk, and she looked up as he approached.

"Crikey, sir, you look worse than me."

"How're you doing, Kate?" he asked as he slung his coat on the back of his chair.

Her faint smile was accompanied by a shrug.

"Not sure. Last night was..."

"It was bad," said Kett. "I'm sorry. It was my fault."

"You were following a hunch, sir," said Savage. "If we hadn't ended up at the church, then it might have been somebody else, and they might not have been able to stop Darcey from throwing herself off the tower."

Kett nodded.

"You saved that girl, Kate, and her baby," he said. "Any word on her?"

"She's doing okay, sir," said Savage. "All things considered. She's in hospital. Baby is fine. It's going to take some time, but I think she'll be able to recover. If *anyone* can recover from that."

Kett looked up, searching the almost empty room.

"Where is everyone?"

"Incident Room, sir," said Savage, collecting a sheet of paper from the printer. "I was just about to head there myself."

"The smell's gone?"

"I guess we're about to find out."

They made their way through the bullpen and up the corridor, hearing Clare's voice long before they'd walked through the door. The Super was patrolling the front of the room like a puffed-up cockerel, his bulging eyes sweeping between Porter, Spalding, Duke and a couple of uniformed officers who seemed to have found themselves in the wrong place but were too frightened to do anything about it. Kett scuttled to the nearest empty desk, hoping Clare wouldn't notice him. It was a futile wish.

"Ah, and here he is. Queen Mab, lady of our dreams."

"Sir?" said Kett.

"Enjoy your nap?"

"I was... working from home," Kett said without much conviction. "Important stuff."

Clare looked like he was going to continue his tirade, dismissing Kett with a snort instead.

"Carry on, Alison."

"We've conducted a thorough search of Darcey's house," said Spalding. "There's nothing of any consequence at all. But she's a romantic, that's for sure. She's got a box containing every letter and card she's ever received from Briggs, and every book we found in her room is a romance novel or an instruction book for relationships."

"Nothing to suggest Briggs was a killer?" said Clare.

Spalding scratched behind her ear with a pencil.

"Nothing, sir. Briggs seemed as devoted to her as she was to him, and every testimony we've received from friends says likewise. Other than one."

"His brother," said Kett, and Spalding frowned.

"How did you know that, sir?"

"He dreamed it," said Clare. "During his nap."

"Just a guess," said Kett. "I get the impression Luke didn't like the fact that Will was spending so much time with Darcey. Odling said they had plans to move away, start fresh."

"Enough of a reason to kill him?" asked Clare.

"No, sir. I don't think Luke would have murdered his own brother, and he was a witness at their wedding so he can't have hated it too much. But Perry Paul is a different matter. They're operating a brothel. If Will had left the fold to be with his girlfriend—"

"Wife, sir," said Savage.

"Wife, yeah. Paul might have worried he would betray them, grass them up. He needed a way of getting rid of him that didn't come back to bite him."

Clare gurned his disapproval.

"So he lured him and his girlfriend out to—"

"Wife, sir," said Savage.

"Tossing *wife*, then, out to a lorry, set fire to it, made them fight to the death? And he did the same to another couple just to make it less suspicious?"

"When you say it like that, sir..." said Kett. "I agree, it doesn't fit. Even if Paul wanted to get rid of William and copycat the Dankworth murder, he wouldn't have had time to prepare. The killings were only hours apart. This feels like something else."

"Serial killer," said Porter.

As much as Kett hated to agree, he found himself nodding.

"Go toss on a cabbage," said Clare, stamping his foot. "These can't be random attacks, I won't allow it. One of you must have found a link between the Dankworths and DeCarlo and Briggs."

"I did," said Porter.

"See." Clare grinned in triumph. "I knew it. What have you got?"

"Karen Dankworth used to live in Lowestoft, sir," Porter said. "But she came up to Yarmouth to use the gym. It's the same gym where DeCarlo worked for three months last year, as a personal trainer."

"They knew each other," said Clare. "There's a connection."

"Not exactly, sir," said Porter. "Dankworth lived in Yarmouth from 2005 to 2008. DeCarlo would have been a child."

"So they never met?" Clare said.

"I don't think so."

"Remind me to do something later, Porter," said Clare, seething.

"What, sir?"

"Castrate you with my hole punch. Any other links? Anything at all?"

"There's no indication that any of our victims knew each other," said Spalding. "The Dankworths were in their forties, they'd been together nearly ten years, married for seven. They were childless. DeCarlo and Briggs were a new couple in their early twenties, married last week, a baby on the way. Different employment fields, different parts of the county, no shared interests, no mutual friends."

Clare glared at her too.

"My hole punch is going to be busy this afternoon," he muttered.

"Not sure I'm castratable, sir," said Spalding.

Clare slumped into a chair, immediately propelling it back onto two legs. Everyone in the room lurched as it looked like he was about to tumble back, but he recovered quickly.

"Any word on the body in lorry number two?"

"Franklin's report has just come in, sir," said Savage, holding up the sheet of paper she'd walked in with. "She's still waiting for DNA, but she's verified that the victim was a man, and she's put his age at somewhere in his early twenties."

"It's almost certainly Briggs," said Clare.

"He was killed by a knife wound to the heart," Savage said, reading off the sheet. "There doesn't seem to be any hesitation, so either he did it with full conviction, or somebody else killed him. Franklin says either is possible, but murder is more likely than suicide. Might explain why Darcey was so afraid of us."

"I don't know," said Kett. "I got the feeling she was telling the truth."

"Father Odling backs up her story," said Porter, who was rocking back on *his* chair. "I spoke to him again this morning."

"While you were having a nap," said Clare, frowning at Kett.

"I wasn't napping, sir! I was working. From home."

"And he backed up everything he told you last night, sir.

Darcey claimed Briggs killed himself so that she wouldn't have to do it. The priest is utterly convinced she's innocent, and he doesn't seem in any state of mind to be lying. He said that if he'd had any suggestion she was guilty, he would have called us straightaway."

"Hay found fingerprints at the lorry," said Spalding. "They match the ones we have on record for William Briggs. She's still looking for Darcey's, but the killer doesn't seem to have left anything for us. Other than the registration plates, that is."

"Any more news on them?" asked Kett. "Or the Beetle? Darcey said the car was stolen, or borrowed."

"We've just had that conversation," said Clare. "You missed it. Because of your nap. No record of the Beetle anywhere, but if the killer changed the plates we wouldn't spot it on the system. The campervan's owner, Anna Greer, and the ex-girlfriend who used it, Jaye Moore, are both accounted for, and have alibis for the thirteenth. We found the place it's being stored. The plates are missing, but forensics have looked it over and there's nothing that can help us. There's no link between Greer and Moore and any of our victims."

"Nobody else used the vehicle?" asked Kett.

"I don't know," said Clare. "Why don't you ask the sleep fairies? The dream pixies? Maybe they can tell you?"

"Who spoke to Greer?" asked Kett, ignoring him.

Everyone turned to look at Duke, who was studying the end of his finger with some intensity.

"Huh?" the PC said when he realised he was the centre of attention.

"Moore, Greer?" asked Kett.

"More what?"

"The camper," said Kett.

"What camper?"

"Jesus Christ, Duke, the Renault, Anna Greer, Jaye Moore. Did anyone else use the van?"

It took a moment more before the light came on.

"No, sir," he said.

"That leaves us at a complete dead end," said Clare. "We—"

"Oh, they did say it had been broken into, sir," said Duke. "A couple of months ago."

"And you're only mentioning this now because..." said Clare, furious.

"Didn't seem relevant, sir," said Duke with a shrug. "They said nothing was taken."

"Where is the van?" said Kett.

"Yard just outside of Aylsham," said Clare. "Forensics didn't say anything about a break-in. Van was intact."

"Might be worth another look," said Kett. "The killer used the plates from William Briggs' car on the first lorry, and he was the second victim. They're using them to make a point, and I don't see why this is any different."

"You're assuming our suspect is planning to kill again," said Clare. The Super's phone was ringing, and he pulled it out of his pocket, jabbing a finger on the screen like he was trying to crush a poisonous spider. "What the toss do you want?"

"You think he's going to kill again, sir?" asked Savage as Clare ranted into his phone.

Kett didn't have time to answer before Clare practically jumped off his chair, slamming his phone on the desk.

"That was the fire service," he said. "There's another tossing lorry on fire."

Kett looked at Savage with a sigh.

"I guess that's a yes," he said.

CHAPTER TWENTY-TWO

THEY RODE OUT IN CONVOY, HEADING SOUTHEAST INTO the morning sun. Savage drove the IRV, Clare in the front seat and Kett sandwiched between Porter and Duke in the back, feeling like he was being crushed to death every time they turned a corner.

Luckily, it was only a short drive, the car peeling through a narrow stretch of countryside before coming to a halt behind the first of two fire engines blocking the narrow road. Kett had been expecting to find himself by a field again, somewhere in the middle of nowhere. Instead, he saw a street lined with houses. On the left was what looked like an abandoned garden centre, and behind the tall wall and the crumbling reception building, rose an enormous pillar of smoke, thick enough to blot out the sun. He could hear the shouts of the firefighters over the roar of the inferno.

Duke was out first, Kett tumbling after him, doing everything he could to expand his compressed lungs. He jogged towards the open gate, only to be intercepted by a firefighter who was running over from his engine.

"Oi, mate, not a chance," the man yelled, waving him back. "It's too dangerous."

The guy was bigger than Duke, and Kett wasn't in any shape to argue with him. He stopped running. Clare walked up to his side.

"You know who I am?" the Superintendent asked the firefighter.

"I know you're not fireproof," he replied. "So until it's out, stay here."

The man walked off, Clare shooting daggers into his back.

"I *am* fireproof," he muttered. "Kett, see if you can get around the side. I want to know what we're dealing with."

"Sir," said Kett, more than a little uncertain.

He doubled back along the wall, reaching the corner of the plot where the yard met the neighbouring houses. A narrow, weed-strewn alleyway separated them, and it was already full of goggle-eyed people who were watching the fire.

"Police," Kett yelled as he forced his way past them. "Move."

The brick wall continued for another dozen yards before a drooping chain-link fence took over. Through it, a stone's throw away, sat the lorry. It was drowning in flames too bright to look at. Smoke poured off it as thick as ink. The heat was incredible, like standing next to a furnace.

There was no mistaking how similar the vehicle was to the two they'd found already.

"Fuck me," said Porter as the DI caught up to him, one hand shielding his eyes. Savage and Duke were right behind him, both coughing as tendrils of smoke curled through the fence.

The firefighters had their hoses on, the sky full of rainbows, but it wasn't having much effect. The conflagration was so intense that it was spreading along the dirt in the yard, stretching its fingers towards rows of parked cars on the far side. If they didn't manage to get it out, there was a chance the entire street could go up in flames.

"Same lorry, isn't it, sir?" said Savage. "I can see the DAF logo at the front."

"Got to be our killer," said Porter.

"We don't know that," said Kett.

He stared down the alley, seeing a street at the far end of it.

"Kate, stay here and see if you can get any information out of the firefighters," he said. "Duke, Porter, with me."

He set off up the alleyway, making it a dozen or so steps before an explosion rocked the abandoned garden centre. The firefighters scrambled back from the spreading flames, people scurrying out of the alleyway as the smoke churned towards them. Kett left them to it, reaching the end of the track a few seconds later and running onto the street.

It was busier here, maybe twenty people watching the fire from the safety of the garden centre's back fence. On the other side of the road sat a sprawling nursing home, the windows full of frightened faces. More people were gathered on the street, including a posse of builders in fluorescent jackets.

"What are we looking for, sir?" asked Duke.

"Anything," said Kett as they walked along the fence. "Just look."

They had to be fifty yards away from the lorry here, with scattered outbuildings in between them, but Kett could still feel the heat of it. He pushed through the crowd, most of whom were wearing pale scrubs with the name of the nursing home on them. There were a handful of teenagers too, and a mother with a baby in her pram.

"Stay back," he told them. "The whole thing might blow."

Nobody seemed to be listening, their eyes full of fire as they watched the lorry burn. There was no sign of anybody in the garden centre other than the firefighters, and the gate on this side was chained and padlocked.

Kett turned his attention to the far side of the road. Elderly folk were emerging from the home like the walking dead, some in wheelchairs, others using Zimmer frames. The staff were doing their best to lure them back, but they seemed to have sensed a chance at freedom. They spilled onto the road, mingling with the builders.

At least, Kett thought they were builders. Four of them definitely were, their combat trousers and boots splashed with mud from a housing development that was springing up next to the care home. A fifth was dressed in jeans and trainers and was wearing a yellow safety vest over his black hoodie. His hood was pulled up, his face wreathed in shadow. He stood apart from the others by a good ten yards, his fists clenched, his body tense enough to set Kett's Spidey-sense tingling.

He turned away before the man could see that he was watching him, trying to alert Porter. The DI was a few paces ahead, his attention still on the fire. Duke was behind them, one hand on his Taser as he surveyed the crowd.

"Pete," hissed Kett.

Porter turned around, waiting for Kett to catch up.

"Across the street, yellow vest, black hoodie, you see him?"

Porter stared, a little too obviously.

"That guy?" he said, nodding.

"Yeah, don't scare him off."

Porter looked at his feet, then subtly back again.

"You think it's him, sir?" he said.

"Not sure," said Kett. "Just getting a vibe from him."

"He's in his trainers," said Porter. "Can't be working."

"You seen something?" said Duke, leaning in to form a huddle.

"Guy over there in the yellow vest," said Porter.

Duke was even more obvious than Porter had been, actually shielding his eyes with his hand even though the sun was behind him.

"Christ, Aaron, you ever heard of the word subtle?" said Kett.

"Sorry, sir," Duke said. "The guy who's standing on his own? I think he saw me."

Kett looked back—they all looked back—in time to see the man staggering away. Even inside the shadow of his hood, Kett saw the panic on his face.

"Oi!" he yelled. "Stop there. Police."

Kett's shout sent the man running, his trainers slipping on the gritty street before finding purchase. He barrelled towards the building site, the wind blowing the hood off his head to reveal a nest of sandy hair.

"Go!" Kett yelled.

Duke was already moving, chuffing hard as he sprinted down the street. Porter was close behind, both of them yelling as they closed in on the guy. It took a little longer for Kett to get his body moving, every joint resisting. By the time he'd reached a run, Duke had caught up to the man and pinned him against the fence of the care home.

"I didn't do it," the guy was yelling. "I didn't do anything!"

"Then why are you running?" Kett said, stepping up to him.

The man was shorter than him by a few inches, and dwarfed by Duke. He'd broken into a sweat, despite the chill of the day, and his watery blue eyes held no hint of violence. He lifted his hands in front of him in surrender.

"Because you were all looking at me," he said.

"What are you doing here?"

The man nodded to a blue Amazon Prime van parked a little way down the street.

"Delivering parcels," he said.

"Fuck," Kett said beneath his breath.

He turned to the crowd, seeing an ancient woman in a wheelchair crossing the street. A man wearing a care home tunic peeled away from the fence to help her. Other people were drifting away, the poisoned air too much for them as the smoke continued to pour from the burning lorry, carried this way by the wind. The teenagers laughed as they retreated, the woman with the baby crossing the street and using a hand to waft away the smoke. Even the builders had grown bored, two of them smoking, the other two staring at their phones.

"Can you round them all up, Pete?" said Kett. "Get some statements out of them. Somebody must have seen how the fire started."

Porter nodded, heading towards the teenagers. Duke still had his hand on the man's chest.

"You can let him go now, Aaron," he said. "He's—"

He stopped, aware of a shout that was coming from the direction of the care home.

"Help!"

It was the woman in the wheelchair, he saw. She had almost reached the driveway, pushed by the member of staff in scrubs. She seemed upset at the fact she was being taken home. She kept craning back to look behind her, her hands grasping at the arms of her wheelchair.

"Stop, please!"

"She really wants to escape," said Duke. "Can't say I blame her."

"Stop," she said. "Help, I don't know you. I don't know you."

It was the cry of somebody who'd lost track of reality, a patient with dementia, and Kett would have ignored it if the man pushing her wheelchair hadn't glanced around and looked at him. He was in his early thirties, handsome, his dark hair cut short, his beard neatly trimmed. He was tall, the muscles of his back clearly defined through the fabric of the care home tunic, tattoos peeking from both sleeves. Just an average guy doing a difficult job.

But his eyes gave him away.

Kett met them, just for a second, but long enough to see the knowledge written into that dark stare. The *challenge.*

"Help!" the woman cried, struggling in her wheelchair. "Please! I don't know you."

"Hey," said Kett.

He started walking towards the man, pointing a finger at him.

"Stop, now."

The guy smiled. He angled the wheelchair around and gave the woman a hefty shove, sending her careening down the street towards Kett.

Then he was off, tearing into the driveway of the care home and vanishing behind the fence.

"Fuck," said Kett, a charge of adrenaline detonating inside him. "That's him!"

He began to sprint, stopping for long enough to catch

the runaway wheelchair before it could hit the kerb. Several of the other care home staff were piling towards the woman and he left her to them, reaching the driveway in a matter of seconds.

The man had vanished, the front door of the care home wide open.

"Fuck," he said again. "Porter, round the back. Duke, with me."

Porter cut left, heading across the front lawn towards the side of the building. Duke trod on Kett's shadow as they crunched down the gravel drive, calling for backup on his radio.

Kett reached the door, peering cautiously through it before entering a small lobby. It was deserted, but the door on the other side was still swinging closed.

Kett wrenched it open, the corridor beyond empty. The hammer of footsteps echoed back. He set off, passing a dining room full of elderly people and shocked staff.

"You see a guy run past here?" he called to them. "Dark hair, beard?"

Every single person in the room pointed—all in different directions.

Kett ignored them, running along the corridor to the door at the end just as a scream spilled through it. He opened the door to find a much larger space, half a dozen old people sitting in the sofas and two more playing pool. A woman in pink scrubs lay on her back on the far side of the room, the door beside her open.

"Hey!" Kett yelled, crossing the room as quickly as he could. The woman was halfway up by the time he reached her.

"Where'd he go?" he asked.

She was too shocked to reply, but the answer was obvious. Kett walked through the door into another corridor, Duke right beside him. The PC had his Taser out, his face deadly serious. Ahead, Kett heard another shout, the clatter of something metallic. Duke took the lead, running through the open door.

"Careful," Kett called after him.

Beyond the corridor was a kitchen, three men in chef's whites standing beside the right-hand wall. Saucepans lay on the floor, a lid still rolling. There were three other doors in the room, all of them closed.

"Where did he go?" Kett asked them.

"That way," said one of the men, pointing at a door bearing a green fire escape sign. "He grabbed a knife."

"Shit," said Kett, pulling out his phone and calling Porter's number. He crossed the cramped kitchen to the door, Duke behind him now. Beyond was yet another corridor, a door in both walls and a third at the end. This one was open, the back garden of the care home visible beyond.

Porter wasn't answering.

Kett ended the call and tried again.

"Pete?" he shouted, jogging down the corridor and hoping his voice would carry. "He's armed!"

He slowed down as he reached the open back door, letting Duke take the lead again. The PC edged through, angling his Taser left, then right.

"No sign of him, sir," he said. "Hang on..."

Footsteps. Somebody pelting this way. Duke stepped out of the door and Kett followed, seeing an enormous, empty garden. To the left was a fenced area containing several bins. Whoever was running was coming from that direction.

"Police!" yelled Kett. "Stop where you are!"

Somebody burst out from behind the fence, lunging at

them. Duke jumped back, discharging his Taser. The barbs went well wide—which was fortunate, because it was Porter who clattered to a halt, his cheeks red, his eyes bulging.

"Jesus Christ, Duke!" he yelled. "You almost bloody shot me!"

Kett swore, scanning the garden for a second before doubling back into the care home. He wrenched open the door to his right to find a cupboard stacked with toilet paper, then tried the one opposite to see yet another corridor that led along the back of the building.

"This way," he yelled, not waiting for a reply.

He reached the far door in seconds, the warren of the care home continuing beyond. The place was a maze, three more doors here. The first was locked, and when he tried the second he found himself inside a small toilet block with three empty stalls.

The window over the sinks was wide open, the chill of the day cutting through.

Kett used the sink to climb onto the window ledge, craning out of it to see a path sheltered between the main building and an annexe. If the man had escaped this way, he was long gone.

"Fuck," he said again.

He climbed through, sat on the ledge, and dropped to the path, the pain jarring up his legs as he landed. He listened past the roar of his pulse, but there were no more shouts of alarm, no more footsteps.

"You see him, sir?" asked Porter, who was leaning through the window overhead.

"No," said Kett, the dread leeching the warmth from his body.

"What do you want us to do?"

"Double back, make sure he isn't still in the building," said Kett.

Porter vanished. Kett made his way down the path, stopping at a locked gate. He grabbed the top and tried to hoist himself up, but his boots couldn't get purchase on the smooth metal. Dropping down, he ran back the way he'd come, only to find himself in the garden again. Two uniformed constables were running past the bins, and both of them met him with a shrug.

"Fuck!" Kett roared. "He's not here, get back around the front. Find him!"

But they were too late, he knew.

The killer was gone.

CHAPTER TWENTY-THREE

It took an hour to search the care home and its sprawling collection of outbuildings, and by the time Kett walked out of the front door, the inferno across the road had finally been put out.

But that wasn't the only fire that had been started here.

Kett felt the heat of it in his cheeks, the embarrassment of having had the killer in his sights, only to let him slip through his fingers. Despite the cold, he felt his body burn with shame.

"Nothing, sir," said Porter as he stepped outside. "He's well and truly fucked off."

Kett's phone rang inside his pocket, but he ignored it. He knew who was calling, and he had no desire to receive the bollocking that would come his way. Savage appeared from behind the fence, out of breath.

"I've searched every garden on the street, sir, and the building site. He's not there. You're sure it was our guy?"

Kett chewed on it for a moment, seeing the way the man had looked at him when he'd wheeled the woman back towards the home, seeing the dare in his expression.

Catch me if you can.

"It's him," he said. "None of the care home staff know who he is; he doesn't work here. He stole the uniform so that he could stand and watch the lorry burn without anyone noticing him."

He thought of those eyes again, the way the man had smiled.

"I think he wanted to be close to us when we arrived. I think he was getting off on it."

"He thinks he's smarter than us, sir," said Savage. "He's playing a game. That's why he switched the plates on the lorries. He's leaving us clues. He wants us to get close."

"Why?" asked Porter. "What kind of prick commits a crime only to lead the police right to him?"

"Classic psychopath, sir," said Savage. "Doesn't believe anyone is clever enough to catch him, but his ego is too inflated for him to remain anonymous. He wants the world to see him, to know what he's capable of."

"He should be in cuffs," said Kett. "We were too slow."

"Speak for yourself, sir," said Porter. "I'd have had him if Duke hadn't shot me."

"I didn't shoot you, sir," said Duke as he ducked out of the door.

"You came very bloody close."

"Yeah, and then I deliberately missed when I saw that it was you," said Duke. "That takes a lot of skill."

"You had your eyes closed, Aaron," said Porter. "I saw you. You missed because you're a shit shot."

"I missed on *purpose*, sir," said Duke.

"You couldn't shoot a porpoise, mate, if it was two feet in front of—"

"Enough," said Kett, hearing his phone again. "We all

messed up. I messed up. I should have caught him. Getting too old for this."

He resigned himself to the fact he was going to have to answer his phone, pulling it out of his pocket. Sure enough, the Superintendent's name was on the screen. Even the letters looked angry.

"We're going to have to explain this to the boss," he said. "Pete, can you do it?"

He answered the call and passed the phone to Porter, who looked at him in horror before passing the phone to Duke. The big PC almost dropped it like it was a hot potato, but Kett didn't wait to see what happened next. He checked for traffic and jogged across the road, Savage and Porter alongside him. He'd just reached the opposite kerb when a uniformed officer appeared from the alleyway beside the derelict garden centre and hailed him with a raised hand.

"Smokies want to talk with you, sir," she said. "They're out the front."

"Thanks," Kett told her, following the alleyway. He could see the lorry through the fence, nothing but a hulk of charred and twisted metal. The hose was still running, the ground around the wreck a swamp of blackened sludge.

"This feels different, sir," said Savage.

"How so?"

"The last two lorries had their tanks emptied. There was hardly any fuel. The fire was designed to scare, not to kill. But this thing went up like a bonfire."

"Why?" said Porter.

"Maybe he didn't have time to drain it, sir," Savage said as they walked out onto the road. "This isn't a field, it's a garden centre on a residential street. Those houses are close enough for people to see the yard. And it's daytime, not the middle of the night."

"He's getting careless," said Kett. "It's like you said, Kate, he thinks he's smarter than us. He thinks we're too stupid to catch him."

He sighed.

"And as of this moment in time, he's right."

He walked past the crumbling brick reception office and through the open gate, the garden centre's large, empty yard opening up in front of him. The firefighters had formed a semi-circle a safe distance from the ruined lorry, two braced against the force of the hose.

"It's safe?" Kett called out as he approached them.

"It's out," said the same man who had warned him before, his voice muffled by his mask. "But I wouldn't get too close."

"You have any idea how it started?"

"Arson, for sure," the man replied. "Looks like somebody lit up a barrel under the petrol tank. Would have gone up in a couple of minutes."

"Fuel tank was full?" Kett asked.

"Probably a quarter of a tank," said the man. "Full one would have blown the whole street to kingdom come."

Kett nodded, taking a deep, smoke-filled breath before asking the next question.

"Do you know if there was anyone inside?"

The firefighter didn't answer, his expression etched with worry beneath the sheen of his visor.

"I don't," he said after a moment. "Heard about the other lorries, though, crossed my mind that there might be somebody in there. If there was, they're dead. Heat would have killed them in no time, long before we got here."

He shrugged.

"Sorry."

"Can you get it open?" Kett asked him.

He didn't look like he wanted to, but he nodded. He called to another firefighter, who ran back onto the street, returning a few seconds later with a crowbar in one hand and a set of bolt cutters in the other. The first guy took the crowbar, and they approached the lorry with caution. The hose shut down before they got there, plunging the yard into an uneasy silence.

There were no plates on the back of the lorry, Kett saw, not even burnt ones.

"Still a chance this might not be him," said Porter.

"It's him," Kett replied.

The doors were secured with a padlock, and the firefighter with the bolt cutters snipped it free. The other man jammed the crowbar into the crack between the doors and leaned hard. The fire-damaged lorry didn't have any fight left in it, the right-hand door squealing open and then dropping clean off its hinges. The firefighters danced away as it clattered to the ground, a wave of soot and smoke rolling out.

All eyes turned to the oil-black interior of the lorry.

And to the twisted sculpture of charred flesh that sat in the middle of it.

"It's him," Kett said again, running a hand over his face.

The firefighters looked back, as if expecting him to tell them what to do. Kett walked towards them, every footstep deafening in the silence of the yard. The closer he got to the lorry, the less he wanted to be there. It was the smell, the acrid, chemical stench of the smoke mixed with something so much worse—something like overdone barbeque. He had to stop a dozen yards from the wreck or risk his stomach unfolding.

But that was close enough.

He put his hand to his face again, clamping it over his mouth even though he couldn't think of a single word to say.

There wasn't just one body in the lorry, there were two. They were slumped against the right-hand wall, locked in what might have been an embrace. It was almost impossible to tell that they had once been human, nothing left of their faces but the crude angle of a nose, the greasy yellow memory of teeth. Every inch of skin had been rendered black, cloth burned away, plastic melted into flesh. The only recognisable thing in the entire harrowing display was a single shoe on the foot of the corpse on the left: a trainer, the Adidas logo still visible. Kett had no idea how it had survived.

"Oh God," said Savage. She walked to his side, close enough for their arms to touch, and he felt the weight of her as she leaned into him.

"What were they doing?" asked Porter from his other side. "Hugging?"

Kett thought so too, until he took another couple of steps forward and looked closer. The corpse with the trainer had pinned the other body against the wall, one arm looped around its neck, the other resting against its stomach. There was something clutched in its fingers, something black that had fused itself between the ribs of the second victim.

"Knife?" he said.

"Looks like it, sir," Savage answered. "They were fighting. He gave them the same rules. One person dies, or you both burn."

"But they didn't have time," said Kett. "The lorry went up too quickly."

The truth of it was right there in the contorted bodies, in the angle of their limbs, in the hollows of their melted faces where their mouths had been open, in one final, airless scream. Kett had to close his eyes, he had to turn away, but it only made it worse because he saw it play out against the black canvas of his mind—the violence, the fear, the rising heat.

The unfathomable, unthinkable horror of it.

And they'd almost had him.

"Nobody goes any closer," he said, opening his eyes and walking away. "Not until forensics have been."

By the time he'd reached the half-moon of firefighters, Duke had appeared. His face had paled, although Kett thought it had more to do with the phone in his hand than the bodies in the back of the lorry.

"He really wants to talk to you, sir," Duke said, holding the mobile out.

Kett puffed out a sigh as he took it, using the call as an excuse to head away from the crime scene and back onto the street.

"Sir," he said.

"Zipper, if I'd wanted to talk to a testicle-faced gremlin, then I'd have called one," he said. "Can you tell me why Duke is answering your phone?"

"I was busy, sir, sorry."

"You lost our suspect?" Clare said. "You had him, and you lost him. Is this correct?"

There was no way of sugar-coating it, so Kett didn't even try.

"And he's killed again?" Clare asked, his anger audible as a tremor in his voice.

"Twice," said Kett. "There are two bodies in the lorry. Looks like they were fighting, but the fire got them first."

"And he stayed to watch?"

"Yeah," said Kett. "He stole a uniform from the care

home opposite, was mingling with the crowd. It was a sheer fluke we spotted him at all."

"You remember what he looks like?" said Clare.

His face was right there, burned into Kett's retinas.

"Yes, sir."

"Then I need you back here for the sketch artist. Now."

"On my way, sir," he said. "I'll leave the rest of the team here."

"Negative, Zippy," said Clare. "We've got a lead on these new victims. The campervan whose plates were on the last lorry was in storage, but it was still being used. Uniforms found evidence of somebody living inside it."

"Really, sir? Who?"

"That's what I need one of your team to find out," Clare said. "Send Porter, or Savage. Anyone except for Duke, because that hedgehog's turd missed this the first time around."

The Super took a breath that rattled the line, his voice softening.

"There's a chance that whoever was squatting in the van is the same person who's in the back of the lorry."

CHAPTER TWENTY-FOUR

Savage was more than happy to be given the chance to escape the crime scene. She commandeered an IRV, fleeing the garden centre like it was still on fire. Only when she was a couple of miles away from the lorry—and the bodies inside it—did she force herself to slow down, taking deep, calming breaths until her pulse had settled.

The peace was almost worse than the panic, though, because images crowded into the void of her thoughts, a song of blood and fire and death that lasted the entire thirty-minute journey to the outskirts of Aylsham. When she pulled the car up outside the address that Clare had texted her, she felt utterly exhausted.

But this was the job. She couldn't stop now.

She got out, slamming the door and shivering in the sudden cold. It was welcome, though, clearing her head as she walked up to the front gate of an industrial lot to the north of the town. The sign told her that it was a self-storage facility called Baron's, although the fact that half the sign had fallen also told her that the place was severely neglected. There was an intercom on the mesh gate, but when she reached out to press the button, she saw that the wires had been cut. It wasn't needed, anyway, because a gentle nudge sent the gate wobbling inwards.

"Hello?" Savage called as she made her way inside.

To the left was a warehouse, *Barons* written over the shuttered door. She wondered if the apostrophe had been put into storage. The rest of the land was taken up by an open lot where around twenty cars sat in neat rows, all of them looking like they'd seen better days. There were four campers here, but only one that had once been a Renault van.

She walked towards it, making it halfway before she heard a door open behind her. Turning, she spotted a young man beetling across the yard from the direction of the warehouse, slinging on a bright purple windcheater as he went. He was holding his lunch in his hand, the contents of his sandwich falling as he ran, leaving a Hansel and Gretel trail of lettuce, cheese and tomato.

"No," he said. "No, no, you can't be here."

Savage pulled her warrant card out of her pocket, offering it to him as he puffed his way over. She wasn't sure if the expression on his face was shock or relief. He couldn't have been older than sixteen, wisps of bumfluff battling it out with the acne on his face. He kept shaking his head like he was trying to shoo away a fly, and she wondered if he had a tic.

"Again?" he said.

"Again," she told him, putting the warrant card away. "I know you've already spoken to a couple of my colleagues, but I was hoping I could ask you a couple of questions about the camper over there. The Renault."

The kid winced, twisting his hands together, his head still twitching.

"I've already told you everything I know," he said. "I'm sorry."

"Can you go over it again for me, Mr..."

"Josh," said the kid. "Not Mr Josh, I mean just Josh."

"Take your time, Josh. You've got the key?"

He scratched at the angry spots on his face, then shook his head.

"Don't need one. Lock's jammed, has been since it got here. Nobody ever comes here though unless they're storing stuff, so don't matter. Place is pretty secure."

"I didn't have any trouble getting in," said Savage. "Gate wasn't locked, buzzer is broken, and if I'm not mistaken you're missing a whole chunk of fence over there."

She wasn't mistaken. The entire panel had been removed, the street beyond visible. They both watched a man walk past with a snorting pug. Josh cleared his throat nervously. His head twitched a little more. Definitely a tic.

"We're going to fix that," he croaked.

"Security cameras?" Savage asked, not seeing any.

"Overrated," said the boy. "And the people who store stuff here don't always want to be watched, if you know what I mean."

He tapped the side of his greasy nose, and Savage shook her head.

"Nope, don't know what you mean," she said. "Are you saying there are illegal things here?"

"Uh..." Josh went so pale Savage could almost see through him. His tic was so pronounced it looked like he was nodding. "No?"

"You run this place, Josh?" asked Savage. "How old are you?"

"Twenty-two," he said, surprising her. "Dad owns it."

"Where is he?"

"Asleep. He works the night shift."

"Well, I won't mention the illegal stuff if you start talking about the camper," said Savage. She started walking, Josh shuffling along behind her, making a series of odd gulping noises. "When did it get here?"

"Two years ago," he said. "I already told your friends earlier. It belongs to a woman in the town. She didn't want to pay to tax it and didn't want to sell it. Let her girlfriend or something drive it for a while, but then she didn't want to neither, so she dropped it off here. Pays us a hundred quid a month to keep it safe."

"But you're not keeping it safe," said Savage. "It was broken into, wasn't it?"

She reached the camper, realising for the first time what a sorry state it was in. Three of the four wheels were completely flat, the hubcaps missing. The passenger side front door was open, the frame buckled, and a crack ran the full width of the windscreen diagonally. The windows were caked with filth, mouldering net curtains concealing the interior. There were no registration plates, of course.

"It *was*," said Josh. "But they didn't take anything. I don't even know how they got in."

Savage nodded at the broken fence panel again.

"I'm guessing through there. They didn't take anything?"

"Wasn't anything to take," he said. "Just a van full of somebody's rubbish."

"They didn't take the plates?"

"Uh..."

Savage grabbed the door and pulled, although the vehicle seemed reluctant to let her in. She put her back into it, the squeal of the door as it finally surrendered enough to chase a small army of birds from the roof of the storage facility.

"You don't have to look in there," said Josh, twitching madly. "Do you?"

"Is it a problem?" she asked.

"No, I mean of course not, but..."

He didn't seem to know what to do with himself, jiggling on the spot like he was desperate for the toilet.

"You hiding something in here, Josh?" Savage asked, and his eyes grew so wide they looked like they were going to roll out of their sockets. "Is it anything dangerous?"

"No," he said. "I'm not... I wouldn't..."

Savage left him to his wittering and climbed into the van. It wasn't as bad in here as she'd been expecting, although the damp had made its home in the fabric of the chairs and in the carpet. She breathed through her mouth as she stepped around the passenger seat and into the back of the van.

The weak yellow light that filtered through the windows revealed a pine cabin bed with a sofa beneath it, a driftwood coffee table, a pull-down desk with a single chair, and a kitchenette in the far corner. Orange wallpaper peeled from the panels, a couple of velvet lampshades hanging from the ceiling. It was actually pretty nice.

"When was the break-in?" Savage asked.

"What?" Josh replied from outside.

"The break-in," she yelled. "When was it?"

"Just before Christmas," he called back.

Savage used the toe of her boot to root through the piles of detritus on the van floor—clothes and books and empty cigarette packets. She checked the sofa and hoisted herself up the ladder to look at the bed. The sheets were rumpled, but they seemed fresh.

Dropping back down, she walked to the desk and unhooked it from the wall, lowering it onto a folding leg. A stack of papers had been tucked into a pocket on the tabletop and she rifled through them. The handwritten notes were neat enough, but the writing was so small she could barely read it in the gloom of the van.

She wriggled the bolt on the back doors and opened them, dropping into the day. Out here, it didn't take long for her to find a note with a date on it.

"Josh," she said, walking around the side of the van. "Are you sure it was a break-in?"

"Yeah," he said, squirming. "Why?"

"Because it looks like somebody was living in this van, and pretty recently too."

The boy's mouth opened like he'd been accused of wearing his grandmother's underwear.

"No!" he breathed, possibly the most unconvincing denial in the history of the human race. "That's... that's so not... Absolutely not."

"Right," said Savage. "You knew?"

"I did not know a thing," he replied slowly.

"I'll make you a deal," said Savage. "You tell me who it was, and I won't mention any of the illegal stuff, okay?"

"There's no illegal—"

"And I won't tell your dad you said anything," Savage finished.

"Deal," said Josh. "You promise?"

"On my life," she said. "Is somebody living here?"

Josh glanced over his shoulder, then nodded.

"Who?"

"Just a mate," he said. "From the town."

"He have a name?"

"Gregg," said Josh. "Two Gs at the end, like the sausage rolls."

"Surname?"

Josh frowned.

"I want to say Peachy?" he said. "Peachman? Pearson? It's something like that. I don't even know him that well, just from the pub. He was kicked out his house last year, didn't have anywhere to go. I told him he could stay in the van for a few notes a week."

"Why didn't you mention this to the police?" Savage asked.

"Didn't want Dad to find out I was earning on the side. Gregg said he'd never come out at night, he'd lock himself up. Dad's plastered most of the time anyway, sleeps in the office. But he'd've wanted a slice of it if he knew."

He shrugged his bony shoulders.

"Not against the law, is it? Offering a man a place to stay."

"No," said Savage. "But not answering a police officer's questions to the fullest of your ability *is* against the law, Josh. And you keeping your mouth shut might have cost somebody their life."

Josh reeled back, the bonnet of the next car over stopping him from falling.

"I didn't..." he said, struggling.

"I know you didn't," said Savage. "How old is Gregg?"

"Never asked. Bit grey. He's big, too. Like, chunky big."

"When did you last see him?"

"Like, a couple of days ago," said Josh. "I bring him food sometimes. I took him some lunch because Dad was working the weekend shift and Gregg couldn't get out."

"Sunday?"

"Yeah. Took him a Gregg's. Gregg's for Gregg. So many Greggs."

He frowned like he'd malfunctioned.

"Greggs," he said a final time.

"Does he normally leave the van?" Savage asked.

"He goes up the pub in the afternoon, usually. He's got a boyfriend too, in the town."

Savage's pulse quickened.

"What's his name?"

"Gregg."

"The boyfriend's name is Gregg?"

"Oh, no, sorry. Thought you meant Gregg. Don't know the other fella's name, sorry. He's in the pub most days n'all, though. Younger."

"Can you tell me anything else about them?" Savage said. "And this is important, Josh. This could save a life."

He stared up at the cold sky like he was watching a plane fly by, the tics making his body jerk. It seemed to take him an age before he remembered to speak.

"No."

"Nothing at all?"

"He's nice," said Josh. "Nice lad. I don't care that he's gay or nuffink, he always treats me with respect, pays on time, never causes any fuss."

He seemed to cotton onto the point of the conversation for the first time.

"He alright?"

Savage thought of the lorry she'd just left behind, the two bodies locked in an embrace in the back, a sculpture of flesh made permanent by the fire.

She didn't answer.

"Last question, Josh," she said instead. "You happen to see who took the van's plates?"

He didn't have a clue, that was clear as day. She handed him a card.

"If you think of anything else, you call me," she said. "I mean it, Josh. If I find out you've been hiding something from me, then we're going to come down on this place like a bomb."

He looked back at the little office with a sigh.

"Maybe that wouldn't be such a bad thing," he said quietly. "I'll let you out."

"No need," Savage told him, heading across the yard. "Fence is wide open."

CHAPTER TWENTY-FIVE

Kett sat in the Incident Room back at HQ, so tired that he was tempted to lie on the floor and take a power nap. Unfortunately, he wasn't alone.

Sitting across the table from him was Clara Clare, one of the sketch artists they used to turn the vague memories of victims and witnesses into something that might actually be used to identify a criminal. Clara also happened to be the oldest child of the Superintendent, and was currently doing a Fine Arts degree at the university in the city. Right now, she seemed like she was seriously considering a change in career.

And possibly a change in parent, too.

For the last half an hour, Kett had been searching the adrenaline-stripped mess of his thoughts in an effort to describe the man who'd run away from him at the care home. By the look on Superintendent Clare's face, as he loomed over his unfortunate daughter, he wasn't doing a very good job.

"That's not what a person looks like, Clara," Clare went on. "Those eyes are far too close together."

"Robbie said they were close together," Clara replied, leaning back in her chair and scooping her wavy hair behind her ear. "That's what you told me, that the eyes seemed close together."

"They were," said Kett. "I *think*. I only saw him once, and only for a second."

"Because you were too bloody slow to keep up with him!" roared Clare. "What's that thing supposed to be around his mouth?"

"The beard?" asked Clara.

"That's a beard?"

"It's *obviously* a beard, sir," said Kett. "Maybe the eyes weren't that close together, Clara, sorry. But you've got the shape of his head right."

"His head was shaped like a turnip?" said Clare.

Clara was on the verge of tears.

"Sir, give her a break," said Kett, and Clare harumphed. "Try the eyes again. You've almost got them. A little wider, but the intensity is there."

Clara had got that spot on, the expression on the man's face that said: 'What are you going to do about it?' She used a rubber to scrub out the eyes, setting to work again while the Super breathed down her collar like a constipated walrus.

"Two eyes," said the Super.

"What?" Clara replied.

"He had two eyes."

"She knows that, sir," said Kett. "She can only draw one at a time."

Clare grumbled beneath his breath.

"He was good looking," said Kett. "Striking. It's a face that would draw attention."

"Like mine," said Clare, with apparently no sense of irony.

"I mean, your face *does* draw attention, sir," said Kett. He lowered his voice to a whisper. "For all the wrong reasons."

Clara laughed as she sketched in the eyebrows.

"This is pointless!" Clare said, clicking his fingers. "Give me some of that paper."

He didn't wait for anyone to respond, snatching a notepad and one of his daughter's pencils before crashing down onto a chair at the next desk over. He clenched the pencil in his fist like it was a knife, scrawling onto the paper with some force.

"It'll keep him busy," Kett said to Clara. "The man's hair was groomed, looked like he'd had it cut recently. Very dark."

Sophie continued to draw, making fine sweeps of her pencil. Slowly, the face on the page came to life.

"How's the nose?" she asked.

"It was bigger, and it had a bump."

"Like it was broken?"

Kett shook his head.

"I don't think so. Like I said, he was handsome, a kind of Leonardo DiCaprio look about him, but with darker hair."

She added some final details, then spun the paper to face him. The portrait was almost perfect, real enough to make Kett's skin crawl. Beneath the man's beard flashed an unkind smile, and the glint in his eye made it look like he was about to leap out of the paper and start running again.

"That's amazing," said Kett.

"And this?" said Clare, reaching over and slapping his own drawing onto the table. "I had quite a flair for art in sixth form."

"You wouldn't know it, sir," said Kett. "This looks like a Picasso. Why's one ear so much higher than the other? And what's his nose doing all the way over there?"

To be fair, Clare hadn't done a bad job in the time he'd had, but it paled in comparison to his daughter's effort, and it didn't look a thing like their killer.

"You've kind of caught him, sir," said Kett. "This looks like our guy, if he'd been put through a car crusher."

"Kind of looks like a chimpanzee with diarrhoea, Dad," said Clara, who was enjoying her revenge. "Why's he got that expression on his face?"

Clare snatched his illustration back and scrunched it into a ball, hurling it across the room.

"That's him?" he asked, nodding to Clara's work.

"That's him," said Kett.

"I'll get it out to the papers. Somebody will know who he is."

Clare took Clara's drawing and lurched out of the room, slamming the door so hard Kett felt the tremor of it run up his legs.

"He's so angry at the moment," she said. "Do you know why?"

"Uh... no," said Kett, assuming Clara wouldn't want to know the truth about her mother's celibacy streak. "Thanks so much for this."

"Any time," she said. "This isn't anything to do with the bodies in the lorries, is it? I saw it on the news. It's awful."

Kett didn't know how to answer, heading out of the room instead. He made his way back to his desk, surprised to find a steaming cup of tea waiting for him there. He looked around the bullpen, but the only other person in sight was Spalding. She glanced up from where she was photocopying something and caught him looking.

"What, sir?"

"Did you make me this, Alison?"

"Uh..."

"Thanks," he said, a genuine smile on his face. "That's the first time you've made me a cuppa in the three years I've known you."

She didn't reply, turning back to the photocopier with a frown on her face.

He sat down, cradling the cup in both hands to soak up some of its warmth. The joy of it lasted the few seconds it took him to have a sip, and quickly wore off. The tea wasn't quite as bad as Porter's—nobody could reach those awful depths—but it was close. There was sugar in it too.

"I don't take sugar, Alison," he said.

She was still glowering at him.

He held his hands to the radiator to warm them up, noticing a handful of things on his desk that definitely hadn't been there yesterday—including a hole punch and a stapler that both had 'Spalding' written on them in black Sharpie. Some of her case files were here as well, tucked beneath his computer.

"Are you missing these, Alison?" he asked.

He missed her reply because his phone started ringing.

"Pete," he said when he answered it. "How's it going?"

"Not good, sir," said Porter. "Franklin's just shown up. She's confirmed there are two bodies in the lorry. She thinks they were both men, and she's fairly sure they were fighting. One's holding a knife, and there's an axe head on the floor by the other guy, handle's burned away."

"Nasty," said Kett.

"She's waiting for Hay to get here before she gets any closer. The rest of the lorry's too messed up. Got something, though."

"What?" said Kett, working down a sip of disgustingly sweet tea.

"Duke's been interviewing the care home staff. You know our suspect ran through the kitchen?"

"Yeah."

"He'd taken off his shirt by then, must have dumped it. He was wearing a vest underneath, and two of the cooks said he had tattoos up both arms. Proper sleeves, by the sounds of it."

"Helpful," said Kett. "They notice anything in particular?"

"That's where it gets interesting," Porter went on, his voice crackling. "One of them said that when the suspect grabbed the knife off the counter, he noticed a heart tattoo on his forearm. A big one, bright red."

"He's sure that's what he saw?"

"Well, the chef was wearing a pair of Mr Magoo glasses, but he seemed pretty certain. And that's too much of a coincidence to ignore, right?"

"It is," said Kett. "Good work."

"Well, it was mainly Duke," said Porter. "But I'll happily take the credit. You heard from Kate?"

"Not yet," said Kett, opening the desk in his drawer and shuffling through the mess of papers. "You?"

"She just called, sir, said there was somebody living inside the camper whose plates were on the second lorry. A man called Gregg something. He was in a relationship with a guy. Savage is trying to get hold of the boyfriend now."

Kett found what he was looking for, laying Madelaine Fielding's book of Norfolk myths and legends on his desk and leaning back in his chair.

"You think these are the men we found in lorry number three?" he asked.

"Makes sense, sir," said Porter. "Sounds like Gregg was homeless. If the killer found him living in the van, then he might have assumed it was his, taken the plates and left them on the lorry as a clue. We'll know as soon as Savage makes contact with the boyfriend."

"Or if she can't make contact," said Kett.

"Exactly, sir. I'll keep you updated."

Kett hung up, resting the phone on his desk and picking up the book. He opened it to the chapter on Jack Valentine, scanning the text again in the hope of finding something he'd missed before. He was so tired that the illustrations seemed to dance over the page, Jack's unkind face and insane, spiralling eyes boring into Kett. He didn't care if it was a well-meaning tradition, there was something very strange about the idea of this supernatural creature knocking on your door and offering you a gift. It was like he told his kids time after time after time.

Never take presents from strangers.

Unless the victims and the killer *weren't* strangers, of course.

Unless the killer somehow knew the people he was burning alive.

He ignored the pictures, reading the dense text that sat alongside them. He'd flicked through it before, but he went slow this time, reading about the darker side of the legend. Jack, or Snatch, would lure you out of your home by pretending to be a loved one, or by leaving a note that looked like it had been written by your Valentine. Then he'd carry you away to his home where he'd force you to be his romantic partner and keep you forever.

"Listen to this," he shouted across to Spalding. "'*Some versions of the tale present Jack as a loner, somebody who couldn't find a romantic interest of his own and who preyed on couples that he saw as perfect, or who embodied the core principles of true love. Unable to lure a man or woman with his own attempts at chivalry, Jack would kidnap a pure romantic soul and attempt to make them fall in love with him.'"*

"Sounds like an incel," said Spalding from her desk. She looked cold, and she was still giving him evils.

"Sounds like Norman Balls," said Kett, although he immediately felt bad for saying it. "'*Invariably, this forced coupling would not work. It would only make the victim despise Jack more, fuelling his cycle of loneliness and despair. There is only one fictional example of this pattern of behaviour reaching a murderous conclusion. In a short story written in 1903, author Katherine Blowers describes Jack Valentine as a young man who loved the daughter of the owner of the estate where he worked. He wooed her over the course of three years, but with each gift, each poem, and each progressively extravagant attempt at seduction she retreated further into herself, before taking her own life on the night he asked her to marry him.'"*

"Cheery," said Spalding.

"'*Jack was so distraught by her passing that he shunned people forevermore, eventually shedding his humanity and becoming a shadow that lurked by the homes of devoted couples, presenting gifts to them as a way of atoning for his sins. This particular story was, according to a diary entry by Blowers, specific to the small Norfolk town in which she grew up, Sea Palling. It is by far the most sinister interpretation of the legend I have come across in my studies.*"

"So our killer might be targeting couples he thinks are perfect?" said Spalding. "Taking out his anger on people he thinks are more fortunate than him."

"Maybe," said Kett.

"But that doesn't work, sir," Spalding went on. "Because Grant Dankworth told us that he and Karen practically hated each other. He was cheating on her. I'm not exactly an expert on relationships, but I don't think many people will be looking up to theirs as a paradigm of true love."

"Same with Briggs and DeCarlo," said Kett. "Deeply religious and pregnant out of wedlock. But would you have known that if you were looking in from the outside? The Dankworths looked pretty happy. No kids, nice house, good money, holidays. And Will and Darcey would have resembled any young, happy couple. The killer might have seen them and assumed their relationships were perfect. He never would have known the truth."

Spalding shrugged.

"But where is he seeing them?" she asked. "The Dankworths lived in Taverham, Will and Darcey in Yarmouth. This Gregg guy lives in Aylsham. They're miles apart."

"I don't know," said Kett.

His phone began to vibrate its way across the desk, squealing its awful tune. It was Savage, and he answered it.

"Kate, Porter's just updated me. You found the boyfriend yet?"

"I'm heading to the pub where Gregg goes to drink," said Savage. "But there's a lot of ground to cover."

"You want some help?" he asked.

"I mean, it's grunt work, sir. Are you sure?"

"Well, if I sit at this warm, cosy desk any longer, I'm going to fall asleep."

There was absolutely no missing the look that Spalding threw him from her cold, dark corner of the bullpen.

"Text me the address," he told Savage, grabbing his coat from the back of the chair. "I'll meet you there."

CHAPTER TWENTY-SIX

KETT WAS DRIVING THE VOLVO INTO AYLSHAM HALF AN hour later when Savage called, her voice so loud through the hands-free that it made the car's speakers vibrate.

"Hang on, Kate," he said, dialling the volume down. "Say that again?"

"I think I've found the boyfriend, sir," she said. "I went to the pub where they drink and the landlord says it sounds like a man called Alan Jemc. He was in there with Gregg a fair bit. He says they were well known as a couple, even though Gregg wasn't technically 'out.' He didn't know much about them, says they were both in their late twenties, maybe early thirties. He last saw them a couple of nights ago for karaoke, seemed happy enough. Gave me a rough address for Jemc. He's just outside of town. Want me to go look?"

"I'll come with you," said Kett. "I'm here. What's the address?"

"He's in a village called Tuttington, sir."

"Tuttington? Surely that's not a real name."

Savage laughed.

"Head east, it's the next village over from Aylsham."

He followed her directions, reaching the village in five minutes. It was every bit as quaint as its name suggested, a couple of long streets filled with impressive houses and enormous front gardens. He turned off the Aylsham road onto the Norwich road, spotting Savage's Audi up ahead. He parked behind her, giving her a wave when she glanced into the rear-view mirror. They got out together, both of them shivering in perfect unison.

"Thanks for coming, sir," she said.

"No worries. Better than twiddling my thumbs in the office. I have no idea what's going on with this case."

"Makes two of us, sir," she said. "But it's interesting, right?"

Kett opened the low gate of a detached, red-brick house and let Savage through first. The garden was as immaculate as the rest of the street. The flowerbeds had been turned over in preparation for spring and a small water feature gurgled contentedly beside the driveway.

"Interesting how?" he asked as they crossed the lawn.

"Just that—"

She fell quiet as the front door of the house opened, just a crack. It was hard to see who had opened it, but there was definitely somebody standing there wearing a cloak of shadow. Kett slowed his pace, putting a hand on Savage's arm to stop her as well.

"Hello?" he called out. "Police."

The person didn't move, just a flash of light on their glasses as they turned their head.

"We're looking for Alan, uh..."

"Jemc," whispered Savage.

"Alan Jemc," Kett said. "Is he here? He's not in any trouble."

It took a few quiet seconds for the door to open fully, revealing a woman in her late seventies who couldn't have been more than five feet tall. She was wearing a smart grey dress that bulged a little around her substantial middle, and her silver hair was pulled back into a severe ponytail. She was drying her hands on a tea towel, and she used her forearm to push her glasses onto the bridge of her nose. She squinted into the garden, more than a little fear written into her wrinkled face.

"Police?" she asked with an accent.

Kett started walking again, nodding as he went.

"Are you a relation?" he asked, and she frowned. "Are you related to Alan?"

"Grandmother," she said, rolling the *r*. "Is he okay?"

Kett saw Savage glance at him, but he didn't meet her eye.

"He's not home?" he asked.

The woman continued to dry her hands with the towel, almost compulsively.

"He went out," she said as they reached the front door. Kett could smell something amazing cooking inside, sweet and doughy. "This morning."

"Was he alone?" asked Kett. "Mrs?"

"Ursula," she said. "Call me Ursula. Yes, he was alone, but he was supposed to be meeting somebody."

"Gregg?" asked Savage. "His friend?"

Ursula freed a hand from the towel to swipe it through the air, dismissing her words.

"Call it what it is, young lady. His boyfriend." She turned in a lumbering half-circle, waddling into the house with no small amount of pain. "You know, back when I was his age, we couldn't say the 'gay' word, not without a wooden spoon to the back of the hand."

Kett walked through the open door, Savage closing it behind them. They followed their noses down the hallway to a small but perfectly ordered kitchen. A rack of buns sat on the counter, steaming, and Kett felt the saliva gather in his mouth.

"It's like they thought that if they hid the word from us, we wouldn't know how to be that way. Words have power, yes, but not that much. We *were*."

She positioned herself next to a high sofa and groaned as she fell into it. There, she continued to dry her hands with the towel, all the while studying Kett and Savage with milky eyes. Kett wondered if she was even older than he'd first thought.

"Yes," she said when she realised they were still waiting for an answer. "He left to meet Gregg."

"Do you know Gregg's surname, by any chance?" said Savage.

"Peterson," she said.

"He seemed okay this morning?" Kett asked. "It was a normal kind of meet-up?"

"As normal as anything ever was for those two," she said. "But it isn't easy, is it? Even these days. Alan embraced his being gay years ago, before he was even a teenager. We encouraged it, of course. Gregg is not so happy in himself. Not his fault, of course. When you grow up being told that the way you love another human being is wrong, it can take a long time to remember that you can love whichever human being you like, so long as they love you back."

"They're in love?" asked Kett.

"Oh, when I see them together, I do not doubt it. Only in those moments when nobody is watching, though. Then, they are in love."

Kett leaned against the counter, forcing himself not to

reach back and grab a bun. The fruity smell of them was driving him to distraction.

"They've been together a while?" he said.

"No, not long. A year or so. They met a long time before that, in the pub, but I don't think Gregg was willing to admit to feeling anything for Alan for many years. They have been friends since the word go, but last summer was when it blossomed into something more tender."

"Have you noticed any changes in them the last couple of weeks?" Kett asked. "Anything different, anything new. Arguments, anything like that?"

Ursula considered the question, folding the tea towel neatly and setting it on her lap.

"Can you tell me why you are asking these questions?" she said. "Is my grandson alright?"

Kett ran a hand through his hair.

"I don't know," he said. "Is there any way for you to reach him? A phone number?"

"I tried his phone before lunch," she said. "To see if he and Gregg were coming for tea. I tried again an hour or so ago. He did not answer."

"Does he usually answer?" asked Savage.

"No. He is young, and busy. But he always calls me back." She swallowed, her head rocking gently back and forth like a nodding dog. "He has not called me back."

Kett felt Savage look at him again, and this time he met her eye.

Ursula must have plucked their unspoken words from the air because she let out a gasp like she'd been punched. For a few seconds, she spoke in her native tongue, a language Kett couldn't make head nor tail of, making the sign of the cross over her chest.

"We don't know anything yet," said Kett. "We're just trying to work out where he is."

"I felt it," Ursula said, her tremor spreading into her arms, so bad that she couldn't pick up the towel. "I felt it, and I knew. It's why I was watching the road, why I saw you coming. He's gone."

She choked back a sob, her rheumy eyes full of steel.

"It doesn't matter," she said. "It is how it is meant to be. I lost my mother and father in the war, my Jovic to cancer. I lost my beautiful daughter too, and her husband. Both in New York, in 2001 when the towers fell. We are a family marked by death, but it does not matter. Alan is with his mother now, and his father, and his grandfather, and all who came before. It will not be long before I join them."

"We don't know—" Savage started, but the old woman hammered a fist against her own chest.

"*I* know," she said. "I know."

Silence dropped into the kitchen like a guillotine, just the bubbling of whatever was on the stove. Ursula stared up at them from where she sat, her body hunched as if she could compress herself into oblivion, pack herself away for the afterlife.

Kett took a deep breath, exhaling it as a sigh.

"I'm sorry," he told her. "I really am."

"Gregg?" said Ursula. "He's okay?"

"We're not sure," he told her. "Was anything delivered to the house this morning? A package, or a gift, in purple paper?"

"No," she said.

"Can we take a look at Alan's room?"

"He won't be needing it," said Ursula. "It's the first one on the right, up the steps."

Kett left the kitchen like his life depended on it. The

corridor beyond was mercifully cool, but he was still sweating by the time he made it to the top of the stairs. Savage walked up behind him, the pain and sadness etched into her face. She opened her mouth to speak, then decided not to.

Kett didn't blame her. What was there to say?

He used his knuckles to push open the door, finding a small room with a low ceiling. A double bed took centre stage, the floral quilt more suited to an elderly couple than a man in his late twenties. A teak wardrobe sat next to it, a matching dresser on the opposite wall beside a low door that probably led into an *en suite*. The only new thing in the room was an electric standing desk beneath the window, currently set for somebody very tall. There was no computer on it, just a scattering of papers.

"Can you check the bathroom, Kate?" asked Kett.

He walked to the desk, finding a pile of bills and bank statements and receipts on the left, all with Jemc's name on them. The paperwork on the right was more personal, a couple of handwritten letters.

Kett leafed through them, seeing one addressed to a woman called Gemma and another to a man by the name of Raiph. Both were dated yesterday, and detailed some of the happier aspects of Alan's life, including the fact that he was in a relationship, as well as some wishes for the future such as finding a house of his own—as much as he loved his grandmother. Neither went any deeper than that, and he'd signed his name beneath with a flourish. Envelopes sat open, already stamped.

"Nothing," said Savage. "Enough toiletries to stock a branch of Superdrug, though. You found anything?"

"Not yet," he said.

He moved the letters to one side, hearing the squeal of

the wardrobe doors and the clink of hangers being moved as Savage searched. There were more papers beneath the letters, including a couple of drafted notes covered in crossing-outs and edits. These were harder to decipher because the handwriting was so sloppy, but Kett did his best to read them aloud.

"'*It's not you, it's me... I can't be with somebody who won't accept me for what I am... Until you take better care of yourself, how can I expect you to take care of me... I know you'll find happiness in the arms of somebody else, but only when...*' I can't read that, but it's pretty obvious what this is."

"Breakup letter?" asked Savage, her head deep inside the wardrobe. "Is there a name on it?"

"No. Handwriting's the same as the other stuff, just not as neat. Looks like he was rehearsing what he wanted to say."

Savage closed the wardrobe doors.

"Gregg had quite a few notes in his camper too, sir," she said. "I had a quick look at them in the car. He was quite the romantic, a lot of poetry, some short stories, and letters too. It's quite sweet, to be honest. Who does that anymore?"

She laughed quietly.

"Can you imagine Aaron writing me a love letter?"

"He'd write it in crayon," said Kett.

Savage opened the top drawer of the dresser.

"Got some photos here, sir," she said, hefting out a couple of albums.

Kett peered over her shoulder as she flicked through them. Alan was a tall, lean, handsome man with sandy hair and his grandmother's round face. There wasn't a single photograph in the album where he wasn't smiling. He shared most of the photos in the first album with another man, obviously a boyfriend.

"Is that Gregg?" he asked.

"I don't think so, sir," said Savage. "Gregg is white."

She pulled out another album, and a photograph slipped free, falling to the carpet. She picked it up and held it out to reveal two men sitting behind a pub table. One was Alan, older than in the other photographs, a patchy beard matching his hair. The other was a guy a few years his senior, markedly overweight with streaks of grey in his dark hair and his beard. They were sitting as if they were saving the seat between them for somebody else, Alan's smile a little faded and the other man leaning away, as uncomfortable as it was possible to be.

"I think that's Gregg," said Savage. "Matches the description from the landlord, and this is the pub I was just in."

Kett closed the drawer and opened the next one down to find more papers; countless letters stuffed into a shoebox and reams of handwritten material. There were magazines here too, a stack of tacky lifestyle rags with the crosswords completed, a few local periodicals called Norfolk Living, and some outdoor running magazines that looked as if they had been well-read. The bottom drawer held only clothes.

"Let's get all this back to HQ," said Kett. "There must be something here that can help us."

"I'll get some bags from the car, sir," said Savage.

She started for the door, but Kett called her back.

"You said something was interesting, Kate, out in the garden. What was it?"

"I'm not sure, sir," she said, leaning on the doorjamb and keeping her voice low. "If Alan and Gregg really are the men we found in the lorry, that makes three very different relationships that the killer has targeted. We've got a couple that have been together for ten years, we've got a young couple that have only just got married, but are expecting a child, and now we've got two gay men who aren't married, as far as I know, and who look like they're on the verge of breaking up."

She shrugged.

"I thought maybe the killer was targeting people because he was jealous or something."

"That's the line I'm going down," said Kett. "I was reading up on Jack Valentine. There are some stories where he kidnaps people who he thinks are in a perfect relationship because he wants one too."

"These are anything but perfect, sir," she said.

"Agreed. But the killer doesn't know what we know. He can't see the cracks."

"I think he can, sir," said Savage. "I think somehow he knows that these relationships are in trouble, and that's why he's going after them."

"Maybe," said Kett. "But it doesn't fit what we know about Jack Valentine, and more importantly, how would the killer know that these couples were having problems? They live miles apart, they have no shared contacts, no common locations. He'd have to be everywhere at once."

Savage didn't have an answer for this. She pushed herself off the door, the old steps creaking as she jogged down them. Kett turned his attention back to the box of papers, rifling through some of the letters. It would take days to go through it all.

He flipped through the pages of the magazines in case anything had been hidden in them. The running ones he could understand, it fit the photos they had found of an athletic young man. The local periodicals seemed too inane to be enjoyed by anyone, nothing but articles about life in the county mixed with advice about money and health. The lifestyle magazines were full of lurid stories about murderous boyfriends and killer pets and tragic deaths, the kind that leapt off the shelves of newsagents with headlines like *Locked in a Box by My Teacher!* or *My Grandfather Ate My Sister!* It was a weird thing for a man in his late twenties to read.

Kett dropped the magazine he was holding and picked up another, finding the same thing. Readers' photos were dropped in amongst the articles, but he didn't see anyone he recognised. There was a double-page spread of horoscopes, and crosswords and word searches filled the rest of the wrinkled pages.

"What am I missing?" he asked the room, but it didn't answer.

Tucking the magazines under his arm with the letters, he made his way down the stairs and back into the kitchen. There was no sign of Savage, but Ursula was beetling between the counters, loading the hot buns into a Tupperware container. She looked around as he entered the room, an expression of hope on her face as if she had expected to see her grandson there. It was quickly erased, swallowed by the soft folds of her face. She sighed, her back so bent it was like she was preparing to bow. Kett wanted to tell her they didn't know for sure that Alan had died, but he couldn't bring himself to do it.

Besides, who was he to doubt an old woman's instincts? She knew.

So did he.

"I really am sorry," he said. "If there's anything else you can tell us that might help..."

"Nothing will help, so don't you worry," she said, returning to the task of moving the buns into the tub. "Some things are destined to be. Such is life."

He didn't know what to say to that.

Ursula used her crooked hands to work a lid onto the tub, the effort exhausting her.

"Here, let me help," said Kett, moving to her side.

"It is done," she replied, hefting up the box and offering it to him. "Take them."

"I can't," said Kett, but she pushed the box into his stomach.

"Take them. They were for Alan, his favourite. But he won't be needing them."

The sadness found a crack, escaping as a sob. The woman quickly subdued it, clearing her throat.

"And neither will I. Take them. Eat them. Bin them. I just don't want them here."

Kett took the box, holding it to his chest. He rested the magazines on top, and Ursula looked at them fondly.

"Alan and his magazines," she said. "Always so horrible, those stories, but he couldn't get enough of them."

She smiled.

"He didn't read them for the death, though. He read them for the love."

"How so?" asked Kett.

"Because everyone there lived to tell their tale, no? They survived. They found happiness after evil. Love won. That is what he enjoyed."

Her face fell again, the woman seeming to grow smaller with every breath.

"I can send somebody to speak with you," said Kett. "We have Family Support Officers who can help you get through this."

He heard how empty his words were, and so did Ursula. She shuffled to the corridor, studying the kitchen as if she knew it was the last time she would see it.

"What can they teach me about death that I do not already know?" she said. "It comes to us all, in the end."

And with that, she was gone.

Kett made his way out of the front door, almost colliding with Savage as she walked back in. She was wearing forensic gloves and carrying an armful of bags, and she frowned at the box.

"What've you got there, sir?"

"Lunch, I think," he said. "Gather what you can. I'm going to call an FSO, she's in a bad way. You mind staying with her until they get here?"

"Of course, sir," said Savage. "I thought the same thing."

"You want one of these?" he asked, offering the box.

She looked up at the house.

"Not hungry, sir. Sorry."

They parted, Savage heading through the door and Kett walking back onto the street. He laid the box on the passenger seat of his Volvo, resisting for all of five seconds before peeling off the lid and collecting a bun from inside. Still warm, and filled with apricot jelly, it was without a doubt one of the best things he'd ever put in his mouth. He polished it off and was biting into his second one when his phone rang. A dollop of jam landed on his shirt as he pulled out his phone.

"Shit," he said through a mouthful of bun. "Pete? What's up?"

"What are you eating, sir?" Porter asked.

"Nothing," said Kett, wiping his face with his sleeve. He swallowed the last of the bun. "What do you need?"

"You, sir," said Porter. "I think we've found something."

CHAPTER TWENTY-SEVEN

Porter put his phone away, taking a moment to catch his breath. He was standing down the street from the care home, in the bony shadow of an apple tree that was hanging over the fence of one of the neighbouring houses.

Further up, the road that ran along the back of the garden centre where the lorry had been found was a zoo of police, fire fighters and paramedics, as well as a good helping of news reporters who'd caught the scent of blood. They were in danger of demolishing the flimsy police perimeter that had been set up.

Behind him, another fifty or so yards along the street, another perimeter was being set up, this one around a ten-year-old Audi A4. He could hear the shouts of the constables as they unwound the police tape, as well as the constant barrage of questions from the handful of journalists who had made their way down.

Porter enjoyed another few seconds of quiet before returning to the car. Duke was standing beside it, his chest puffed out, his arms tense by his sides. He had good reason to be proud because he was the one who had found the

Audi on a routine search of the street, but he still looked ridiculous.

"Aaron, why are you standing like that?" said Porter when he was in earshot.

Duke angled his body slightly to the side, keeping his arms tense. He didn't look at Porter, his attention was squarely on the reporters as they snapped photos and filmed footage.

"Just giving them what they want, sir," he said, his biceps bulging as he scratched the back of his head.

"Giving who what they want?"

"The cameras," said Duke. "This is going to be on the TV later, I want to look good."

"You look like a prat," said Porter.

He glanced at the reporters, who had their cameras aimed his way, and sucked in his gut. Duke continued to show off his arms, the fabric of his jacket almost splitting.

"Anyone heard from the Super, yet?" Porter asked, struggling to speak as he held in his stomach. "We need that warrant."

"No, sir," said Duke, twisting around like a bodybuilder on stage. Porter heard a murmur of appreciation from the direction of the reporters.

He stepped in front of the giant PC, expanding his shoulders and puffing out his chest. He could have opened the Audi himself in a heartbeat, but he didn't want to do it without a warrant, or at least the go-ahead from Clare. He had no excuse to Kett this one up, especially given the DCI wasn't even here.

But there were definitely reasonable grounds for searching the car. On the front seat was a black hoodie, streaked with paint. And lying beneath it, peeking through a fold of fabric, was what was almost certainly a paper box, the same colour as the one they had found in Darcey DeCarlo's house. They'd knocked on every door along the street, and spoken to everyone inside the nursing home, and nobody knew who the car belonged to.

"It has to be his," Porter said, thinking aloud. "He parked it here in case he had to make a quick getaway from the garden centre. He set fire to the lorry, then stayed to watch, thinking nobody would spot him. By the time we'd chased him, there was too much heat for him to drive off, so he legged it."

Duke was still staring at the reporters, his face deadly serious, his lips pouting.

"Yeah?" Porter said.

"Sorry, sir," said Duke, still not looking. "Sounds right."

"Unbelievable," said Porter. "Nobody bloody cares what you look like, mate."

"Excuse me," came a shout from the other side of the street. Porter turned to see one of the reporters waving at him. "Can you move a little to the side, please?"

"Me?" said Porter, pointing at himself.

"Yes, you," she said.

"Why?" he asked.

It was pretty bloody obvious why. There was nothing behind Porter except for Duke, who was contorting himself like an ape in an effort to flex his muscles.

"Fuck's sake," Porter muttered, making his way to the Audi and hearing the rapid-fire click of the cameras. He pulled out his phone and tried Clare again, and this time the call went through.

"Speak!" boomed the Super.

"Can we enter the car yet, sir?" Porter asked.

"It's definitely his?"

"Like, ninety percent, sir," Porter said. He cupped his hand to the glass, seeing the purple box beneath the jumper.

"Did you say a hundred percent?" Clare asked.

"Ninety, sir."

"I'm hearing a definite one hundred."

"There's no way I could know for sure, sir," said Porter.

"Did you just say you know for sure?" asked Clare. "In that case, do it."

"I didn't—"

"I heard what I heard, you tossjockey. You're on record. Open the bloody car."

Porter hung up, then called out to Duke.

"Hey, Fabio, if you're not too busy, mind throwing me your baton?"

Duke pulled out his weapon in slow motion and flicked it out with a flourish. One of the reporters actually started clapping. Porter opened his mouth to tell him to hurry up, but was caught short when Duke lobbed the baton towards him. He tried to snatch it out of the air but he missed, the baton pinging off the end of his fingers before sliding under the car.

"You absolute..." he started, only to realise that he was now the focus of the cameras. "Have you lot not got anything better to do?" he roared at them.

He bent over so hard that he thought he'd split the seat of his trousers. He retrieved the baton from beneath the car, moving to the rear driver's side window.

"Stand back," he told nobody in particular, his voice a little lower than it normally was. "This could be dangerous."

He whacked the baton into the glass, only for nothing to happen. He tried again, the Audi resisting.

"Need some help, sir?" asked Duke, loud enough for everyone to hear.

Porter glared at him, then imagined Duke's face in the car window. This time, when he struck it, the glass exploded into chunks, filling the back seat. He folded the baton up and dropped it into his pocket, leaning in to pop the central locking. He worked some gloves onto his hands before opening the driver's door, sliding behind the wheel and closing it behind him. He nudged the jumper to the floor.

The little paper box sat alone on the chair next to him, partially open. Porter picked it up, spinning it in his fingers until he saw the JV inside the heart on the underside. The tape had already been picked away, so he unfolded the box to reveal a few lines of handwritten text on the inside.

I'm ready to commit, I'm ready to give you everything I am. Come find me.

Beneath the words was a postcode that he knew belonged to the garden centre where the lorry had been burned out.

Porter turned the paper over in his hands, looking for something else, but that was all there was. He laid it back on the seat, checking the glove box to find that it had been emptied. When he sat back up, there was a face looming into his window, a mobile phone held up in front of it—one of the reporters.

"Back off," he yelled, the words steaming up the window. "This is a crime scene."

Duke led them away, more constables plunging the car into darkness as they surrounded it. Porter craned back, finding nothing on the back seat or in the footwell. He opened his door, almost knocking over the young PC who stood there.

"Sorry, sir," she said as she scampered out of the way.

Porter walked to the boot, opening it to find a mountain of old clothes. There were jeans, jumpers and a couple of T-shirts on the top, a yellow high-vis vest to the right and a pile of shoes at the back. There was a duffel bag full of hats and gloves, as well as several pairs of sunglasses. He rummaged through them carefully, pulling the garments apart and checking pockets when he found them. The clothes were clean, the strong smell of fabric conditioner making his nose run.

It was only at the bottom of the pile that he found something that wasn't fabric. It was cold and hard and sharp, and he withdrew his hand like he'd been bitten by a snake, expecting to see blood. He looked closer, finding a straight metal ridge that was too colourful to be a weapon.

When he pulled it out, he saw that it was a bright yellow vehicle registration plate.

"Shit," he said, laying it to the side and feeling for another one. He found it beneath the duffel bag, the front plate from the same car.

He placed it with the first, his gloved hands fumbling his phone out of his pocket. He sat on the edge of the boot, calling Clare.

"It's him, sir," he said before the Super could speak. "Another Jack Valentine box in the front with a note."

"What did it say?" asked Clare.

"I'll send you a photo, sir. But it's a message for Alan, I think. There's something else, I found a set of registration plates in the boot."

"From a different car?" asked Clare.

"Yes, sir," Porter said, but he had to stand up and close the boot to make sure. "Definitely. We've found number plates on every lorry so far, and they've all been from the next set of victims, right? The lorry we found today didn't have plates at all, maybe these were supposed to be on it."

"Give me the number, Pete, I'll run it. Be ready to move."

"Always, sir," said Porter.

He read the licence plate out twice before hanging up, then made his way up the street, ignoring the barrage of questions from the reporters as he passed them. One of them was yelling his name with some intensity, and when he turned in the direction of the garden centre he saw that it wasn't a reporter at all, it was Emily Franklin.

"Peter Porter!" she yelled, her hands cupped to her mouth. "Stop ignoring me!"

"Sorry," he shouted back. He crossed the road to the chain-link fence that separated the street from the garden centre's yard. Franklin was hovering on the other side of it, and she grabbed hold of the fence, weeping dramatically.

"Don't lock me in here, Pete," she wailed, as if she was performing on stage. "Oh, what did I ever do to you? Set me free!"

"What have you found?" he asked.

"No appreciation for the dramatic arts," she said, letting go of the fence. "Why does that not surprise me? Well, your two men in the lorry were definitely fighting. Bloke A is the one with the knife in his chest. I think the blade entered his heart, he would have bled out in a minute or so. But he's also got stab wounds to the left shoulder, his left arm, and his left flank. This last one grazed his ribs and left a nasty wound."

"Shit," said Porter.

"It was very shit for him, yes. It's going to be hard to pinpoint exactly what happened because of the damage the fire did to his tissues. But Bloke B has injuries too, including a very nasty dent in his head and some missing teeth, probably sustained by a blow with a blunt object."

"Shit," Porter said again.

"Extremely shit, yes. I found a hammer close to the bodies. The handle has burned away, but there's evidence of blood on the head. Bloke A got some good shots in before Bloke B stuck him with the knife."

"So Bloke A died first?" said Porter. Franklin nodded. "Why wouldn't the killer let him out, then? When Grant Dankworth murdered his wife, the killer opened the door. When William died, Darcey was set free. If Bloke B killed his boyfriend like he'd been asked to, why did the killer let them both burn?"

"You're asking the wrong person," said Franklin. "I only deal with the gory stuff."

She shuddered, her bright eyes growing dull.

"It must have been vicious," she said quietly. "These men were lovers?"

"We think so, yeah," said Porter.

"The things we do to the ones we love," she said. "I'm going to take them back to my lab now, unless you need them to stay."

"Take them," said Porter. "One thing, though, can you tell me which bloke was which? Gregg was on the larger side, Alan was taller and leaner, I think."

"Gregg's your Bloke B," she said.

"Thanks, Emily."

She gave him a wave as she set off, her walk becoming a childlike skip halfway across the yard.

"She is so weird," Porter muttered.

He pulled out his phone to call Kett, only to find that Clare was already ringing him.

"The plates belong to a man called Frank Hopkins," said the Super. "They should be on a 2003 Skoda Octavia. He's not too far from you, next town over, Brundall. I've dispatched some units. Get over there."

"Yes, sir," Porter said, although Clare had already hung up.

He jogged for the alley that led down the side of the yard, yelling as he went.

"Duke, stop showing off, you great twat. We've got to move!"

CHAPTER TWENTY-EIGHT

Kett got the call when he was driving. He did a U-turn on the deserted Aylsham road and headed southeast.

"Brundall?" he said to Superintendent Clare.

"That's right. The man who owns the car is in his sixties, lives with his wife Eileen just outside of town. No history with us at all. It's weird. Why would the killer go after an older couple?"

"Savage was talking about this a second ago, sir," said Kett. "Every victim is different. We've got a husband and wife in their forties, a newly married couple in their early twenties, a pair of men in their thirties. It's like the killer's going after completely different demographics. It's like he's..."

He paused as he overtook a truck, his heart revving alongside the Volvo's engine as he pulled in just in time to miss an oncoming lorry.

"It's like he's testing them, sir," he said.

"Testing what?"

"Testing their love for each other," said Kett.

"You sound like a barrel of wet toss, Kett," said Clare. "Pull it together. Let me know when you're there."

"Sir?" said Kett, but the Super had already hung up.

"A barrel of wet toss?" said Kett, grimacing.

He slowed down as he reached the roundabout, taking a right onto a road called Cucumber Lane. Just two minutes later he turned a corner onto a residential street that should have been quiet, but which bristled with police. Three IRVs straddled the middle of the road, their lights flashing, and uniformed coppers congregated on the pavement outside a new build. Trees boxed in the driveway, including an enormous conifer outside the front window.

A couple of the PCs looked at his car suspiciously as he pulled up, then waved when they realised who he was.

"We got them?" he asked as he climbed out.

"We got the wife," said a PC. "She's inside. She doesn't know where her husband is."

Kett jogged halfway to the house, then walked the rest when the ache in his spine grew too much. The front door was open, two PCs parting ways to let him through. The house was freezing, cold air from outside cutting right through the meagre warmth from the radiators. Kett shooed the two constables outside and closed the door, only for it to open again almost immediately.

"I'm trying to keep the heat—" he started, before he saw Porter and Duke there. He opened the door for them, both shivering as they darted inside.

"Was calling you from halfway up the road, sir," said Porter.

"Didn't hear you," said Kett.

He stepped into the living room to find that it was already crowded. Eileen Hopkins sat in the middle of a sofa that still bore its plastic wrap, her face knotted into a fist of worry. Four uniformed police officers made the room look like a matchbox, none of them seeming to know what to do with themselves. Two more stood in the kitchen on the opposite side of an archway, one of them in the final stages of making a cup of tea.

"Give us some space, lads," said Kett, waving the constables out of the living room. He waited for them to leave before perching on the edge of a pink velvet chair. The smell of potpourri was so strong it gave him an instant headache.

Eileen was too busy staring at the carpet to even notice him. She was made up to the nines, with what must have been an entire pack of blusher on her cheeks and bright blue eye shadow. Her silvery hair had been rinsed an odd shade of green.

"Mrs Hopkins?" he said gently.

She frowned up at him.

"I hope somebody's going to clean my carpets," she said, her accent as local as it was possible to be. "They've only been in two months. Mud everywhere."

"I'll make sure they're cleaned after we've gone," said Kett. "But right now I need to know where Frank is."

"You and me both," said Eileen, sniffing. "Supposed to have been back for his lunch, but he never showed. He'll be off perving at the ladies in the gym, no doubt."

"The gym?" said Kett.

"He don't go to the gym, he just orders a cuppa at the café, so he can ogle them when they're coming out the changing rooms. The man hasn't had a hard-on for thirty years, so I don't know what he's planning on doing with them."

Duke snorted with laughter from the back of the room, covering it with a cough.

"Has he got a phone we can call?" asked Kett.

"Yeah."

"You know the number?"

"Yeah."

"Can we have it?" Kett said, the impatience gnawing at his nerves.

"Won't do you any good. His phone's here."

"What's the name of the gym?" Kett asked. "It's local?"

The woman shrugged, delicately running a finger along an eyelash that was caked with mascara. Kett looked at Porter.

"Check any gyms in the area, Pete, see if anyone's seen him."

"What's he done?" asked Eileen. "Don't tell me he finally worked up the courage to grab a tit or something."

Duke choked out another laugh, and this time Kett glared at him.

"He might be in danger," said Kett. "You too. Has a man been to the house in the last few days, a man you don't know? Tall, dark, handsome."

"I wish," said Eileen. "No."

"Has anyone left anything on the doorstep, a box made out of paper with a heart on it? A note inside that sounds like it was written by your husband?"

"You know what Frank gave me for my Valentine's this year?" said Eileen with a huff of laughter. "A pair of his soiled boxers soaking in the bathroom sink."

"But no box?"

"No box, no nothing," said Eileen, tracing her finger along her eyelash again. "But he never was one for grand gestures. We've been together forty-two years, and in all that time he's bought me three Valentine's cards. Two of them were in the same year, because he'd forgotten he'd already given me one."

She sat forward, pointing a crooked finger at Kett like this was all his fault.

"All my life people told me I could do better. My friends, my family, a dozen agony aunts and even a therapist, once. She was supposed to be impartial, but we had one session with her and she told me to leave him. Did I, though?"

She paused, as if expecting a reply, then answered herself.

"Of course I didn't. Why do we settle? Why do we think we're not worth something more, eh? One life we get here, one chance at happiness, and how many of us spend it with somebody we don't love? Somebody we don't even *like*? It's madness. Is he dead?"

"Frank?" said Kett. "No, I don't think so."

Eileen sat back and folded her arms over her chest like she was disappointed.

"Did Frank take the car when he left the house today?" asked Kett.

"Well he ain't walking to the gym, not with his knees," said Eileen, staring once again at the filthy carpet.

"Did you happen to notice if it still had its number plates this morning?"

She wrinkled her face at the question, an obvious *no*.

"Has anything unusual—"

"Sir?" Another PC stuck her head through the living room door. "Husband's back. He's just pulling up now."

Eileen groaned.

It took Kett a couple of attempts to get up from the soft chair, and he walked outside to see a shit-coloured Skoda Octavia trying to squeeze between two IRVs. It was doing a bad job, the car squealing as it took the paint off the side of a police car.

There was no licence plate on the front of the Skoda.

A man in his late sixties sat in the driver's seat—so short that he could barely see over the wheel. Three constables were waving at the driver and calling for him to stop, but he was ignoring them.

Kett jogged over, slamming his hands on the bonnet.

"Stop," he ordered. "Frank, turn off the engine."

The man left the car running, winding down his window instead.

"You're blocking me driveway," he said, his cheeks mottled with age and anger. "Bloody arses."

"Engine off, *now*," Kett said, leaving no more room for argument.

Frank grumbled a reply, but did as he was told. It was impossible for him to open any doors because of the IRVs on either side, but Kett couldn't see anyone else in the car.

"Check the boot," he told Porter, who had followed him out. "Frank, where have you been?"

"Getting a cuppa," said the man, his hands still on the wheel. "No crime in that."

"At the gym?"

"Oh for fuck's sake," he said. "What's that jealous old hag told you? It's not a crime to look, it's why God gave us eyes. Fucking woke brigade showing up. What next? Can't breathe the same air they do? Can't give a bum a little tickle when they walk past? Give a man a break, eh? What's the world come to?"

There was far too much there for Kett to even begin unpacking.

"This isn't about you being a pervert," he said. "Not yet, anyway. Where are your plates, Frank?"

"Plates?" he said. "In the kitchen. What's that got to do with anything?"

"Number plates, for the car."

"On the fucking car!" he said. "Hey, what's he doing?"

Porter had opened the Skoda's boot, but he closed it again after a moment.

"No back plate," the DI said.

"What are you on about?" said Frank. "They're on the bloody car."

"You haven't seen anyone interfering with your car?" Kett said. "A man, tall and dark, well built, tattoos. It would have been in the last couple of days."

"No."

"Has anyone of that description approached you recently? Asked you about your relationship, maybe, your wife?"

"No!"

"You haven't seen anyone of that description at all?"

"Half the so-called men in the gym are tall and dark and built like Sylvester Stallone, but none of them have asked me about my wife. Why would they? Have you seen her? Looks like a grenade went off in a carrier bag full of makeup and tripe."

Kett had to bite his tongue. He was glad Savage wasn't here, because he was pretty sure she'd have dragged the man out through the Skoda's open window.

"Nobody's left anything on the doorstep? A paper box with a heart on it."

"You're fucking mad," said Frank, looping a finger around his ear. "Go on, piss off, let me park my car."

Kett waited a moment more, then he stood back and nodded to the constable behind the wheel of one of the IRVs. The PC reversed it, leaving enough space for Frank to get through. The man pulled onto his driveway with no little aggression, yelling obscenities out the window as he did so. Unfortunately for him, he was going too fast to stop.

The Skoda slammed into the trunk of the conifer tree and Kett heard the dull pop of the exploding airbag, followed by a gargled cry of outrage. A few seconds later, the driver's door opened and Frank all but fell out, his face so white with dust that he could have been a ghost. A few coppers ran to help him, but Kett wasn't one of them. He was trying his hardest not to laugh as Frank teetered like a punch-drunk boxer towards his front door.

"Don't you wish the universe dealt with all the arseholes like that, sir?" said Porter, grinning.

"It would save us a lot of work," said Kett. "Call him an ambulance, will you, Pete?"

Frank had collapsed onto his arse, his arms flapping in the air like a chicken's wings. Eileen was watching her husband through the living room window, a broad smile on her face.

"What's going on?" said Kett. "The killer had their plates in his car but he didn't attach them to the third lorry, and he hasn't tried to approach Frank or Eileen. You think he ran out of time?"

"He's definitely rushing, sir," said Porter. "He might not have had a chance to change the plates."

"Or drain the petrol tank," said Kett. "Public place, broad daylight. Yeah, he's rushing. Maybe that's why he didn't use the plates, because he knew he wouldn't have time to snatch Frank and Eileen."

"You think he's done then, sir?" asked Porter. "You think he's finished?"

Kett thought about it for all of three seconds, then shook his head.

"You didn't see him, Pete," he said. "The man at the care home, the way he looked at me. He's not done, he's just adapting. The number plates aren't a compulsion, it's not a rule. He did it to help us out because he thought we needed it, it's part of his game. Now that he knows we're catching up with him, he's only going to move faster, take more risks. He might not have even wanted Frank and Eileen. He might just be fucking with us. He might be..."

The temperature seemed to plummet, goosebumps breaking out on his arm as he stepped into the street, searching.

"Might be watching us right now," he finished, scanning the parked cars, trying to make sense of the dark windows of the neighbouring houses. "Pete, can you do a sweep of the road just to make sure? He stayed to watch once. He likes to be in the thick of it. Remember, he thinks he's smarter than us."

"He's smarter than one of us for sure, sir," said Porter, nodding to Duke, who was picking his nose outside the front door of the Hopkins house. "Sure, will do."

The DI ran off, barking orders to the idling constables. Kett studied the Skoda, puffing out a breath and trying to work out what to do next. There were too many pieces in this case, and they were all moving too fast to make sense of. And right at the heart of it was a man whose motive for putting couples through hell was what? Jealousy? Or anger? Or some twisted desire to make them prove their love for each other in the face of death?

It was madness. The whole thing was insane.

But it couldn't be random. It couldn't be sheer chaos.

There had to be a link between the victims.

Kett called the Superintendent, kicking loose chips of gravel down the road as he waited for an answer.

"Zipper," said Clare. "What have you got?"

"A headache, sir. Frank and Eileen are both accounted for. Neither of them know anything about the killer."

"Well that's no tossing use to us, is it?"

"Sorry, sir."

"So what now?" the Super asked.

"I think we need to go back to the beginning," said Kett. "Is Dankworth still in custody?"

CHAPTER TWENTY-NINE

IT FELT LIKE A MILLION YEARS AGO THAT KETT HAD last sat face to face with Grant Dankworth, and he looked like an entirely different man. A night in holding often made people resemble ghosts of themselves, but Grant looked like he'd been cut in half and hollowed out. He limped into the interview room like the living dead, his face sallow, the bags under his eyes big enough to camp in. Kett had seen people like this before, mostly after a few years in prison.

He wondered if Grant was rehearsing for the same fate.

"Take a seat, mate," said Duke, who had fetched Dankworth from his cell.

Grant collapsed into the chair like every bone had been filleted from his body, curling his arms on the table and resting his head there. He closed his eyes, his breathing levelling out so much it was like he'd gone to sleep. Kett started the recorder, giving the names of everyone present.

"And DI Peter Porter," he said, looking at the door. Porter stood outside, staring at something on his phone. Kett cleared his throat and tried again. "And DI Peter Porter."

Porter finished what he was doing and scurried into the room, closing the door behind him. He stood against the back wall, muttering quiet obscenities at Duke, who had taken the seat next to Kett.

"How are you holding up, Grant?" Kett asked the shadow of the man on the other side of the table. He didn't press him, counting down the seconds until Grant muttered an unintelligible reply.

"Gonna have to do a little better than that," said Kett. "Head up, speak clearly. How are you holding up?"

Grant sniffed, lifting his head out of the nest of his arms. His eyes were more red than white, swollen by tears.

"What's the point?" he said. "Said all I can think of to say. Won't be enough, will it? Won't be enough to let me walk out of here."

"Or bring your wife back," said Kett. "Remember her?"

Grant stared at Kett with those bloodshot eyes.

"Yeah," he said, although it hadn't been a serious question. "Told you all I know. So just get it over with."

"Doesn't work that way," said Kett. "You have to wait, just like any other criminal. Anything you want to add to your statement?"

"I was in shock," he said, sniffing.

"When?"

"When it happened," he went on. "That's why it took me so long to come to you. I was in my car, I was in shock, I couldn't think straight."

"Right," said Kett, unconvinced. "We can come back to that. I don't want to talk to you about what happened the other night. I want to talk to you about your relationship with Karen before all of this happened."

"Why?"

"Because whoever did this to you has done it to two other couples," said Kett.

Grant sat up, shocked.

"What?" he croaked.

"A young couple were locked in a van just after you, on Sunday night. It was set on fire. She was pregnant."

Grant swallowed, looking between Kett and Duke and Porter.

"She died?" he asked eventually.

"*He* died," said Kett. "Her husband killed himself so that she wouldn't have to."

The guilt cut into Grant's face as cleanly as a knife, just for a second, before defiance set in. He started to defend himself only for Kett to cut him off.

"And another couple was murdered in the same way this afternoon. They fought each other, but they both died in the fire. Two men, this time."

Grant licked his lips.

"Why?" he asked.

"That's what we want to know," said Kett. "The killer is picking his victims for a reason. If we can figure out what it is, we can find him before he does it again."

Grant lifted his hands like they weighed a hundred tonnes, barely able to force a shrug.

"It could be anything," he said. "We'd never done anything wrong, we weren't special. We weren't *anything*."

"What do you mean?" asked Kett, shifting his position in the uncomfortable chair.

"What I'm saying. There's no reason somebody would pick us. We're boring. We didn't even like each other half the time. We didn't piss anyone off, we didn't do anything wrong."

"You were cheating," said Kett. "How many times?"

Grant spat out a laugh.

"You say cheating like it means anything," he said. "It's not cheating if you're not in love with them."

"Say what?" said Porter. "How'd you figure that one out?"

"Like you've never cheated," Grant said.

"Never," Porter told him.

Grant looked at Duke.

"Wouldn't do it," the PC told him.

"Yeah, right," he scoffed, turning to Kett.

"We're not all like you, Grant," said Kett.

"Well, we had an agreement, Karen and I," he blustered. "As long as I didn't love them, it was okay."

"She told you that?" said Kett.

"No, but she knew. I knew she knew. She didn't care."

"Right," said Kett. "How long was it going on?"

"That's not really any of your..." Grant started, but the wall of anger he was facing battered him into submission. He bit his lip for a moment before carrying on. "Years. Two or three. I don't remember."

"How many women?"

He spread his arms to his side like he was measuring a fish.

A *big* fish.

"And who knew?"

"They did," he said.

"The women? I hope so. Any of them want more than sex? Any of them threaten you or Karen?"

"No," he said. "They just wanted what I wanted. It was a bit of fun."

"You say Karen didn't know about the women, but she did," said Kett. "She knew your marriage was in trouble. Did she ever speak to anyone about it?"

Grant shrugged like he couldn't have cared less.

"Her mum, probably. Her friends. You think one of them did this? Why would they make us fight, though? Why wouldn't they just kill me?"

"Who else?" asked Kett, ignoring his question.

"Fuck knows," he said. "She was always bad mouthing me to people. Little snidey remarks, always undercutting me, making me look like shit."

"I wonder why she did that," said Porter.

"Because she was jealous," Grant said, missing the DI's sarcasm. "Not my fault she aged so badly, is it? She was proper fit when we got together, and up for anything. Age just treats men and women differently, doesn't it? Marriage should take that into account."

"Christ," said Kett, the rage stewing inside him. "I have met some real charmers on this case."

Grant shrugged again, staring at his hands.

"Who else?" Kett said again. "Think."

"We had therapy," he said. "A couple of times."

It felt like something had ignited in the middle of Kett's head, and he leaned forward.

"Therapy?"

"Yeah. Karen was always into that sort of thing. Always thinking other people could help her. She was on the phone all the time to fucking horoscopes, fortune tellers, all those automated things you see in the back of newspapers. Spent a fortune. Always writing to those magazines, always buying books. She wanted everyone else to do the hard work for her, could never be arsed to do anything herself."

"Who was the therapy with?"

"That charity," said Grant. "I can't remember what they're called. They help couples get over shit."

"When?"

"Last year," he said. "Autumn time. We'd just got back from Lanzarote and things were shit. Karen suggested it. She'd spent the whole holiday ignoring me, making cunty little digs, then blamed me for making it shit. She lost it when we got back, told me we could either get therapy or get divorced."

He laughed miserably.

"Wish I'd fucking taken her up on the divorce. Only reason I didn't is because of the house. She put in more money than I did and it would have ruined me, buying her out. At least staying together was cheaper. Just thought maybe one day she'd pop her..."

He croaked, his eyes bulging at the tape recorder, then at Kett.

"Clogs," Kett finished for him. "Thanks, that will make our lives a lot easier."

"No," he said, leaning on the desk. "That's not what I was saying. I just meant I didn't want to get divorced. Look, I know this sounds shit, but I loved Karen, I did. Things had just been bad for a while, but I thought they'd get better eventually. You don't stop loving somebody just like that. She was just... She'd changed, but I still..."

He groaned, the reality of what had happened pushing against the dam he'd built up against it.

"Who was the therapist?" Kett asked.

"I can't remember. There were two. One was a guy, but we only went to one session because she fucking fancied him, I could tell. He was taking her side on everything."

"What did he look like?"

"Like, not ugly. Tall." He clicked his fingers. "His name was Carey."

"Dark hair?"

"Like, kind of. Not black. Brown."

"Well built? Tattoos?"

Here, Grant shook his head.

"Nah, skinny."

"You're sure?"

"I don't know. It's not like I was into him or anything. He was just a guy. Can't think if he had tattoos or not."

"Where was this?"

"Somewhere in the city. They've got a place there, a house."

"And the woman you saw?"

"Some old biddy called Sandra," said Grant. "Same place. Relate, that's the name of it. They both worked for Relate. I wasn't really paying any attention."

He squinted at Kett.

"You think *they* did this? That guy?" He was shaking his head. "It wasn't him. He was soft, the man who took me, he was... I didn't see him, but I know he was different. Felt like a..."

He was struggling, but Kett gave him time.

"Like a predator, you know? Not a sexual one, but something else. Something *bigger* than us. I don't know what I'm saying."

Kett knew. He thought of the man's eyes, his shark's smile.

Something bigger than us.

"There's nothing else you can tell me?" he asked. "Nobody else who would know what you were going through? Who would think to target you?"

"Nobody," said Grant, almost a whisper. "Like I said, we were nothing. We meant nothing."

After a handful of awkward seconds, Kett ended the interview and stood up, making his way out of the room.

"Put him back in his cell," he told Duke.

"Come on," said Grant, lifting his arms in protest. "I talked, give me something back. Let me out of here."

Kett ignored him, stepping into the corridor. He waited for Porter to join him, leaning in to speak quietly.

"Eileen Hopkins spoke about therapy too," he said. "Her and Frank tried it out. Can you find out who they spoke with? That's a link."

"There's a chance Will and Darcey might have too, sir," said Porter. "Young couple, unexpected pregnancy, difficult family life and highly religious. We know they confided in the priest, but maybe he wasn't the only one they spoke to."

"Good thinking," said Kett. He checked his watch to see that it was coming up for three. "I'll go speak with her now."

He pushed through the doors, shouting back.

"This might be it, Pete. We're closing in."

CHAPTER THIRTY

Kett called Savage from HQ to find that she was already on her way back into the city.

"Meet me at the hospital, will you, Kate?" he asked. "I think Darcey will open up to you more than she will me."

"Sure, sir," she said. "The FSO is with Alan Jemc's grandmother. She's calmed down, but she's still talking like she's going to end it all." She sniffed sadly, although it may have been static from the call. "Her whole family is gone. Can't imagine it."

"Me neither," said Kett. "Drive safe."

He'd almost made it to the lobby when he heard a bellow behind him.

"Zipper!"

He turned to see Clare flapping down the corridor, his face puce, his teeth bared.

"Christ alive, I was calling you for about five minutes."

"Would help if you used my name, sir," said Kett.

"Zipper *is* your name," he said. "I filed the Deed Poll myself, it's official. Your new warrant card is arriving next week and I've ordered a nameplate for your desk. Where are we?"

"We might have a lead, sir," said Kett. "Both the Hopkins and the Dankworths had therapy to help with their marriage problems. Grant's given me the names of the two people he and Karen spoke with. A woman called Sandra and a man called Carey, both working for Relate in the city."

"Therapy?" said Clare, disappointed. "What's that got to do with our killer? I've had therapy, I've never killed anyone."

"Good to know, sir," said Kett. "It's the only link I can find between the couples. If the killer is testing them, testing their love for each other, then—"

"Bucket of toss," said Clare. "Like I've already told you."

"I'm not so sure, sir," Kett said. "Why else would he pit them against each other like that? Like they were gladiators."

"Still sounds like bullshit to me," said Clare, looking around. "But I'll look into it. Where's Goblin?"

"Goblin, sir?"

"Goblin. Tim Nice-But-Dim."

Kett shook his head, too tired to try to remember the Super's long list of nicknames. Clare started to bounce around, doing a reasonably good gorilla impression.

"You know, Lord King Kong Dong, Shit-My-Pants, Toss-Flossing McMonkey Nuts the Third."

"Duke?" said Kett.

"Yes, Duke. I need a word with that prat."

"What's he done now?" said Kett.

"What's he done?" echoed Clare. The Superintendent pulled out his phone, jabbing furiously at the screen before holding it up.

Kett had to put on his glasses to make any sense of what he was looking at, and even then he struggled. It was an article on an online news site, and the main image at the top of the page was of Duke. He looked like he was standing on the stage at a bodybuilding contest, his biceps tensed and bulging through the sleeves of his uniform, his annoyingly handsome face aimed right at the camera.

The headline read: *Valentine's Day Copper Arrests Our Hearts!*

Porter was in the photo too, Kett realised, although it was a terrible shot of the DI. He was hunched over next to Duke, his mouth open in what might have been a shout or a yawn, one eye bulging, the other half shut. He could have been auditioning to be the Hunchback of Notre Dame.

Before Kett could read the article, Clare snatched the phone away, returning it a second later with a different site on the screen. This one was from the Metro website, and there was another photo of Duke in an even more ridiculous pose. Porter was there too, caught mid-movement and looking like some kind of bleary-eyed sock puppet as he stumbled towards the photographer. The headline for this article was a little more down to earth, but the caption beneath the picture struck a different tone.

Many online reactions to the case focussed on one of the constables sent to secure the scene, with viewers commenting on the fact that Norfolk Constabulary had brought out their best for Valentine's week.

"Jesus," said Kett.

"Quite," Clare replied, holding the phone so tightly the screen was in danger of shattering. "That swollen donkey's bollock is making the rest of us look bad."

"He's putting Grant Dankworth back in holding, sir," said Kett, checking his watch again. "Look, I really need to go. I'm hoping Darcey DeCarlo can confirm the therapist angle."

"Well bloody go then, Zipper," said Clare. "What are you arsing around here for?"

"You..." Kett shook his head, realising it was pointless. He walked into the lobby before Clare could say another word, shouting back, "I'll keep you updated, sir."

HE REACHED the hospital half an hour later, finding it busier than he'd ever seen it. The main car park was mobbed, everyone double parked and even more cars mounted along the kerb, providing a veritable smorgasbord for the traffic warden who was on patrol. Kett left the Volvo in a bus stop, flashing his warrant card at the warden, and then at an apoplectic bus driver, as he ran for the main doors.

Navigating the crowds inside proved challenging, but it was easy enough to find the ward where Darcey was recovering. PC Felicity Niven sat by the door, looking at something on her phone. She leapt out of her chair when she saw Kett approaching.

"Sorry, sir," she said. "I was paying attention, honest. I just got a message. From the boss."

"You're alright, Flick," he said. "Any trouble?"

"No," she said. "Been people in and out, but no sign of anyone tall, dark and handsome."

"Sir," came a shout from behind him, and he turned to see Savage running down the corridor.

"Good timing," he said.

He pressed the doorbell, waiting for the nurse at the

desk to buzz them through. She pointed to her right before he could even introduce himself.

"Room 3," she said. "She's awake, doing okay."

"Thanks," said Kett. "You want to lead on this, Kate? I think she'll respond to you, given that you saved her life."

"Not sure she appreciated it at the time, sir," said Savage. "But sure, of course."

They stopped outside the room, peering through the open door to see Darcey DeCarlo sitting upright in her bed, her hands resting on her belly. She was staring out of the window at the grey sky, and she looked around when Kett knocked. Her face was strangely expressionless, and Kett wondered if she had been sedated.

"Hey, Darcey," he said quietly. "You mind if we come in?"

She nodded once, a loose strand of hair falling in front of her face. She made no effort to tuck it away. Kett let Savage into the room first before following, leaving the door open. He stood at the foot of the bed while Savage perched on the edge, a little closer to the young woman. A small, gold cross hung over Darcey's hospital gown, casting a reflection on the far wall that rose and fell with every breath.

"Hi," said Savage, offering Darcey a warm smile. "You're doing okay?"

Darcey nodded again, and this time she swept her hair back behind her ear.

"And the baby?" said Savage.

Darcey returned her hand to her stomach, giving it a gentle rub.

"They checked her heart." She spoke slowly, as if she needed to remember how to pronounce each word. "They said she's strong. They said I didn't hurt her."

"That's good," said Savage. "That's great, Darcey. You're both going to be fine."

The young woman's brow furrowed, but only for a second or two.

"I guess," she said.

"We're still trying to find the person who did this to you," Savage went on. "To William. But we need your help. Is that okay?"

"I guess," she said again.

Savage rested her hand on Darcey's arm, giving it a soft squeeze.

"Thank you. This is Robbie, do you remember him?"

Darcey nodded without looking up.

"Hi," said Kett. "We just need to ask a couple of questions, okay?"

Another nod.

"I know it can't be easy, the pregnancy. I know you were concerned about it happening before you and Will were married."

Darcey winced as if he had accused her of something terrible.

"I know you must have been worried. Did you and Will ever seek any kind of professional help? Somebody to talk to about it all. Any kind of therapy?"

Darcey lifted her head, studying him as if he was talking in a foreign language.

"Lots of people do it," said Savage. "It's a great way of talking through your problems, finding ways to work together."

"We spoke to Father Odling," she said. "Sometimes to Val."

"Nobody else?" asked Kett.

"I asked a few people for advice," she said. "Just chat

rooms on the internet. MumsNet, that kind of thing. But we never had therapy. Willy would never have done it, he wasn't that kind of person."

"Wasn't the kind of person who wanted to solve problems?" said Kett. "To fix things?"

The look Darcey gave him this time had anger in it.

"He wanted to solve everyone's problems," she said. "You don't get it. He wasn't like his brother. He was nothing like him or any of them."

"What problems was he trying to solve, Darcey?" said Kett.

She held onto the question, her eyes reading invisible lines.

"I'm safe here, aren't I?" she said eventually.

"Safest place in the world," he told her. "There's a police officer right outside the door."

She laughed, but there was no warmth in it.

"Doesn't make me feel any better," she said. "The police are the problem."

"What do you mean?" Kett asked, but he had a feeling he already knew.

Darcey shot a look at the door as if she expected somebody to be standing there.

"You went to the house, didn't you?" she said.

"Will's house? In Yarmouth?"

"Yeah. You saw what they were doing there?"

"The women," said Kett. "I saw."

"And?" she said, the anger returning.

"And it's bad," said Kett. "I don't know exactly what's going on there, but I know it's bad. We're aware of it now, we're going to look into it, I promise."

"Look into it?" she said, disgusted. "You know those girls

get shipped in from Europe? They take their passports from them, make them do all kinds of horrible things. They don't let them leave, they keep them prisoner, make them do all that then take all their money from them. They're slaves."

"You know this for sure?" said Kett.

"Yeah, because Willy knew it. Luke was running the place, but Willy didn't want anything to do with it. He just set up the online stuff for them but he hated it. Luke and that..."

Here her voice dropped to a whisper, as if she was afraid somebody else might hear her.

"That man who calls himself the Archduke. You met him?"

Kett nodded.

"They beat up anyone who threatens them, probably worse. Willy wanted to leave but they wouldn't let him, said they'd mess him up if he ever went behind their backs. He was scared of them. We were going to..."

She stopped as the memory of his death began to seep through whatever drugs they'd given her. Kett could see her reliving it.

"You were going to leave?" said Savage, reading her mind, bringing her back.

"Yeah, we were going to leave. But then I realised I was pregnant, I couldn't... I couldn't leave before we were married, because I didn't know anywhere else that would do it. It's my fault we stayed, my fault he died."

"It's not," said Savage, giving her arm another squeeze. "It's not your fault, or Will's fault. The blame lies with the man who did this to you, nobody else, and we're going to make him pay for what he did."

"But we need to find him," said Kett. "As soon as we do,

I'll open an investigation into Luke Briggs and the Archduke. You have my word, we'll bring them down."

"You won't," she said. "Half of you are in on it."

"You're talking about Dawson, right?" said Kett. "The detective?"

Darcey nodded, her hair falling over her face again. Savage gently swept it back for her. She looked paler at the mention of Dawson.

"He's part of it?" said Kett.

"He's the biggest part. He runs the whole thing, but he's got this act he does, makes himself look like an idiot, like he can't even drink a cup of coffee without spilling it down himself. He doesn't care if people think he looks stupid, he doesn't even care if people think he's a bad guy, but he doesn't want people to know that he's the one who brings the girls in, that he's the one who locks them up and makes them work. He's..."

She checked the door again.

"You believe in the Devil?"

"No," said Kett. "Not the one you're talking about, anyway."

"I do," she said. "I think it's him. I think he's evil. They say the greatest trick the Devil ever pulled is convincing people he doesn't exist, don't they? Well that's what he's doing. Nobody believes that he's capable of it, but Willy saw it up close. He knew."

"Dawson won't get away with it," said Kett. "You have my word. I'll bring him down. But I can't do it until we catch William's killer. We need to do that first, before he does the same thing to somebody else."

"It won't wait," said Darcey. "Chuckles knows you know about the house, about the girls. He'll shut everything down and start up someplace else. He'll make it disappear. You have to go after him now."

"We will."

Darcey screwed her eyes shut, shaking her head.

"You don't understand," she said. "You're not getting it."

"I am," said Kett. "I know you want to stop these men from—"

She snapped open her eyes, and she looked wild.

"Dawson killed Willy," she said.

"*What?*"

"It was him. He was at the lorry. He... he didn't think I'd seen him, he thought he was hiding, but he wasn't. I saw him there."

Kett and Savage frowned at each other.

"I don't think so, Darcey," said Kett. "We've seen the killer, we know what he looks like."

"Because Dawson isn't..." The words caught in her throat and she choked on them, coughing for a handful of seconds. "He doesn't work alone, does he? He used Willy and the Archduke and Luke to run the house, he uses a million people to do his dirty work in the town. He was there, but there was another man as well."

"What did he look like?" asked Kett.

"It was dark," she said. "I couldn't see, and then I was inside the lorry. But he was big, he had a deep voice. I *recognised* his voice, I've heard it before."

"Why didn't you tell us this?" said Kett, grabbing the end of the bed in both hands.

"Because I didn't know if you were one of *his*," she said, her words frantic now. "I didn't know if you were good or bad."

"Where did you hear his voice before?" asked Savage.

"At the house," she said, one hand leaving her belly to grab the golden cross around her neck. "I heard him speaking to Willy and to Luke, heard him laughing. He's Dawson's man, I know it. Dawson used him to kidnap Willy because he was threatening to leave. He knew he wouldn't let me die, that he'd... that he'd take his own life. He probably thought we'd both die in there. It's him, I'm telling you. *Please* listen to me."

"Okay," said Kett. "I hear you. I'm going to send somebody to pick up Dawson right now, and somebody else to William's house. Okay?"

"You'll be too late," she said. "Nobody will be there. He'll have moved everyone out. But..."

She swallowed, thinking hard.

"But what?" asked Kett.

"He's got another place," she said. "Willy always spoke about it. A warehouse somewhere. He'll have moved the girls there until he finds them a new place to work from."

"Where?" said Kett.

"I don't know. Not for definite. But it was down by the port, I know that much. He'll be there, I'm sure of it. Him and Luke and the Archduke and the man who locked us in the lorry. They're all in on it."

"You're sure about this?" he asked her.

Darcey met his eye, as fierce as anyone he'd ever met.

"I'm sure," she said. "It's him. And you can catch him. But you have to move fast."

CHAPTER THIRTY-ONE

Kett left the Volvo at the hospital, riding in Savage's Audi. He called Clare on speakerphone as they thumped over the roundabout.

"Sir," he said when the call connected. "Darcey DeCarlo thinks DI Charles Dawson is behind the Valentine's killings."

"Suck my tosspipe, Kett," Clare roared back. "Dawson can barely tie his own shoes. I once saw him try to smoke a pipe by putting the wrong end in his mouth."

"I thought the same thing, sir. She says it's just an act. The clever man plays the fool, and all that. He's been running the brothel in Yarmouth with the Briggs brothers and Perry Paul, the Archduke. Darcey says he uses other people to do his dirty work, but that he's smarter than he looks. She saw him alongside our killer on the night she and Will were loaded into the lorry."

"She actually said that?" said Clare. "You didn't hit your head too hard and imagine it?"

"She said it, sir. I don't think she has any reason to lie."

He felt Savage's eyes on him and he turned to her. She was frowning, but she didn't speak.

"Everyone has a reason to lie," said Clare. "Why would Charles Dawson kill Will?"

"Because Will wanted to leave the operation, and Darcey wanted him to talk to the police, to shut the whole thing down. I'm guessing Dawson couldn't just order a hit on him because of Luke. He needed it to look like a random killing."

"What kind of moron forces two people into mortal combat in a burning lorry just to make a death look like an accident?" said Clare. "Not to mention putting two other couples through the same thing. What's the link?"

"I don't know, sir," said Kett.

"Bucket. Of. Toss."

"Darcey thinks they'll have abandoned the house on the seafront," Kett went on. "But she told us Dawson owns a warehouse by the port. He'll be keeping the girls there until he has a new place to operate out of. If he's there, there's a chance our killer is too."

"You've got an address?"

"Not yet, sir," said Kett. "Savage and I are heading out to try and find it."

"I'll send the rest of the team to meet you," said Clare. "I asked for Dawson to be tailed, but I haven't had any updates. I don't think anyone took it seriously, because it's *Chuckles*."

He grunted his annoyance.

"I'd call bullshit on this, because everything I know about Chuckles tells me he couldn't take charge of a cup of his own asparagus-scented piss, let alone something like this. But your therapy leads came up dead."

"The therapists are *dead*, sir?" said Kett.

"No, you suppurating badger cock, the *leads* are dead. Cold. Fucked. Carey Rose lives in Brighton and is accounted for. Sandra Macclesfield passed away last year from complications due to diabetes. Your only link between our victims was a dud. We've nothing else to go on. Get to Yarmouth, I'll see if I can get hold of Dawson."

"Yes, sir," said Kett. "And send Gorski. I think we're going to need tactical."

"Of course you are," said Clare, his voice cold. "Because there's a ninety-nine percent chance you're going to Kett this whole thing up. Now, begone!"

The line went dead.

"Begone?" said Kett as they hit the dual carriageway, Savage accelerating so hard he thought his guts were going to explode out of his backside. She still had that look on her face. "What's up?" he asked.

"I don't know, sir," she said. "Something about this isn't right."

"You think Darcey's lying to us?"

"It's not that," she said. "I think she's telling the truth about Dawson, about the brothel. We're missing something, though. I can't figure out what."

Kett gripped the strap above the door as the countryside flashed past.

"Me neither," he said. "But I get the feeling we're about to find out."

THEY TORE into Yarmouth twenty-five minutes later, following the tangled roads east. A couple of IRVs had caught up to them on the Acle Straight, their sirens off but their lights flashing, and they tailed them all the way to the seafront. There was a mob of police cars outside the Briggs' house already, and Savage pulled the car over beside them. They'd breached the enormous gate, flooding the yard, and Kett could see an army of PCs through the dirty windows as they conducted a search.

He wound his window down, yelling to the closest constable. The man trotted over, one hand on his Taser to stop it from rattling.

"What's going on?" Kett asked, holding out his warrant card.

"Raid," said the PC. "But they must have known we were coming. Place is deserted."

"Is DI Dawson here?" he asked.

"Chuckles, sir?" The PC looked back into the crowd, then shook his head. "Haven't seen him."

"If he shows up, tell him to call me," said Kett, fishing a card from his wallet and handing it to the man.

"Yes, sir," he said. "Is there a reason?"

"He'll know it."

Kett wound his window up and Savage took off again, the setting sun casting the long shadow of their car out to sea as they made their way along the quiet promenade, past the huge, deserted beaches and the skeletal piers, past the lonely arcades whose lights did their best to ward away the inevitable dark, past the shuttered amusement parks with their abandoned rides.

The port rose in the windscreen like an industrial wasteland, enormous warehouses and smoking chimneys and vast cranes that punctured the sky. There had to be a square mile of land here, and hundreds of buildings, so Kett pointed to the side of the road and told Savage to pull over. She did as she was asked, keeping the engine running.

"No point rushing in," he said. "Not until we know where he is. Don't want to risk scaring him off again."

He pulled out his phone and called Spalding, counting nine rings before she answered.

"I know what you're going to ask me for, sir," she said, her words muffled like she was chewing on a pencil. "And believe me, you calling up right now isn't going to make me go any quicker."

"Would anything make you go quicker, Alison?" he said. "Because we're running out of time. If Dawson knows we're onto him, he'll be in the wind."

Spalding didn't reply. He could hear her typing, and past that the growl of an engine from outside the car. He craned around to see a tactical police van slow to a halt behind them. There was no mistaking the explosion of red hair he could make out through the windscreen. He lifted a hand, but if Gorski saw him she didn't respond.

"Can you call me back?" he asked Spalding, one hand on the door.

"I can," she said. "But I think I've got it. Dawson's listed as a director for a dormant company called Happy Clown Enterprises Ltd. Why clowns?"

"He calls himself Chuckles," said Kett. "They've got property?"

"A storage facility by the port," she said. "Bell's Marsh Road, by the waterfront. There's no number."

"Bell's Marsh Road?" said Kett. "I'll find it. Thank you."

"It's right there," said Savage, Google Maps open on her phone. "Next street over."

Kett let himself out of the car, the frozen wind hunting him from the churning sea. Night sat on the horizon, a wave of inky darkness that was moving this way fast. Gorski wound down her window as he walked over, giving him a nod.

"Hey, Julia," he said. "Thanks for coming."

"What have you got, sir?"

He leaned against the door and pointed to the buildings across the street. There was a line of smaller premises here, dwarfed by the bigger warehouses behind.

"We think we've got some women being kept against their will," he said. "Probably two or three men holding them, I don't know if they're armed."

"Doesn't sound too bad," said Gorski.

"There's a chance that one of those men is a copper," Kett said. "DI Charles Dawson."

"That makes it harder," she said. "Crooked?"

"As they come. But we have intel that puts him at the scene of the Valentine's killings, too."

Gorski nodded, her eyes narrowing.

"How do you want to do it?" Kett asked her.

Gorski glanced at the man in the seat next to her, an unspoken exchange between them.

"With extreme prejudice, sir," she said. "We'll go on foot, you guys seal off the road and stay out of the way."

Kett stood back as Gorski dropped out. She thumped the side of the van a couple of times and the back opened up, a file of officers in tactical uniforms appearing. The soft rattle of their weapons was the only noise they made as they congregated on the pavement. They formed a huddle around Gorski as she relayed her orders.

Kett made his way back to the car, calling to the constables that had followed.

"Close the road, would you?" he told them. "Both directions, and get a block on the next street over as well, in case they make a run for it."

They ran off, both of them waving at a Mondeo that was approaching from the north. They had a quick word with the driver, then let it through. The car joined the end of the line of vehicles, Porter and Duke emerging from it. Porter did *not* look happy.

"It's really not your fault, sir," Duke said as they walked over. "Some faces just aren't made for the cameras."

"My face is bloody golden, mate," Porter grumbled back. "You just make me so miserable that every time I appear in a photo with you, I look like shit. You're the problem, not me." He tilted his head at Kett. "Sir, you moving in?"

"Imminently," said Kett.

"You really think it's Dawson?" Porter asked. "He doesn't strike me as the kind of man who'd lock two people in a burning lorry and make them fight to the death."

Kett shrugged. Savage had made her way over to join them.

"We're not sure, sir," she said. "It's what Darcey DeCarlo told us, and she's a credible witness."

"There's no link between Dawson and the other couples, though?"

"Nothing we've found," said Kett. "Doesn't mean he wasn't involved."

"We're ready, sir," said Gorski. "Which building is it?"

"No number," said Kett. "But it belongs to a company called Happy Clowns Enterprises."

"Shouldn't be too hard to find," said Duke. "You can spot clowns from a mile off."

"What?" said Porter, staring at him.

"The outfits, sir, they're pretty bright."

"Unlike you," said Porter. "There won't be any actual clowns there, Aaron."

Duke frowned.

"Let's move," said Kett.

Gorski took the lead, the head of a black snake that slid soundlessly across the road. The night had rolled over the town in the time they'd been standing here, the streetlights on but struggling. A short line of traffic had built up behind the police barricades, people out of their cars and watching. But this part of Yarmouth was quiet, the warehouses abandoned. The only sound Kett could hear over the patter of feet and the crash of the waves behind him was a soft, melodic sound.

"Is somebody *humming*?" he asked.

The sound stopped immediately.

"No," said Duke.

They made their way slowly forward. The right-hand side of the road was residential, a row of houses, most of which had their lights on. On the left, though, were nothing but warehouses and industrial units. Most of these were shuttered, their gates chained, the rusting signs bearing the names of businesses long dead. Kett passed a couple of car showrooms, a garage, and a bathroom store, then he stopped.

The next building along was a low warehouse, its walls brick, its roof corrugated iron. There were no windows, but an aura of yellow light spilled out through the crack between the double front doors. There was no sign on the wall, no number, no indication at all who owned the building.

But sitting in the middle of the car park, between a couple of beat-up Fords and a white van, was a lurid green Audi R8.

"Saw that car back at the house, sir," said Porter.

"This is it," Kett said, approaching Gorski.

She nodded, and pulled her visor down.

"Stay back," she told him.

He had no intention of doing otherwise.

The gates were chained, but a tactical officer with a set of giant bolt cutters made short work of the padlock. Gorski hefted the gate open and her team funnelled through, their weapons up.

Kett leaned against the chain-link fence, the cold air and the first spray of drizzle doing little to cool his blood. The adrenaline was roaring, his head pounding as he watched the team reach the warehouse. They seemed to take a collective breath, a moment of calm before the storm.

Then Gorski opened the door and they moved in, fast and hard.

"Armed police!" they shouted, an onslaught of sound. "Do not move!"

Screams tore into the night, a lot of them. In a heartbeat, all but two of the tactical team had vanished into the building, their shouts drowned out by the cries of panic from inside.

A gunshot.

The screams rose in volume, one woman flying out of the door so fast that she tripped and fell, her head bouncing off the ground. Another followed, a tactical officer trying to stop her, but missing. She bolted for the gate, saw the army of police that waited outside it.

"Come on," Kett told her. "It's safe."

She must have thought otherwise, doubling back towards the warehouse just as another gun went off. She ducked to her knees, her hands on her ears. More women were pouring through the door, too many for the tactical officers to contain.

"Over here," Kett yelled, waving them on. "Hurry!"

They were too terrified to hear him, scattering in a dozen different directions, vanishing into the shadows. The gunfire was coming thick and fast from inside, too frenzied to be Gorski and her team.

Somebody was shooting back.

The two officers by the door had entered the warehouse to join the fight. Kett ran through the gate towards the woman who was on her knees, grabbing her hand.

"Come on," he said. "Move."

She didn't look like she was going to, then Savage appeared, taking her gently under the arm.

"It's too dangerous here," she said, more gunfire emphasising her point. "Let's go."

The woman stood up, holding Savage's hand as they ran for the street.

"Hey!" Kett called out to another huddle of women. "Let's go!"

Somebody was running towards him, and he recognised the woman he'd met inside the Briggs house. She looked scared, but there was a wild defiance in her eyes.

"Help me," Kett told her. "Get them out of there."

"To go where?" she spat. "Prison? Back home? Better to run."

"No, it's not," said Kett. He flinched as another round of gunfire split the night.

The woman studied him a moment more before turning and shouting something in her own language. One by one, the women that had fled to the darkest corners of the car park began to emerge, following the woman's call towards the gate. Kett helped them along, Savage and Duke and Porter gathering them on the other side of the fence. The young woman was the last to go, and she pointed her finger at Kett.

"You fuck us over, your life won't be worth living."

"Noted," said Kett.

She ran off after the others, a tide of uniformed officers leading them up the street and around the corner.

Kett turned back to the warehouse just as another barrage of gunfire exploded from inside. This time it was followed by a scream of pain, too raw and too wet to work out whether it came from a man or a woman. A series of shouts followed, muted by the walls of the building.

"What is going on in there?" said Porter from Kett's side.

Before Kett could answer, he heard the clatter of a door opening from the flank of the warehouse, footsteps drumming. A shadow peeled itself away from the building, crossing the car park as fast as it could go. Kett waited for the tactical team to follow, but gunfire had opened up again from deep inside the building. They were too busy to notice that somebody had escaped.

"Shit," said Kett. "Hey!"

The man glanced back, barely missing a step.

It was Perry Paul, the Archduke.

"Hey!" Kett roared again. "Stop!"

Paul made it to the edge of the car park, grabbing the drooping fence and hauling himself up it. It was harder than it should have been, mainly because he was holding something in his hand.

"Get on the radio," Kett told Duke. "Tell Gorski she's lost one."

He started running, ignoring Savage as she called out after him. Paul was struggling to get over the fence, and after a few seconds he dropped back down. He tried again, his grunts echoing across the car park, concealing the sound of Kett's footsteps until he was twenty yards away. He stopped next to the white van so that he'd have somewhere to take cover.

Because now that he was this close, he could see that Paul was holding a gun.

"Hey," Kett shouted. "Perry, stop. It's over."

Paul made one last effort to scale the fence, then howled his fury into the air. He turned around, his fist clenched around the handle of the pistol, his finger on the trigger. There was blood on the shoulder of his expensive, camouflaged tracksuit, more dripping from his sleeve and pattering onto the ground. He'd paled considerably since the last time Kett had seen him, but he still managed a leering smile.

"Drop the gun," said Kett, half his body still protected by the van.

"Or what?" said Paul. He hawked up a ball of bloody spit, lobbing it halfway to where Kett was standing. He made no effort to lift the gun. "What are you going to do?"

"I'm going to come over there and take it," said Kett.

Paul's smile grew, his teeth crimson.

"Now that's something I'd like to see," he said.

He doubled up, groaning. The stain on his tracksuit top was spreading fast. Kett could see the trail of blood he'd left from the warehouse door to the fence.

"Just drop it," Kett said. "We can get you into an ambulance before you bleed to death."

"Fuck you," the Archduke said, straightening up with no small effort. "I'd rather go out in a blaze of glory."

He lifted the gun to his head with the same sick smile.

"Don't you dare," said Kett.

Paul pulled the trigger.

Nothing happened.

"Ran dry a while ago," Paul said, dropping his hand to his side. "Bad luck for me."

Kett stepped out from behind the van, his pulse like a jackhammer.

"Then drop it," he said. "We're not even after you. It's Dawson we want."

"You got him," he said, nodding to the warehouse. "Not sure if he'll make it, though."

"He's in charge of all this?" Kett asked.

"If you can believe it," Paul replied, spitting more blood.

"Then help me take him down," said Kett. "Help me get him behind bars for all of this, and for the couples he burned inside the lorries."

Paul frowned, sagging against the fence as if his legs were struggling to hold him up.

"What?" he said.

"Drop the gun, Perry. We can help each other."

The side door of the warehouse sprung open with a crack that almost made Kett leap right out of his boots. He turned to see Gorski stride into the car park, her rifle to her shoulder. Two more members of the team followed, pointing their weapons at Paul.

"Nah," said Paul. "I'm a dead man either way. At least this will be quick."

He lifted the revolver and pointed it at the approaching tactical team.

"It's emp—" Kett shouted, then Gorski's rifle snapped and Paul collapsed against the fence, a perfect hole punched in the centre of his chest. He slumped backwards, folding like a ragdoll, his unseeing eyes staring at the dark sky.

"Man down," yelled Gorski, running towards Paul, her rifle still up. "Kett, back the fuck away."

"It was empty," said Kett, both hands in his hair.

"Sir?" said Savage. She was making her way across the car park, Porter and Duke beside her.

Gorski kicked the gun away, crouching down in order to

check Perry Paul's pulse. For a handful of seconds, nobody breathed. Then Gorski shook her head.

"Fuck," Kett said. "His gun was empty."

"Wasn't going to take that chance, sir," said Gorski, cradling her rifle against her flank and pulling up her visor. She looked exhausted. "Warehouse is secure. We've got one man in custody, another with a gunshot wound."

"Your team okay?" he asked.

No answer.

"Is it safe to go in?"

It took Gorski a while to reply, her serious eyes locked on the dead man at her feet.

"It's all yours, sir," she said quietly. "Knock yourself out."

CHAPTER THIRTY-TWO

By the time Kett had made it to the warehouse's main doors, an ambulance was rolling through the open gates into the car park.

And when he walked into the building and heard the screams, he understood why it was here.

It was absolute carnage inside the warehouse, the vast, windowless space shredded by gunfire, the cold air heavy with the smell of smoke. The middle of the building was made up like an apartment, with four assorted sofas arranged in a square next to a small kitchenette and a long dining table. It was hemmed in by dozens of cots which had been lined up along both long walls, most stripped bare, but ten or so made up to sleep in, with suitcases tucked underneath.

A man sat on one of the beds, his hands cuffed behind his back. From here, Kett couldn't see his face, but the colour of his hair and the studs in his ears told him it was Luke Briggs. Three of the tactical team stood beside him, all of them alert even though their rifles had been stowed. Two more officers stood beside an internal door that probably led to a toilet.

It was from this door that a harrowing chorus of sobs and shrieks radiated.

"Somebody isn't happy," said Porter as he strode in behind him.

Kett crossed the warehouse, trying not to slip on the hail of shell casings that had been strewn across the floor. The tactical officers by the door stood to attention as he approached them.

"You all okay?" Kett asked, speaking up so that his voice wasn't drowned out by the gargled screams.

"We are, sir," said one of the men, his voice muffled by his balaclava. "Ambulance on its way?"

"It's here," said Kett. "What happened?"

"You kind of have to see it for yourself," said the man. "It isn't pretty."

They moved aside to let Kett and Porter through the door. Ahead was a short corridor, the whitewashed wall marked by a streak of blood that looked too bright to be real in the buzzing fluorescents. In the confined space, the screams were almost deafening. There was another voice too, speaking calmly and quietly.

"Stop moving. If you don't stop moving, you're going to lose it."

There was a door on the right, and Kett pushed it open with his fingertips to see a small bathroom. A man lay on the tiled floor in a puddle of blood, curled so tightly into himself that only his filthy overcoat gave away his identity. Two more officers knelt beside him, one trying to hold him still as he rocked back and forth, the other fumbling with a first aid kit. They both looked around when they heard the door open.

"What happened?" said Kett.

The answer was pretty obvious in the way Charles Dawson had both hands clamped over his crotch, his fingers slick with blood.

"He got shot," said the firearms officer with the first aid kit. "He opened fire on us, ran in here for cover. Loose round caught him as he was running."

"Caught him where?" said Porter, ashen faced.

"Caught him someplace you really don't want to get caught."

Dawson howled, writhing in agony.

"Stop moving!" the other man told him. "Christ, where are the paramedics?"

"I'll go check," said Kett. "You think there's any chance of him talking?"

"He's just had his knob shot off, sir," said the first officer. "I doubt it."

Dawson arched his back in pain, his face sliding into view. His mouth twisted open, his round eyes full of horror as they met Kett's.

"Right," said Kett, trying not to imagine what the man was going through.

He walked back the way he'd come. Porter trotted next to him, one hand on his crotch as if he was expecting another round of gunfire.

"That's..." the DI started, and he couldn't seem to find the words to finish.

Luckily for Dawson, the paramedics had made their way through the door.

"Over here," said Kett, and they charged across the room, their bags swinging. He pointed in the direction of the screams. "Through there. I think he's had his... his, uh..."

"His *penis*," said Porter. He opened his fist in an imitation of something exploding, and he added the sound effect to boot.

"Shot in the penis," Kett said.

"Right in the penis," Porter added.

The paramedics ran into the corridor, and Kett wiped the sweat from his cool brow. His stomach was roiling, the stench of gunpowder and blood making him want to vomit. He closed his eyes for a moment to compose himself, then made his way to where Luke Briggs sat on the edge of the bed. The man didn't look up, even when Kett stood over him.

"Luke," said Kett.

Luke sniffed, his head almost resting in his lap. Kett sat on the bed next to him, taking a moment to study the dingy warehouse, the filthy floors, the stained bedding. He wondered if this wasn't just a place they took the women to stay when they weren't in the house, if maybe this was a place they were sent to *work*. The thought of it, of Dawson and Briggs and Paul forcing the women into prostitution in this awful building, made the screams that came from the bathroom a little more bearable.

"Luke," he said again. "It's over. Your brother is dead. Perry Paul is dead. Dawson's finished. You're the only one left, so it's up to you, I'm afraid."

Luke swallowed, still staring at his own knees. Kett could hear the rattle of the handcuffs as he trembled.

"Only one left for what?" he said quietly.

"To tell me what the hell is going on," Kett said. "It's your story now. So talk."

Luke sniffed, a tear dripping from the end of his nose.

"Willy's dead?"

"Yeah. Sorry."

"You're sure?"

"We're sure," said Kett. "We found his body in a lorry that had been set on fire. Darcey was in there too, but she got out. Somebody locked them in and made them fight, told them the door would only be opened when one of them was dead."

Luke looked up, his eyes dark hollows in his face.

"What?"

"According to Darcey, Will killed himself so that she could go free."

"Why?" Luke asked.

"Why what?" said Kett. "Why'd he kill himself?"

"Why would somebody do that to him?" Luke said. "He wasn't a bad guy, didn't even want any part of this. He wanted to go and *I* wanted him to go. To get out. Why would..."

His voice had grown weaker with every word, and finally tailed off.

"Charles Dawson was running your operation?" asked Kett.

It took him a while, but eventually he nodded.

"You and William and Paul, you were working for him?"

Dawson screamed from the bathroom, as if he was denying it. But Luke nodded again.

"Did Dawson know that Will wanted out?" said Kett.

"No," Luke said. "No, Willy wouldn't have dared say anything. Dawson would have..."

He sat up, tensing his arms as if trying to break out of the handcuffs.

"*Chuckles* did that to my brother?"

"I don't know," said Kett. "Not for sure. Was he capable of something like that?"

Luke scoffed, and when he spoke again it was a whisper, as if he was afraid that Dawson might hear him.

"He's evil. You have no idea. You say Willy was burned?"

"After he'd stabbed himself, yeah," said Kett.

"I've seen Chuckles do that to a man before," said Luke. "Out at sea. Tied him to a boat and set fire to it, watched him burn to death, watched him scream until his throat..."

He stalled.

"Seen him do too many bad things to people. Some of them deserved it, most of them didn't. Some just looked at him the wrong way."

He hung his head.

"But how did he know?" said Luke. "How did he know Willy wanted out? He only told me. I didn't think he'd even spoken to Darcey about it. He didn't want to worry her, with the baby and everything."

"You knew about the baby?"

One of the paramedics jogged out of the door, heading for the exit with the look of somebody about to throw up.

"Yeah, of course," said Luke. "Willy told me everything. He was worried because Darcey was a nut. She told him they had to get married or the baby would be conceived in sin, or something like that. I told him he was a little late to change that. He got married, though. Last week."

"I know," said Kett. "Did anyone else know he wanted out?"

Luke frowned.

"When did it happen? When did he die?"

"Sunday night," said Kett. "Around midnight, we think."

Luke's frown deepened, and he shook his head.

"Dawson was with me on Sunday," he said.

"All night?"

"Yeah. I mean most of it. He'd brought in a couple of new girls off the boat and he... I mean, he wanted to try them out."

"Try them out?" said Kett, his anger growing. Luke seemed to sense it, edging away from him on the bed.

"He always wanted to try out the new girls," he said. "Just him, though, none of the rest of us were allowed to touch them."

Kett didn't believe him, not one bit.

"I swear," said Luke. "Chuckles was in the house all night, got fucked off his face and fell asleep in the bath. I saw him leave for work the next morning."

"You didn't see him leave all night?"

"No," said Luke. "He was in the room with the girls till after midnight, and I know he was in there because I could hear him. I could hear *them*. He always makes them cry, it's fucking horrible. When he came out, he could barely walk he was so drunk, he never left the house."

"Darcey told us she saw Dawson outside the lorry where she was held captive."

"She couldn't've," he said. "She got it wrong."

The adrenaline was starting to swim through Kett's veins again, but it was nothing to do with gunfire this time.

"She said there was another man with him," he went on. "He's tall, well built, dark hair, trimmed beard, tattoos on both arms."

He pulled out his phone, finding the photo he had taken of Clara Clare's sketch.

"You know anyone like this who works with Dawson?"

Luke studied the sketch for a moment, and Kett could see the answer in his expression before he spoke it.

"No. Never seen him before."

Shit, thought Kett, putting the phone away.

"You know where Dawson was this morning? Between nine and eleven?"

"No," Luke said. "Didn't see him, but the Archduke did. He had a meeting with him this morning, told me about it when he came back to the house. It was in town."

"What time was that?"

"Like, ten? Maybe before. I don't know. I was asleep when he left the house."

Kett swore silently again. The paramedic had returned with a stretcher, a uniformed constable helping him into the warehouse. He wheeled it through the door to where Dawson's screams were starting to fade.

"Do the names Grant and Karen Dankworth mean anything to you, Luke? Or Alan Jemc and Gregg Peterson?"

"No," the young man said.

"You're sure?"

"I don't know them. Don't know anything about the lorry, or what happened to my brother." He sniffed, the cuffs rattling. "I don't doubt for a second that Chuckles would have killed Willy if he'd known he was bailing on us. And he would have made it hurt. We're all fucking terrified of him, Willy especially. Took a beating from him more than once. But he didn't know. There's no way he could have known."

The screams picked up again, accompanied by shouts from the paramedics. They were probably trying to get him on the stretcher, Kett thought.

"Is that him?" Luke asked, staring at the door.

"Dawson? Yeah."

"What happened to him?"

"I think somebody shot his dick off," said Kett.

Luke reacted with a simple nod.

"Good," he said.

Kett pushed himself off the bed, feeling like somebody was sliding daggers into his spine.

"Will you testify against him, Luke? It will help your case."

Luke breathed out a laugh, his eyes locked on something in the middle distance.

"Ain't nothing going to help my case," he said. "Not after this. But fuck it. Not like I got anything to lose. Better than going to jail."

"You're still going to jail," said Kett.

He walked towards Porter, who was waiting for him by the main doors. Halfway there, though, he turned around and made his way back.

"Luke, you say Dawson killed a lot of people."

Luke nodded.

"Last night he showed up at the church, St Margaret's, when Will's girlfriend tried to throw herself off the roof. You hear about that?"

The expression on the young man's face made it very clear he hadn't.

"A woman died while we were there. Not at the church, but just up the road."

"Hit-and-run?" said Luke. Kett nodded.

"How'd you know?"

"Chuckles had me drive a car over to the scrapyard in the middle of the night, blood and shit all over it. Who was it?"

"A woman called Valerie. She worked at the church. Why would he kill her?"

Luke shrugged.

"Could be a million reasons. Like I said, I've seen him have somebody killed because they gave him the stink eye in the street. He's a mad cunt, no doubt. My guess, though, is if she worked at the church, then she heard something she shouldn't've."

"From Will or Darcey?" said Kett. "Something about your house, about the girls. Makes sense. But they spoke to the priest, too. Why didn't Dawson go after him?"

At this, Luke actually laughed.

"You need me to answer that, then there's no hope for you."

"Odling is in on it?"

"Not part of the crew. He's just a customer."

"Fuck's sake," muttered Kett.

He made his way to the door again, standing back as the paramedics appeared from the corridor that led to the bathroom. They were wheeling the stretcher, one of them holding an IV that had been plugged into Charles Dawson's arm. It was a small mercy that the man was now unconscious, his tongue lolling out of his mouth, one eye partially open and staring at the roof.

"He okay?" asked Kett as they manoeuvred him towards the exit. "How's his, you know?"

"Cock's still there," said the paramedic at the back of the stretcher. He nodded to a hazardous waste box that was resting on Dawson's blanketed legs. "But what's left of his testicle is in there."

"Christ," said Kett, one hand to his mouth.

"Bad news, sir?" asked Porter as Kett reached him. It was a zoo out here, three ambulances in the car park and a forest of IRVs outside the gates, their blue lights making the night swim. Kett heard a coarse voice rise over the hum of chatter and the growl of engines, seeing Superintendent Clare practically running towards them.

"It is now," he said. "Brace yourself."

"Zipper! KitKat! What in the name of Satan's arse biscuits is going on?"

"It's going to take a while to explain, sir," said Kett. "But Darcey DeCarlo's tip paid off. Dawson and his associates were keeping women here, forcing them into prostitution. Dawson was in charge, the Briggs brothers and Perry Paul were working for him, certainly others as well."

"Where is that prick?" Clare said, searching the crowd with red eyes.

"Dawson's in an ambulance," said Kett. "Somebody shot his bollock off."

"Who the fuck's Izbollokov?" said Clare. "Are the Russians in on this?"

"No, sir, somebody shot Dawson in the crotch. He's lost a bollock."

Clare paled noticeably.

"Perry Paul is dead, the tactical team took them both out."

"His *bollock*?" said Clare.

"No, Paul was shot in the chest."

"But Dawson really lost a bollock?"

"At least one, sir," said Kett. "The whole... crotchal area was a mess."

"Christ alive," said Clare. "I almost feel sorry for him. But this is good, because Dawson's our Valentine's killer? Right?"

Kett took a breath.

"*Right*?"

"No, sir. He's not. Luke said Dawson was at the Briggs house all night on the thirteenth, drunk off his face. He was *testing* some new girls, apparently, so we can check with the women we found here tonight."

"Testing?" said Porter, the anger inside him visible.

"Yeah," said Kett. "Safe to say he won't be doing that again. He has an alibi for the third lorry this morning as well, sir. It's not him. But he probably killed Valerie so she wouldn't pass on whatever Darcey and Will spoke to her about. Luke dumped the car that Dawson used to kill her."

"And the priest?" said Clare.

"In on it, sir," said Kett. "He's a punter."

"Is there any fucking thing you don't make more complicated than it needs to be, Kett?" Clare said, furious.

"I didn't make him—"

"So what's the link?" Clare said, stamping his brogue on the tarmac. "If this isn't Charles Dawson then why did the killer go after William Briggs and his girlfriend? What else do we have?"

Kett searched his mind for an answer, but his thoughts were a sandstorm of exhaustion and confusion. He couldn't see a single logical thing in the chaos. Fortunately, he was saved from answering as Savage and Duke walked over from the street. The pair of them looked miserable.

"We've rounded up sixteen women, sir," she said. "All European or Russian, most don't speak English, or at least not very well. The ones that do aren't talking, I think they're scared of us."

"They're scared of Dawson," said Kett. "Let's get them someplace safe, someplace warm. They'll open up when they know he's not coming after them."

"I saw him on the stretcher, sir. What happened to him?"

"Shot right in the todger," said Porter. "You couldn't ask for a better punishment."

Savage winced.

"But he's not our man?" she said.

Kett shook his head.

"Darcey DeCarlo played us, sir," she said.

"What's that?" barked Clare.

"Darcey told us about the women that were being kept in the house, told us about Luke and Paul and Dawson. We told her we needed to prioritise the Valentine's case and she didn't seem happy about it."

"She knew Dawson would be on the run, sir," said Kett. "Knew he'd be pushing the whole operation into hiding. She didn't think we'd get to him in time if we waited."

"That's why she told us Dawson was at the lorry," said Savage. "It's the only way she could get us to come after him."

"Clever girl," said Clare. "She did good. Dawson's finished, and this is a decent bust."

"Thanks, sir," said Porter.

"I said Darcey did good. You lot fucked the whole thing up. Who starts a gunfight in Great Yarmouth?"

"Technically, we didn't start—"

"Stick a bollock in it, Kett," said Clare. "Preferably Dawson's, if you can find it."

The Super spluttered out a sigh.

"So we've got nothing, then? No clue as to why our killer targeted William Briggs and Darcey DeCarlo? No connection to the other victims? That's what you're telling me?"

Nobody answered. Kett watched one of the ambulances pull away, followed by a couple of IRVs. The frightened faces of the women peered back through the dark windows of the cars like ghosts. They were safe, at least, but there was still a killer out there, and if they didn't hurry, then somebody else was going to die an unthinkable death.

"He's not finished," said Kett.

"I know," said Clare. "He's going to strike again, and he's going to keep doing it until we catch him."

The Superintendent kicked a stone across the car park, then turned the angry blisters of his eyes to Kett.

"So go and bloody catch him."

CHAPTER THIRTY-THREE

THE JOURNEY BACK TO HQ WAS A QUIET ONE. KETT drove, Porter in the passenger seat and Savage and Duke in the back, nobody speaking more than a handful of words as they cut through the congested evening traffic. It was after six by the time they walked into the MIT bullpen, and Kett was surprised to find that it was almost deserted. DS Spalding sat alone at Kett's desk, chewing on her pencil like she hadn't eaten in a month. She looked up as they entered.

"Isn't that my spot, Alison?" said Kett as he walked over.

"Yes, sir, but it's the only one by the radiator, and it's bloody freezing in here."

"Fair enough."

He hung his coat on the back of the next chair over, rubbing his face as if he could scrub away the exhaustion.

"Dawson isn't our guy, then?" said Spalding.

"Not for the Valentine's case, Sarge," said Savage as she walked over. "But we've got him for a lot of other stuff."

"Plus, he got his bollock shot off," said Porter, as he took a seat at his own desk.

"I heard it was his cock, sir?" said Spalding.

"Probably a bit of both," said Kett, grimacing. "Big bullet, small target. You found any other leads? I've got to admit, I'm struggling with this one."

"Possibly," said Spalding, giving Kett's computer screen a tap. He slipped on his glasses, realising that it wasn't his computer at all.

"Wait, Alison, did you move all your stuff to my desk?"

"Yes, sir," she said. "I asked the Super, and he told me it was fine. His exact words were, 'The further that arse-flavoured tossmuffin is from my office, the happier I will be.'"

"Right," said Kett.

"Your stuff is on my old desk, sir," she went on. "Over there, in the cold bit of the room. By the toilets."

"Thanks," he said, too tired to argue. "What did you find?"

"Might have a lead on the lorries, sir," she said, tapping the monitor again. "The killer switched the plates and did a pretty good job of filing off the chassis number, but they must have forgotten about the VIN on the dash. Two were too damaged to read, but Hay's managed to work out the other one, although it's only a partial."

"That's big," said Kett. "Did it lead anywhere?"

"Yeah," she said. "If the partial's correct, the lorry came from a trucking firm just outside of Birmingham. It was sold to a company in Norfolk last April, and registered SORN in September."

"What company?"

"It's a logistics outfit in Dereham, sir," she said. "But they went bankrupt late last year, got struck off. I've contacted the Dereham police to see if they can find anything, but that was just half an hour or so ago, I haven't heard. Company has one director, Mehmet Cevher, but he lives in Egypt and he hasn't been in the UK for six months. There's a warrant out for him for non-payment of insolvency fees, so I can't see him visiting anytime soon."

"Staff?" asked Kett.

"Nothing so far, sir. There's nobody else on the Companies House register, and nobody on his payroll. But he bought a dozen lorries, all of them older models, and eight of them were DAFs like the ones our killer used."

"Shit."

"My guess is he was using freelance drivers to ship things in his lorries, probably paid them in cash, nothing on record."

"Dead end?" said Kett.

"Hopefully the woodentops will find something when they get there, sir," she said.

"Hey!" Duke exclaimed from where he was perched on Savage's desk. "Less of the insults, please, Sarge."

"Sorry," she said. "You know what I mean. The plods."

Duke did not look impressed.

"Thanks, Alison," said Kett. "This is something. This is good."

He made his way to Porter's desk, the room swaying under a sudden attack of vertigo.

"You alright, sir?" Porter asked. "You look like shit."

"Feel it," said Kett. "Last night is catching up with me. I don't trust the local coppers to find anything in Dereham, gonna head out there now and have a look."

"Sir, if you try to drive in this state you'll be plastered over the side of the road," said Porter, getting out of his chair and slinging on his coat. "I'll go."

"You sure, Pete?"

Porter nodded, making his way out of the bullpen. Kett stifled a yawn with the back of his hand.

"What about me, sir?" Savage asked. "I can go over the leads, see if we missed anything."

Duke checked his watch with a sigh.

"Or I can talk to Dankworth again," Savage went on. "Some more time in his cell might have reawakened his memories."

"No, it's okay," said Kett. "We're all exhausted. Why don't you both go home, get a little rest."

"Sir—" said Savage, at the same time that Duke practically propelled himself from the desk, blurting out, "Good idea, sir!"

"Aaron!" said Savage. "We can't just go home. We don't know when the killer is going to attack again. We—"

"Exactly," said Kett. "It could be tonight, it could be tomorrow, it might not be until a week from now. We rest while we can. We've been through a lot tonight. Go home. Just make sure you leave your phone on loud."

Savage wasn't happy about it, but she nodded. Duke offered her his hand.

"My lady," he said.

She took it, and he hauled her out of her chair so fast a laugh escaped her. She slapped him on his shoulder, then gave Kett a solemn look.

"You'll call me as soon as you hear anything, sir?"

"I will," he said. "I promise."

She slid her arm through Duke's and they left the room together, Savage throwing one last look back before she disappeared through the door.

"I'm going to make a move too, sir," said Spalding. "If that's okay?"

"Sure," he said. "I'll let you know what Porter finds."

"If you have to, sir," she said, stretching her arms over her head. "Lovely and cosy over here, isn't it?"

He gave her a stern look before crossing the bullpen and heading for the Incident Room. He closed the door behind him, sealing himself in the quiet gloom and feeling his exhaustion like a weighted blanket over his head. The dead watched him from the opposite wall, full of horror, full of grief. The photographs howled their silent accusations across the room. He'd let them down. He hadn't been able to find the man who had done this to them.

"I'm sorry," he said, his eyes sliding shut of their own accord. "I will. I promise."

He just had to find the link between the victims, the thing that connected them, the missing piece of the puzzle. Why these three couples—or four, if you included the Hopkins, who had been targeted but not attacked? All different ages, in different stages of their relationships, and miles apart from each other.

But all of them in trouble in some way.

Grant Dankworth had been cheating on his wife. Darcey DeCarlo had been panicking about her baby. Alan had struggled with the fact that Gregg hadn't come to terms with his sexuality yet. And Eileen Hopkins seemed to hate her husband for being a pervert. But these were private problems, shared with family and friends and, in Darcey's case, the priest. Who else would have known?

And what did it matter, because didn't all relationships have problems? Even when you were madly in love, you still fought. It was just what humans did.

There was no such thing as a perfect couple.

The room jolted to one side and Kett only just managed

to catch himself before he fell. He'd almost fallen asleep right here, standing up.

He took a seat at the nearest desk, rubbing his eyes until fireworks exploded. It was almost seven, and he thought about Billie and the kids, about his own family waiting for him to come home. How many times had his late nights led to an argument with his wife? How many times had she told him, in the heat of the moment, that there wasn't room for her and the girls in his head alongside the madness of the job?

No such thing as a perfect couple, not even him and Billie.

And yet those two words circled his mind like drifting birds.

Perfect couple.

He tried to watch them, tried to find some meaning in their movements, but the birds were too far away, lost in the glare of the sun, and in the crash of the waves, and—

He startled awake again, the room impossibly quiet, not a single sound from the bullpen. He'd only dozed off for a second, hadn't he? But when he checked his watch, he saw that almost half an hour had passed.

"Come on, Robbie," he said, wiping the drool from his mouth.

He stood up, his joints like castanets. He was no good to anyone like this. Taking one last look at the faces of the men and women on the Incident Room wall, he switched off the light and left the room.

It was time to go home.

"WHAT A SHITHOLE."

Porter peered through the window of the small industrial unit they'd found on the outskirts of Dereham. It had been a petrol station at one point, concrete scars on the forecourt where the pumps had once been, the canopy punctured by giant holes. There was a small booth where payments had been made, and past that a large brick and corrugated iron garage, its rickety doors chained.

The entire place had become a dumping ground, with bags of festering waste piled up against the walls and a dozen sofas and duvets congregating down the side of the building. The smell was so bad that Porter half expected to find a dead body, although it might just have been the mounds of dog shit that crisscrossed the cracked asphalt.

He couldn't see anything through the filthy glass, so he aimed his torch backwards, blinding the trio of constables who stood behind him. They'd been here when he'd arrived, and according to them they'd already searched the grounds and found, as they put it, 'nothing dodgy.' But all three of them were young lads, one of whom could barely stop yawning, and he wasn't sure he could trust them.

"Any of you got bolt cutters in your car?" he asked.

"Sure, sir," said one of the officers, jogging back to the street.

Porter tried the door of the booth again, just in case it had spontaneously opened, then made his way to the garage. Despite his heavy overcoat, the cold had settled into his bones, so brutal it was painful.

"Can either of you tell me why I'm freezing my arse off in this miserable bloody country?" Porter muttered. "I bet I could get a job in the Bahamas."

The constables didn't answer, traipsing after him like

unhappy children. The garage didn't have any windows but the crack between the doors was big enough for Porter to peer through. It looked empty.

"Nothing there, sir," said one of the men. "Place is deserted."

The first officer jogged back over, offering a sturdy pair of bolt cutters. Porter stared at them, then at the constable, and after a few seconds the man got the message.

"Right you are, sir," he said.

He snapped the bolt cutters against the enormous chain like he was lopping branches from a bush. It kept dancing out of the way, jingling like the bells on Santa's sleigh.

"For fuck's sake," Porter said, resting his torch on the ground. "Give it here."

The constable handed the bolt cutters over, and Porter clamped them onto the padlock. He braced one arm of the tool against the wall, then leaned on it, the shackle giving up the fight almost immediately. He handed them back.

"Most dickheads use giant chains and cheap locks," he said as he fed the chain out through the handles and dropped it to the floor. "Worth remembering."

"Yes, sir."

He pulled the right-hand door open, both sets of hinges almost coming out of the frame, and a wave of debris hailing down from the ceiling. He coughed his way inside, his torch peeling apart layers of dust and darkness and letting him know that his first hunch was correct.

The building was completely and utterly empty.

He did a circuit of the space anyway, skirting around the mechanic's pit and stepping over a handful of loose tools. There were a couple of internal doors that led to a toilet and to some storage areas, but the whole place looked like it had either been stripped by the owners or looted.

He called Kett as he made his way back out of the doors, only for it to go to voicemail. He tried Clare instead.

"Speak," boomed the Superintendent. "Unless you've got more bad news, that is, in which case, toss off."

"I'm in Dereham, sir, the garage where the lorries came from. Dead end, it's deserted."

"What did I say, Porter?" grumbled Clare. "If it's bad news, toss the toss off."

The line went dead and Porter pocketed his phone. He stood on the forecourt for a moment, puffing clouds of cold air from his lips as he tried to figure out where to go next. The garage was located on a small industrial estate, sandwiched between a pet store and an office building that looked like it was the headquarters of a local printing company. Both were closed for the night. There was another wide, low commercial building opposite, but he couldn't figure out what it was. He started back towards the car, only for one of the constables to shout out.

"Security camera over there, sir, worth looking at?"

Porter stared at the building across the road, the one he'd just checked out.

"Right there, sir," said the constable from behind him.

"I see it," Porter snapped back, although he still couldn't figure out where it was.

"On the left, sir."

"I know it's on the bloody left," he said, finally finding it. "It's right there."

He crossed the street, the constables treading on his shadow as if afraid to be left in the dark.

Porter walked into the small car park, shining his torch onto the face of the ugly, single-storey building. The security camera sat beneath the guttering, pointing directly at the floor beneath it as if it had given up on life. It looked like it hadn't worked in years.

There was no signage on the building at all, or evidence that there ever had been on its filthy, pebble-dashed walls. The only sign of life was a string of multicoloured, solar-powered fairy lights that had been fastened around the door, glowing weakly. The ends of the building connected to a wooden fence that was taller than Porter, the lot stretching maybe fifty yards in both directions.

Porter cupped his hand to the glass window in the door and squinted into the dark. He could just about discern a small reception area with a desk and a couple of chairs, some posters on the walls. A sizable collection of mail had built up beneath the letterbox, but it was too dark for Porter to read any names.

He stepped back from the building, tapping his torch on his leg and causing shadows to dance in every direction. There was nothing here of any note, and yet something about the place was tugging on his nerves.

The fairy lights, he realised. He'd seen them before.

He crossed the front of the building to the closest fence panel, then hefted himself off the ground in order to look over the top.

"Holy shit," he said.

Past the fence was a yard. Two white lorries sat in the middle of it, cloaked in shadow. He grunted as he dropped back down.

"Can one of you give me a foot up?"

"Sir?" said the youngest of the PCs, a lad who barely looked old enough to have left school.

"Bend over, let me get on you," Porter said.

"*Sir?*" the man squeaked.

"Not like that, mate," said Porter. "What's your name?"

"Atkins, sir."

"Get over here."

Atkins shuffled to the fence, unsure, and Porter bent him over to fashion a crude platform. He slid his torch into his pocket, took hold of the fence, planted a knee on the officer's back and hoisted himself up. The young man squirmed, groaning, the other two coppers doing their best not to break down in a fit of giggles.

Porter ignored them all, slinging a leg over the fence, then straddling it. It felt like he was being cut in two with a length of cheese wire, so he dropped down the other side, landing awkwardly on concrete.

"Ouch," he said, massaging his groin.

"You want us to hop over too, sir?" came a shout. "Atkins won't mind if we use him as a stepladder."

"Bloody would," PC Atkins grumbled.

"I'm fine," said Porter. "Nobody here."

At least he didn't *think* there was, but there were no lights on, and even when he pulled out his torch and aimed it across the yard he couldn't see the end of it. Anything could have been lurking in those shadows, and his imagination painted leering grins against the dark; wild eyes and sharp blades.

"But be ready just in case," he shouted back.

"Yes, sir," they replied in chorus.

He aimed the torch at the closest lorry and followed the light to it. It was an old one, the white walls caked in dirt, the passenger side window in the cab smashed, but it was impossible to guess the year because the licence plates had been removed. He passed the first lorry and illuminated the second to see that this one had no plates either.

There were a couple of butchered vehicles in the yard, two cars without their wheels or doors, plus wide barricades of other junk. Porter navigated the maze, heading for the main building. It was bigger than it had looked from the road, a sprawling, boxy structure pocked with dirty windows and a single fire exit. There were no lights on inside. Anyone could have been watching him.

I'm watching you too, he thought, trying to lend himself a little courage as he ran for the door. It was locked, of course, so he made his way around the corner to investigate the back of the building. There was another door here, also locked. He patrolled the row of windows, giving each a rattle until he found one that felt a little less secure than the others. Even when he worked his fingers into the frame, though, he couldn't wrench it open.

"Fuck this," he said, searching the yard until he found a length of metal inside a pile of car parts. He carried it back to the window and jammed it under the frame, sliding it back and forth in the hope of releasing a catch. After a minute or so he gave up, frustration gnawing at his nerves. He looked at the metal in his hands, then at the window, then over at the lorries. Then he cracked the pole into the glass.

The noise it made seemed to split the night in two, surely loud enough for every single person in a ten-mile radius to hear.

"You okay, sir?" shouted one of the PCs.

"Yeah, I'm fine. Just... slipped."

He used the pole to knock out the loose glass before climbing through the window, finding himself in a small room that was empty apart from a stack of chairs against one wall. He peeked his head through the open door to see a short corridor.

"Hello?" he called out, his voice muted by the close

walls, by the carpet beneath his feet. "Police. Is anyone here?"

No reply, and for that he was eternally grateful. He didn't get the sense that anyone was here, but unlike Kett, he didn't seem to have the ability to read buildings. There could have been a dozen armed men right behind the next door and he wouldn't have known anything about it.

He stepped into the corridor, opening the doors as he walked and finding more empty rooms. After a dozen yards, the hallway angled to the right, and he crept towards the front of the building, ready to use the heavy Maglite as a weapon if he needed to.

The door at the end opened into the reception area. He could see the three constables messing around in the car park, one of them giving Atkins a cuff around the back of his head that sent his hat flying.

Porter walked to the door and rapped the torch on the glass. All three of them looked like they'd shit themselves.

"Behave," he told them.

He crouched by the door, picking up a couple of letters until he found a name: Gavin Dove. There were some companies listed on the envelopes, including Ad-*van*-ture Times and Mountbatten's, and he tore open a couple that looked like bills. Despite the fact the office didn't look like it had been used for a few years, every payment was up to date.

He turned back to the room, sweeping the torch from wall to wall. The posters were all for a travel company that seemed to specialise in UK trips, with images of the rolling peaks and the glorious lakes and the wide sandy beaches of Cornwall. Each one had a camper in the middle of it, families grinning through the windows.

"Ad-*van*-ture Times," he said, reading the print. "The adventure starts with the turn of a key."

It was about as shit a slogan as any he'd ever seen.

He walked to the desk, which had been recently polished. There was no computer, but when he lifted the phone he heard a dial tone. He opened the top drawer to find a ream of documents: financial statements and customer contracts, Gavin Dove's name cropping up over and over.

He closed the drawer and opened the one beneath it.

"Holy motherfucking shit," he said.

Staring up at him from a badly printed photo were two familiar faces, both smiling as they embraced one another.

Karen and Grant Dankworth.

He pulled the wad of documents out of the drawer and laid them on the desk, peeling the photograph off the top to reveal a picture of another couple, one he hadn't seen before. They stood in the door of what looked like a church, their hands resting on the shoulders of a blonde-haired child. The man, in his thirties and handsome, was looking at the camera with a broad smile. The woman, who was also striking, was staring at her husband.

Porter flicked to the next photo, seeing Darcey DeCarlo standing on the beach, squinting at the camera. There was a man behind her, walking away along the long line of her shadow, that could have been William Briggs. Both were blurred, as if the photographer had caught them in the middle of some kind of dance. Like the others, this one was printed on plain A4 paper, although there were images and text beneath the photo that could only have come from Facebook.

He laid the torch on the desk and pulled out his phone, calling Clare.

"Shall I tell you what happens to KitKats that waste my time?" the Super said. "They get snapped in half, then eaten."

"I'm not wasting your time, sir," Porter told him. "I'm in a commercial premises across the road from the garage where the lorries were stored. There are two more lorries in the yard at the back of this place, both DAFs with no plates, and I've found a load of photographs in a drawer in reception. They're our victims, sir."

There was no reply from the Super, just quiet chatter from the coppers outside the door.

"Sir?" said Porter.

He lifted the photo of Darcey and William, finding another couple he didn't recognise, this time two women holding hands at a zoo, a giraffe leaning in as if trying to photobomb them. This had been taken from Facebook as well, the next post visible beneath it. The name of the account was Julia Gerritsen.

"You're certain?" said Clare eventually. "You've found photographs of the victims?"

"Yeah, I've found DeCarlo and Briggs so far, plus the Dankworths." He lifted the paper to reveal the next print-out, two men standing outside a pub. Porter never would have guessed they were in a relationship if he didn't already know it. "Here's Gregg and Alan Jemc."

He licked his fingers in order to sweep this photo off the pile, and there he stopped, because for a moment he had forgotten how to move.

"Oh shit," he said.

"What is it?" asked Clare.

"Where's Robbie, sir?"

"Why?"

On the next sheet was another photograph, this one

taken from a newspaper. Porter knew that because he'd seen it a hundred times, and he'd been there when it was taken. Kett stood outside the main doors of Police HQ, red faced and harassed because of the onslaught of questions he'd just answered after the Three Little Pigs case. Next to him, her hand wrapped around his, her face steely, was Billie.

"Because I think he's in trouble, sir," said Porter. "I think he's in serious fucking trouble."

CHAPTER THIRTY-FOUR

"I'M HOME!"

Kett stepped into the welcome warmth of his house, slamming the door shut behind him to keep the February chill outside. He hung up his coat on the overflowing peg and kicked his shoes into the pile by the door, leaving his wallet and his phone on the hallway console. He took a moment to stretch his neck, to arch his aching back, to *breathe*. He could hear his girls upstairs, an unmistakeable serenade of screams as they argued about something.

"Hello!" he called out. "I said I'm home!"

If they heard him, they didn't show it. He walked past the living room and peeked inside to find it empty. The kitchen was deserted too.

"Billie?"

He did a quick tour of the downstairs before heading up, every muscle in his body protesting. He wasn't sure what squeaked more, the steps or his knees. By the time he was on the landing, the screams had reached a crescendo, and they were coming from the bathroom. When he peeked around the door, his jaw almost hit the floor.

Evie had her head in the sink, Alice standing over her with both hands on her shoulders like she was trying to dunk her. The water was running so hard it was nearly overflowing. Alice was the one doing most of the screaming, although Evie was doing her best to join in when her face wasn't underwater.

Moira was sitting on the toilet, her pyjama bottoms around her ankles. She had a piece of toilet paper in her hands and she was waving it at her sisters, cackling like a lunatic.

"What on Earth is going on in here?" Kett said, and all three of them spun around to face him, their screams dying out long enough for them to catch their breath before starting again.

"It's Moira!" said Alice, her face twisted into an expression of horror. "She threw toilet paper at us!"

"I didn't!" Moira shouted back, her cheeks crimson as she threw the paper she was holding to the floor.

"It went in Evie's hair!" Alice went on.

"It went in my hair!" Evie confirmed, water dripping from her face.

"I didn't!" Moira roared.

"It had poo on it!" hissed Alice, apoplectic with panic.

"What?" said Kett. "Moira, that's—"

"I didn't!" Moira roared, her voice demonic. "I was tricking them."

Evie dunked her head into the sink again, blowing bubbles. Alice scrubbed her hair for her, using hand soap as shampoo.

"Unbelievable," said Kett, walking into the bathroom and gently steering Alice out of the way. "Evie, you're going to drown yourself. Come here."

He pulled the hand towel from the rail and scrubbed Evie's hair.

"Moira, can you come off the toilet please?"

"I did a poo," she said, still crimson.

"Where's your mum?"

"She went out," said Alice from the door.

The fear was a tickle inside Kett's gut.

"Out? When?"

"Ages ago," said Moira from the toilet. "She said she'd be back to wipe my bum, but she's been *ages*."

"It wasn't ages," said Evie, squirming in his hands as he tried to dry her hair. "It was just now. Somebody came to the door. She said she'd just be a second."

The tickle of fear became a kick to the guts, almost enough to double him over. He handed Evie the towel and left the room.

"What about my bum?" wailed Moira behind him.

Kett dropped down the stairs so fast he almost fell, grabbing the bannister to hold himself up. He pulled on his boots, wrenching open the front door and running into the night. Gravel ground through his wet socks into the soft flesh of his feet.

"Billie?" he yelled.

It was like he'd been ripped back in time, to all those years ago when he'd found out.

It's your wife, she's been taken.

"Billie!" he almost screamed.

And she answered him.

"Robbie?"

There she was, stepping around the corner of their drive, past the bare magnolia tree. He stumbled to her and wrapped her in his arms so tightly that she gasped.

"Fuck," he said, breathing the word into her hair, his body electric with terror. "You're okay. You're okay."

"I'm fine," she said, pulling herself away with no small force. She laid a hand on his cheek. "What's got into you? What's wrong?"

He sucked in frozen air until the adrenaline began to ebb away.

"The girls said you'd gone; they said you'd left with someone."

"Yeah, Albert," she said, nodding down the road. "He got confused again. I just walked him home, made sure his heating was on, made him a cuppa. He thinks we're married, bless him."

She pulled a face.

"Although I'm not sure 'bless him' is the right phrase, he did ask me up to his bedroom."

Kett laughed, still not ready to let go of her. He grabbed her hand, holding it tight as they walked back to the door.

"It's this case, Billie," he said, glancing back to the street to make sure nobody was following them. "It's getting to me. I can't figure it out."

She stopped at the threshold, squeezing his hand.

"You will," she said. "You always do."

He let her go through first, closing the door behind him and twisting both locks. The girls were still arguing upstairs.

"What did I miss?" Billie asked. "I was only gone a few minutes."

"A poo emergency," said Kett, heading for the stairs.

"When isn't there a poo emergency?"

He took care of Moira's bum and helped her wash her hands, checking Evie's sodden hair for any sign of toilet paper. Then he went to the bedroom to find fresh socks. By the time he'd made his way downstairs, his daughters were best friends again, piling around the kitchen table and asking for cereal.

"It's a bit late," said Kett, but he gave them a bowl each and divided the last of the Cheerios between them.

"Really?" said Billie as she carried two cups of tea to the table. "Evie didn't finish her dinner. I told her no more food."

"Sorry," said Kett, giving Evie a stern look that she ignored. "Nobody mentioned that."

"Daddy's in trouble," said Alice.

"Daddy is always in trouble," said Moira, matter-of-factly.

"I am not!"

"You need to write Mummy a card to say sorry," said Alice, crunching her cereal.

Kett took a sip of his tea, feeling it wash away some of the horror of the day.

"Huh?" he said.

"It's what we've been doing at school," explained Evie. "If we get in trouble or if we make somebody sad or if we want to say something, we write a card, or a letter."

"Daddy doesn't need to say sorry," said Billie, taking her seat. "He just didn't know."

"Mummy needs to write a letter," said Evie, spraying Cheerios. "To say sorry."

"What for?" asked Kett.

"Dear Daddy," said Evie. "I'm sorry, but I have a new boyfriend."

Kett almost sprayed tea across the table.

"Evie!" said Billie.

"He's old," their middle daughter went on. "And creepy. I don't like him."

"Albert?" said Kett.

"Yeah," Billie answered. "We're engaged to be married. He's going to be your new Dad, Evie. Sorry."

"Gross!" said Alice. "Dear Daddy, sorry my new boyfriend is old and smelly, but at least he isn't at work all day."

That one stung a little.

"Sorry," said Kett.

"You have to write a letter," said Alice.

"Dear Alice," Kett said, pretending to write on the table. "And Evie, and Moira, and Billie. I'm sorry I spend so much time at work, but..."

He tailed off, something tugging at a loose thread inside his skull.

"But what?" said Evie.

He didn't reply, searching his head, looking for the thing that had called to him.

"But I have a very important job," Billie said, speaking for him. "And lots of people rely on me, and I love my family very much, but sometimes I need to stay on late to help solve a crime. If it was up to me, I'd be home all day every day playing with my children, but sadly, I can't. I will make more of an effort in the future to limit my working hours, because I know that my kids are only young once and I'll be sad if I miss it all, and also my wife is very, very tired."

She laughed.

"I sound more like an—"

"Agony aunt," said Kett, a supernova detonating inside his thoughts. "You sound like an agony aunt."

"What's an agony aunt?" said Evie.

Kett stood up, his hands on his head to try and physically restrain the thought before it left him. Four couples, all from different parts of the county, all completely unknown to each other, no connection at all other than the fact that they were having problems.

"Dada?" said Moira.

"Hang on," he said, feeling it slip through his fingers like sand. "Hang on, give me a sec."

He walked out of the kitchen into the hall, talking to himself as he went.

"Letters, letters."

He'd thought the link might have been therapy, and what if he was right? Not a therapist you saw face to face, but somebody you wrote to. He'd found letters at Alan Jemc's house.

He'd found magazines, too.

"Shit," he said, pulling on his boots.

He opened the front door and ran to the car. The box of cakes that Jemc's grandmother had given him was still on the passenger seat, and underneath it was the pile of paperwork he'd taken from the young man's bedroom.

He pulled out the collection of magazines, squinting at them in the weak glow from the car's interior lights. Even when he put on his glasses, he could barely read the microscopic print.

He clutched them tight, carrying them back to the house, then pausing when he realised he could hear sirens.

A *lot* of sirens.

He walked to the end of the drive instead, looking down the street to see half a dozen IRVs thumping past traffic and heading this way inside a bubble of blue light. A couple of uniformed officers were crossing the street from the satellite station on the other side of the road, running towards his house. Kett patted his pocket, looking for his phone, and remembered he'd left it by the door. He lifted a hand to wave at the approaching coppers.

"Everything alright?" he shouted when they were close enough.

Their answer was drowned out by the growl of engines and the howl of sirens as the IRVs arrived. A dozen more officers climbed out, surrounding Kett with a cacophony of shouts. He stepped back onto the gravel, worried for a moment that they'd come to arrest *him*. Then a familiar voice rose above the chatter, booming down the street.

"Kett! What the toss is going on?"

Clare was peeling himself out of a police car, and he lurched down the street to where Kett was standing.

"Sir?" said Kett.

The Super flapped his arms like a drowning pelican.

"Turn those bloody sirens off!" he roared.

When the street had fallen silent, he approached Kett, giving him a hefty prod in the chest.

"I said what the toss is going on?"

"I actually have no idea, sir," said Kett. "I've only just got back, I—"

"You haven't been taken by the killer?" Clare asked.

"I mean… no, I am quite obviously still here," he said.

"And Billie?"

"In the kitchen, with the girls."

That was a lie, he realised when he looked at the house. All four of them were standing in the open front door, their eyes wide and their mouths open.

"She's fine," said Kett. "Why?"

Clare seemed to deflate with relief.

"Because your twat of a friend, Peter Porter, found the building our killer has been operating from. We think his name is Gavin Dove. There are photographs there of all of our couples, plus you and your wife."

The roar of panic in Kett's head could have been a jumbo jet.

"What?" he said, just a whisper.

"Porter says there are photographs of more than twenty couples there, we think they're all Dove's potential targets. He's been scoping them out, gathering intel."

"Shit," said Kett. "You're serious? Me and Billie are there?"

Clare nodded, his face deathly pale.

"You weren't answering your phone, you great puddle of horse toss. We thought he was going after you."

"It's inside," said Kett, pointing at the house as if that would help. "We had a... poo emergency."

"I'll show you a poo emergency," growled Clare. "I'm going to toss you off so hard you'll shit yourself."

"*What?*"

"The job," said Clare, looking down the street for a second before turning back to Kett. "Toss you off the job. Fuck me. I'm going to need you back in. We have to track down every person in those photographs before Dove goes after them, because we have no idea where he is, or who he's going to target next."

"You've got his home address, sir?"

"Nobody there, no idea where he's heading. No record of a mobile phone. We've lost too much time coming after you, we're probably too late to stop another attack."

"Sorry, sir," said Kett.

He lifted the magazines he was holding.

"I think I might have something," he said. "It literally just came to me."

Kett took the top magazine and dumped the rest on the bonnet of his car. He flicked through the greasy pages, ignoring the articles, the crosswords, the sudoku puzzles and the horoscopes, finding what he was looking for a couple of pages from the back.

There were three short letters from readers, and when he scanned through them, he saw that they were all asking for relationship advice.

And each one had an answer.

"This, sir," he said, pointing. "We couldn't find a link between the couples, a reason the killer was targeting these specific people. I thought it might have been random, but it's not. Then I thought it might be some kind of therapist they'd all seen, but nothing fit. It's *this*, I'm sure of it."

"An agony aunt? Have you lost your mind?"

Clare took the magazine and scanned the page.

"Ask Annie," he said, reading the title and looking at the photograph of a round-faced, middle-aged woman wearing a turban and a pearl necklace. "Are you telling me this Annie person is our killer?"

"No, sir," said Kett. "Not her."

He lifted the rest of the magazines from the car.

"Because Annie looks like she'd lose a battle against a wet paper bag," Clare went on. "Dove's our man."

Kett ignored him, checking the titles of the magazines—Take a Break, That's Life—and stopping at the local one, Norfolk Living. He opened it up, managing to drop the rest onto the driveway in his haste. His numb fingers struggled with the thin paper as he browsed the pages.

"There's another one here, sir," he said, using his arm to push his glasses back up his nose. "Another agony aunt page. *Truly, Madly, Deeply*."

"This is bloody useless, Kett," Clare replied. "These don't mean a thing. Our killer owns an industrial lot across town, he runs adventure holidays or some shit, he's not a dotty old biddy solving other people's problems in a local rag."

Kett read through the first letter, shivering so hard in the cold he could barely see straight.

"Can I borrow a torch?" he said to the parade of constables who were waiting for orders. One obliged, shining the light on the page.

The first letter was from a woman who suspected her husband fancied the neighbour. The second was from a guy who needed help to escape his boring relationship. The third, though, was a man who desperately wanted his boyfriend to stop hiding their love from his friends and family.

"This letter, sir, it's from a man called Alan J. I found this at Jemc's house. It has to be him."

Clare muttered beneath his breath as he took the magazine.

"It could be anyone," he said. "I know at least twelve people called Alan, and they're all hopeless tossers."

"No, sir," said Kett. "It's him. This is how they're connected, I'm sure of it. Grant Dankworth told us his wife was always asking people for advice about how to save their relationship. He told us she wrote to people, to magazines. I bet if we look hard enough we'll find a letter from her in another issue of this magazine. Darcey DeCarlo too, she needed help with her situation. She was looking for it everywhere."

He closed the magazine and held it up.

"Norfolk Living, it's local. If our killer's obsessed with love, with Valentine's Day, with relationships, then this is how they'd find couples in trouble. Every letter they read would have led them to a new set of victims."

This time, Clare didn't argue.

"Who is it, then?" he asked. "What's the name of the agony aunt?"

Kett flicked his way back to the right page.

"'*Truly, Madly, Deeply*,'" he read aloud. "'*Let our world famous agony aunt help you with your deepest darkest secrets.*' It doesn't say her name."

"Yes, it does," said Clare, jabbing the page with a long fingernail. "Right there, you're reading it wrong."

He was, he realised.

"Truly, *Maddy*, Deeply," he said. He navigated back to the beginning of the magazine, to the list of contributors. "Here, it says the agony aunt is Maddy F."

And the dark night seemed to glow like it was dawn.

"Holy shit," he said. "Maddy F? Madelaine Fielding."

"Who?" said Clare.

"Madelaine, Norman Balls' friend, the one who wrote the book on local urban legends, she had a whole chapter on Jack Valentine. I spoke with her."

He slapped a hand to his forehead.

"She told us she wrote other things. She's a writer, a journalist. I'm sure she said she had a self-help column too. That's just another word for agony aunt, right?"

"You think *she* did this?" said Clare. "This woman managed to subdue our victims, transport them to the kill site, get them into a lorry and set fire to it?"

"Not on her own," said Kett. "She has a boyfriend. He was outside her house yesterday, in a campervan. She said he was picking her up for a date, but what if they're working together? What if Dove is the man she was meeting? What if they were on their way to target another couple? Maddy F. Shit, he was right there. They were *both* right there. This is too much of a coincidence for it to be anything else, sir."

"Then let's go get her," said Clare, heading back to his IRV. "I'll call the others."

Kett turned to the house, his family perfectly framed in the front door. They looked too small, too far away, and when Moira offered a little wave, it was all he could do not to run to her, to barricade them all inside where the world couldn't touch them.

In another life, he thought, he would do exactly that. He'd close the door on the job and never go back. He'd be a husband, and a dad, and nothing more.

In this life, though, he simply waved back.

And turned away.

"I need you to stay here," he told the constable who'd given him the torch. "Keep them safe."

"Yes, sir," the man said.

Kett ran to the IRV, sliding into the back. Clare was just hanging up on a call.

"Can't reach Savage or Duke," he said. "Porter's on his way back into the city. You remember where she lives?"

"Yes, sir," said Kett.

"Then let's fucking end this."

CHAPTER THIRTY-FIVE

"No peeking," said Duke.

Savage shut her eyes so tightly that little bolts of light flickered to and fro against the black canvas. She could hear Duke thumping around in the kitchen of her flat, where he'd spent the last twenty minutes trying to rustle up a romantic dinner. So far she'd counted at least four pieces of cutlery dropping to the floor and one broken plate, but the smell that was wafting through to the living room wasn't unpleasant.

"You'd better be hungry," he shouted.

Colin was a dead weight on her lap, and the little dog barked as if to answer him.

"Starving," she replied, stroking Colin's head. It wasn't a lie. She'd barely eaten all day, and it had been a *long* day. Her stomach felt like a living thing that was trying to gnaw its way out of her. "How much longer?"

"It's ready," he said. "But it's no duck *à l'orange* this time, I'm afraid. I didn't have much to work with."

That was an understatement. Savage was pretty sure all she had in the kitchen was an old loaf of bread and some beans, maybe a rind of cheese somewhere at the back of the fridge. Still, she'd been impressed with Duke's cooking so far. It certainly put hers to shame.

"Keep those peepers closed," he said from right outside the door.

He clomped his way in, Colin propelling herself from Savage's lap in order to go on a raid.

"Back off," said Duke, setting the plate down on the coffee table. "Uh-uh, not for you, bad doggy."

Colin barked so loud it made Savage's ears ring. She opened her eyes to see Duke standing there, dressed in his uniform because technically he was still on duty. Colin was a mass of tangled limbs and bulging eyes in his arms, trying desperately to wriggle free. Beneath them was a plate of steaming food. Savage felt excited for the fraction of a second before she realised what it was.

"Beans on toast?" she said.

"No," said Duke, grimacing as Colin licked his face. "It's Duke's Seasonal Rarebit. Artisanal bread—"

"Toast," said Savage.

"With haricot beans and a pureed tomato dressing."

"Beans on toast."

"And a layer of the finest melted *fromage*."

"Cheesy beans on toast," said Savage, picking up the plate.

"Cheesy beans on toast," he confirmed with a laugh. "I didn't have a lot to work with."

"I'm too hungry to care," she said. "Thank you."

Savage used the knife to rip off a hunk of dinner, shovelling it into her mouth. It was hotter than the sun, but she worked it down, her eyes watering.

"It's hot," said Duke.

"Yeah," she croaked. "Thanks for the warning."

"Thought the steam might give it away, and the fact the beans are still bubbling."

She blew on it, hacking off another forkful.

"I ordered a Maccy D's as well," said Duke. "In case you're still hungry."

"Have I ever told you how much I love you, Aaron?" she said through a mouthful of beans.

"Not enough," he replied, grinning. He dropped the dog gently onto the floor and she leapt instantly onto the sofa, staring at Savage like she hadn't been fed in months. Duke seemed to be chewing on something too, although it wasn't food.

"You okay?" Savage asked him. "You eating?"

"I'm saving myself for the burger," he said, perching on the chair opposite. "Look, Kate. There's something I've been trying to tell you for ages now. Something I wanted to ask you yesterday. I wanted it to be romantic, I wanted it to be special, and this case kind of threw a spanner in the works. But I figured it doesn't have to be anything special, because this *is* special, you know? However it happens, it's special."

Savage paused, her fork halfway to her mouth. Her heart was revving like an engine, and she wasn't sure why.

"Aaron..."

"Hang on," he said, sliding his hand into his pocket. "Just let me say it."

From the bedroom where it was charging, Savage heard her phone ring.

"I should—"

"It will only take a second," said Duke. "Kate, you know how much I love you, right?"

"Right..." she said. "Aaron, I—"

"This has been the most magical year and a half of my

life. I've never felt this connected to somebody, like a part of me is a part of you, and—"

Somebody thumped on the door and Colin bounded out of the room, barking her head off.

"And I really want to take this moment to—"

"We should probably get that," said Savage as the knock came again.

"It can wait," said Duke, his voice raised over Colin's barks. "It's the burger. I just want to—"

Somebody pounded on the door a third time, Colin howling now. Duke threw back his head and groaned.

"I'll go grab it," said Savage, putting her plate on the table.

"I'll do it," said Duke, stomping out of the room. "Eat your rarebit."

"Beans on toast," she said.

She could hear Duke wrestling the dog into the kitchen while shouting to the delivery driver and her smile grew, along with a blossom of warmth inside her that seemed to make the whole flat feel warmer. She knew Duke well enough now to know exactly what he was going to ask her, and even though it made her skin prickle with excitement and her heart swell, it filled her with panic, too. Because in all her years she'd never once felt as close to somebody as she did to him, she'd never before felt this, felt *love*, and that thought was terrifying.

"Hang on!" Duke yelled as he ran down the stairs. "We're in, don't leave."

It was terrifying because she knew how fragile these things were, how prone they were to fracturing, or dissolving, or burning up. Love was so hard to build, but so easy to destroy, a fact that the Jack Valentine case had made clearer than ever—she could still see Darcey tumbling over the edge of the roof in search of a quick death rather than be without Will. She could still see the mangled, scorched forms of Gregg and Alan as they'd fought to the death, and Grant Dankworth's smug smile as he talked about all the times he'd cheated on his wife.

Wasn't it easier to never fall in love at all?

She cut off another section of cheesy bread but her stomach was churning, and after a second or two she dropped it back onto the plate. She wasn't sure if it was the case, or Duke's fumbling speech, or the fact she felt like she hadn't properly slept for so long, but the emotion was ballooning inside her chest, a lump in her throat, a pressure behind her eyes. All she wanted to do right now was cry,

Colin was still howling in the kitchen, scratching the door so hard she was about to pull it off its hinges. Savage hadn't heard the front door close, and she couldn't make out Duke's voice. He'd be scrabbling in his pockets for a tip, she knew, apologising to whoever was waiting patiently on the doorstep. He was sweet like that.

Her stomach did another somersault, and she stood up, making her way to the door.

"Aaron? You okay?"

No answer, just the endless barks of the dog and the rumble of the delivery driver's car from the street outside. Cold air was pouring up the stairwell from the open door.

"Aaron?"

She heard her phone ringing again, but she didn't want to open the kitchen door to get it because then Colin would bolt. She dropped onto the first step and peered over the handrail. The stairs doubled back, the front door right beneath her, but there was nobody there.

"Way to let all the heat out," she grumbled as she made her way down. "Aaron, what are you doing?"

She reached the door, leaning into the cold night. It was pitch black out there, the closest streetlight broken and the moon a smudge behind the clouds. Past the tangled mess of her downstairs neighbour's front garden was the street, but it wasn't a car or a scooter that waited there, its lights on and its engine running. It was a campervan, hand-painted in shades of pink and green with 'Happy Wheels' written along the side.

"Aaron?" she called out.

She walked over the threshold, something crunching weakly beneath her bare foot. Recoiling, she spotted a paper box on the step. She had crushed it, but it was impossible to miss what was drawn on the lid.

A heart.

Two letters: *J* and *V*.

"Shit," she said, the word caught in the snapping beartrap of her throat. She backed into the safety of the stairwell, instinctively reaching for the baton she hadn't carried in years.

And she saw him, a lump of shadow half hidden by the bushes of the front garden.

Duke, lying on his stomach, out cold.

Or worse.

"Aaron!" she screamed, and she almost ran to him before she stopped herself.

She couldn't help him if something happened to her.

She grabbed the door, slammed it shut, ran for the stairs.

Something smashed through the glass window of the door and she tripped, collapsing onto the steps. She looked over her shoulder to see a hand reach through, saw it twist the latch, saw the door swing open.

A man ran into her home, his face hidden by the hood of his raincoat. He was so wide he nearly filled the entire hallway, so tall his hooded head seemed to scrape the ceiling.

"No!" she screamed, rolling onto her back, kicking herself up the stairs.

The man reached her in a single stride, something bright yellow in his hands.

Duke's Taser.

"No!"

"Yes," the man said, a shark's grin visible beneath his hood.

He pulled the trigger, and Savage felt a second of unimaginable pain as her body spasmed, every muscle rigid with agony, every cell on fire.

Then the man's fist struck her in the side of the head, and her world went black.

CHAPTER THIRTY-SIX

They tore through the night, riding a wave of sound and fury across the city. The constable driving the IRV did so with frightening intensity, Clare holding onto the strap over the door like his life depended on it. Kett sat in the back, his head hitting the ceiling every time they went over a speed bump. He had his phone to his ear for most of the journey, but no matter how many times he tried Savage and Duke, neither of them answered.

That same knot of panic was starting to form in his stomach, because Savage always answered her phone. He called Porter instead.

"Sir?"

"You back in the city yet, Pete?"

"Almost."

"Can you swing by Kate's place, see if she's there? I can't get hold of her."

"They're probably doing Valentine's stuff, sir," said Porter. "I don't really want to—"

"Do it," Kett said, hanging up.

"What's wrong?" Clare asked, looking back.

"I don't know, sir," he said as they peeled off the dual carriageway, accelerating up the ramp into Cringleford. "Hopefully nothing. It's left here, then the next right."

"You're sure?" said Clare, almost sliding into the constable's lap as they turned. The squeal of tyres was loud enough to cut through the sirens.

Kett nodded.

"She's going to hear us coming," he said.

Clare switched off the siren, and one by one the convoy of IRVs followed suit. The silence that followed was almost worse, the anticipation dumping so much adrenaline into Kett's system that he felt sick. The PC took the next right so hard the IRV bumped off the curb.

"Halfway down," said Kett, massaging the top of his head.

The car juddered to a halt, Clare out before they'd fully stopped. The Superintendent opened Kett's door, and he exited into the frozen night. He looked at the identical houses that sat along the side of the road, and for a second he couldn't remember which one belonged to Madelaine.

Then he saw her through the upstairs window, a pale face beneath a crown of red hair, a defiant smile that perfectly mirrored the one he'd seen on the man back at the care home.

He saw her, and he *knew*.

"There," he yelled, pointing.

Madelaine vanished, the curtain billowing in her wake. Kett reached the front door and didn't stop, his shoulder crunching into the lock. The window cracked, but the door didn't give, the pain roaring through him as he bounced back. A constable took his place, shattering the glass with his baton, reaching through, then shaking his head.

"Deadlock," he said.

"Move!" bellowed Clare.

The Superintendent was jogging up the driveway with an enforcer ram in his hands. Kett barely had time to stagger back before he crunched it into the door. The uPVC buckled instantly, and a second strike sent the door reeling into the wall.

Kett pushed past Clare, entering the house.

"Madelaine, it's over!" he yelled.

He grabbed the handrail and hauled himself up the stairs, hearing the thunder of feet behind him as the Force followed. Madelaine was running across the landing, her phone in her hand. She screamed when she saw Kett, hurling herself towards the open bathroom door.

He lunged for her, snatched the sleeve of her shirt. She wrenched herself free, her phone hitting the floor and bouncing past his feet, clattering down the stairs. She fell through the door and kicked it shut. He reached it just as the lock clicked.

"Fuck," he said, pounding on the door. "You've got to the count of three to get out here. You hear me? One."

He took a step back, glancing to the stairs to see Clare halfway up them.

"Two."

The Super gave him a nod.

"Time's up."

Kett drove his boot into the bathroom door directly beneath the handle and it exploded out of its frame, wobbling inwards. Madelaine stood by the sink, one hand clutching something, the other to her mouth. She was chewing furiously, her eyes bulging beneath coils of copper-coloured hair.

Kett lunged for her and she staggered back, tripping on the toilet and collapsing against the wall. She dropped what she was holding—a white container, pills scattering—and laughed, white foam exploding from her lips.

"No, you bloody don't," said Kett.

He grabbed her by the scruff of the neck and yanked her up, her fists battering him as he spun her across the room. She screamed, releasing a storm of white dust from the tablets she'd been chewing. He drove his foot into the back of her leg and she dropped hard, doubling over the edge of the bath.

"Spit them up," he growled.

Madelaine shrieked an insane laugh.

"You're too late," she said. "You're too—"

Kett grabbed the back of her head with one hand and rammed his fingers into her mouth. Her entire body buckled and a jet of warm vomit sprayed past his hand, hitting the back of the bath. He tried to do it again, but she clamped her mouth shut, grinding his fingers between her teeth.

"Shit!" he hissed, ripping his hand away.

It had done the trick, though. Madelaine heaved again, the sick dribbling over her chin. Kett held onto her as she struggled, one hand on her arm, the other gripping the back of her neck.

Clare had entered the room, and he picked up whatever Madelaine had dropped. It was a white tub, the kind you got chewing gum in.

"Painkillers," he said.

Kett turned to the woman beneath him, the stench of vomit making his stomach churn.

"You knew we'd be coming," he said. "Right? You were going to end it all before we could arrest you."

Madelaine laughed again, a desperate sound. She tried to push herself up but Kett drove her back down against the side of the bath.

"We need some cuffs in here," he said, and a second later a constable squeezed in next to him. Between them, they managed to twist Madelaine's arms behind her back and secure them there. Her laughter became a shriek of pain, but she wasn't giving in. Her body writhed in Kett's grip, every muscle flexing as she tried to stand up.

"Enough," Kett told her. "It's over. Where's Gavin?"

"Who?" she said, spitting into the bath.

"Gavin, the man you're working with. Where is he?"

Another laugh. Madelaine said something that he couldn't make out, and he moved his hand from her neck to her hair, lifting her head.

"What?"

"You know I'll never tell you," she said. "I'll die before I tell you."

"Why?" said Kett.

"You wouldn't understand."

Kett looked past the constable to where Clare stood by the sink. The Superintendent looked as lost as he felt.

"Tell me what he's doing, then," said Kett. "Tell me why."

"Like I said, you wouldn't understand."

The smell of vomit was becoming overpowering. Kett stood back.

"Get her up," he told the constable. "Take her onto the landing."

The PC grabbed Madelaine beneath the arms and dragged her out of the room. She kicked as she went, one boot connecting with Kett's knee hard enough to make him grunt with pain. Her eyes flashed at him beneath her hair, full of insane fury. He wondered how she'd managed to hide it so well when he'd visited her before, because this kind of madness was surely enough to split even the most carefully crafted mask.

The constable dropped the woman by the bedroom door, where she shuffled back against the wall like a cornered animal. Her head snapped from side to side as she took in the men who surrounded her, her teeth bared.

"Calm down," Kett said as he walked out of the bathroom. He crouched down on the other side of the landing, well out of reach of her feet. "There's nothing you can do right now. You have to accept that. We've caught you, and we're going to catch Gavin, too. But if you don't want anything bad to happen to him, you need to tell us where we can find him, right now."

"You're too late," she said again. "I texted him, told him you'd found me. You can't touch him."

"He's going to run?" said Clare from the bathroom door.

"In a way," said Madelaine, that smug smile returning.

"He's going to do what you tried to do," said Kett. "He's going to kill himself."

She laughed.

"Why?" he asked.

"You know why," she told him, sniffing. "It's love."

"Love?"

"It's how all the great lovers meet their fate," she said. "Romeo and Juliet, Tristan and Isolde. They chose to leave the world rather than lose each other."

"That's insane," said Kett.

"It's love," said Madelaine.

It was pointless arguing with her.

"Then tell me why you're doing what you're doing," he said. "Explain it to me."

"Why?" she asked with a casual shrug.

"You're doing this for a reason. It's important to you. It's a... a mission, right? You're trying to prove something to yourself, to the world."

She cocked her head, studying him intently.

"You're trying to show us something by targeting these couples," Kett went on. "They wrote to you, didn't they? To your column in the magazine. Maddy F. They asked for your help."

"And I gave it," she said. A little of the woman he'd met before was returning to her features as she calmed herself down. "I told them how to fix their relationships. I gave them what they needed. Or at least I thought I had."

"Sir?" somebody called from downstairs. Kett ignored them.

"I thought you could fix anything when it came to love," Madelaine went on. "I thought love was the strongest thing in the universe. And it *is*."

Her smile was the brightest thing in the house.

"I only saw that when I met *him*, though. He showed me what love is, what it can do. And I realised the reason I couldn't help these people was because what they had wasn't love at all, it was... it was false, it was a lie they told each other to get through the day."

She leaned forward, speaking faster with every word.

"What they had wasn't love, it wasn't even friendship. They weren't soulmates. They *hated* each other, you could see that in every word they wrote to me, in every spiteful thing they said to each other. Why do we do it?"

The words were coming so fast now she was tripping over them.

"Why do we fool ourselves that we love somebody when we can barely even stand to be in the same room as them? When we argue and fight and talk shit about each other. No, that's not love. How can it be? But I didn't see it until I met *him*. He showed me true love. He showed me what it means, what it can do. You've never..."

She had to stop, her eyes wheeling in their sockets, her face manic with joy.

"God, you've never known love like this, you've never felt it. It's... There are no words. But it makes you see the lies in other people, makes you see how weak they are, how wrong they are to call what they have *love*."

The cuffs snapped tight behind her back as she tried to move her hands.

"Let me go," she said. "Let me go to him."

"No," said Kett. "Not until you tell me *why*."

"But it's so obvious why," she said, confused. "Can't you see it?"

"You were testing them?" said Kett. "The couples who wrote to you, you were testing their love."

"It's not a test," she said. "Because I already knew what they'd do. I already knew they'd choose themselves over the person they claim to love. It's not a test."

"It's a punishment," said Kett.

She didn't answer, but he saw the truth in her face.

"You were wrong, Madelaine, they didn't all choose themselves. William Briggs, you remember him?"

There wasn't a scrap of recognition in her expression.

"Your second victim, you locked him in a lorry with his wife, Darcey."

"His girlfriend," she said. "They weren't married."

"They were," said Kett. "She's pregnant too, did you know that?"

She hadn't known, that much was clear in the moment of horror before she could compose herself.

"William killed himself, Madelaine. He drove a knife

into his heart so that Darcey wouldn't have to do it. What's that, if not love?"

And her face opened with rancid delight.

"So you *do* get it," she said. "That is love. We showed them that, we gave it to them, and..."

She faltered, her mouth forming silent words.

"And maybe... maybe they shouldn't have died," she went on after a moment. "But how would they have known if we hadn't shown them? How would *we* have known?"

She looked at Kett as if he had an answer.

"You have no idea," she said when he didn't give her one. "Until you've done what we've done, until you've seen what we've seen, you have no idea what true love is. Every time we..."

"Murdered somebody," said Kett.

"No, it was never murder," she protested. "We never touched them. They did this to themselves, and every time they did it, it made us stronger. It was like we... like we took the scraps of their love and we fed on them. It made us..."

She was euphoric.

"It made us whole. It made us perfect."

Kett rocked back, glancing at Clare to see the same thoughts on the Super's face.

She's lost her mind.

"Gavin sounds remarkable," Kett said, changing tack. "Where is he?"

Madelaine opened her mouth as if to answer, then clamped it shut again. She shook her head.

"Tell me," said Kett. "Don't you want the world to know what you're doing? It's all for nothing, otherwise."

"No," she said.

"Where is he?"

"You'll find out soon enough," she said. "When he's finished."

"He's taken another couple?"

That same smile.

"He's going to make them fight?"

Her eyes blazed with excitement through the tangled mess of her hair.

"Sir?" came the same voice. Porter stood at the top of the stairs, holding Madelaine's phone.

"Hang on," Kett told him. "Who has he taken?"

Her smile grew, and she rested her head against the wall, sighing.

"It was going to be you," she said, her quiet words turning his blood to ice.

"*What*?"

"Don't ask me why. This one was nothing to do with me. But he knew all about you, Robert. He told me you'd let your wife be taken, years ago, that nobody would do that if they were truly in love. He said you needed to prove yourself."

The words had jammed themselves into Kett's throat, he couldn't speak. The image of Billie inside a burning lorry filled his head, and it was all he could do not to wrap his hand around Madelaine's throat and choke the smile from her face.

"But we saw the children," she said. "When we came to your house. We couldn't do it. *I* wouldn't do it."

"Who does he have?" Kett asked, just a whisper. "We found his place, we found the photos. Who is it? It's not too late to stop this, to save them."

"What makes you think they deserve to be saved?"

"Sir," said Porter, leaning in. "I went by Savage's house, she's not there. Door was open, dog's locked in the kitchen."

He faltered, his face deathly pale.

"Neighbours said they heard shouts, saw a campervan driving off about thirty minutes ago."

"Fuck," said Kett. He turned back to Madelaine to see that she was laughing quietly.

"This is you?" he said. "This is *him*?"

"He said it was the best way of showing you what we were doing," she said. "The best way of showing you we were right."

"Fuck," Kett said again, pushing himself up. "Where are they?"

"You're too late," she said.

The fury possessed him. He grabbed the woman by the hair, twisting her head up.

"Tell me where they are, or I swear to God."

And she answered him with another laugh.

"There's nothing you can say or do to me," she told him. "I'm his, body and soul. We'll be together again soon, some place you can never find us."

"Where is he?" he growled, ringing her head off the wall.

"Kett!" said Superintendent Clare.

"Body and soul," Madelaine whispered, curling into herself. "Body and soul. Body and soul."

Kett let go of her, looking at Clare, and then at Porter.

"Search the house," he said. "Tear the place apart. Give me the phone, Pete."

Porter handed it to him and he swiped his thumb up the screen, only to see that it was locked.

"Look at me, Madelaine," he said.

She burrowed into herself, and he grabbed her chin, forcing her head up. He held the phone in front of her until he heard the click of it unlocking. There was a text message on the screen:

They've found me. I love you. See you on the other side.

By some miracle, it hadn't been sent. He must have knocked the phone out of her hands before she could fire it off.

"It's Dove," he said, reading the name of the contact. "She didn't get a chance to send it. He doesn't know."

The look Madelaine gave him was full of madness. She tried to heave her body up to get to the phone, but a pair of constables intercepted her, pushing her back down.

"Doesn't matter," she screamed. "You can't stop him, you can't stop us. There's nothing you can do. You're too late."

"Must be a burner," said Clare. "What's the number?"

Kett found Dove's information, passing the phone over.

"We can track it, sir," he said. "We can find out where they are."

"I'll need to get a warrant, it will—"

"It's *Kate*, sir," said Kett.

Clare nodded, heading for the stairs.

"There's still time," Kett said to Porter.

But he had a terrible feeling that Madelaine was right.

They were already too late.

CHAPTER THIRTY-SEVEN

"KATE."

Her name was a whisper, spoken into the void.

"Kate."

She could almost *see* it, a sliver of light against the unbearable dark.

"Kate, *please*."

Was she drowning? Because the world around her felt too cold. She couldn't breathe, and she kicked upwards, heading for the silver glow of her name.

"Kate!"

Bursting through the surface of the water and gasping for air. She sat up, one hand to her throat, seeing not an ocean around her but a large, white room, illuminated by fairy lights.

A lorry, she thought, and the horror of it flooded back into her head: the knock on the door, the man with the Taser, Duke's body on the ground.

"Aaron!" she cried out, and the pain flooded her skull like boiling water.

She turned her head slowly, groaning. Duke was behind

her, sitting on a chair that had been bolted to the floor of the lorry. His hands and legs were secured with ropes, his muscles straining as he fought to free himself. He was still in his uniform, but his equipment was gone.

"You're okay?" he asked. "You're okay?"

"I'm okay," she told him, her voice thick, her tongue too big for her mouth.

She tried to stand up, the lorry cartwheeling around her, the agony unbearable. She moved to her hands and knees instead, crawling to Duke.

"I think they gave us something," he said. "I just woke up. You've been out cold."

"For how long?" she said.

"I don't know."

Duke heaved in a breath, fighting to free himself.

"There are weapons behind me," he said, throwing his head back.

Savage used his chair to pull herself up. Behind him was a wooden table, and on it was a collection of tools that made her stomach churn—old hammers, crowbars, an axe, and a butcher's collection of knives. The shock of waking here had kept her mind busy, but now the reality of what was happening hit her like another fist.

"He's outside," said Duke. "He'll know you're awake. We don't have long."

He tried to smile, but Savage saw the fear there. She put a hand to his face.

"It's going to be okay," she said. "We're going to get out of this. Just stay calm, Aaron, okay?"

He nodded, his eyes wide.

Savage crossed from the chair to the table like she was on a boat in a storm, holding onto it to stop herself from falling. She ran her hand along the weapons that had been left there until she landed on a wicked kitchen knife with a seven-inch blade. She picked it up and carried it back to Duke, dropping onto her knees behind him.

"Hold still," she told him. "I—"

Something hit the side of the lorry like a cannon shot, the echo rumbling back and forth like thunder.

Then, a shout from outside.

"Kate Savage and Aaron Duke. I bring you here tonight in the name of love."

The man struck the side of the lorry again.

"In the name of everything that love stands for."

Savage ignored him as best she could, sawing through the ropes. The knife was sharp, and in a matter of seconds Duke's arms were free. She handed him the knife, and he worked on the ropes that secured his legs. Savage ran to the lorry's doors and tried the handle. It took a good few kicks to tell her what she already knew.

They were locked.

"What would you do for love, Kate?" the man outside continued, his voice now coming from somewhere to the left, muffled by the lorry's thick walls. "What would you do for love, Aaron?"

Duke stood up, clutching the knife in his hand. He strode to Savage's side and drove his boot into the door only to stagger back.

"That won't work," said Savage.

"You claim to love one another," said the voice from outside. "But that is a lie."

"Fucker," growled Duke, running to the table. "There's a crowbar here, will that do it?"

Savage didn't answer, trying to slow the tornado of her thoughts.

"Love means nothing to either of you," came the voice. "This is your trial."

And she smelled it, a bitter aroma that made her blood run cold.

Smoke.

"And I, Jack Valentine, am your judge," said the voice. "If love means nothing to you, then you are not worthy of it. Kill it dead."

Duke had picked up the crowbar and was heading for the door.

"Come on," he said. "We can get it open."

"One person dies," said the voice. "The other leaves. The choice is yours."

The man struck the lorry again, two times, as if banging a gong. The smoke was thick now, pouring in through the cracks in the door, clawing into Savage's lungs, making it hard to see. She pulled off her jacket and held it to her mouth. Duke was trying to ram the crowbar into the crack between the doors, but he was coughing too hard to get any force behind it.

"Aaron," she said, taking his arm. "It won't work."

He shrugged her off, tried again, the crowbar spinning out of his hands. She grabbed him more forcefully, pulling him to the other end of the cargo bay, both of them hacking up black phlegm as the smoke pooled at their feet. It was getting hot fast, the air swimming. Savage could feel the soles of her boots sticking to the metal floor.

"What are we going to do, Kate?" Duke said, his words muffled by the arm he held over his mouth. Tears ran down his face, leaving streaks in the dirt.

"There's a way," she said, the panic churning inside her. "There's always a way."

"There is," said Duke, still holding the knife. "I'll do it, Kate."

She took his arm, shaking her head.

"Not that," she told him. "Never that."

Savage sipped the poisoned air, forced herself to stay calm. The door was locked tight. The walls were solid metal. The fire burned beneath them, no way out through the floor.

She angled her head up.

"The roof," she said. "It's our only shot."

Duke nodded. They turned to the table together, Duke climbing onto it and offering Savage a hand up. Even from here, with their arms extended, the ceiling was well out of reach.

"Come on," said Duke, crouching down and offering Savage his knee. "I'll—"

He had to stop, the coughs tearing from him. The smoke was so thick now that Savage couldn't see the door anymore. Her head was ringing like she was standing inside a cathedral bell.

She took Aaron's hand, planted a boot on his thigh, then swung her leg around his shoulders. He held her ankles like her granddad had done when she was a child, grunting as he straightened up.

She stretched out her fingers, pressed them into the roof, saw the bulge they made.

"It's canvas," she said, the roar of the fire drowning out her words. "Give me the knife."

He passed it up and she took it, driving the point into the roof. The material resisted for a second, then tore, cold air dropping through the gap. She sawed frantically, cutting a rough circle into the roof, ripping the material free. She heaved in a lungful of clean air before dropping her head back into the smoke.

"We can get out," she said. "Give me a push and I'll..."

And she fell silent, because she suddenly realised what the problem would be.

"Get me down," she said.

"Just go!" coughed Duke.

She wriggled her way off his shoulders, sliding down beside him on the tabletop, the knife tumbling out of her fingers and onto the floor. The air felt like boiling water against her skin.

"I'll help you out first," she said. "Pull me up after you."

"It won't work, Kate," said Duke, his eyes bloodshot but still full of that kindness she'd fallen in love with.

"It will work," she said.

She laced her hands together into a cat's cradle.

"I can do it, Aaron, just *try*."

"It's too high," he said.

He took her hands in his own, holding tight.

"It's too high," he said again. "I'm sorry, but please let me say this. I've been trying for so long and..."

He doubled over, coughing, and when he dropped down onto his knee, she thought he'd collapsed.

"Aaron?" she said, trying to pull her hands free only for him to hold them even tighter.

He looked up at her.

"Kate, you make me the happiest man in the world."

"What?" she said. "Aaron, not now. You don't have to do this now, you—"

"There's not going to be another time," he said. "Please."

It was like a dam had broken in her chest, the sob tearing its way out of her as violently as the coughs. Duke was crying too, but there was a smile on his face. He reached into his pocket and pulled out a little crocheted bag. The smoke was so thick that even when he opened it, she couldn't see what was inside.

"I love you, Kate Savage," he said. "Would you do me the honour of becoming my wife?"

She pulled her hand free and rested it on his cheek, using her thumb to smudge away a tear. She was sobbing so hard she could barely speak, but somehow she managed it.

"Yes, you dope. Of course I will. I love you."

He pulled a ring from the bag and slid it onto her finger. Then he leaned up and kissed her, tasting of salt and smoke.

"Now go," he said when he'd pulled away. "Go."

It crossed her mind that it would be better to stay, to pass together.

But only for a moment.

Duke was still on one knee and she climbed onto his shoulders again, feeling the strength of him as he stood. She stretched her arms through the hole she'd made in the roof, finding the frame and clinging onto it.

"You got it?" Duke said.

"Yeah."

"Hold on."

He ducked out from beneath her and she started to slip, then she felt his hands under her boots, taking her weight. She pushed upwards until she could hook her elbows over the edge of the hole, then she swung a leg over, clambering onto the roof.

She filled her lungs with air and crawled back to the hole, peering in.

"Aaron, give me the crowbar, I'll open the doors from outside."

Duke's face was only just visible, flecked with firelight

as the flames started to eat their way through the lorry's shell.

"I can't... see it," he said. "Just go, it's okay."

His arm covered his mouth, but those kind, gentle eyes watched her.

"Come on, Aaron," she sobbed, lying on her stomach and offering him her hand even though she knew she wasn't strong enough to pull him up. "Come on! Please!"

She felt his fingers touch hers, a squeeze.

"Go!" he shouted.

Then he disappeared into the churning smoke.

"No!" she screamed. "Aaron, no!"

She started to climb back in, but the heat was too much, blistering her skin. There was nothing she could do but back away from the hole, still screaming Duke's name as she went. She reached the edge of the roof, a wall of smoke that was darker than the night sky. Sliding her legs off first, she clung on until her lungs started screaming, then she let go.

She seemed to fall forever before she hit the ground, the impact driving the last of the air from her lungs. Flames reached for her from beneath the lorry, but she tumbled out of their way, rolling onto her hands and knees, making it to her feet.

The lorry was a pyre, almost lost in the fury of the fire. Savage sucked in air, screaming.

"Aaron!"

She took a step towards the inferno, heading for the back doors.

Then the world blazed white as the petrol tank exploded.

A concussive fist of heat and noise punched her backwards, rolling her over and over until she couldn't work out what was sky and what was ground.

Somehow, she sat up.

Somehow, she opened her eyes.

"Aaron..." she said, reaching for the lorry, hoping to see him inside that hellscape of fire and smoke.

Knowing she wouldn't.

She wasn't alone, though.

A shadow stood by the trees a little way off, watching the burning lorry from the hood of his raincoat.

Jack Valentine, she thought.

She pushed herself up, the pain almost too much to be real.

It didn't matter anymore.

Nothing mattered anymore.

"Hey," she said, just a whisper.

She took a step, then another, feeling the machine of her body come back online.

Jack turned and saw her. His eyes widened.

"Hey," she said again, breaking into a run.

The man turned, slipping into the darkness of the woods. Savage followed, gaining speed with every step, driven by rage, driven by loss, driven by heartbreak.

Nothing mattered anymore.

Except *this*.

Duke wasn't the only one who was going to die tonight.

CHAPTER THIRTY-EIGHT

KETT DROVE, BECAUSE HE DIDN'T TRUST ANYONE ELSE to get him there fast enough. He took the roads at breakneck speed, riding the wail of the siren through the night and leading a tail of police cars behind him.

"Keep going, Kett," said Superintendent Clare from the passenger seat. He had his phone to his ear, his eyes like a hawk's as he stared at the road ahead. Spalding had managed to give them the rough location of Gavin Dove's phone before they'd even left the house, following the ping from a cell tower to the east of the city. "You're sure, Alison?"

"Savage still isn't answering, sir," said Porter from the back. He was leaning between the seats, his phone clutched in his hand. "If that prick has so much as touched a hair on her head..."

He left the threat unfinished because there was nothing else to say. They'd seen the killer at work, they knew how he operated.

There was every chance that Savage and Duke were already dead.

"Spalding's found Dove on the system," Clare said. "He's ex-military, Green Beret. Discharged in 2019 on medical grounds, he failed the psych evaluation."

"No shit," said Kett.

"He's been living in Norfolk ever since, runs a camper rental company, the one that you found, Porter. He was renovating some of the lorries we found in his yard. The headquarters for the magazine Madelaine works for is on the same street."

"That's how they met," said Kett.

"Take the next exit," said Clare, bracing one hand on the dash as Kett overtook the car in front. "Spalding's narrowed it down to a mile or so outside of Blofield. The chopper's inbound, the Fire Service is on its way, and Gorski's deployed."

Too slow, Kett thought. *We're not going to get to them in time.*

He peeled the car off the dual carriageway, the convoy of vehicles tailing him. He had to brake hard as he entered the roundabout, almost losing control.

"Easy, Robbie," said Clare. "We're no use to them dead."

He pumped the brakes, following the signs and accelerating hard onto the country lane. The world beyond the headlights was so ink-black it might as well not have been there at all.

"It's left ahead," Clare said.

Kett slowed down, seeing the junction and steering hard into it. The IRV thumped over the verge, almost taking off. Then Kett floored it, the BMW's big engine growling.

"What's that?" said Porter, pointing through the windscreen. There was a glow on the horizon that looked bright enough to be sunrise.

"Shit," said Kett. "It's fire."

The road curved wildly left and right, as if trying to slow them down. But there was no danger of getting lost. The flames rose higher than the trees, a beacon that could be seen for miles.

A funeral pyre that burned a hole in the sky.

"Fuck me," said Porter, his ashen face even paler thanks to the rippling blue lights.

"It's not over yet," said Clare, but the tone of his voice undermined his words. When Kett glanced at the Superintendent, there was fear on his face—something he didn't think he'd ever seen before, not even in those times when Clare's own life had been in danger.

He steered the IRV around a tight bend, the street ahead lit up like a stage thanks to a break in the hedge. When he pulled the car through the gap into the field beyond, the burning lorry filled the windscreen, the roar of it audible even over the growl of the engine, over the tuning fork ring of panic in his skull. He braked, only for Clare to backhand him on the arm.

"Leave room for the fire engine," the Super shouted, his eyes wild.

Kett pulled the car over to the side, getting out. The heat pouring off the lorry was phenomenal even from thirty yards away, his skin prickling, the sweat breaking out on his face. He had to lift a hand to shield his eyes as he stumbled over the rough ground.

"Kate!" he yelled, his voice swallowed by the fire. "Christ."

He had to stop, to take a step back. The heat was just too much.

He turned to see Clare and Porter charging across the field, lit up brilliantly by the inferno. A dozen police officers followed, all wearing the same expressions of shock and horror.

None of them could help.

If anyone had been inside the lorry, they were long dead.

Kett turned back to the inferno. From here he could only see the cab, the windscreen shattered and the seats burned out. A stone's throw away was a campervan, one that he'd seen before parked outside Madelaine Fielding's house. Kett jogged towards it, slipping on the ridges of the field.

You fucking idiot, Robbie, he thought. *You missed him, twice. This is your fault.*

"Careful, Kett," Clare called out. "We don't know where he is."

Kett reached the camper, cupping his hand to the dark window to see that it was empty. He ran to the back and opened the doors, but there was nothing there other than loose coils of rope.

"Fuck," he said. "He's gone. Spread out, search the woods. If he hasn't driven away then he might be on foot. Where's the helicopter?"

"Minutes away," said Clare, checking his watch.

"We're too late," said Kett, staring at the burning lorry until it felt like his eyes were being scorched out of their sockets.

He turned away, but the fire still raged, seared into his retinas. He imagined Savage there, Duke too, both of them screaming as the fire consumed them. It was all he could do not to hurl himself into the blaze.

"We can't do anything for them other than pray they weren't inside," said Clare. "But we can catch Dove. The fire's recent, he hasn't taken his van. We can find him."

Kett nodded, blinking the last of the light from his eyes. The uniformed coppers had spread out, charging into the woods that surrounded the field, their torches scattering the shadows.

"Pete, with me," Kett shouted, running towards the trees.

He stopped when he heard a shout behind him.

"Sir!"

One of the coppers was standing to the side of the lorry, waving at the Superintendent.

"Sir, over here!" he said. "Hurry!"

Kett started towards him, only to stop in his tracks when another sound cut through the night, barely audible over the shouts, over the snap and crack of the fire.

A *scream*.

He spun around, running for the woods.

"Kate!"

"STOP!"

Savage screamed the word into the night even though her throat was red raw, even though her lungs were ruined.

"Stop!"

She wasn't sure how long she'd been running, but she'd left the glow of the fire behind her. The woods were so dark she may as well have been blind, just the occasional glimpse of the cloud-wrapped moon between the skeletal canopies letting her know she hadn't fallen off the edge of the world.

Somewhere behind her she thought she could hear sirens, shouts too. They'd found her, but they hadn't got here fast enough.

They hadn't arrived in time to save Duke.

And they hadn't arrived in time to stop her doing what she needed to do.

Something jabbed into the soft flesh of her cheek—a branch, she realised as she recoiled—and she slowed to a walk. Her heart drummed harder than she'd ever felt it, the rhythm like it was calling his name: *Aa-ron, Aa-ron, Aa-ron.* The devastation coursed through her, the grief, the fury.

"Where are you?" she screamed into the woods.

She had to hold her breath in order to get her answer, listening past the sirens, past the growing volume of voices behind her, hearing the snap of branches from over to her right.

She set off towards the sound, stumbling on roots. Twigs tangled in her hair like fingers, trying to hold her tight. She skinned her knuckles on the rough trunks as she fought for something to hold onto. But the pain wasn't important. It wasn't forever.

Only *death* was forever.

There was a grunt from up ahead, something heavy falling.

"Fuck," said the man.

He was close, but Savage didn't realise how close until she saw the ghostly light of a mobile phone from behind a tree maybe fifteen yards away. It shone left, then right, then angled back, so bright after the dark woods that it blinded her.

"Shit," she heard the man say. He was panting hard, struggling to his feet.

"Stop," Savage ordered. "Don't move. This ends here, with you and me."

There must have been something in her voice because he didn't run. He stepped out from the tree, his phone creating a perfect pocket of light.

Savage walked towards him, closing the gap. Her fists were clenched so tightly she wasn't sure she'd ever be able to open them again.

The man who called himself Jack Valentine welcomed her with a tight smile, his dark eyes alert. He was tall, taller even than Duke had been, and broad too, dressed in jeans and boots and a black roll-neck jumper. He was in his thirties, his hair and his beard black. He pulled something from his pocket with his free hand, something that glinted.

A knife.

But still she didn't stop. She *couldn't* stop.

All she could think about was Aaron, his smile as he drowned in smoke, the way he'd squeezed her fingers.

Would you do me the honour of becoming my wife?

And now she'd never see him again, never hear his voice, his goofy laugh, never feel his strong arms around her. She'd never be safe again, she'd never be loved again.

The pain of it was worse than anything she'd ever felt.

"Back off," said the man.

She kept walking, her boots slipping in the dirt. Ten yards now.

The man lifted the knife.

"I don't want to have to do this to you," he said.

"Just tell me why," she replied, a branch snapping underfoot like a gunshot. Her voice was so low it scared her. It was a dog's growl. "Tell me why he had to die."

The man laughed, that smile still plastered on his face.

"You kill him?"

"No," she said.

"Then there's your answer. He died for you. He died because of how much he loved you. Don't you see what we've given you?"

"What you've *given* me?" she said.

She took another few steps, just five yards away now, almost close enough to touch. Only when he lifted the knife and pointed it at her throat, did she finally stop.

"You'll thank us for it one day," he said. "You'll thank us for showing you what real love is. How else would you have known how he felt about you? *Really* felt?"

"I knew," she said.

She met his eye and held it.

"What now?" he asked, the knife still pointed at her neck.

"You know what," she told him. "You don't get to do that. Not to him."

He nodded, looking past her to where the shouts of the approaching police were growing louder.

"I guess I owe you a shot," he said. "Better make it quick, though. I'm not getting caught today."

"It will be quick," she said.

He beckoned her with the knife, adjusting his stance in a way that made it clear he was no stranger to a fight. Savage hesitated, suddenly unsure. She could hold her own in most situations, but she was exhausted, consumed by emotion, stripped bare by the adrenaline. There was a tremor that ran through her entire body, an engine about to stall.

"Not too late to turn around and fuck off," the man said. "You'll thank us later."

She couldn't do that to Duke, even though she knew he'd have begged her to leave.

"Us," she said, the man's words catching up with her.

"Huh?"

"You said us, just now. You'll thank *us*."

He nodded, the knife point perfectly steady, waiting to bury itself into the soft meat of her throat.

"You're doing this with somebody you love?" Savage said, just a guess. "Somebody special?"

He didn't answer, licking his lips as he looked once again over her shoulder. The shouts were close enough now that she could hear her name. There were more lights in the trees, she realised, the faintest of auroras dancing between the branches, finding the man's face. Savage wondered for the first time how they'd got here so quickly, working it out in a heartbeat.

"They know," she said.

"Know what?"

"That you're not working alone. They know about your... what? Girlfriend? Boyfriend? Wife?"

"It's more than that," he said. "Somebody like you wouldn't get it."

"Soulmate?" Savage said.

"More than that. You wouldn't—"

"Oh, no, I get it," she said. "I've seen it a million times. Two people whose relationship is so empty they have to find ways of keeping themselves together. It's not usually murder."

"You don't understand," he said, and this time he was the one who took a step towards her.

"She means a lot to you, right?" Savage said, retreating. Her heel caught the root of a tree and she almost fell.

"More than you'll ever know," he said, lifting his arm like a scorpion's tail. She had to take another step backwards as he advanced.

"You stop to wonder how they found us so fast?"

The lights were growing stronger, the voices louder. She didn't dare take her eyes off the man to look, but she knew they were close.

"What do you mean?" he said.

"I mean, how did they know where we were?"

"The fire," he said. "They must have seen it."

Savage shook her head.

"Uh-uh. I don't know how far out of the city we are, but I'm guessing a few miles. No way they'd have got here so fast."

The man's smile fell away, and Savage nodded.

"They found her," she said. "Whoever she is, they found her. Either she told them where you were, or she gave them your number so they could track your phone."

It was like he'd frozen, only his blinking eyes giving him away.

"She wouldn't," he said after a few seconds. "There's no way."

"She did," said Savage.

The man released a long breath, the knife wavering.

"Kate!" came a voice behind her, beautifully familiar. This time she risked a glance back, seeing Porter between the trees. Kett was there too, an army of coppers right behind them. They stopped when they saw the knife.

"Drop it," said Kett. "Nowhere to go, Gavin."

Savage turned back to the man.

"It's over," she said.

He nodded. Sniffed.

"She told you where I was?" he called out.

"Yeah," said Kett. "Gave you right up. So drop the fucking knife."

The man—Gavin—licked his lips. He looked at Savage, a softer smile appearing on his face.

"I meant it," he said. "You'll thank us for what we did, one day. Most love ends, but your love will be eternal. You'll have it for the rest of your life."

He dropped his phone, flipped the knife inwards with practised ease, took it in both hands.

"You're one of the lucky ones," he said, and his body tensed.

She knew what he was going to do, it was etched into every harrowed line of his face, in the insane gleam of his eyes.

And all she could think was, *let him do it,* because some people didn't deserve to be saved.

But there was Duke again, standing right beside her. She could almost feel his big hand in hers, she could almost hear his calm voice in her ear.

Everyone deserves to be saved.

She moved before she was even aware of it, throwing herself at Gavin and grabbing his hands. She felt the sudden lurch as he pulled the blade towards his throat, but she dropped to the ground, letting her body weight pull his arms down.

"Kate!" somebody yelled.

Gavin lost his footing, falling onto her, pinning her to the forest floor. The knife was sandwiched between them, the blade slicing through her clothes, her skin.

"Fuck off!" he roared, his face pressed against hers.

Savage ground her forehead into his nose until he gargled with pain, keeping her hands locked around his so he couldn't get purchase on the weapon.

"Let me go!" he said.

"No," she told him.

He was too strong, pushing himself up, twisting the knife towards his own body.

Savage snapped her head up, her teeth clamping onto his cheek, hard enough to draw blood.

He screamed, the most wretched sound she'd ever heard.

Then somebody thumped into him, pulling him away. Savage sat up to see Porter there, his knee in the man's throat as another constable wrestled the knife away. She spat blood from her mouth.

"Come on," said Kett, grabbing her arms, hauling her to her feet.

Gavin was putting up a hell of a fight, but it was a battle he couldn't win. In less than five seconds, he was swamped beneath a wave of black uniforms, his cries drowned out by their shouts. Kett steered her away, one arm around her shoulders.

"You okay?" he asked.

There were no words to answer him with. She stopped walking, burrowing her head into his chest, the sobs too big to fit up her throat. Kett held her so hard she could barely breathe, his voice drowned out by the roar of her pulse. He held her until there was nothing left, until she was empty.

It was a million years later that she peeled herself away, Kett's face just a blur past the tears—a blur that, for a second that broke her heart clean in two, could have been Duke.

"Aaron," she whispered, and she knew from Kett's silence that it was true, that he wasn't coming back.

"You're safe," he said. "You're safe. You're safe."

He walked her into the trees, the shouts of the police ebbing away, replaced with their quiet footsteps. Savage felt numb, as if her body had turned to plastic. She felt *broken*.

"Kett?" came another voice, the Superintendent.

"Over here, sir," said Kett.

"Where? I can't see a tossing thing."

Savage looked up, smudging a hand over her eyes to see a flickering glow through the trees.

The fire, she knew. The lorry.

"We're coming to you, sir," said Kett. "I've got Kate, she's..."

He was going to say okay, she knew, but that was a lie.

"She's *alive.*"

Savage spotted Clare's outline limping through the woods.

"Thank God," the Superintendent said when he saw her. "I thought we'd lost you."

She took a breath, the stench of smoke making her gag.

"Not me, sir," she said. "But Aaron... He's..."

"He's alive," said Clare.

Savage's heart seemed to stop.

"*What?*" she said, shaking her head.

"I said the Bollock Goblin's alive," Clare repeated. "But unconscious. One of our officers found him in the field by the back of the lorry."

"That's impossible," said Savage, pushing herself away from Kett. "He was trapped, he... I saw him, sir, he was inside the lorry when it exploded."

"Then they must have found some other musclebound goat vagina with a ridiculous beard and legs like Spanish hams," said Clare, hitching a thumb over his shoulder. "Go on."

She didn't need to be told twice, using the last of her energy to break into a run. It was like she was moving inside a dream, the woods too big, the air too thick, her legs not carrying her fast enough.

Then she burst out of the trees, seeing the lorry right ahead, the fading fire painting the field in soft light. Dozens of police officers surrounded it, turned into mirages by the shimmering air and the smoke.

"Aaron?" she called.

The officers pointed, and she followed their fingers around the circumference of the pyre, around the circle of blackened earth, seeing a huddle of uniforms standing there.

And another on the ground beneath them.

She pushed between the PCs, dropping to her knees beside Duke, her hands on his chest, on his neck, on his face. His uniform was ripped to shreds, his skin burned raw in places, patches of his beard and his hair seared away.

But he was alive. He was breathing.

The sobs ripped out of her, the tears falling too fast for her to wipe away. She moved her hands from his face to his chest and back again to make sure he was real.

"Aaron?"

"He's out cold," said one of the PCs. "Must have got out somehow."

Savage glanced at the back of the lorry. One door was closed, the other lay on the ground ten yards away as if it had been shot off by a cannon.

"Aaron, it's me," she said, running her hands over his face. "Aaron?"

Duke groaned.

"Thank God," Savage said, leaning back, looking at the smoke-scarred sky. "Thank you, thank you."

"Kate?"

Duke opened one bloodshot eye, peering at her.

"*How*?" she said. "I saw you, I..."

Despite everything, he managed a smile. He moved his chapped lips, the words a whisper she had to lean in to hear.

"Explosion... blew the bloody... doors off."

Savage laughed, still stroking his face.

"You..." Duke started, then coughed weakly.

"I what?" she said.

She heard the bleep of a siren, looking back to see an ambulance bumping onto the field.

"You..." Duke said again. "You said yes, right?"

Savage laughed, bending over to plant a kiss on his lips. She remembered the ring he'd given her, looking at it for the first time. It sat on her soot-black finger, the little diamond the brightest thing in the world.

"Yes," she said.

Kett jogged into sight, shielding his eyes from the blaze. Porter and Clare followed, all of them looking at her.

"He okay?" Kett asked, and she nodded.

"I think so."

Duke closed his eye, smiling.

"We're going to get married?" he said.

Savage lay down beside him, the ground beautifully cold against her back, the dwindling fire painting the tops of the trees. She took Duke's hand and held it tight, feeling him squeeze her fingers until the beat of her heart had returned to normal. The exhaustion was so immense that she could barely speak, but she managed.

"Yeah," she said. "We are."

CHAPTER THIRTY-NINE

Wednesday

"Okay, prepare to be amazed."

Savage used her hip to open the door, careful not to tip the tray she was holding.

Inside the hospital room, Duke did his best to shuffle up the bed, groaning in pain with every movement. After a second or two, he gave up, resting his bruised and battered head on the pillow. He studied Savage with one eye, the other one hidden by a bandage. The smile he gave her almost made her drop the tray, because for a moment she felt like she was dreaming, like she would wake up and remember that he was gone.

But there he was. Her Aaron.

"I'm so ready for this," he said, his voice a feeble croak. "I'm ready to be amazed, ready to have my socks blown off, in fact."

"Poor choice of words," said Savage, setting the tray on

Duke's bedside table and perching on the edge of the bed. She found the control and pressed the button to raise his top half. "Given that you pretty much did have your socks blown off."

Duke's laugh lasted a handful of seconds before it turned into a cough. Savage waited until he was almost upright before offering him the plastic cup of apple juice she had brought for his lunch. He sipped gently, his lips red raw.

"Should have brought you a straw, sorry," she said.

"You can't drink champers out of a straw," he said.

"Huh?"

"Champagne," Duke said. "This is the first date of our engagement, I'm celebrating. That's not apple juice, it's Bollinger."

Savage laughed, setting the cup back down.

"What did you make me, then?" he asked, trying to turn his head to look at the tray.

"Oh, it's an epic feast," Savage said. "A testament to my love for you."

She lifted the plate onto his lap, both of them staring at the solitary slice of buttered toast.

"Fit for a king," said Duke. "Thank you."

"There's custard for pudding," she said. "I can smell it."

"Yum."

He laughed again, but it was weaker now. He closed his eye, taking a few moments to recover his breath. He'd spent the last twelve hours or so flitting in and out of sleep while the doctors had examined him, his list of injuries growing longer with every test and scan.

He'd suffered burns to nearly thirty percent of his body, mainly his face and neck and arms, but fortunately they were mild. Only the ones on his scalp were second-degree.

The heat had damaged his eye, although the doctor that Savage had shadowed that morning said it would recover, and the explosion had ruptured the eardrum on the same side. He'd sustained two broken ribs when he'd thrown himself out of the back of the lorry, plus a torn tendon in his knee.

Given all that, he was surprisingly upbeat.

"Can I see it again?" he asked, ignoring the toast and nodding to Savage's hand. She held it up proudly, the ring catching the bright light of the room and sparkling fiercely. Duke took it in his trembling hand, his fingers still black from the fire. His smile faltered. "I'm sorry it's not very big."

"It's perfect, Aaron," she said. "It's perfect because it came from you."

"You really like it?"

"I love it," she said, leaning over to kiss him on the cheek. "I love you."

"Ow," he said.

"I feel like I should ask you properly," he said, shuffling in the bed. "It wasn't exactly romantic, given the fire and everything."

"And the explosion," said Savage.

"The serial killer outside the doors."

"And that lorry was filthy."

"Yeah. Give me a second."

Duke looked like he was trying to get out of bed, and Savage planted a hand on his chest to stop him.

"You can ask me when you're out of hospital," she said. "Yeah? You can ask me every day if you like. I'll always give you the same answer."

He beamed at her.

"And what answer is that?"

"Yes, you dope."

She kissed him again, this time on his lips.

"Ow," he said again. "This is nice, though. Having some alone time. It feels like a proper date."

"It does," she said. "Which is why you should eat the delicious meal I've lovingly made for you."

He didn't have a chance to answer because somebody knocked on the door. Savage glanced over to see DCI Kett there. He was so tired he looked like he was sleepwalking.

"Bad time?" he asked, the words becoming a yawn that he covered with the back of his hand.

"No, sir," said Savage, at the exact same time Duke said, "Yes!"

"Any word, sir?" Savage asked as Kett collapsed into the chair in the corner of the room.

"Too many words to say them all now," he said, yawning again. "But I can give you the CliffsNotes. Both Madelaine Fielding and Gavin Dove are well and truly finished. We interviewed them both this morning, and within about five minutes they'd turned on each other. Both are blaming the other one for everything that happened."

"So much for true love, sir," said Savage.

"Quite," said Kett. "They met because their workplaces were on the same street, fell hard for each other. A proper infatuation. Dove was the one who pushed the relationship to a dark place. Forensics found a couple of laptops at his house, a lot of horrible shit on there, bondage and torture and some dark web chatroom logs that are seriously messed up. Kidnapping, murder, rape. You name it, he's had a fantasy about it. I don't think any of it is real, not the early stuff anyway, but we'll know soon enough."

"Not nice," said Savage.

"Not at all. There's a bunch of emails and messages between Maddy and Gavin, thousands of them. He started sharing his fantasies with her after they met, and it turns out she was willing to go along with it. Seems like the more they spoke, the harder she fell for him. By the time he suggested killing somebody, I think she probably would have done anything he said."

"But she still did it, sir," said Savage.

"She did, and she'll go to prison for it. You can blame love for a lot of things, but not for murder. Besides, the whole 'sticking two people inside a burning lorry and making them fight to the death' was her idea. She honestly thought it would be romantic."

"What?" croaked Duke.

"She was a fantasist too," said Kett. "And a compulsive liar. I asked around, the book she wrote for her dissertation was almost entirely made up, including her sources. Jack Valentine never kidnapped people. That was a lie. She created her own version of the story and used it to justify what she was doing."

He shook his head.

"We dug up Dove's garden this morning, found a burned corpse that almost certainly belongs to Karen Dankworth. It wasn't alone."

"What, sir?" said Savage. "All the other bodies were accounted for, weren't they?"

"All the ones we knew about," he said. "But Dove and Fielding have been doing this for longer than we assumed. There are three older bodies in the garden, all burned beyond recognition."

Savage put her hand to her mouth.

"I think he planned to remove all the bodies from the lorries, like he did with Karen, but he was getting careless. He didn't have time."

"This is all fascinating, sir," said Duke. "But can it wait?

We were just enjoying some alone time. Our first date as an engaged couple."

"Oh, right, of course," said Kett, sitting forward in the chair as if preparing himself for the arduous task of standing up. "Sure, I just wanted to update you. I was here to see Darcey. She's getting out today."

"She's okay, sir?" asked Savage.

"She will be, I think," Kett replied. "Time heals all wounds."

Savage wasn't so sure about that. Time couldn't erase everything.

"She did confess that she'd lied about Dawson being at the lorry when Will died," Kett said. "Clare's right, it was a clever thing to do. Probably saved those women a lot of pain, and possibly their lives. Not to mention the fact that a lot of bad men are now behind bars, including Father Odling."

"She did good, sir," said Savage.

"How are you holding up, Aaron?" Kett asked as he groaned his way back to his feet, his joints popping like distant gunfire.

"I'll be great, when we're on our own," Aaron replied. "Sir."

"Received and understood."

Kett opened the door only to find Porter standing there. He stood back to let the DI in, the room starting to feel a little crowded.

"How're you doing, mate?" Porter asked Duke. "You look like shit."

"Still better looking than you, sir," Duke replied. "I was just saying, Kate and I were enjoying some alone—"

"Oh, are you going to eat that?" Porter asked, spying the toast. He didn't wait for a reply, snatching it from the plate and biting off half of it in one go. He looked like he was having trouble working it down.

"Christ, it's a little dry," he said, spraying crumbs and glaring at Duke like it was his fault.

"What do you need, Pete?" Kett said, sitting back down in the chair.

"Just here to see if DI 'Dickless' Dawson's ready for an interview yet, sir," he said, sitting on the end of the bed and causing Duke to moan in pain. Porter was oblivious to it, biting off another mouthful of toast. "I don't think they'll be calling him Chuckles anymore. One bollock's gone, but apparently there's some serious damage to his knob as well. The nurse I spoke to said they might have to amputate."

A collective groan rippled across the room.

"Deserves it," said Kett.

Porter nodded, swallowing painfully.

"This is the worst toast I've ever had," he said.

He picked up Duke's juice and downed it, thumping a fist into his chest.

"Bit better."

"You've eaten our romantic lunch, sir," said Duke, glowering at Porter. "You can leave now."

"I'm going, I'm going," said Porter, giving Duke's leg a hefty pat. "Glad to see you're alright, mate. Thought we'd lost you for a while there."

He gave Duke a genuine smile of friendship.

"And congrats on the engagement. Always thought you were too vacant to be engaged, but you live and learn."

Duke's forehead creased as he struggled to understand the insult.

"Right, back to HQ," said Porter. "I have a meeting with God."

"God?" said Kett.

"Yeah, God. Clare's nickname for himself, remember? Although I think Satan's probably a better one."

"God will do just fine," said Clare, who appeared in the open door so dramatically that everyone in the room jumped in fright. He walked in, flashing Porter a grin that was positively demonic. "Although I can be a devil if you poke me too hard, Detective. I can make your life hell, I can toss you off into the fiery pits over and over again until you're a dry, shrivelled husk."

"*What?*" squeaked Porter.

"Doesn't mean what you think it means, sir," said Kett.

"Shut it, Zipper," said Clare, closing the door behind him and shooing Porter from the bed.

Duke barely had time to shift out of the way before the Super sat down. He slapped a hand onto the PC's arm with no small force, his smile growing.

"Looking good, Constable," he said. "You were lucky. Cara examined the truck you were in, it had a reinforced steel bed for heavy loads. Pure chance. I don't think even Dove knew about it. It blocked the full force of the explosion, channelled the heat out to the sides. The frame buckled, and the door popped off."

He patted Duke's arm again.

"Somebody's looking out for you."

"Good to know," said Duke, his eye watering. "Is that all? Because I'm not feeling great, and I just wanted some time with Kate."

"Ah, yes," said Clare. "I haven't had a chance to say it yet, but congratulations! Really weird time to propose, Hodenkobold, but still a reason to celebrate."

Duke nodded, the pain etched into his face.

"Do you think I could have a new nickname, sir?" he asked. "Given everything that's happened."

Clare thought about it for all of a second.

"No, I like that one just fine."

Duke pouted as well as his battered face would allow. Clare was still smiling, and it was making Savage uneasy. Kett must have felt it too, because he leaned forward in the chair.

"Are you okay, sir?" he asked. "You seem a little... different."

Clare grinned, his eyebrows wiggling.

"It's funny you should ask," he said. "Because when I got home this morning Fiona decided that—"

"No!" yelled Kett, throwing up a hand as if Clare was coming at him with a bat.

"Decided that her celibacy streak was—"

"No!" said Porter, putting his hands over his ears. "I don't want to hear it!"

"Was not something she wished to pursue anymore, and let's just say that after such a long time away from each other we—"

Duke's heartbeat monitor made it seem like he was having some kind of fit as he attempted to hide himself in his blankets.

"Sir!" said Savage, resisting the urge to clamp her fingers over Clare's mouth. "Please, can we leave this conversation for another time?"

"Like a century from now," said Kett. "A *millennia*."

"It's too late," said Porter, his hands still over his ears. "It's in my head, I can't get it out."

Clare roared with laughter, a noise Savage had never heard before and never wanted to hear again. He pushed himself off the bed and stretched leisurely, wiggling his eyebrows again.

"I'll see you all back at HQ," he said, doing a strange little dance on the spot. "Sharpish."

But even he couldn't get out of the room, because when he opened the door, Norman Balls was standing outside, one hand cupped to his ear as if he had been eavesdropping. He stood bolt upright, his eyes wide, his mouth open.

"Uh..." he said.

"What are you doing, Balls?" barked Clare, his good mood evaporating.

"What are *you* doing?" Balls said, entering the room even though there was barely any space for him. "If this party is to celebrate the satisfactory conclusion of the case, then I should be here too."

"Why?" said Porter.

"Because I solved it!" said Balls, pointing at himself. "I took you right to the killer."

"But you didn't know she was the killer," said Kett.

"No, I didn't," said Balls, his head dropping. "I thought she was the love of my life."

"I think you had a lucky escape, Norman," said Savage.

"You really had no idea?" said Kett, forcing himself out of the chair again. "All the times you met her, you had no clue she was a monster?"

"Oh, I'd never met her before this week," he said. "Just a few online chats, and it was mainly me doing the chatting. But we were soulmates, I could feel it. I loved everything about her."

He frowned.

"Well, apart from all the terrible murders and stuff."

Duke really was starting to struggle, and Savage rested a gentle hand on his cheek before turning to the others.

"I think it's time to leave," she said. "But thank you all for stopping by."

Balls caught sight of the ring, nodding appreciatively.

"I heard about the engagement," he said. "Congratulations. I just want to point out that my Rover is available for weddings. As an official deputy for the Force—"

"Not a deputy," said Clare.

"And as a dear friend to you all—"

"Not a friend," muttered Kett.

"I will gladly chauffeur you to wherever you need to be."

"No," groaned Duke.

"Thank you," Savage said. "We'll have a think."

Balls tipped an imaginary cap to her and left the room.

Clare followed, looking back from the corridor.

"That reminds me, I'm not sure if I ever told you this, but I'm an ordained minister. And yes, I will happily conduct the ceremony."

"No!" said Duke from the bed.

"Can we let you know, sir?" said Savage, ushering Porter to the door.

"I'll be the best man, obviously," the DI said. "Thanks, Aaron."

"No," Duke yelled. "I didn't say—"

But Porter had gone. Kett stopped by the door, laughing quietly.

"It's going to be quite a day," he said. "And you deserve it, both of you. You going to be okay?"

Savage glanced at Duke.

"Yes, sir. I think we are."

"I do too," he said. "You got through the worst thing that will ever happen to you last night, and believe me, I know how much that changes you. But..."

He seemed to struggle to find the words, and Savage noticed for the first time how much older he looked than when she'd first met him—the lines around his eyes deeper, so much more grey in his hair.

"But something like this, it gives you a strength that most people don't have. Most couples don't have. It's the same with me and Billie, what we went through made us unbreakable."

"Thank you, sir," said Savage.

Kett nodded to her and left the room, closing the door behind him. The sudden quiet—just the gentle beep of Duke's monitors, his hoarse breaths, the distant hum of the hospital—didn't feel real.

Savage sat next to Duke on the bed and held his hand. It seemed to take every ounce of strength he had to keep his eye open.

"Did they just plan our wedding for us?" he said.

"I think so," she replied. "Can you imagine Colin Clare being our minister?"

"You may now toss the bride," said Duke, laughing so hard he started coughing again.

Savage rested her hand on his face until it stopped.

"Get some sleep, Aaron," she said.

He closed his eye and nodded.

"I don't care how we get married," he whispered. "I just want to be with you."

"You will be," she said.

She felt her own exhaustion catching up with her, and she lifted her legs onto the bed, resting her head on Duke's chest, feeling the steady rise and fall of it as he drifted into sleep.

Unbreakable, she thought. She liked the sound of that.

"You will be," she said again, yawning. "I love you."

PAPER GIRLS
ALEX SMITH
BAD DOG
ALEX SMITH
THREE LITTLE PIGS
ALEX SMITH
WHIP CRACK
ALEX SMITH
RUN RABBIT RUN
ALEX SMITH
STONE COLD DEAD
ALEX SMITH
EVERY MOTHER'S SON
ALEX SMITH
SWEET BRIAR ROSE
ALEX SMITH
JAW BREAKER
ALEX SMITH
KNOCK KNOCK
ALEX SMITH
KING RAT
ALEX SMITH
KNUCKLE BONES
ALEX SMITH
LUCKY NUMBER SEVEN
ALEX SMITH
UNHOLY SAINTS
ALEX SMITH
TRULY MADLY DEADLY
ALEX SMITH
READ THE FIRST FIFTEEN BOOKS NOW!

ABOUT THE AUTHOR

Alex Smith wrote his first book when he was six. It wasn't particularly good, but it did have some supernatural monsters in it. His latest books, the DCI Robert Kett thrillers, have monsters in them too, although these monsters are very human, and all the more terrifying for it. In between, he has published fourteen novels for children and teenagers under his full name, Alexander Gordon Smith—including the number one bestselling series Escape From Furnace, which is loved by millions of readers worldwide and which is soon to become a motion picture. He lives in Norwich with his wife and three young daughters.

Find out more at alexsmithbooks.com

RELENTLESS
MEDIA

Printed in Great Britain
by Amazon

40362705R00260